M000074575

INSIDE A KILLER'S LAIR

The wall above the work area was covered with newspaper and magazine stories. Time had yellowed many of them, others appeared to have been photocopied. The oldest and most brittle was Chapa's original piece that ran the morning after Grubb's capture. Annie's name had been circled in black pencil and the newspaper story was neatly taped in place, next to a page out of *TV Guide* that listed a cable documentary on Kenny Lee Grubb.

There were several other photos on the wall, including one of a man he recognized, Officer Pete Rudman mowing the lawn of a simple ranch home. Two additional photos of an unsuspecting Rudman showed him coming out of a grocery store with his wife and casually getting in a few holes of golf.

Chapa now realized, maybe for the first time, that staying with the Kenny Lee Grubb story all those years had probably saved his life. Two of the people who were connected to Grubb's capture had been murdered. He didn't want to think about Annie already being dead, too, but he knew it was more than a possibility. So there it was, like a circle formed by connecting the dots, and, as the reporter who broke the story of that capture, he had to place himself in that group. Chapa was still alive only because Grubb wanted him to finish telling his story.

What had Grubb said to him a few days ago? *The circle will be complete.*

KILLING RED

HENRY PEREZ

PINNACLE BOOKS
KENSINGTON PUBLISHING CORP.
www.kensingtonbooks.com

PINNACLE BOOKS are published by

Kensington Publishing Corp.
119 West 40th Street
New York, NY 10018

All Kensington titles, imprints, and distributed lines are available at special quantity discounts for bulk purchases for sales promotions, premiums, fund-raising, educational, or institutional use. Special book excerpts or customized printings can also be created to fit specific needs. For details, write or phone the office of the Kensington special sales manager: Kensington Publishing Corp., 119 West 40th Street, New York, NY 10018, attn: Special Sales Department; phone 1-800-221-2647.

PINNACLE BOOKS and the Pinnacle logo are Reg. U.S. Pat. & TM Off.

ISBN-13: 978-0-7860-2032-4
ISBN-10: 0-7860-2032-6

First printing: June 2009

10 9 8 7 6 5 4 3 2 1

Printed in the United States of America

For everyone in my life who always believed this day would come.

PROLOGUE

The night that Grubb buried Annie Sykes he watched and waited behind a cover of young trees. For more than forty-five minutes the child did not move, and Grubb could easily have assumed she was dead. But somehow the killer knew that wasn't the case.

Grubb didn't make a habit of sticking around after disposing of his victims, and none of the other bodies were dealt with in such a public manner. Annie was different. She had been more resistant and stubborn than the others. From the moment he'd snatched the ten-year-old, there was something about her he found unsettling.

Annie wasn't buried in the traditional sense. Grubb had taken her limp body to a clearing in a small patch of woods a couple of miles from his house. There he opened a hole in the cold dirt just big enough to fit the child in head first, past her shoulders and almost up to her elbows, but not all the way in. He then meticulously fastened her head to the ground by putting a dog collar around her neck and securing it with tent spikes. But that was just a precaution and a bit of symbolism. The job of terminating Grubb's tenth victim belonged to what should have been a lethal mixture of depressants that he'd injected into Annie's thin veins.

From the withering tree branches above, to the lifeless autumn soil below, death was at home in this place. Something about that gave Grubb a rare feeling of tranquility. A sense of relief was slowly beginning to come over him as the minutes passed and he detected no movement that would suggest the child was still breathing. That changed when he saw Annie's small body twitch.

At first, Grubb told himself it was just a trick of the full moon's light. He had carefully measured out the right amount of each of the three drugs, then added a little more. But she twitched again, then again, and Kenny Lee Grubb was frightened for one of the few times in his life.

A curtain of sweat gathered along Grubb's brow, though he was anything but warm. He quietly circled around the edge of the woods as the child struggled to free herself, too spooked by the way she appeared to have come back to life to get any closer. Then suddenly she was free. When she rose from the dirt, Grubb became convinced he was watching a ghost. He had believed all along that this child was more evil than the others, and this confirmed it.

Of the many images in Grubb's life that would haunt anyone else, the one that lingered most was of Annie Sykes standing in that field, covered in dried blood and fresh dirt. She looked around, then looked in his direction. Pretending she didn't see him, Grubb thought. Toying with him. Evil.

With as little movement as possible, he searched the area immediately around him until he found what he was looking for. Autumn was only a few weeks old, but dead leaves had already covered much of the thick, three-foot length of broken branch that lay just beyond Grubb's reach.

He took a cautious step in its direction, while keeping his eyes on the child, then leaned down and picked up the heavy shaft of cold wood. Grubb squeezed his makeshift weapon until his palms burned, and he liked the way that felt.

Then he tightened his grip even more and began searching for the best angle from which to attack.

Annie's mind was racing with questions. What time was it? How long had she been there? Why did someone bury her head in the ground? Maybe the rest of her didn't fit. Maybe someone needed a bigger shovel to open a larger hole for the rest of her. In that case, they'd be back. Soon.

Where was she? She removed enough dirt from her eyes to be able to look around and see it was a clear night, but none of what she saw looked familiar. Maybe she was in a faraway place, or it could be she was in the backyard of that house.

Wait, what house? She remembered. The one where the man who always smelled like he'd been sweating a lot had taken her. Annie thought that she'd seen the same tall man at her school a few times. Now she remembered more things about him. Things that she never wanted to think about again.

Annie decided that she wasn't going to be scared any more. Just like her dad had taught her when she was younger, and couldn't go to sleep without a night-light because she was certain there were monsters in the world, and something horrible hiding in the dark. She'd reluctantly accepted her father's view that the monsters were created in her mind, and learned how to take charge of her fear and gradually make it go away.

It was time to shove those fears aside and go home. But she stood up too quickly, and pain flared across her chest. In the moonlight, Annie saw that the front of her dress was stained dark brown with dirt and sweat. It was the same dress she'd been wearing since the last time she was home. For a moment Annie worried her mother might get angry with her for ruining it. She tried to pull the cloth away from her cold skin, but that hurt more than anything.

Annie looked down at her bare feet and saw that the hole her head had been buried in wasn't as deep as she'd expected. The spikes that pinned the collar to the ground were barely visible. Only a small portion of each was exposed, the rest had been swallowed up by dirt. Annie knew she could never have pulled them out, and was proud of herself for having figured out another way.

The clearing she was standing in was surrounded by what looked like a forest. The onset of fall had not yet stripped the trees all the way down to their skeletal limbs. A fierce wind blowing though the leaves startled her. Then she heard a sound that was not made by the wind. Then another.

She was not alone.

Annie thought about trying to stand as perfectly still as she could and maybe whoever or whatever was out there would not see her. A crackling sound, then another, closer, and Annie knew she had to start running—now.

To her left, Annie saw a small opening through a collection of thin trees. She ran faster, until the wind was rushing past her face. As she weaved through the narrow trail, a tangle of unforgiving, sharp branches tore at her bare ankles. Ignoring the pain, she headed for a path just a little to her right. Every few strides, one of her feet would land on something coarse, but Annie knew she couldn't let that slow her down.

Annie wanted to look back, but thought better of it.

Then she realized that whatever was after her wasn't trailing behind, it was just on the other side of a long row of trees on her right. It was running *with* her, no more than thirty feet away.

Nothing that her mom or dad had ever taught Annie could keep her from being afraid now. Why did Dad send her into that store all by herself? Was it because he believed Annie was old enough, or because he didn't want to interrupt the conversation he was having on his phone? Why had he left Annie unprotected, giving that man the chance to talk a young girl into going to the storage room, then out the back door?

Can't think about that now. It's getting closer.

Out of the corner of her eye Annie thought she saw the monster cut through the row of trees and move in behind her. Without slowing down, Annie allowed herself a quick glance back, and saw she was right. Whatever was chasing her appeared to be made of shadows and night. It was tall and fast, and Annie thought she'd seen that one arm was longer than the other. But then she understood what she'd really seen. The monster was holding something long and thick up over its head. And it was closing in on Annie—fast.

Annie felt the footsteps closely tracing her own, and realized she could not outrun it. There was no place to duck into, no gap in the bushes and trees, so Annie decided to make an opening. She rushed into a tiny space between two thick bushes, kept her balance, and pushed through what seemed like a forest of angry branches, until she finally came to a clearing on the other side.

She willed herself to run faster than she ever had before, but nearly tripped over her own feet. Through the muck that the sweat from her brow had carried into her eyes Annie saw a building in the distance, beyond the scattered lights of a parking lot. Running toward the first sign of civilization she had seen in a long time, Annie thought she heard the monster yell something, but couldn't make out what it was and didn't care.

Monsters trick you with their lies.

The building was getting closer now, and beyond it Annie saw a row of homes, but nothing that she recognized. As she came up around the side of the building, Annie realized that the noises of the night, real and imagined, were gone. She heard her heavy breathing, then the sound of her small wounded feet slapping the pavement.

A moment later she was standing under the large well-lit sign above the door. It was the kind of small store her mom and dad shopped at when it was late and they needed to get something after all the other places had closed. She couldn't remember ever seeing this one before, though.

When she reached the doors, Annie turned and looked back toward the woods for the first time. She could barely make out a vague shape within the darkness of the trees. And though she could not see its face, Annie was certain the monster was staring back at her.

Dominic Delacruz wasn't supposed to be at the store that Tuesday, the one he would refer to as *That Night*, for the rest of his life. One of his workers had called in sick, another needed to leave early, and he didn't like his son to work on school nights. That meant Dominic had to fill in until his replacement arrived at 5:00 A.M.

It was just shy of midnight, and he had almost finished stocking the magazine rack when he noticed the small figure standing outside the store, just beyond the reach of the automatic door sensor. Moving closer, Dominic saw it was a girl in a dress, and he immediately knew something wasn't right. Her long hair appeared to be matted down, like something was covering it, and she wasn't wearing a coat, though it could not have been more than thirty-five degrees out there.

The fact that she was alone was certainly unusual, but Dominic figured that the girl had probably raced her father or mother from the car to the door. Or maybe something was wrong.

She wasn't moving, just standing in place. Though Dominic was free of superstitions, he decided at that moment that if ghosts really did exist, this child could be the genuine article.

That thought chilled him to the core.

Walking toward the front, he was just a few feet from the door when the child abruptly turned and quickly entered the store. She stopped when she saw Dominic, and he froze at the sight of her stained dress and muddy legs.

Through the dirt that covered her head he could see patches of what appeared to be vibrant red hair. He instinctively reached forward and wiped some of the filth from the girl's face, then stopped, thinking that some of this might be evidence of a crime.

"I need your help," she said suddenly, though it seemed like getting those few words out was hard work for the child.

Dominic squatted down to her eye level.

"What is your name?"

"I need your help," she repeated, and looked back toward the door. This time Dominic saw the terror in her eyes. He could almost feel her fear, and realized whatever was happening might not yet be over.

Dominic touched her arms and was stunned by how cold they were, as though she'd been lying in a grave. He took off his work smock and wrapped it around her shoulders. That's when he noticed the deep scratches on the child's arms and how the dress stuck to her trembling body in those areas where it seemed to be painted a shiny dark brown.

He stared at the wounded child for a moment until he thought he saw something move outside of the store. Dominic slowly walked in the direction of the movement, each step measured. He stopped before reaching the automatic door sensor, and carefully studied the area just outside the front of his store, but saw only darkness beyond the parking lot lights. There had been several frightening nights back when he owned a store in Chicago, but nothing that had prepared him for this.

Dominic thought about taking the child into the back room, hidden away from whoever might still be out there. But he didn't want to let her out of his sight. So he walked her to the narrow stretch behind the counter and told her to sit down on the floor, which she did without hesitation.

After another long look in the direction of the parking lot, Dominic reached into a small drawer under the register, pulled out the .44, and checked to make sure it was loaded. Dominic knew that whoever had done such terrible things to this little girl would be looking for her, and maybe already knew exactly where she was.

He dialed 9-1-1, and did his best to explain what was happening. After he hung up, Dominic wondered if he should offer her some ice cream, or anything. That could wait.

"You'll be all right now," he said to the girl without taking his eyes off the door or loosening his grip on the gun.

That was sixteen years ago, and not a night has gone by since without Dominic thinking about that frightened, broken little girl. Sometimes, when he's alone at the store late at night and the door opens, it startles him for just a moment and he imagines that she's about to walk in again.

Then Dominic goes home and prays for the gift of forgetting. But that prayer never gets answered.

Alex Chapa, just a little more than a year out of college, was hiding in a corner of the cramped newsroom. The only other writer in the office that night was playing Tetris on one of the two computers in the room. Down the hall, Betty the Layout Lady—few at the *Tri-Cities Bulletin* seemed to know her last name—was putting the final touches on section one.

Back turned to Murphy and the annoying sounds of his game, Chapa was working on a feature story that wouldn't earn him an extra penny, but might at least help him feel better about his job. So far, the newspaper business hadn't been as fulfilling as he'd imagined—personally, professionally, or financially.

A phone rang two desks away.

"Wrong number," Murphy barked, refusing to break eye-contact with the monitor.

Chapa leaned back in his office chair and looked over at his colleague.

"Might be Carter checking in. He does that."

"Not during his fishing trips, he doesn't. Let it go, Alex."

Ross Carter was the *Bulletin*'s lone columnist. A respected pro who had been in the business longer than the lakes he loved to fish had been wet. Chapa looked up to Carter a little bit when he first started at the paper. But over time Chapa had starting wondering if the guy was just drifting along on cruise control. Counting the days until his last byline.

Another ring.

"Oh, hell." Chapa rolled over to Carter's desk.

"You touch it, you own it," Murphy said as Chapa reached for the phone, lifting the handset just before the next ring cut out.

"*Tri-Cities Bulletin*, news desk."

"Carter?"

"No, Alex Chapa. Carter's not here."

"Shit."

"Can I help you?"

"How soon will Carter be back?"

"Not till next week."

"Shit. Do you have a number I can get him at?"

"Not really. He's on a lake, up in Wisconsin."

A thick sigh.

"I can take a message if you like."

"No. It'll all be over by the time Carter gets it."

Chapa turned away from Murphy and lowered his voice. "Whatever it is, I'm certain that I can help you."

"And what makes you think that?"

"Because the urgency in your voice suggests that whatever this is about, matters, and not in a selfish way, no, it's not about you, it's bigger than any one person, and you have the clarity to understand that, which means you also understand that it's bigger than Carter, or any reporter." Chapa turned away from the mouthpiece, drew a breath, heard Murphy ask him if he was all right, ignored the question.

"Yeah, okay, buddy. But Carter has to know that this came from Bulldog."

"Bulldog?"

"He'll know who you're talking about."

"So what are we talking about, Bulldog?" Chapa asked, straining to sound casual.

Silence. And Chapa feared he'd lost the guy.

"It's a police raid. Going down in about forty-five minutes. Maybe less."

"Where?"

More silence.

"Look, I'll be sure and let Carter know this came from Bulldog. I've already written it down. Now, while it still matters, where is this going to happen?"

He gave Chapa the address, but it was hard to believe that anything criminal could be happening in that corner of Chicago's suburbs. It was a place populated by folks with membership cards to clubs, and close ties to their church affiliations, living in color coordinated houses on clean, freshly resurfaced streets.

"It's about that missing girl, Annie Sykes."

Chapa knew the case. A week ago, on the evening of October 7, the ten-year-old had gone missing after she walked into Rudi's Foods in West Chicago and was never seen walking out.

"They found her?"

"Not exactly. She sort of found them, more or less. Escaped from some psycho late last night."

"*Last* night?"

"Yeah, she walked into some convenience store, and the owner called the cops." There was a slight wheeze in Bulldog's voice, leading Chapa to decide he was a long-time smoker. "Then she spent last night and all day today in the hospital for observation. The cops kept that under wraps. But now, tonight, about an hour ago, she led them to where the guy lives."

"You know what that guy's name is?"

"Yes, Grubb, Kenneth L. They got the house under heavy surveillance while they put a team together."

Across the room, Murphy yelled something about finishing a level, then, "You still on the phone, Alex?"

Chapa nodded casually, rolling his eyes, feigning exasperation.

"I'll tell you what, Bulldog, I'll talk you up to Carter, big time, if you forget all of this right now, and no other reporter gets a phone call tonight."

"You mean that?"

"Absolutely."

Chapa hung up the phone, grabbed his jacket and note pads, and headed for the door like it was nothing at all.

"You got something, Alex, or just making a food run?"

"Maybe something, we'll see."

"I warned you."

"That you did, Murph."

Chapa sprinted across the parking lot and into his car. He pounded the accelerator of his old Honda Civic, tearing down country roads, quickly narrowing the distance to the address Bulldog had given him, while keeping an eye out for any squads.

Can't afford to get a ticket. Can't afford to lose time, either. The house was only a few miles away, but the minutes seemed to be passing by faster than the darkened Midwestern landscape.

Once he crossed Route 59 and the Grandville city limits, Chapa let rip and did fifty down quiet residential streets, confident that every available cop in town would be part of the team gathering to storm a sleepy, well-manicured neighborhood.

Chapa pulled into the Pleasant Highlands subdivision less than twenty minutes after he'd left the newspaper office. Grubb's house was at the far end of a labyrinth of short, narrow streets near the middle of a longer center drive. Chapa tried to get as close as possible. But the cops had blocked off both ends of the wide, curving street and he had to park around the corner and a block and a half down from the house.

Choosing his palm-size notebook instead of a larger more conspicuous one, Chapa grabbed a couple of pens, took a calming breath, and stepped out of his car. He decided to try the most direct path first, and walked down a street that ran parallel to the one he needed to get to. Folks in nightgowns and sweats drifted like moths in the direction of the police activity, only to be turned away before they could get near enough to see what was going on. Chapa couldn't afford to be turned away, couldn't risk drawing that much attention to himself. He needed to find another way.

As he walked with a smattering of half-awake neighbors who were quietly speculating on what all the fuss was about, Chapa kept looking around for a way in. He was getting closer to the police barricade than he wanted to be, when he spotted a small park nestled between a cluster of houses.

Ducking away from the would-be gawkers, he cut down a driveway, and through a backyard, drawing a response from a set of motion sensors that rousted security lights. Ignoring the sudden unwanted attention, Chapa slipped past a row of bushes and emerged on the other side, no more than twenty yards from a jungle gym.

The park was quiet, empty. A lone light post illuminated the area around the swings. Chapa thought about the children who played in this park. Wondered if their parents would ever again feel safe there. Or if the place would now have a taint.

Locating the paved path that led from the park to a sidewalk beyond, Chapa eyed the street where all of the heavy action was going down. He knew he wouldn't fit in with any group of officials at the scene. His faded jeans, the fabric starting to split at the cuff, and University of Iowa sweatshirt couldn't pass as anyone's official uniform. Except maybe that of a recent college grad trying to make it as a reporter. But Chapa just played it cool, like he had a hall pass in his back pocket, and strolled down the sidewalk and past huddles of heavily armed officers.

"How the hell did you get here?"

Officer Steven Zirbel's voice startled Chapa, but the

reporter was already working on his response before realizing who was talking.

"Steve, you're out late tonight."

"And you're where you don't belong, Alex."

The two men had gotten to know each other a couple of months back when Chapa spent the night with a
police detail at a roadside checkpoint. Zirbel, who over-
saw the operation, liked the way the story turned out,
and though he was always cautious, the lieutenant had
become somewhat of a source Chapa could rely on.

"I understand you guys are about to bring in a very
bad guy."

"And how do you know that?"

Chapa smiled and shrugged as Zirbel moved in close.

"Look, Alex, you need to move on," he said, his voice
measured. "I'll give you a call in the morning after the
smoke clears."

"That's no good, Steve. I'm holding up page one
right now. I've got to have something."

Zirbel looked away, in the direction of the house,
then to where a group of men from various jurisdictions had assembled. When he focused his attention
back on Chapa, the reporter could almost hear the
wheels turning inside the cop's head.

"You keep my name out of it, unless I call you and
tell you otherwise," the officer jabbed an index finger
at Chapa, who nodded. He knew Zirbel had been angling for a promotion and the right story could put him
over the top. The wrong one might knock him back to
the overnight shift at the evidence desk.

Zirbel laid out how twenty-four hours ago Annie
Sykes walked into Dominic Delacruz's store and everything that followed and how she had led them here.

"You're going in awfully hard on one girl's word,
Steve."

"She's a very convincing little girl."

Chapa followed Zirbel's eyes to the three people standing by a cruiser's open door. He recognized Roger Sykes, a man in his midthirties who dressed like the middle manager that he was.

"Is that her?" Chapa asked, pointing to the small red-headed child wedged between her parents.

"They insisted on being here when we take him. We told them to stay in the car, but they weren't too interested in anything we had to say."

A guy decked out in protective gear called for Zirbel.

"Go back to where you came from, Alex," Zirbel said, then walked over to a group that looked like it was primed to go into battle.

Cloaked in as much confidence as he could conjure, Chapa walked down the sidewalk in the direction of the Sykes family. He nodded to a uniformed who was staring at him, but didn't break stride. Making sure Roger Sykes saw him as he approached, Chapa pulled out the small notebook and a pen, then introduced himself.

"My wife and I have appreciated how the newspapers publicized Annie's disappearance, but not the way you guys came after me and her mother."

"I know my paper may have been off base, but—"

Michelle Sykes cut Chapa off. "It was those incompetent jerks in the police department." She was pleasant looking in a fresh, rural Illinois way. "They couldn't find our daughter, and I still don't know how anyone could have thought Roger was involved. That was just a terrible thing for us. People should be ashamed of themselves."

Annie Sykes had been looking up at Chapa the entire time. When he returned the attention she took it as a cue that it was her turn.

"I'm looking forward to going home," her tone strong, voice driven by determination. "But first I want to see the police get that terrible man."

"You got away from him, didn't you?" Chapa asked, kneeling to meet her at eye-level.

She nodded, "I wasn't afraid, not too much," and almost smiled.

"How did you recognize the house from the outside?"

"I remembered some of the streets that he turned on when he brought me here in his van." Then she pointed to an area of fencing that Chapa could barely make out in the darkness. "And I remember seeing that through a window in the basement. I have a really good memory."

"It's been a horrible time, and we'll be talking to our attorney after all this is over," Roger said, then put a protective arm around his daughter, as though it could shield her from everything. "But we're just thankful that Annie's back and we can put all this behind us. I love Annie very much. She's a strong person, and she's my little girl. I don't care what anyone said about me, I'm just so glad she's back."

A shot exploded inside the house. Now the police were rushing around like scattered ants, ordering each other to get down, get back, get ready. Chapa got shoved aside as Annie and her parents were hustled into the squad car. He made his way around to the back of the vehicle so he could get a decent view of the house. Leaning on the trunk of the car, Chapa quickly took notes as the police rushed the house.

A chaotic minute passed. Then a guy wearing a flak jacket over a gray suit appeared on the front porch. "It's all over," he said, then signaled for paramedics to move in.

Chapa was also on the move. Getting as close as he could without drawing attention, he stopped just beyond the reach of a streetlight. He waited there until

Zirbel walked out of the house and was crossing the front yard.

"Steve, who got shot?"

"Didn't I tell you to get out of here?"

"And I was doing just that when I heard the shot. You can't hold this back now."

Zirbel appeared to take stock of the situation.

"I assume one of your officers shot the suspect, let's start with that, Steve."

"One shot, in the chest."

"So the suspect was armed?"

"When we entered the house we found Kenneth Lee Grubb in the dining room. The moment the suspect saw us, he put down a piece of bread he was eating and appeared to reach for a weapon even though he'd been told to remain still, that's when the officer fired."

Chapa's hand was racing across the yellow tablet, as he made certain he didn't miss a word.

"What kind of weapon?"

Zirbel hesitated for a moment as he surveyed the immediate area.

"Damnedest thing I've ever seen. A large animal collar with long metal spikes sticking out of it." Zirbel leaned in close to Chapa and used his height advantage to cast a shadow over the reporter. "But I'd appreciate it if you kept that detail to yourself for the time being."

"I will, Steve," Chapa said, drawing a large oval around the last part of Zirbel's statement, then writing the word *No* in large letters next to it.

"Do right by the department, Alex," Zirbel added, then turned to a uniformed and told him to escort Chapa to his vehicle.

Once he was back in his car, it took Chapa a moment to regain his bearings and find the fastest way out of the subdivision. Then he quickly drove away, stopped at a pay phone six blocks later, and called the office. It took some coaxing to talk Betty the Layout Lady into delaying the printing of page one, even more to convince her to do a redesign.

"You got eight hundred words, young man, give or take a dozen, no more, and one hour to get them to me."

He thanked her, then dialed information and got a home number for Dominic Delacruz. The store owner didn't sound like he'd been sleeping, but he wasn't anxious to get media attention, either. Still, Chapa managed to squeeze a solid, if reluctant, quote out of him.

Winded and running on high octane, Chapa had just sat down at his desk to write his story when he got a call from Zirbel, who gave him the okay to use his name and filled in a few more of the details.

"After we secured the rest of the house, we cautiously headed for the basement, and found evidence that someone had been kept down there," Zirbel said. "We believe that at least one other child had been held there."

"Why, what did you find?"

After another hesitation, Zirbel said, "Children's snacks, a boy's T-shirt, and a dozen or so comic books in a small room in the basement."

"There was more than one room?"

"Several. Each appears to have been used for a different purpose. It's going to take a while to sort everything out, but we believe that some of the victims may have started out in a makeshift guest room before being transferred to other parts of the large basement."

He told Chapa that the officers removed several bottles of a liquid that had yet to be identified.

"We're waiting for the lab results, but we're reasonably certain the bottles contain whatever drug the suspect used on his victims," Zirbel said.

"So if there were other kids down there, where are they now?"

"We don't know yet. Grubb is considered a suspect in at least four other disappearances over the past three months," Zirbel said. "But that's the first question I'm going to ask him when the son-of-a-bitch comes out of intensive care."

The story came in at 844 words, and Betty the Layout Lady forgave him for that. It would be one of the last Chapa would ever write for the *Tri-Cities Bulletin*.

The reporter didn't sleep that night as he waited for the morning's *Bulletin* to arrive. Sleep would become precious and uneasy in the days and months that followed. For a while he took comfort in the certainty that it would all pass in time. But he was wrong.

Sixteen years and millions of printed words later, spanning hundreds of topics, the story that launched Alex Chapa's career still dogged him.

Six Days Before the Execution

CHAPTER 1

The heavy door closed as tightly as the lid of a casket. But the sliding of large metal bolts that secured it in place was never as loud as Alex Chapa expected. There was no echo, and the sounds from the rest of the world were immediately shut out, leaving this most secure cage within a cage in the grip of a stifling silence.

The reporter had visited Pennington Correctional a number of times before, always in a professional capacity, but it never got any easier. Beneath the well-crafted illusion of order and security, but never too far from the surface, lay a pit of anger and violence populated by men who had long ago discarded whatever tattered humanity they ever possessed.

Chapa had to remind himself that he would be leaving, and could go whenever he chose. That was comforting, but not as much as the knowledge that Kenny Lee Grubb did not have any of those options.

It had been an hour's drive to the prison from the *Chicago Record*'s main office in Larkin, a midsized town about thirty miles west of Cook County, nestled among the city's largest suburbs. The drive had given Chapa a chance to gather his thoughts, but all the time in the world would never be enough to fully prepare for something like this.

The uniformed guard escorting him through the prison was built like a thick rectangular dining table that had been stood on one end. Chapa listened to the man's stories about the three riots he'd survived during his eighteen years at Pennington.

"But I don't think we're due for one anytime soon," the guard added.

Things started looking familiar once they turned a corner and headed down a narrow hall. They passed a con working broom detail. The guy looked up and locked eyes with Chapa, who instantly knew he'd been sized-up and judged in a fraction of a second. Chapa didn't break eye contact, he just stared through the guy like no one was there. He had no fear of this asshole in prison garb. Wouldn't show any even if he did.

The mirror by the door to the special visiting room was covered with a month's worth of finger marks. Chapa used it to straighten the collar of his navy blue shirt, but didn't give a damn about anything else the mirror showed him. His early forties were passing by without leaving any new marks. Most of his hair was still naturally dark brown, and he'd determined earlier that morning that he didn't look a day over thirty-nine.

"This is as far as you go."

The guard's badge identified him simply as Harker. He had a well-traveled face punctuated by an overgrown mustache that contrasted with his cleanly shaved head. Harker opened the door and ushered Chapa into the cramped but clean space.

"You sit there," Harker said, pointing one of his callused fingers to the only chair on Chapa's half of the room. "Keep on your side of the table, and don't hand him anything."

Chapa did as he was told, then reached into his black

leather satchel and pulled out a notepad, two pens, and his black, lighter-size digital recorder.

"You can't use that here," Harker said.

Chapa slipped the recorder back into the case, discreetly pushing the record button as he tucked it into place. He took a quick inventory of how many weapons Harker had on his person. Four—that Chapa could see.

He hadn't spoken with Grubb for six years. That was when the paper asked him to do a piece on the ten-year anniversary of the capture of one of Illinois' most notorious mass murderers. It wasn't an assignment that Chapa had welcomed, but he knew it was coming. Every time a new Kenny Lee Grubb feature needed to be written, Alex Chapa was the *Chicago Record*'s logical choice to write it.

The original story had fallen to Chapa when he was still a newbie at the smaller *Tri-Cities Bulletin*, and it helped him make a name for himself. A few weeks later he was introduced as the *Chicago Record*'s newest columnist. The new job with the Chicago area's number two paper brought Chapa more than a significant boost in salary. But nothing matched the notoriety he gained from the Grubb story. There had been book offers, which Chapa had turned down because they would detract from the day-to-day reporting that he loved. He did short appearances on the ten o'clock news during Grubb's trial, and even considered an offer to host a cable network show before coming to his senses and getting on with his newspaper career.

It had been a very good career so far, and Chapa was confident his best work was still ahead of him. He had spent the years since trying to put some distance between himself and Grubb, and much of what had come with that early success. He had grown weary of the references to a sixteen-year-old story every time he was introduced at a speaking engagement. In the same way that musicians sometimes grow to despise that break-through single their fans demand they play at every concert, so it was that Chapa had become tired of being identified with his first big hit.

But in the quietest moments, Chapa understood that if he had been anywhere but at that news desk when the tip came in about Grubb's arrest he might still be a grunt reporter, covering restaurant openings and board meetings. Instead, he was able to devote his time and column inches to the subjects he cared about—the street gang infestation of the Midwest and the best efforts to solve the problem, failing schools and inspiring success stories, the struggles of immigrants and the plight of displaced American workers. There had been awards, as well as the resentment from some of his peers that often follows success. He'd been lucky, then good.

Chapa's head was pounding from not getting much sleep the night before. He'd spent most of it in the dark, staring at his ceiling and wondering why the murderer of nine children had asked to see him, and only him, just six days before his execution.

Getting face time with anyone on death row wasn't easy, even harder when the subject is the prison's most infamous resident. But Chapa had been in the game long enough to know how to get meetings arranged and things done.

The small room had a heavy detergent smell, and there was something grotesque about that antiseptic odor in a place like this. It wasn't the room usually reserved for visits with the irredeemable. That one had thick glass between visitor and con, and communication was strictly through telephones. Here, Chapa and Grubb would be face to face with nothing but a four-foot, white laminate–top table and Officer Harker between them. Apparently, the warden was pleased with that series of stories the *Record* had run about Illinois' successful prison system.

Opening the notepad to a fresh page and uncapping each pen, Chapa laid it all out the way he wanted. Part of him knew this was just an attempt to feel like he was in control of a situation that he wasn't sure he wanted any part of.

Chapa was thinking about the murderers and rapists who shared the same secondhand air now snaking through his lungs, when the door leading to the rest of the prison squealed open and Grubb appeared. He was dressed in a bright orange jumpsuit, his expression as blank as a dead man's mind. The silver metal handcuffs that bound Grubb's wrists matched the frame of his wheelchair.

A heavy chain connected the cuffs to the thick shackles around the killer's ankles, even though Grubb's legs were useless to him. His pasty skin and sharp features were capped by jet black hair and underscored by a chin that looked like it had sliced its way down from the rest of his face.

Grubb invaded Chapa's personal space with a long stare that seemed to have no origin or intent. Trying to stay cool, or at least create the impression that he was, Chapa reached for his pen without taking his eyes off Grubb, but came up empty and instead knocked one of them to the floor. Grubb's demeanor suddenly changed as a smile knifed across his waxy face and cut its way into that narrow space between Chapa's skin and everything that lay beneath.

CHAPTER 2

"I killed her."

"You killed a lot of *hers*, Kenny."

Ten minutes into the interview, Chapa had not yet heard anything worth writing down. That was unusual. Grubb was many things, virtually all of them horrible, but he had never been a bad interview subject. This, however, was not turning out to be a typical interview.

"I mean the talker, the cheater, the one who gave you your career," Grubb said, and captured Chapa's eyes with his own. "I killed Red."

This was how Grubb described each of the children he had murdered, even at his sentencing when he was supposed to deliver something in the way of an apology to the families of his young victims. There were nine bodies in all, seven girls and two boys, and nine families that no longer had the pieces to put it all back together.

The children's parents had named them Ellie, Ryan, Shelly, two were named Heather, another was named Maria, and there was also a Mary, and a Carson, as well as his first victim, a frail but happy nine-year-old named Stephanie. But Grubb reduced them to physical attributes, so the shattered parents had to hear about *Dark Eyes*, *Little Knees*, and *Short Fingers*.

Chapa knew every one of the perverse nicknames their executioner had given them, but he had also made damned sure to never forget their birth names. This was especially true with Annie Sykes, the girl who Grubb called "Red."

It was Annie who escaped and somehow gave the police a perfect description of Grubb's house, his neighborhood, and enough landmarks that they were able to find it within a few short hours.

"I know when a piece of meat has been rendered," Grubb said, inching closer before looking over to see if Harker was watching from where he sat, some twenty feet away, then slowly easing back into his chair.

His killing technique had varied somewhat from victim to victim, though all but two were drugged using a mixture of depressants and barbiturates including Rohypnol. In Grubb's harrowed mind, each child deserved to be killed in a way that was specific to them.

In Annie Sykes' case Grubb explained, "I was sending her back to where she came from."

Those were the only words he spoke about Annie at the trial. The parents of other children were not so fortunate. They sat there, in that indistinct courtroom, as Grubb coldly described what he had done to each child, and how their sons and daughters had died.

He had not publicly spoken about Annie since that one instance at his trial. Until now.

"Red belonged in the sacred ground where I planted her. I never trusted the little bitch, so I gave her more of the medicine than any of the others. She was no longer of this world."

"Well, I tell you what, Kenny, for a ghost she sure did a hell of a job of leading the cops to your house."

Grubb smiled broadly and Chapa could see that the killer had fewer teeth than when he arrived at Pennington.

"Alex, can I call you Alex? It's been some time since we last spoke, but I feel like we're brethren."

Chapa did not respond.

"You see me here, a cripple, my wrists and ankles chained together, and that helps you and your readers feel safe, don't it?"

"Shouldn't it?"

"Perhaps," Grubb said. His arms had become thick from years of working out, but remained free of prison ink.

Chapa looked down at his blank notepad and felt an urge to write something, but so far this was looking like nothing more than a disturbing waste of time. That was about to change.

Grubb just sat there and stared at him for a few seconds, and out of the corner of his eye Chapa saw Harker was getting ready to bring the meeting to an end.

"If I tell you the truth, will you print it?"

"We always print the truth," Chapa said picking up the only pen that was still sitting on the table.

"The hell you do. If you did, all of those sleepwalkers out there would take up arms and fortify their homes."

"Would they?"

"You bet they would. Because the truth is, my work continues. Right now, just beyond these walls."

Chapa started taking notes, knowing that at any moment Harker, or any one of the other four guards who were standing outside the doors, could decide that time was up.

"What are you talking about, Kenny? You're not going to go into some diatribe about the violence in society or crap like that, are you?"

Grubb forced out a deep laugh.

"No, asshole," Grubb lowered his voice so it was just above what would be a suspicious whisper. "I'm talking about what you folks mistakenly refer to as a copycat killer."

Chapa stopped writing. While, contrary to common belief around the profession, he had no deep fascination with killers like Grubb, Chapa did keep an eye out for reports of pattern killings from around the country. It was a habit he had fallen into after the Grubb case. He was relieved when months passed and none turned up.

He chose to not respond to Grubb's last comment, knowing that the killer would not be able to stand the silence for long. It worked.

"If you think about it, Alex, the term *copycat* is insulting to both the original and the disciple. I prefer the word *tribute*. You know, like bands that expertly re-create another band's music. Because that's what's been going down across the Rust Belt during the past few months. Somebody is replaying my greatest hits."

Grubb had to be blowing smoke. A desperate attempt to generate some attention for himself in the few remaining days he had left. What Chapa expected to hear next was an offer of assistance in exchange for more time. An offer he figured the authorities had already turned down.

"You shouldn't try to bullshit me. I'm not the one who's trapped in a cage. I read the news reports online and on the wire. I would've noticed anything like that."

Grubb settled in, folded his arms, and said, "Pick up your pen, not the one you've been using, the other one, the better one. I wouldn't want you to miss this." Then Grubb winked at him.

Chapa ignored the suggestion. He knew some experts believed the best way to deal with a person like Grubb was to act subservient and give his ego some room to stretch out and move around. But Chapa had never been able to do that during any of his interviews with the killer, and he wasn't interested in starting now. Knowing what Annie looked like on that night, what she and her family and all the other families had gone through, Chapa could never show anything but contempt for the man on the other side of the table.

A look over at Harker resulted in the guard giving him the five minute signal.

"This pen will do just fine."

Grubb slowly leaned forward. So casual.

"I'll tell you where to find everything you'll need for your story, but I want you to report the truth, that's why you were summoned here."

The reporter nodded, matching the killer's ease.

"Check out what happened in Grand Rapids in February, Zanesville, Ohio in late August of last year, down in Jackson, Tennessee this summer, and Marion, Iowa more than two years ago."

Chapa wrote down each location, though he felt more than a little uneasy about taking information from Grubb.

"Look up a boy named Mike Connor who took his last breath a week before Christmas in Ortonville, Minnesota. You can find the rest on your own, Alex."

"How many more?"

"Eight total for sure, but I think number nine has already been rendered."

Chapa tried to ignore the obvious pleasure the monster in front of him was getting from this. If by some chance Grubb was right, then this was anything but a simple death row rant.

"All innocent children like the ones you murdered?"

"Those animals that I rendered were bad to the core." He had gotten under Grubb's skin, and this pleased Chapa, though the raised voice brought Harker to his feet.

"Look newsman, I didn't want to believe it at first, either. They were so small and soft, but I tested them and learned the truth. I knew the things they would've done once they grew and became powerful. Now I know I'm not the only one who understands that."

Signaling to Harker that it was okay, Chapa silently pleaded for just another minute. The guard nodded, but did not sit back down.

"Maybe you don't believe me yet, but you will when my disciple gives me his greatest gift."

Chapa thought of his own daughter. Nikki was beyond Grubb's reach, but predators were everywhere, always hunting for innocent prey.

"So let's hope that if there is some vile creature out there doing this he'll run into a tough little kid like Annie. Just like you did."

Grubb laughed silently as Chapa felt what sparse warmth there might have been in the room disappear into the killer's gaping smile.

"Don't you see? He's leaving *her* for last. Before they put me out of all of you people's misery he's going to finish Red for me." Grubb wasn't smiling now. "And then the circle will be complete."

"She's not a child anymore, Grubb."

"No, but she's still mine and I want her back," Grubb said, and Chapa could see he was barely keeping it together. Something that came from a place no light could ever sneak into was seeping to the surface, threatening to betray the killer's façade.

"What makes you think I won't go to the cops? Turn this all over to them, and let a bunch of feds tear into the last few days of your worthless life?"

"Because you won't, not right away. Because you're never satisfied trailing a story when you can get ahead of it. Because that's who you are. It's the one thing you're good at."

Harker walked around to the back of the wheelchair

and wrapped his heavy hands around the grips. Grubb tried to wave him off, and when that didn't work he clutched the tabletop and strained to pull himself forward. The chair did not budge.

"You know, Alex, ninety-nine out of a hundred reporters would have written that story without using her name, without interviewing Red's parents. They might have mentioned that a child tipped-off the police, but after that their discretion would've taken over. But not you."

Harker reached forward and gradually put the squeeze on Grubb's shoulder, while sliding his other hand to a holster that cradled a taser.

"And, Alex, do allow yourself some personal satisfaction when the news comes that everything has been put right. After all, you will have had a hand in it. You made her famous enough to be worth rendering a second time."

With that, Grubb pushed away from the table, forcing Harker to take an abrupt step back. Grubb then turned the wheels and rolled away, as though the decision was his and Harker had no say in the matter. A loud buzz sounded, and the guard opened the door.

"I'm hoping to see the story in print before they kill me in six days. But that's really not what's important, is it?"

Grubb disappeared into the rest of the prison as Chapa was still working on a comeback.

CHAPTER 3

Grubb had clawed his way under Chapa's skin, something the reporter had long ago promised himself he'd never allow.

But he knew once you bring someone like that into your life, there's no turning back. Chapa had used cons for sources on several occasions. A few had tried to follow him into his everyday life after they got out. None had as powerful an effect on him as Grubb.

Like Charles Manson before him, Grubb had developed a cult following, a twisted reality Chapa had long ago given up trying to understand. There was something about life-takers who claimed to kill with a purpose that seemed to motivate some folks to put out the welcome mat and open their doors.

Grubb had further cultivated that by playing up his disability, and becoming something of an unlikely advocate for prisoners' rights. Some thought this murderer of children was as much a victim as he was a criminal. Chapa would have gladly volunteered to take those people on a tour of nine small graves, each stained with Grubb's bloody fingerprints.

To Chapa, Grubb was neither complex nor mysterious. And he sometimes wondered how any of his readers could find Grubb interesting. As far as Chapa was concerned, Grubb was nothing more than a disease with a pulse.

The image of Grubb chained and restricted to a wheelchair lingered in Chapa's mind. The disability and the years on death row had reduced Grubb to a snarl of contempt and hostility in their purest form. Unable to act on the violence that Chapa knew still coursed through the killer. A mass of hate in the steel cage Police Officer Pete Rudman had condemned him to.

Though it struck Grubb in the chest, the bullet from Rudman's gun did only minor damage until it reached the spinal column, strategically lodging itself where no surgeon dared cut. The small piece of lead took away all use of his legs, and left Grubb without feeling from the waist down. It had taken months for Grubb to recover enough to leave the hospital so the state could take the next step toward executing him.

An investigation determined Rudman was justified in firing his weapon, though there were no guns in the house, let alone within Grubb's reach when the police arrived at his suburban home. As officers moved in and surrounded the wounded suspect, his blood painting the beige ceramic floor tiles, they saw his fingers curled tight around a thick dog collar, long silver tent spikes clinging to its side.

Rudman retired about a decade later, closing out a career filled with honors and citations, but one that was always defined by a single moment in a dark house on a quiet street. He and his wife moved to a planned community in Myrtle Beach and filled their days with golf, swimming, and general relaxation, until a few months ago when he'd been shot during a botched home invasion.

How tragic that a decorated officer lost his life that

way, just a victim to some crackhead's cravings, Chapa had thought as he helped write Rudman's obit. And how unjust it was that Grubb had not died first. It should not have worked out that way, but Grubb's attorney successfully petitioned the court to delay his client's execution for nearly a year because of various issues relating to the killer's disability.

Leaving Pennington Correctional, Chapa knew he would spend much of the next few days following up on the information he'd been given. Sleep was always tough for Chapa to come by, and it would be even harder until he'd dismissed the possibility that there might be anything to Grubb's claim.

Before hitting the interstate, Chapa stopped at a library he had seen on his way to the prison. It was an older brick building, but that was just the outside. The interior looked modern and newly renovated. After walking through a well-lit entryway, Chapa found himself in a large, open area rimmed with bookcases. The place smelled of fresh paint and printer ink. Long rows of computer monitors filled the middle of the room. He was pleased to find an open public terminal and a friendly employee willing to help an out-of-towner get online.

But that's as far as his good fortune got him. He could find no listing for Annie Sykes anywhere in the Chicago area. He expanded his search to the Midwest, then the nation. Nothing. She had probably gotten married, probably took her husband's name. Further research would have to wait until he got back to his office.

It was an hour-long drive to any place Chapa might want to go, and that gave him time to organize his thoughts and figure out what to do next. The breezy rock of Nick Lowe's *The Convincer* accompanied him on his trip through Illinois farm country, and by the time he passed through the toll booth in DeKalb, Chapa knew where his first stop would be.

The *Chicago Record*'s coverage area extended from the upscale towns along the North Shore of Lake Michigan, through the heart of the city, to the hardscrabble roads that led to the western suburbs and down to Joliet. During Chapa's time working there, the *Record* had emerged as a major player in the Chicago area media market, and the newspaper that covered more ground than any other periodical in the state.

From early on in his now sixteen-year career with the paper, Chapa had become known for his profiles of regular people, and exposés of some seriously irregular ones. For a time, his stories were consistently picked up for syndication, but that had cooled a bit, as it had for many journalists.

Mergers and cost-cutting measures had taken hold throughout the industry, and newspapers were relying more on wire stories and less on their own journalists. The past five years had been especially difficult. The *Record* was slowly creeping toward a more homogenized product that emphasized the brand over the individual writer.

As far as the suits were concerned, news columnists didn't sell papers anymore. Less than two decades into the only career he had ever wanted, Chapa sometimes felt like a dinosaur in an industry facing extinction.

Still, he knew how to conduct a one-on-one with the best of them. Understanding that the key to being a skilled interviewer is knowing how to become an active part of a one-way conversation. As he exited onto Route 59, Chapa anticipated that those skills would soon be put to the test.

Dominic Delacruz's business had grown into a chain of six convenience stores. They spanned a thirty-mile stretch of sprawl along DuPage County's southern edge. Chapa was certain he could find Dominic's original store, anything else was a wild card.

In the weeks following Grubb's capture, Chapa had done a couple of feel good follow-up stories about Dominic, his store, and his family. But as much as Chapa had tried to build up that part of the story, Dominic always refused to take credit for having done anything exceptional, and wouldn't tolerate being called a hero.

Dominic was four years old when his family came to the United States from central Mexico. His father worked at a manufacturing plant in the Chicago suburbs, and his mother was employed as a seamstress. Unable to get a job delivering papers, or stocking shelves at the nearby shopping center, like a lot of the other kids in his neighborhood did, Dominic started mowing lawns in the summer and shoveling snow in winter by the age of twelve.

He didn't play Little League, or go to movies, or become a Scout. Dominic spent his free time at a nearby branch of the library. With dreams of becoming an engineer, he read every book he could find on the subject. Still, he knew deep down that the money to send him to college would never be there. When his father died at the age of fifty-two, it was time to set his dreams aside and go to work.

But Dominic and his brother, Antonio, were determined to have a better life than the one they'd seen their father struggle through. So they saved their money and started figuring out what it would take to open a Mexican restaurant in the western suburbs of Chicago.

Those plans changed the day they drove past a recently closed convenience store on the way to a friend's house on the far east end of the city's Pilsen neighborhood. Delacruz Brothers opened three months later, and was an immediate success.

The brothers made a good deal of money, much of it from selling cigarettes and lottery tickets. But they eventually got tired of being held up late at night and chasing away gangbangers all day long.

Antonio took his money and moved to Tucson where he opened that restaurant they had always planned. Dominic, usually the more conservative of the two, believed that the convenience store business had been too good to risk trying something else.

After he had prayed for guidance and believed in his heart that he'd received an answer, Dominic sold the store and began looking for a new location in the suburbs, the sort of area where he wanted his kids to grow up. He found it in rural DuPage County, at the far end of a new subdivision.

Initially, business was slow at The Late Stop, but things began to pick up as the surrounding woods started giving way to new homes. Soon, what was once a thick forest would be just a memory as more shopping strips followed the construction of half-million dollar homes.

Dominic and his wife were happy in their new home, and he settled into a nice routine. He had five employees, including his eldest son, and worked four days, plus just one night a week at the store. But as the owner, he would have to step in on nights when one of his regular workers couldn't make it.

One of those nights turned out to be far from routine.

Chapa had heard that Delacruz had left the area some time ago, but could not remember if that was the son, or the old man. It didn't matter either way. There couldn't be much Chapa did not already know about what had happened that night, but he needed a starting point, and the place where Annie Sykes found refuge seemed as good as any.

CHAPTER 4

The convenience store had changed some since Chapa had last been there more than a decade earlier. The kid behind the counter wasn't old enough to be a regular employee, so he had to be family.

"You're looking for my grandfather, he's in the back," the boy said, then called out, "Papi."

Chapa glanced back toward the door and imagined what Annie must have looked like on that night. Alone, beaten, and bruised, a fighter in need of help. Had Grubb succeeded in breaking her? Chapa had seen no evidence of that back then.

Smooth jazz flowed through the speakers overhead, and the place smelled of flowery air freshener which almost succeeded in masking the odor of cheap, over-brewed coffee. Dominic Delacruz emerged from a backroom and introduced himself. Chapa recognized the man immediately, though his face was much more weathered than before, and his thick wave of hair had turned almost entirely gray.

"Sure, I remember you. I haven't been able to forget anything from that time, you know," Delacruz said. They shook hands, the store owner's fingers were hard and coarse like fine sandpaper. "You're Latino, right?"

Chapa nodded. "Cuban."

This was an exchange that Chapa had grown accustomed to. As a child he observed how Latin American immigrants made a habit of asking each other what country they were from. He always assumed that's what happens when the peoples of twenty-two different nations, loosely tied together by a common language, are tossed into one large mass by their adopted country.

"You don't have an accent. I haven't met many Cubans, but the ones I have all sounded, well, Cuban."

"We left Cuba when I was very young."

Dominic gave him a once-over, offering no sign of approval.

"How old were you?"

"Barely four."

Chapa's mother had been determined to assimilate into American culture, deciding that it was the best way to succeed in the United States. As a result, by the time Chapa was a teenager his Cubanismo had long become something he set aside and brought out only for special occasions, or when family came up from Florida. He sometimes joked that as a Cuban living in the Midwest he was required by federal law to maintain a cadre of relatives in Miami.

On a shelf in the next aisle down from where he and Dominic were standing, alongside the Chef Boyardee Ravioli and Chicken of the Sea Tuna, Chapa spotted a can of black beans. Probably wouldn't find one of those in any other suburban convenience store, he thought, and it reminded him of the cooking shortcuts his mother began relying on as she got older.

Each day Chapa would step out the door of his house and into a different world, one that quickly became more comfortable and familiar. Still, within the confines of the home he grew up in, Chapa was surrounded by the food and culture of his native country.

But that changed over time as his mother made friends at work and around the neighborhood, and even joined the PTA.

In many ways, Chapa had found it more difficult being the kid without a father than the one whose mother spoke with an accent.

"So are you here to do some follow-up story now that they're finally going to kill that animal?"

"Something like that."

Chapa wasn't trying to be smart. He really wasn't certain where any of this was going. When he got the message that Grubb wanted a sit-down, he'd expected to do the standard death row piece—part indignation, part remorse, with the occasional guest appearance by Jesus.

"I realize it was a long time ago, but is there anything about that night you might've overlooked back then? Anything that you've remembered after the fact?"

"You sound more like a detective than a reporter."

Chapa smiled.

"Years come and go, and you make some money, raise children, see them become adults," Dominic said, looking at his grandson. "You take trips, see new places, and meet new people. But some of the things that you've seen and been through, they never go away. The worst of them stay fresh."

Chapa jotted down Dominic's comments in his notepad.

"What about since then?" Chapa asked. "How are things different for you or maybe this store?"

"Ever since that night, I've been more aware of everything that goes on when I'm here. I was in the backroom when that blue beater pulled up to the store," Dominic said, describing the car Chapa had been driving for the past seven years. "But I noticed it the moment I walked out here. That's just how it is."

Chapa considered defending his car, then thought better of it.

"But, for example," Dominic now pointed to a green sedan that was parked at the far end of the store's lot, "the person in that car is probably on the phone, or checking a map, or changing the CD. I noticed them right away because they're here, but maybe they don't want to get too close. At night, I'd have a reason to be suspicious, but even now I'm on alert. Is that better? I don't know."

Dominic started straightening already well-organized shelves of prepackaged pastries.

"That night, I was sure someone was out there, Grubb probably," he said. "The way it was reported, it was like I was just the guy whose store she wandered into, but it wasn't like that."

"What do you mean?"

He stopped lining up Ho Hos and Twinkies and seemed lost in thought for a moment.

"When that little girl walked in she drew me right into it, her fear and the terror that she had been through. There was something really special about her. If someone had come in after her I probably would have shot them."

It was hard to imagine Dominic Delacruz ever drawing down on anyone, but Chapa sensed this conversation was taking the old man back, maybe to a place that he had spent years trying to get away from.

"Do you have any children of your own, Mr. Chapa?"

"I have a daughter."

"Then you know what it's like, but still, that was different. In that moment it was like she might as well have been my child. So naturally I protected her. I've come to believe I was put here on that night for a reason."

"Anyone come around lately to talk to you about that night or the little girl?"

"No, not until today, not until you came in. Why did you come here? What were you hoping to find?"

"Chapa closed his notepad and stared at the door again.

"I'm not sure, really. Some inspiration? I'm trying to finish an old story and make sure that I get it right, that I didn't miss anything."

Dominic finished the display of pastries and turned back in the direction of his office without giving Chapa the opportunity to offer a second handshake.

"I hope you figure it out," Dominic said just before he disappeared into the backroom. "I don't think you did much good the first time you came around."

CHAPTER 5

As far as Chapa was concerned, using the word *beater* to describe his car, as Dominic Delacruz had, was a little unfair. The late 90's Corolla wasn't rusting out yet, and it ran just fine. In fact, the car had not begun to show its age until some punks in Aurora got pissed off about a story he did on the video game culture and broke the driver's side mirror. He found it dangling by the cables, and duct taped it back into place as best he could. More than a year had passed since then, and the money from the insurance claim was long gone, spent on things other than the mirror. But he'd get it taken care of one of these days.

Having received little in the way of useful information from Dominic Delacruz, Chapa was tempted to go work on something else, or maybe call up a buddy and see if they could get together for lunch. His common sense was telling him to get away from this story and all of the baggage that came with it. One call and it would become the feds' problem.

But his instincts were telling him something else, and he couldn't shake the memory of that craven smile on Grubb's face, or how sure of himself the killer had seemed. So instead of ringing up a friend or going into

the office to grab another story, Chapa turned north on
Route 59 and headed toward West Chicago. Though it
had been more than a decade, he still remembered the
Sykes' street address.

That area had grown up over the past several years as
farmland gave way to subdivisions and strip malls. It was
hard to imagine, but Grubb might've had something to
do with the growth.

He'd been born Kenneth Lee Dresder in a rural
Kentucky town to a mother who could never be entirely
certain about the identity of the boy's father, and the
man she'd coaxed into marriage four months earlier.
At age sixteen he ran away for the third time, winding
up in a dusty corner of Arkansas. He drifted back home
a little over a year later. By then, the man he'd long
hated calling "Dad" was dead. His mother had taken
back her maiden name, and also changed his younger
brother's to match. So Kenny asked his mom to take
him to court and change his last name as well. It was his
way of shaking free from the man who had brought him
nothing but violence and pain. The change made him
feel like a new person, at least for a little while.

When he was in his midtwenties, Grubb got his realtor's license at the urging of his mother after she saw a
commercial about it while watching her stories. A few
months later, the realtor who was handling the develop-
ment of several new subdivisions in DuPage County
took a chance on him.

By all accounts, Grubb was the kind of realtor who
could sell a new house to a man in hospice care, and he
experienced a great deal of success in his new profession. But what Grubb really liked about the job was how
people would let him walk through their homes, sometimes unattended. When the police searched his house
after arresting Grubb they found a large plastic bin of
children's clothing and small toys. There were photos,

too, each with his nickname for the child written in marker on the back.

He lost his job after one client too many complained about the amount of attention Grubb paid to their child. At first, he figured that he would hook on with another realtor, but that didn't happen after word quickly spread throughout the industry. Grubb tried to make a go of it as an independent, but all of the established realtors made that tough to do. The only steady job he could get was delivering baked goods to various businesses in the area.

That job also came with its own set of what Grubb considered perks, in the form of three elementary schools and one junior high on his route. He collected candid snapshots of many of the kids at the schools. When police found the photos they assumed that Grubb was stalking those children and had plans for several of them at the time of his capture. The pictures themselves were not lurid, but the fact that he had them at all, tucked neatly into a photo album, was enough to keep any parent up at night.

Annie Sykes was a student at one of those schools, but hers was a crime of opportunity. Driving down some of the same streets that Grubb once cruised as a predator, Chapa thought of how many easy opportunities a creature like that must have had.

As Chapa turned north off busy Roosevelt Road, he was surprised to see colored lights flashing in his side-view mirror. A tap of the patrol car's siren punctuated the moment.

"What the hell?"

It had been some time since Chapa had been pulled over. Then again, he hadn't been in this area for a few months. Chapa's tense relationship with the local police dated back to his coverage of the Grubb case, and had just grown worse over time. He watched the cop get out of the cruiser, and shook his head when he recognized him.

Chapa rolled the window down.

"License and registration, Mr. Chapa."

"What's the matter, Tate, you get all worn out from not catching the bangers who pulled off that carjacking a couple weeks back?"

"Don't need a conversation."

"Then why are we having one at all?"

Streaks of gray were shuffled in with the cop's naturally auburn hair. They weren't there the first time Chapa had tangled with him. Or the second. Neither was the solid beer gut that was beginning to encroach on Tate's waistline.

"Maybe I'm cleaning up the streets of my town by dealing with a low-rent, shithole, waste-of-space journalist like yourself."

"See, that's probably why we never got along. You don't understand that part of my job is to protect the rest of us from abuse by anyone in a position of power." Chapa leaned out the window and lowered his voice, like he was about to share something special with the officer. "Actually, Dan, it's the part of my job I like best."

Tate shrugged.

"So why was I pulled over? Think fast."

Tate pointed to the duct taped side-view mirror. "You have a broken piece of safety equipment, and if it should fall off it could present a hazard to other motorists. Now, I'm not asking you again."

Chapa turned over his license and proof of ownership, and Tate walked back to his squad car. He returned ten minutes later with a pink slip of paper in his hand.

"You understand I could let you off with a warning, but this time I just went ahead and wrote you a ticket. Sign here."

Chapa scribbled something approximating a signature, then Tate tossed a pink slip of paper into Chapa's car.

"Not that it matters, officer, but that mirror isn't going to fall off anytime soon."

Without taking his eyes off Chapa, Tate raised his left arm, his hand forming a fist, like he was going to punch himself. Then Tate slammed his left elbow down on the mirror. The duct tape put up little resistance. A piece of Chapa's car was now dangling by a cable, and his ability to mask his anger was quickly waning.

"Like I said, you gotta get that thing fixed."

Chapa knew the smart move was to say nothing and just drive away. Go to the first place he found and have a new mirror installed. Quiet. Uneventful. Smart. He knew that was the thing to do, even gave it a moment's consideration.

And instead, he went with, "Is that what the doctor said to your mother on the day you were born?"

Tate's forehead turned nearly as red as the hairs that lined it. He took a step back and unsnapped his holster.

"Step out of the vehicle, now!"

Chapa undid his seat belt, pausing a moment to show Tate that it had been buckled, then slowly got out of his car. As soon as he emerged from the vehicle, Tate rushed him, and in one well-trained move spun Chapa around and pressed his chest against the side of the Corolla. Before Chapa could make a sound, Tate grabbed the reporter's left arm and yanked it up until his wrist was just below his shoulder blades.

Pain raced across Chapa's back, shoulders, and up into his neck. Even more when Tate let his considerable weight push in against him. But except for an involuntary grunt, there was no way he was going to let Tate know how much this hurt.

"When I saw your shitty little car, I thought, oh happy day."

"Didn't know you cared so much, Dan," Chapa said through teeth that were grinding with every breath.

Tate pressed even harder, jamming Chapa's left shoulder into the metal frame of the rear driver's side window.

"That's *Officer Tate*, asshole."

His breath smelled like Doritos. That, combined with the pain, was starting to have an effect on Chapa's stomach.

"Maybe it's just me, but whenever I'm screwing someone I insist they call me by my first name, Dan."

Tate let up a little, but the relief was only temporary. Chapa knew things were about to get worse when he heard the clanging of handcuffs.

"This is going to be fun," Tate said, and abruptly yanked Chapa's left arm down, then moved in with the cuffs.

But the sound of a woman's voice coming through the speaker-mic attached to Tate's shoulder ruined the officer's mood.

"We've got a four-car collision at the intersection of Sunset and Grand, please respond, Officer Tate."

Tate grunted, then pressed a button on the small device.

"Janet, this is Dan, have we got anyone else who can get to the scene?"

"Sorry, Dan, but it's bad. How soon can you be there?"

Tate sighed.

"I'm on my way."

With that, he pulled the cuffs away, gave Chapa one last shove, then tossed his registration on the ground, but pocketed his license. Chapa didn't take the bait, didn't squat just inches from Tate's knee, didn't even look down.

"Sooner or later. It could be city, county, or state, but one of us is gonna make it very bad for you."

As the cop returned to his cruiser, Chapa tried to casually shake the sting out of his shoulder. He leaned his aches against the battered Corolla as Tate sped by. Once the squad car was out of sight, Chapa picked his registration up off the street and tucked it in his wallet, then did what he could to put the mirror back into place.

Chapa was cold and numb except for the throbbing in his back. Defiance had become natural to him in situations like this, but he paid a price for it. His hand was trembling just a little, which pissed him off most of all.

Before pulling out into traffic, Chapa reached down and snatched the ticket up off the floor, then tossed it in his glove compartment with a dozen or so others of different colors and sizes. Chapa would have a close friend in the Chicago branch of the FBI make a phone call in the next couple of days and the whole thing would go away. Until the next time. His license would arrive in the mail within a week.

Turning left onto Annie's street, Chapa was struck by how little it had changed. The area appeared much as it had more than a decade and a half before, as though the people there were waiting for something to happen before they could move.

The Sykes lived near the end of a long block of upper middle-class homes. Chapa recognized the white house with the stone front and blue window boxes that once cradled flowers. The paint on the windows was all but chipped away, and moisture had crept in and started to warp the frames. A late model Taurus sat in the driveway, making it a safe bet someone was home.

Chapa parked along the curb, kicking up a swirl of dead leaves. Sensing that an October wind was stopping by for a midday visit, he grabbed his brown leather coat, then stepped out of his car and into the past.

CHAPTER 6

"I've seen you before."

She looked like she had seen too much and remembered more than anyone would want to.

Chapa was doing his best to connect the woman behind the dented screen to the one that he had met years before. He remembered Michelle Sykes being attractive, but found it hard to imagine how the person at the door could have ever turned a head.

"We met many years ago, I'm Alex Chapa."

Her facial expression changed, first to recognition, then to something less than approval.

"My daughter left a long time ago. What do you want?"

He put on his most reassuring reporter's face.

"Just to catch up a little. I was doing a story on Grubb and got to wondering if you folks were okay, and how Annie was doing."

He followed that up with an empathetic smile and hoped it would do the trick. She hesitated for a moment, studying the reporter's face, then relented.

"Come on in, but please wipe your feet."

Chapa sat down on a couch that was almost as worn as the carpeting. The faded photos on the wall, old furniture, and even older television and stereo made him feel like he was sitting in a time capsule. She offered him something to drink and retreated to the kitchen to get it, then returned a moment later with a cup of coffee.

"Annie is not here, if that's why you came by."

"When did she move out?"

"The last time we saw her was a little over a year ago. Only heard from her once since then. She called last Mother's Day."

Chapa took a sip of the lifeless coffee, set the cup down, and pulled out a small spiral as though it were nothing at all.

"Where does Annie live now?"

"Don't know, probably somewhere in Chicago. Her name isn't Annie anymore, it's Angela."

"She changed it?"

"I don't know if it's legal, you know through the courts, but that's what she wants to be called."

Chapa wrote down *Angela Sykes, Chicago.*

"Does she have a job? Is she going to school? Is she dating anyone?"

Michelle Sykes shrugged, then slumped down a little and Chapa thought if the woman remained still long enough she might fade into the wallpaper.

"She draws really well, and she mentioned something about working as an artist."

"Do you know who her friends are?"

"She's talked about a friend, but I don't think it's a romantic thing, other than that I have no idea, wish I knew. She and her brother Tyler, he's gone away too. They're my only children. I lost the baby I was carrying, not long after Annie was taken."

"I never knew that."

"Why would you? I never showed much, didn't get

the chance to, and it wasn't something the press needed to know about."

Chapa tucked the notebook back into his coat pocket.

"And how is your husband doing?"

She started to drift away, but then reached across the timeworn coffee table and picked up Chapa's cup.

"I'll refill this, you look like you could use a little more."

He wasn't going to point out that it was only a couple of polite sips away from full. She walked to the kitchen, but stopped in the doorway.

"My husband is doing fine. Thank you for asking."

Chapa watched her drift into the kitchen. He stood up from the sagging couch, which wasn't easy, and wandered over to a row of photos along a far wall. Several had yellowed, all were at least a decade old. Either that, or Michelle Sykes had aged faster than most presidents do while in office.

Annie was in almost every photo. Birthday and Christmas settings breathed life into scenes of parties and family gatherings that appeared to be among the oldest on the wall. Miscellaneous relatives, who resembled one parent or the other, leaned in and smiled. It was all there on the wall, captured inside plastic frames.

Chapa focused on a row of Annie's high school pictures. She'd grown up in a hurry, though there was always a hint of the little girl. Tyler got the same treatment, and Chapa detected a certain consistency to the photos. It didn't matter if Annie was smiling or not, she always had a faraway look. Tyler, on the other hand, usually appeared angry, or frustrated, or like he wanted to be anywhere else.

Through a narrow opening in the kitchen door, Chapa caught a glimpse of Michelle standing at the sink, staring out a window. He considered walking over to her, or asking if everything was okay, then thought better of it.

He remembered his first visit here when the wallpaper was new and the paint on the trim was fresh. The house was full of energy then. The Sykes were not just willing, but anxious to get their story out, and Chapa obliged. Maybe he should have warned them back then that trying to clear Roger's name and assign blame to the police could bring even more unwanted attention. But Chapa had sensed there was more to it. That perhaps Roger Sykes had a mass of guilt he couldn't get free of. Now he wondered if Roger had been the only parent knotted up by dark feelings they could not shake.

Chapa spotted a stack of papers that had been carefully placed on a small side table. Sliding the first one off the top, he saw that they were all the same. Christmas letters, the kind families send each other in hope of giving some meaning to the year that has come and gone.

Glancing over to the kitchen again, and seeing that Michelle had not moved, he picked up one of the letters.

Hello Everyone,

Has another year really passed by? The time moves so quickly now, not like before. We hope this finds all of you well, healthy, and with peace of mind.

Roger and I have come full circle since Annie moved out and is thriving on her own. It's just the two of us here in the old house now, though things are never just like they were before.

Annie is in good health, and she likes her new job. She returns home almost every weekend, and we're thankful for that. She has a wonderful social life and

Roger and I both feel that it won't be long before she introduces us to Mr. Right.

Tyler is off living a life of travel and adventure. You know Tyler, always getting into one thing or another. Though college didn't suit him, he's getting firsthand life experience and meeting new people all the time. Every time he calls our conversations seem to go on and on.

Roger and I marked our 25th wedding anniversary this fall. We kept the celebration to a minimum. As everyone knows, we're not big party people. So I just cooked a nice meal and we had a wonderful time together.

Roger is getting better and the new medication that he's been on for a little over a year is working well. He's up and around on most days, and our times together are some of the best we've had in a while. I believe he has found some solid ground, and for that we are both grateful.

We've been talking about taking a trip next year, our first in a very long time. We're hoping Annie can break away from her busy schedule to join us. Maybe Tyler will realize his folks aren't as old as he remembers and he'll tag along too.

We'd love to hear from you. Christmas is such a special time for us, filled with wonderful old memories from back when we moved into this house and all the fun we had when Annie still believed in Santa Claus.

We hope your year has been rewarding, and that you are with your family during this holiday season.

> *God Bless,*
> *Roger, Michelle, Annie, and Tyler*

"Our Christmas message, I try to put on a good face, no one wants to hear about your problems."

Chapa had not heard her come back into the room and felt a bit guilty about reading the letter.

"It's sad how the number of letters I need to send out seems to shrink each year," she said, handing him the refilled cup of coffee.

He pointed to the bottom of the paper and what appeared to be a crude family crest with a fancy "S" in the middle.

"Tyler drew that a long time ago, before he got so angry about everything."

Chapa returned the page to the top of the small stack.

"And the part about Annie?"

"I didn't want to tell everyone that I don't know where she is or what she does with herself. They would just think we've done a terrible job as parents."

"What about your husband? Did he get hurt, or sick?"

She shook her head.

"There's nothing physically wrong with him. He's one of the fittest men I've ever known." She motioned for Chapa to sit down and he chose a rocker over taking another chance with the couch.

"I think he kept hoping it would all get back to how it was before. It never worked out that way."

"What do you remember about the night Annie disappeared?"

"More than you would want to know."

She looked into his eyes with a long gaze that Chapa knew he could not penetrate. Sensing his time there was through, he took one last, long sip of coffee, mostly to be polite. He gave her his card and the standard, "Give me a call if there's anything else that you can tell me," though he knew he'd never hear from the woman.

He thanked her, and said goodbye as they walked out onto the front porch. But she suddenly grabbed his arm, then recoiled a little, as though physical contact had become alien to her.

"I never blamed my husband, even though everyone else did."

"I'm sure you didn't, why would you have?" Instinctively, Chapa reached into his coat pocket and wrapped his hand around his recorder. "Would you like to talk a little more about that?"

She shook her head, and Chapa responded with a nod, then reached up and squeezed her shoulder in a way he hoped would be reassuring. He was halfway to his car when he heard the screen door open behind him.

"I hope you don't take this the wrong way, but please don't come back."

Chapa didn't turn to look at her, and didn't take it any way at all.

CHAPTER 7

Though the calendar read October 7, 1992, it still smelled a lot like summer in the Midwest. Smoke rose from suburban Illinois backyards, as folks were sneaking in one more night of barbecuing before the inevitable chill took hold. Roger Sykes worked late and came home to find his pregnant wife lying on the couch, slowed by another bout of the indigestion that was becoming a daily ordeal. He volunteered to run to the store and pick up a couple of necessities, namely milk, toilet paper, and a box of crackers to offset the nausea.

He was at the end of the driveway when his daughter Annie came bounding out of the house.

"Mom said I could go with you."

It was a short drive to the store and Annie filled it with talk about school, her friends, and Halloween. When they pulled into the mostly empty lot, the child asked her father if she could run in and get what they needed.

Annie had just about convinced him someone would help her take the gallon of milk to the register, and that she would count the change to make sure it was right. Then his mobile phone started ringing, and he handed

Annie a ten dollar bill and watched her run into the store.

The call lasted less than five minutes, so Roger wasn't alarmed that Annie wasn't back before he was finished. He turned the radio on and listened to an oldies station while waiting. When Fleetwood Mac's "Don't Stop" came on Roger flipped over to sports talk. The old 70's hit was getting more airplay than usual since it had become presidential candidate Bill Clinton's theme song.

Ten minutes passed, then fifteen, and the discussion between the former jocks had grown stale. Roger wasn't quite worried yet, just a bit frustrated that maybe Annie had forgotten which type of milk to get. She'd be too stubborn to admit that, and would likely end up buying the wrong kind. He got out and went to help her.

Roger planned to pretend that he'd forgotten one other item, so as to not embarrass his daughter, or give her the idea he was checking up on her. There were more employees than customers milling around the mid-size grocery store. Roger was a little surprised when he didn't see Annie standing near one of the registers.

He walked the length of the aisle that ran across the front of the store, then more slowly down the one that was parallel at the back. Roger's pace picked up as he weaved up and down the rows that connected the front to the back. When he'd walked each of them, several more than once, he hustled over to the customer service desk.

Had she gone to the bathroom?

"Could you page my little girl? Her name is Annie."

An older woman with unnaturally dark hair framing a blank expression complied. After more than a minute passed without a response, Roger asked one of the employees to check the bathroom, and followed her to where it was located in the rear of the store. He watched as the squat, middle-aged woman pushed the door open, called out to Annie, then returned, shaking her head.

Could she have finished and walked out? Might he have missed her?

When none of the four people working the registers could remember a small girl checking out, Roger switched into panic mode.

"Annie!"

Roger yelled out her name several times as he sprinted down the same aisles he'd confidently walked just minutes before. He then ran toward the store's backroom against the protests of the owner. The smell of stale fruit greeted Roger as he pushed through the door. The large, dimly lit space was littered with boxes and refrigeration units. Roger moved through the room without a sense of direction, stopping at a small brown table that had newspapers and a used Styrofoam cup on it. One of the folding chairs around the table was lying on its side.

Calling out for her again, Roger ran spastically through the cluttered room, tossing boxes aside. He scrambled over to the large freezers and looked inside each one. Roger was sweating, his mind racing, he knew he had to get a grip. He stopped moving just long enough to see a container of milk and a package of toilet paper sitting on the floor, next to a box of Annie's favorite cereal. A box of crackers lay a few feet away from the other discarded things. It had been ripped open, and one of the wrapped stacks was missing.

He squatted down and gently touched the items, as though they were connected to his daughter. Then Roger looked up and saw that the storeroom's back door was just a few feet away, and that it was ajar. He ran outside and into an empty stretch of asphalt.

"Annie! Can you hear me?"

Following the wide drive to where it met the street,

Roger found himself along the side of the building. He could see his car at the other end, and for a moment he hoped Annie would be sitting inside, waiting for him. But he knew better now, and he dropped to his knees and screamed like a wounded animal. Weeping uncontrollably, he drove his fist into the pavement until it went numb.

During those wretched minutes, as he was gutted by emotions that came from some place dark and primitive, Roger Sykes felt himself cross a line that few ever dare to approach.

Though dozens of cars passed by him on the busy street, and some even slowed down a little to stare at the desperate man, Roger had never felt so alone.

Five hours later, Roger Sykes and his wife drove home from the police station in separate cars. All of the store's employees had been accounted for, and the only security cameras were positioned over the registers. Still, the cops did their best to give Annie's parents a bit of hope.

As Roger turned onto his street, that overplayed Fleetwood Mac song came on the radio again. But he didn't notice, and he probably would not have had the strength to reach over and switch stations anyhow.

Six torturous days after the abduction, and twenty hours after Annie Sykes had walked into Dominic Delacruz's store, Alex Chapa took the call that would change his professional life.

The day after Chapa broke the story of Grubb's capture, reporters from other papers went after the crime scene, the killer, and the police investigation. Chapa did that as well, but he instinctively focused on the girl's family, and Annie herself, knowing that the human interest angle would draw in readers. He was right.

As a result, his stories brought the child far more notoriety than any ten-year-old victim and her parents should ever have to deal with. His editors, however, were so impressed with Chapa's work on the initial piece, how he'd managed to talk to the girl, though he refused to quote her directly, as well as her parents, that they allowed him to continue as lead reporter on the story. Soon after, Chapa landed a better job with a bigger paper.

For weeks after Grubb's capture, and then again around the time of his trial, police had to create a barrier around the Sykes' home to keep the curious at something close to a reasonable distance. One person in particular, a grieving father named Jack Whitlock, became especially obsessed with Annie. Whitlock believed Annie and his son had been imprisoned by Grubb at the same time, and he wanted answers to why she had escaped and his boy hadn't.

Forensics proved that Carson Whitlock had been Grubb's fifth victim, brutally murdered more than two months before Annie was taken, but not found until after her capture. Those facts did nothing to sway Whitlock, who confronted Annie as she walked home from school one day, an act that earned him a restraining order.

Chapa had always been concerned about any lingering effect his story might have had on the young girl's already damaged life. For years he had wanted to make it up to Annie Sykes. The guilt would rise up in him each time he was assigned a new story about Grubb.

Maybe Annie had forgiven him by now. The police certainly hadn't. Though Chapa had used only those quotes that were on the record, some of the brass in the various jurisdictions involved with the case saw it otherwise.

There was some aggressive ass-covering involved, which always happens when a reporter breaks a story before it gets spun. And a bit of quiet embarrassment over the way a child helped break a case that had stumped the authorities for months. In time, police departments all over the Chicago area would turn on Chapa for questioning their investigation methods and describing, in detail, how they had failed to put together several significant leads.

No matter the cause, the results were severe. Chapa struggled, more than most reporters, to get any sort of information or even the most basic cooperation from authorities. For years he'd been routinely harassed at crime scenes. That simmering tension spilled over one night when the subject of an exposé he'd been working on assaulted him at a bar, and Chapa was the one who spent the night in jail. It was made clear to him then that he was on his own.

Sometimes Chapa missed the days before the Grubb story, when he was still carving out a career. Back then, his life, personal as well as professional, made a lot more sense to him.

Chapa was thinking about that time now as he drove to the *Record*'s main office to do some research on Annie. He was lost in his thoughts of the past as well as his troubling visit with Michelle Sykes, but still noticed the green sedan in the rearview mirror. Chapa was almost sure it had been there since he pulled out of the Sykes' neighborhood, some twenty minutes earlier.

CHAPTER 8

The green sedan was still there ten minutes and a dozen turns later. Most of those changes in direction had no purpose other than to prove Chapa's suspicions. Though it figured that whoever was following him already knew where Chapa worked, he was feeling territorial, and wanted to lose this asshole before driving on to the *Record*.

Chapa switched off the radio right in the middle of a vintage Warren Zevon howl. He then turned a sharp left onto what he knew was a short street, followed by a quick right, then punched the accelerator. It was midafternoon, and traffic was light.

As he swung left and merged into the flow on northbound Randall Road, Chapa caught just a slice of green in his mirror. He'd left the tail back around the last corner. Maybe the driver hadn't seen him. He kept looking back for about a half mile, but couldn't make out if a green sedan was somewhere in the pack of cars lagging behind.

He turned off Randall a few streets sooner than usual, into a lazy residential area. For two blocks Chapa saw nothing but tree-lined asphalt in his wake. But as he pulled up to a four-way, he spotted the car casually closing in about a block and a half back.

Chapa drove through the intersection and past the next one, then pulled over. The green sedan slowed down, then paused before rolling through the first intersection and coming to a stop against the curb.

Whoever was driving that car had to be connected to Grubb, Chapa figured. Maybe it was the killer Grubb had told him about. The one who was stalking Annie Sykes.

Eyes locked on the busted side-view mirror, wondering what the other driver might do next, fidgeting, drumming his fingers on the steering wheel, and growing tired of this bullshit, Chapa decided to make his move. He drove away from the curb, and turned into the next driveway. A small woman wearing a pale green smock and a lavender bandana looked up from the garden she was working on along the front of her house. He tossed a nod her way, then pulled out and reversed direction.

Chapa figured that as much as the driver of the green sedan wanted to stay on his tail, it had to be even more important that they avoid being seen. Chapa was going to make that more difficult. He had to get a look at the sedan's license plate.

But as he raced back to where the car had come to a stop, Chapa saw no sign of the vehicle. That changed once he reached the next intersection. He turned right and sped up until the green sedan was no more than a block away.

That must've been when the driver spotted him, because he matched Chapa's speed, then accelerated even more. Chapa wasn't comfortable doing fifty, fifty-five, now sixty down narrow neighborhood streets. He slowed at each intersection, a precaution that cost him precious distance every time.

One block gave way to another as the two cars danced around parked vehicles, and maneuvered through curves, conceding a bit of speed until the next straightaway. Tri-level houses and two-car garages rushed by as the Toyota's engine moaned with each press of the accelerator. The gap between them was holding steady, and Chapa's only hope was that the driver would run into a red light or a crowded four-way.

Then he caught a break. Three intersections ahead and almost a full block beyond the green car, a stoplight turned yellow, and Chapa knew there was no chance the driver would get through before it went red. Even if he turned right at the light, it should still slow him down a little, maybe just enough for Chapa to read his plate number.

Chapa watched as the green sedan approached the intersection. The light turned red, but the vehicle kept going, weaving around a car that was making a left turn, serenaded by angry horns as it just barely avoided another.

The car was still in Chapa's sights as he arrived at the intersection. Chapa paused for a moment, just long enough to see that the nearest oncoming car was at least thirty yards away. Then he hit the gas and blew through. A car horn wailed from somewhere behind him.

The green sedan had slowed down some, the driver apparently deciding that he'd ditched Chapa at the light. A block and a half became a dozen car lengths, then even fewer, and Chapa started focusing on the plate. Just a little bit closer.

But the heavy roar of the sedan's engine and the screeching of tires told Chapa he'd been spotted. In an instant, the gap between the two vehicles doubled, then Chapa lost sight of the car as it made a left turn without slowing down.

Chapa was pushing seventy as he closed in on the same corner. He kept his foot off the brake and took the turn at full speed, jamming the wheel hard to the left. But instead of seeing the green sedan, Chapa's vision became a blur of blue as he swerved to miss the massive garbage truck that was a few short feet away and bearing down hard.

He avoided a collision by the narrow width of a heartbeat, but overcompensated in the process. The Toyota's right front tire crashed hard into the curb, and the car went airborne for a moment before slamming back down to the pavement.

The truck rumbled through the intersection as though nothing had happened, but Chapa wasn't sure his car would be able to continue as easily. Chapa's palms, like the middle of his back, were slick with sweat. This had gone far enough. He put the car in park, and took his first good breath since he'd turned around in that driveway.

Two blocks' worth of neatly kept middle-class homes away, the driver of the sedan responded by slowing all the way down to a crawl. He was mocking Chapa, taunting him. Not the least bit shaken by any of this. It was as though the other driver had lured him into another reality, one Chapa wanted to break free of immediately.

But Chapa remembered why he'd gone on the offensive in the first place. The threat to Annie Sykes, maybe others too. Could be the person in that car wanted to hurt Michelle Sykes' little girl. Could be they planned to tear apart whatever was left of Roger Sykes by finishing what Grubb had started. Chapa wasn't going to let that happen. He shifted into drive, straightened the wheel, and accelerated as the green sedan sped off.

A few blocks ahead, the suburban neighborhood opened into large field. In the distance, Chapa could see there was more traffic and movement than what they had encountered up until now.

Then he realized why.

The green sedan was less then a block ahead of him when Chapa drove past the school traffic sign. Chapa immediately slowed down, then abruptly pulled over as Balenger Elementary rose out of its usually tranquil surroundings.

If he thought putting his hands up or waving a white flag would have done any good, Chapa would not have hesitated in doing it. Anything to tell the other driver that this was over. But Chapa knew better. The green sedan wasn't slowing down. It was accelerating.

Chapa watched helplessly as it sped toward a crosswalk. A group of children, still buzzed about the end of their school day, was heading straight for the street. The crossing guard, an older woman whose white hair contrasted with her brightly colored uniform, was paying attention to the kids she was there to protect. Seemingly unaware that death was raging in their direction at more than sixty miles per hour, she began to lead the children into the crosswalk.

One of the kids pointed toward the speeding car as the woman raised her stop sign and took a backward step into the street. Chapa pulled out and headed toward the school, desperate to figure out a way to make the car stop, knowing that he couldn't.

He punched his horn, four quick jabs.

The woman turned as the green sedan charged through the crosswalk at full speed, then she fell down hard. Chapa sped toward her, ready to help in whatever way he could, as the sound of children screaming sliced through the afternoon calm.

But as Chapa got closer he saw the woman sit up, then scramble to her feet like a gymnast who just took a spill. She withdrew a pencil and small notepad from her orange vest, turned toward the green sedan as it disappeared in the distance, and quickly scribbled something.

Chapa rolled down his window as he pulled up and stopped.

"Ma'am, are you okay?"

"I'm fine, I've fallen before and I'm sure I'll fall again. We all fall down sometimes."

She smiled at the kids, and Chapa could see the woman was holding it together for their sake.

"No, really, are you hurt?" Chapa asked, lowering his voice.

"I'm okay, thank you." She brushed a patch of dirt off her hip, picked up her stop sign, and waved the children across.

"I saw you writing something. Did you get the plate number?"

She looked down at her notepad.

"I'm afraid not, but I know it was a green Dodge, and the driver was a large man. Next time I'll get the son—" she started to use a term that was not appropriate for young ears, and stopped herself. "The next time that careless gentleman drives by this school, I will get his license plate and I'll report him."

Chapa liked the woman's grit, and had no doubt she would spend weeks and maybe months looking out for the green sedan. But he was also certain there wouldn't be a next time.

As Chapa drove away, he fought to steady his breathing and pulse rate. Both were racing at speeds faster than any car he'd ever owned could reach.

CHAPTER 9

Duane Wormley was smiling like he'd just taken a stealthy piss in Chapa's coffee.

"The prodigal reporter has returned."

Chapa ignored him, it was something he'd become good at through repetition, but Wormley would have none of it.

"Maybe I should ask for your autograph, while I still have the chance," Wormley said, then leaned back his small, burgundy upholstered office chair that Chapa always thought looked purposely uncomfortable.

"What are you talking about, Duane?"

"Ooh, someone's way out of the loop, so far out he can't even see it, not without a, you know, he needs—"

"What, Duane? A telescope, a compass, an atlas, a GPS system, two Sherpas, whatever, just get there."

Wormley withdrew a little, like a threatened turtle. Pushing his narrow glasses up the bridge of his nose, he looked around the newsroom like he was some sort of secret agent.

"There's a buzz," he said, leaning in toward Chapa, then ran a hand through thinning dishwater blond hair as though he were giving someone a signal.

Zach, an intern Chapa had just about decided was

okay, was sitting a few feet beyond Wormley's sightline. He caught Chapa's eyes, then rolled his.

"What kind of a buzz?" Chapa asked.

"The kind that results in cutbacks. The sort of cutbacks that sometimes put overpaid reporters on the street."

Chapa had heard that sort of talk before. It was a cyclical thing, but over the past few years, as more readers turned to the Internet and ad revenues softened, the cycles had become shorter. It was happening in every newspaper office, all over the country.

"I wouldn't be the first to go."

"I wouldn't be so sure of that." Wormley was feeling his oats again. "You have an office, the rest of us work in cubicles, or at a desk in the middle of a crowded room. You're always out of the building, I'm always on time, and I'm an example to others."

Zach adopted a serious look, tightened his lips, and gave Chapa a mocking nod. Though he had a habit of putting a little too much purple in his prose, Zach had real potential.

Wormley was still talking.

"You have an attitude, I have a purpose. And you're extremely well paid, while others have to count their peanuts."

That last line conjured up an image that Chapa did not want to dwell on. He also opted to not mention that a large portion of his paycheck went toward child support.

"He's Alex Freakin' Chapa," Zach jumped into the fray. Chapa rewarded him with a *Right On* point of his left index finger.

"Big deal," Wormley didn't bother to turn and face the intern. "I got more email responses to my column last week than you did to yours, Alex. Probably more responses than you've gotten all year."

"You ran a column asking people to send in the story

of their most exciting scrapbooking experience," Chapa said, making no effort to mask his disdain.

"That's right, I'm in touch with what readers are into today. You're not."

A few others in the office were doing their best to pretend they weren't tuned in to this exchange. Most of the morning crew was still around. Reporters, editors, and layout artists working the night shift, and others like Chapa who punched their own clocks, were starting to stumble in.

"Duane, you're not a journalist. For shit's sake, you named your column *Wormin' Around.*"

"That's clever."

"It's stupid."

Zach choked back a laugh. Chapa decided the kid was okay.

"Taken literally, it suggests you're either playing in dirt, or having sex with yourself."

A mix of anger and confusion flashed across Duane's slender face.

"What's that supposed to—"

"Worms have both male and female junk down there," Zach chimed in.

Wormley corkscrewed his brow and looked off into the distance, as if he was actually trying to picture how that might work.

"I'm just saying you're going to want to get your résumé together, that's all."

Remembering he had work to do, Chapa shrugged, then started for his office.

"Oh yeah, and Macklin was looking for you, something about needing to have a meeting."

That stopped Chapa, but for just a moment, and he didn't turn to look back.

"You're going to get fired, Alex."

"Not this week."

CHAPTER 10

Chapa learned early on that reporters have streaks which run hot and cold just like athletes and gamblers do. Most of the time there's no rhyme or reason to it. One day a guy is in a slump, then maybe the right story comes along and a week later he's back in a groove.

Over the past couple of months, Chapa had been mired in the mother of all slumps. He knew it too, which made things much worse. Wormley was onto something, the fact that Macklin was looking for him was a concern. Nothing good could come from a sit-down with the *Record*'s managing editor, and Chapa wasn't ready to face it head-on just yet. First, he had a story to write.

He shut the door to his office, and the unruly collection of sounds from the busy newsroom were left on the other side, replaced by the steady swoosh of a ceiling fan. The small space, the same one Chapa had occupied since his first day at the *Record*, was cluttered but not disorganized. At any given moment Chapa could point to which pile or crowded desk drawer contained a particular piece of information or an old clipping. There were several shelves filled with reference books, a few CDs—mostly jazz and blues, his writing music—but none of the awards Chapa had received over the years. Most of those were boxed and stored in Chapa's attic, a few others had been stuffed into a file cabinet drawer awaiting the same fate. Framed photos covered what little wall space there was—all of them were of Nikki. Two of the ten-year-old's drawings were taped to the only window in the office. The light from outside shone through, projecting a series of colors across Chapa's workspace.

He poured himself a cup of coffee from the pot he'd made earlier that morning—the rich black Bustelo that few in the office would dare try and wade through. It was Chapa's morning companion seven days a week. He took a long sip and went to work. The hour Chapa spent online yielded very little. His search turned up a few small mentions of Annie Sykes winning an award or making the honor roll in high school, but nothing that could help him find her now. Substituting *Angela* for *Annie* didn't help. The young woman had somehow managed to stay off the grid. He ran into the same frustrating conclusion sifting through his files on the case, as well as all the other readily available information.

After digging around for a while on several news sites, Chapa tracked down a few stories connecting the names and places Grubb had given him. But very little of it was of any help. The authorities typically kept a lid on how much the media was told while their investigations were ongoing. If Grubb had access to outside information he could just as easily have learned of these cases. Chapa felt like he was being played, but he couldn't afford to be wrong about that.

Around 5:30 he called Joseph Andrews, an agent at the Chicago branch of the FBI.

"You know how I hate asking you for a favor, Joe."

"Not half as much as I hate hearing you ask."

They agreed to meet for dinner in a couple of hours.

It was Chapa's turn to buy, so naturally Andrews chose an upscale steakhouse halfway to the city.

"Will the *Record* be picking up this tab?" Andrews asked.

"I'm going to make sure we talk business so that it does."

"Cheap bastard."

Chapa pulled together his notes from the meeting with Grubb, and typed out the list of names the killer had given him. He didn't have much faith in anything Grubb said, but he would pass the info on to Andrews anyhow.

When he was just about ready to leave he phoned Nikki, and hoped her mother would not answer the child's cell phone. Chapa had no wish to engage in any more conversations with his ex-wife than were absolutely necessary. Another showdown with Carla was the last thing he needed today.

It seemed now, years after it ended, like their marriage had always been more quicksand than bedrock. Chapa had always done his best to avoid fighting with Carla in front of Nikki. But Chapa knew that by the time the child turned three she had developed an acute sense of trouble between her parents. It had worried him every time Nikki tried to overcompensate by being even more clingy and affectionate than usual. Chapa and his daughter had been close until the day she and her mother moved out. No matter how hectic the rest of his life became, he had always made time for Nikki. He had been her comfort parent, the one she would cuddle up on when she wasn't feeling well, the one she would ask to help her with a puzzle, or play a game, or watch a movie. But it wasn't like that anymore.

After a few rings, he heard the sound of his daughter's voice asking the caller to leave a message. They had not spoken in more than two weeks, though Chapa had called at least once a day during that time. He enjoyed hearing her voice, even if it was only a recording that he suspected was being used to avoid a conversation.

"Hey, sweetie, it's Dad again. I miss you so much, I would love to talk to you, even if it's only for a minute. So hey, why don't you give me a call? I love you with all of my heart."

There hadn't been a blow-up or a rift of any kind between them, which made Chapa wonder if Carla was somehow involved. He hung up the phone, but let his hand linger on the receiver, as though it were a connection to his child.

After sitting at his desk for a few lost minutes, he called Erin to let her know he wouldn't be stopping by.

"I was planning on cooking for you, Alex."

"I didn't know that, in fact, I wasn't sure whether you were expecting me tonight."

Though things had steadily become more involved between them, Chapa knew that Erin's commitment level was outpacing his own.

"I'm sure I asked you about tonight a couple of days ago."

"If you're sure, then you probably did, and I probably said I'd be there."

They had been dating for just over six months, and Chapa had done his best to keep a healthy distance between himself and the commitment track. It hadn't worked out the way he'd planned.

Nothing about their first meeting hinted at how attached they would become, though the connection had been immediate. Chapa had gone to his bank after a statement suggested that Carla's name was still on their accounts more than two years after he'd filled out paperwork to remove it. After sitting in the lobby for a while, he was shown to Erin's office. Less than a minute into their discussion, Chapa made a point of checking for a wedding ring.

Before their casual business talk was over he told her, "This is the first truly interesting meeting I've ever had with a bank vice president."

That got a smile out of her, a real one, not the standard customer relations version, and Chapa saw just how lovely she was. An Irish beauty, whose dark chocolate brown hair reached down to caress soft shoulders, and perfectly accentuated her warm hazel eyes. He didn't ask Erin out before leaving the bank, even though she walked him to the door, but he took her card knowing that he would.

Erin's phone was ringing as she walked back into her office. It was Chapa calling from the parking lot. They went out that night, and twice more in the week that followed. She hadn't dated anyone that many times in more than four years. Chapa had promised himself he'd never date anyone exclusively again.

"I'll make it up to you, Erin. I'll be over tomorrow night and I'll stay until you kick me out."

Chapa was beginning to understand that was something she would probably never do.

CHAPTER 11

J.D.'s Grill wasn't really a *grill.* Not when the cheapest steak on the menu checked in at twenty-four bucks and change. The décor was designed to create a rustic vibe, complete with dark wood paneling and ceiling lamps made from antlers. But the dessert tray Chapa was staring at one table over told another story. He wondered how many mountain cabins and hunting lodges were stocked with French pastries.

Chapa had waited nearly half an hour beyond his reservation time before finally being seated in a cramped back corner. Andrews was late, which was unusual, then again, so was the agent's choice of restaurants. Chapa was starting to wonder if he was in the wrong place.

"What, the little kid's table wasn't available?" Joseph Andrews said before Chapa had seen him.

Chapa looked up and was struck by how perfect the federal agent looked in his tailored suit. Like it had been molded to fit his tall, slender frame. Like a superhero's costume. Every one of Andrews' thick brown hairs was in its place, obedient army privates bending to the will of a demanding drill sergeant.

The two men had been friends since college, and had long ago perfected the art of ball-busting. They were opposites in many ways, but it worked somehow. Chapa was quite possibly the only soul on the planet who felt comfortable giving Joseph Andrews shit. The agent, in turn, was the only person who called Chapa "Al."

"Watch this, Al," Andrews said and waved to a guy who had been running the floor as though he was in charge of solving all of the world's seating problems.

To Chapa's amazement, the tightly dressed man rushed to Andrews, greeting him as though he were a rich relative. An instant later, two servers were motioned into action. They scooped up Chapa's menu, and for a moment he thought they were about to kick him out of the restaurant. Instead, the attentive trio led Chapa and Andrews to a table at the other end of the dining room, near a large fireplace.

"Now isn't this better?" Andrews asked.

Chapa gestured to the fireplace. "That must be where they roast the mutton that they hunt in the wilds of Oak Brook."

"Mutton comes from sheep, Al. People don't hunt sheep. You probably meant *venison*."

"No, actually I've gotten a good look at the staff here, and I think hunting sheep would present a major challenge for these folks."

"I know J.D.'s can be a bit high brow, but the food makes the rest of it easier to tolerate," Andrews responded, as attentive servers held chairs out for the two of them. Andrews played along, squatting just enough so that his could be scooted in under him. Chapa, on the other hand, shooed his server away.

"I can handle my own damn seat," he said to Andrews after they'd finally been left alone.

But it didn't last. Andrews had just opened his menu when another server scurried over and offered him dark linen, explaining how it would not clash with his charcoal gray pants. The agent nodded his approval and the young man carefully and evenly spread the deep blue cloth across his lap.

"No one wants to see a white slab across dark slacks, Al."

Chapa looked down at his own pants. Apparently his jeans weren't blue enough to merit a special napkin.

"I'm not going to coax the story out of you, Joe, it's already been way too long a day."

"I had dinner here with the governor Monday night." Tired or not, that got Chapa's attention. "I thought about inviting you along, but I know you don't like politics, and besides, he doesn't seem to like reporters much these days."

Chapa shrugged that off and they both ordered. Taking advantage of the lull before the food arrived, Chapa pulled out the list of names Grubb had given him and slid it across the table.

Andrews examined it closely, but Chapa could tell from his expression that the names were not familiar to him.

"You do know, these psychos pull shit like this all the time," Andrews said. "They seem to go extra crazy in the days before their execution. I once had a psychiatrist explain the reasons for it to me, but I didn't really give a damn, and I didn't listen."

"I understand this is probably a lot of hot air, but knowing what Grubb is capable of—"

"I will look into it. Whenever there's a situation where kids may be involved it immediately becomes a priority."

Andrews folded the sheet of paper into three equal sections and slipped it inside his crisp suit jacket.

"There's something else, too. I want you to help me find Annie Sykes."

Chapa explained about the threat from Grubb, the

name change, and how her mother thought she was living in Chicago.

"If you find her, then what? You'll protect her from some fictional copycat?"

"What if he's not fictional?"

"Then we'd know about it, and you would be in over your head."

Chapa wasn't so sure law enforcement would know about it, not even the Bureau. The apparent randomness of Grubb's crimes had stumped investigators sixteen years earlier. Whatever trait linked the victims to one another existed solely in the killer's mind. If a copycat was following that same blueprint, he wouldn't be any easier to detect.

They were more than halfway through a platter of calamari when the rest of the food arrived. The smell of fresh seafood and spices ribboned their table as Chapa watched Andrews organize the shrimp and linguini on his plate with the care that Tibetan monks take when creating intricate sand art. The twelve crustaceans circled the plate, perfectly spaced apart.

Chapa couldn't resist. He reached across the table and speared three o'clock.

"Delicious," he said through a full mouth.

Andrews just shook his head, then shifted two and four just enough to narrow the gap.

"So when did you decide to become the crime-solving journalist?"

"I'm not interested in solving any crimes, or catching a killer."

"That's good."

"I'm trying to find a young woman because I don't want her to get hurt any more than she already has been."

The two friends then set aside both personal and professional topics and dedicated the rest of the dinner-time conversation to the subjects most guys prefer talking about. After they had spent ten minutes debating what moves the Cubs should make during the off season, it was Andrews who returned to the reason they'd gotten together that night.

"Like I said, I will personally check it out. My division is spread thin right now with this election coming up. Half of my guys are off getting additional training at the request of the Homeland Security suits." Andrews pulled the list out of his pocket, looked at the names once more, then folded it up again and put it back. "Believe me, if this turns out to be something, I will launch an investigation."

Andrews wiped his mouth and tossed the napkin on the table like he was done. Though he hadn't eaten much of his meal.

"Look, Al, I know how you work."

Chapa listened as he slipped the last few bites of New York strip into his mouth.

"You do some research, talk to all sorts of people, screw up a few times, break some rules, piss folks off, then throw it all into a blender. And somehow what comes out is a great story that gets you another award."

Chapa was nodding as though he'd been locked in on Andrews' every word.

"Are you finished with those?" he asked, aiming his fork at the five remaining shrimp.

"Have at it." Andrews pushed his plate across the table. "But this situation is different, and if anything is going on you might get some blood on your hands, maybe your own."

The agent waved off their server's offer to show them the dessert tray, slapping his solid abs, then pointing to Chapa's and shaking his head. Chapa wasn't soft, not much, at least. But he didn't have Andrews' six days a week workout physique, either.

"I know what you can do when you go after a story. Your ability to focus and lock in is inspiring. But this isn't that kind of story, especially at a time when you should be focusing on the other parts of your life."

Chapa couldn't respond right away. He was still chewing the last of the shrimp, which he then washed down with his second glass of merlot.

"Joe, over the past three years I've lost my wife, I've lost my daughter, and any semblance of a normal home. And now it looks like I'll be losing my job."

Andrews flashed a look of concern, but Chapa raised an open palm and continued.

"When it comes to those areas of my life, I don't always understand what's expected of me. But I do know the rules of this game. I know there have been times when I've retreated into my work because it was easy. But now, my work is just about all I have."

Chapa explained the situation at the paper, Andrews mixing a few choice expletives with words of encouragement in response.

After Chapa picked up the check, Andrews said his goodbyes to various staff members, and they walked out to the parking lot.

"When are you going flying with me, Al?"

This was Andrews' latest hobby, and as with all of his previous obsessions, he made a habit of inviting his friend to join him.

"I don't know, Joe. I'm a big fan of keeping two feet planted on solid ground."

Before he'd started working toward earning his pilot's license, three years ago, Andrews had become an accomplished hiker, nature photographer, whitewater rafter, and spelunker. He would study long hours, engage in doctoral level research, and get into intense discussions with experts in each field. Maybe that's why he could not mask his unhappiness the time the two of them went scuba diving in the middle of Lake Michigan, and Chapa looked like a natural the moment he hit the water.

"After all, Al, you *were* born on an island," Andrews had pointed out once they were back on shore.

"So what? That was a long time ago. I don't see what all the excitement is about. You fall in the water, then just keep going."

Or the time Andrews wanted to show his friend how much he had improved since taking up archery some ten months earlier. In less than half an hour Chapa was just about matching him arrow for arrow.

"Big deal, Joe. You pull back, aim the damn thing, and let go."

So as they walked out to where Andrews had parked his Ford Escape, Chapa was thinking that flying a small plane probably wasn't all that difficult.

"Want to see something cool, Al? Get in and open the glove compartment."

Gauging by the size of the door, it was more of a one room apartment than a glove compartment.

"My guess is it didn't come this way from the factory."

Chapa pushed a button, and as the door slowly opened a pair of lights switched on inside. There he saw a collection of office supplies getting the kind of treatment that's usually reserved for cursed diamonds. All six of the pens of varying point sizes lining the door were Parkers, and so was the retractable pencil. Two small framed pictures brightened the base of the door, down by the hinges. One was of Jenny, Andrews' wife of nineteen years, and the other of their two sons. Filling the opening was a compact shelving unit complete with drawers.

"Sweet, isn't it," Andrews said, smiling. "Open the bottom drawer and give me the blue spiral."

Chapa did as instructed. The drawer held three

small spiral notebooks. The one on the right was blue. Andrews opened to a blank page and wrote down the name *Annie/Angela Sykes*, slipped the list of names inside the front cover, then handed the notebook back to Chapa who casually tossed it into the drawer.

"Eh, eh, eh," Andrews said. "Please, as you found it."

"Did you build this, Joe?"

"No, but I designed it," Andrews said. "I'm thinking of filing for a patent. Do you think people would go for it?"

Chapa returned the notebooks to their proper order and closed the door.

"Oh yeah, Joe, it would be huge. Especially if you added a small credenza, maybe off to the side. And a tiny vacuum cleaner so you could keep the whole thing nice and tidy."

Andrews gave his friend a familiar look of disapproval.

"Okay, Al, now you're just being a dick."

CHAPTER 12

The moment Chapa walked into his dark, two-story house he wished that he'd taken Erin up on her offer. The place was showing signs of neglect, and Chapa's to-do list had grown exponentially in the past several weeks.

Chapa looked through his mail—a bill, junk, and a letter he had written to Nikki which was now stamped RETURN TO SENDER. He tossed it, along with a CD package he'd received from a club he had joined after the divorce, on a pile of other unopened mail and other boxes of CDs he had not ordered.

He dropped his notepad and recorder on a small, cluttered table that sat just below a room-length wall of family photos. Before Carla moved out, the picture frames had been neatly hung to form a symmetrical pattern resembling the leafy half of a large tree. But after she had taken some of the pictures, and Chapa removed a few others, the whole thing took on the appearance of a poorly designed building that was threatening to collapse at any moment.

One photo of his daughter in particular caught Chapa's eye. It had been taken at a neighbor's swim-

ming pool the summer before the divorce. The child
was pushing her wet, amber hair away from her face, revealing the small birthmark that sometimes made her a
little self-conscious.

"Nikki, it's just part of you, and it's beautiful," her father had told her, gently touching the raindrop-shaped
mark under her left ear.

Having grown up without a father, Chapa had
made a silent promise to never let Nikki forget how
much he loved her, or how special she was. Now he
couldn't help feeling that he'd broken that promise.
He looked at that photo a little longer, wondering
how much Nikki had changed in the past few months.
The child resembled her mother at birth, but quickly
began to take on many of his facial characteristics,
even though his in-laws insisted the opposite was true.
This gave Chapa a warm feeling and an unbreakable
connection to his daughter long before she knew his
name.

Kicking off his shoes, Chapa headed in the direction
of the rustling sound he'd been hearing since he first
walked in. As he entered the kitchen Chapa was serenaded with a series of high-pitched notes, bringing a
smile to his face.

"Hey, Jimmy, how was your day?"

The yellow and black parakeet had been a gift from
Erin on the one month anniversary of their first date.
She seemed disappointed when he named the bird
after former president Jimmy Carter. She was hoping
for something more romantic. Though generally apolit-
ical, Chapa had recently written a story on the former
president and greatly admired the man, not for his performance in office, but for proving that lives can have a
second act.

The bird didn't talk much, but he loved to sing. He

perched on Chapa's finger, then his shoulder. Leaning in, Jimmy rubbed the top of his head against Chapa's face.

"I'd love to play, but I've still got some work to do."

Chapa returned Jimmy to his cage, which he then covered with an old sheet, and wished him good night.

Digging through his CD collection, Chapa realized that most of his music was in his car. It made sense, that was where he spent most of his time whenever he wasn't at the office or over at Erin's.

After rejecting several dozen albums, Chapa found the perfect CD to match his mood. A few seconds later, Robert Cray's lonesome chords were pouring through the speakers.

It didn't take him long to transcribe his recorded interview with Grubb, even though the device had missed a word or two while hidden away in Chapa's satchel. He read through the notes, then played the interview again, looking for any hidden details or the sort of crazy encoded shit psychos sometimes slip into conversation.

There was nothing there that he hadn't already heard. But there was something about Grubb's tone. He turned off the recorder, closed his eyes, and leaned back into the couch. Chapa sat there for several minutes, going over everything he could remember about the interview, and letting the music take him deeper into his thoughts. Then his eyes snapped open and he sat up. Goddamn it, Chapa believed him, and that meant Annie Sykes' life might now be measured in days.

He thought about calling Andrews, but knew his friend made a habit of going to bed much too early. So instead Chapa heated up a bowl of black beans from a pot he'd cooked the day before, and made sure all of his doors were locked—something told him that was a good idea. He spent a little more than an hour catching up on month-old magazines and thinking about Annie Sykes, then left the empty bowl in the sink and got ready for bed. Though he was tired and it was late, settling in wasn't easy that night. And when sleep finally did come, it proved to be anything but peaceful.

Five Days Before the Execution

CHAPTER 13

The cruel morning sun slipped in through Chapa's curtains, shoving him out of a series of fragmented dreams. He sat up too fast and his head screamed for mercy. When he finally got up at a more reasonable pace, Chapa reached for his cell phone and called Andrews.

"I believe him, Joe."

"I know you do, and I think you might be right."

Two of the names had already checked out, though it was not yet clear if any link existed between them. Andrews was still waiting to hear back about the others.

"It's most likely that Grubb has gotten information from the outside, heard or read about those cases, and tied them together," Andrews said. "But just based on those two we're going to have a couple of our guys talk to Grubb today."

The Bureau handled murderers as well as anyone, but Grubb had an agenda, and Chapa doubted they'd get anywhere.

"We'll get a list of everyone who has been in to see him during the past year," Andrews said. "But there are all sorts of ways to get information into and out of almost any prison."

"Any guesses on who could be paying him *tribute?*" Chapa asked, spitting the last word out as though it were a mouthful of phlegm.

"No clue. I got copies of all his files, but there isn't much there."

"Grubb had family, but no friends," Chapa remembered.

"That's right. The parents have been dead for years. Grubb has a brother, but they checked him out thoroughly back then. For a while there was some thought that Grubb was working with someone. Annie Sykes claimed there was another person in the basement with her and Grubb."

Chapa remembered that detail. Annie had believed there could have been a second person who always stayed hidden in shadows, just beyond her sight. But the police found no evidence of anything like that.

"Al, as far as I can tell the only big mistake Grubb's brother ever made was being born into that family."

"How about that father of one of the other kids Grubb murdered?"

"You mean Jack Whitlock, he went a little nuts, I remember. I don't suspect there's anything there, but I'll run a check on him, anyhow."

Chapa nearly dropped the phone as he maneuvered out of yesterday's clothes.

"You still there?" Andrews asked.

"Yeah, I'm in the process of peeling off the clothes I slept in."

"C'mon, Al, it's already been a tough day for me. I sure as hell don't need that image doggin' me around."

"Were there any surprises in the old police file?"

Chapa could hear the sound of pages ruffling, and files getting slapped down on Andrews' desk.

"Not really, the cops were thorough. You remember. They checked out the family, talked to the neighbors."

"Let me guess, they said he was a *quiet man* who generally kept to himself."

"Bingo. They even questioned a self-proclaimed psychic who'd gotten enough of the details right to be considered a possible suspect."

"I remember her. One of our staffers did a feature about psychics who help the police solve crimes and she was quoted in the story. Her name was Louise."

Andrews had cupped the speaker and was talking to someone in his office. Chapa was too tired to repeat himself and planned to sign off as soon as his friend turned his attention back to him.

"You're right, Al. Louise Jones, she worked out of a small storefront in downtown St. Charles."

Chapa had momentarily forgotten how well Andrews could multitask while in the middle of anything. One of Andrews' former partners used to joke that the agent had shut down a counterfeiting ring, arrested two street gang leaders, and shown a jaywalker the error of his ways all while helping his wife deliver their second child.

He thanked Andrews and reached for the phone book, wondering if there was a listing for Psychics.

"Don't go and do anything stupid," Andrews said, then signed off.

Chapa considered what a copycat might look like. He'd be a very private, but outwardly normal man. That was the secret to survival for predators. It had been one of the reasons Grubb was so difficult to catch. If a killer was out there, Chapa knew he would be no more distinct or noteworthy than the guy in the third cubicle down the hall who tends to keep to himself. The next person in line at the hardware store. That neighbor who's spending another weekend working in his basement.

If he was out there, Chapa was determined to get between the killer and Annie Sykes. But before he could go forward, Chapa knew he'd have to take another step back.

CHAPTER 14

The receding tread on the Toyota's tires swallowed up pieces of white gravel then spit them out as Chapa pulled through the circular drive, and parked a few feet beyond the front door. The property rested in a quiet and established neighborhood at the far west end of Chicago's extended suburbs.

It was one of those old large Midwestern houses that are usually filled with memories and secrets in equal measure. The two-story light blue structure had seen better days. Paint was beginning to flake off in spots, and an effort had been made to cover up the bare areas by slapping on a syrup-thick coat.

Louise Jones had long ago given up her storefront business, and instead performed readings in her home by appointment only. She'd told Chapa on the phone that she could squeeze him in that morning, though he got the sense there were many more openings than clients. He had told her he was a reporter doing a story on local businesses.

There was some truth to that, not much, but some. Chapa had decided that even if Grubb's threat to Annie Sykes didn't amount to anything, he would still get a story out of all this to run on the day of the execution.

"You look like a man with a lot on his mind."

Not bad for a woman her age, probably late fifties, Chapa figured, and he could easily imagine her having been quite attractive once.

"Madam Eva welcomes you to her domain," she said, ushering Chapa into a large but cluttered foyer.

Looking down a long hallway that led to the back of the house, Chapa thought the place appeared to have more than its share of dark corners. You could hide just about anything in those. A family secret, a broken heart, a shattered past. Plants obscured the front of each window, and the amount of furniture in the room could have filled a small apartment. The fresh smell of greenery was fighting a losing battle with the woman's perfume.

"When did you start going by Madam Eva?"

She frowned in a way that suggested his question was out of bounds, and slowly extended an arm in the direction of a parlor at the side of the house. The small room was even more cramped than the foyer. The few strands of light that managed to make their way in had to sneak under a pair of open but partially blocked windows. Every once in a while a fist of wind punched through the thick green curtains and sunlight would momentarily lick the dark wood floor.

The smell of incense drifted in from another room. Louise sat down in an oversize chair covered with a gaudy red fabric, and fanned her dress, reminding Chapa of an aging peacock. She then turned on a small lamp that had a frilly shade. The lamp's stingy smattering of light failed to extend beyond its immediate area.

"I used to be Miss Ballistar, but when the Internet became big that name started popping up on all sorts of websites for mystical worlds, role-playing, and that sort of junk."

"That's too bad, probably cost you a few bucks to get

new business cards made up," Chapa said, and took a seat in a puffy old chair with paisley cushions that turned out to be more comfortable than it looked.

Madam Eva sat across from him, scribbling something in a thin brown journal that was resting on her lap. She straightened the few remaining folds in her silky flowered gown and slowly leaned toward Chapa. Her hand abruptly caressed his as she ran a satin fingertip across his palm and looked into Chapa's eyes.

"Your brown eyes are rich and seductive, but also sad in a way. There is a darkness about you. You carry a burden."

"We all do sooner or later."

She smiled gently, and he thought about pulling his hand back but figured she might be more helpful if he went along for a while.

"What answers do you seek?"

"I'm looking for someone, a young woman."

She ran her thumb along the back of his ring finger.

"You were married once."

Nice guess, Chapa thought. Whatever physical impression his wedding ring had once made was long gone.

"It's not like that. I'm here about a girl named Annie Sykes."

Madam Eva withdrew her hand and retreated into her chair. Her expression growing more serious as she examined his face.

"That girl no longer exists."

"I know she goes by Angela."

She suddenly seemed frightened, and Chapa now realized the woman knew about Annie Sykes' name change, which meant she knew much more. He remembered how the police had once considered her a possible accomplice, even though they knew it was a long shot.

"How did you know so much about what had happened to her?"

"I already told this to the police, years ago. I had a vision, a powerful one, they chose to ignore it."

She started to get up, a nervous response, then caught herself.

"Did you see her in this vision? Did you see Grubb?"

"Who are you? Why are you really here?"

Chapa's eyes had adjusted to the dark room and for the first time he took in the fullness of it. Four bookshelves hugged the walls, and framed posters of abstract art covered what little space was left over.

"I'm a reporter, like I told you, but I'm not here about your business. I covered Annie's case sixteen years ago, and I have reason to believe she could be in great danger now."

She moved closer to him, as though she was seeing Chapa for the first time and wanted to get a better look.

"No, you're not *a* reporter, Mr. Chapa, you're *the* reporter." She smiled, not as gently this time. "Guilt has a long reach, doesn't it?"

She jotted a few more notes.

"Look, Louise, maybe one day you and I can gaze into a crystal ball and examine my hang-ups, but right now I have to know how to find her," Chapa said, then reached out and cupped her hands in his. "If you care about her, then I assure you we're on the same side."

She pressed an open palm to his chest, then closed her eyes.

"Your heart is not entirely pure, Mr. Chapa."

"Whose is?"

"I spoke with you once back then. You were dismissive, and really full of yourself."

"I apologize. I wasn't arrogant, just young and stupid."

"I choose to believe you, but Madam Eva's time is valuable."

Chapa got the message, pulled twin twenties out of his wallet and dropped them on the table. Louise scooped up the money, and it vanished somewhere in the folds of her gown. She then walked to a large book-case, and slid out a journal, similar to one she'd been using, from a long shelf of journals. This one was red, and Chapa wondered if that was intentional.

"She first came to me a couple of years ago, looking for answers to the same question you're asking. I told her what I told the police. I just knew. My visions come through my dreams, and I've had many of them. None as vivid as that one."

"You said Annie *first* came to you. When was the last time you saw her?"

She flipped through the journal.

"Just under a month ago."

"Is there any chance I could look in that book you're holding?"

"None. Psychic-client privilege. But she's not really a client, I've never charged her a penny. What kind of trouble is she in?"

He recounted his discussion with Grubb, giving up most of it, holding back just a few details.

"Is it true? Is someone out there?"

"I think there could be. Has anyone else come around asking about her?"

She paused for a moment, wrinkled her brow, then said, "No, no one."

But the hesitation and hint of uncertainty in Louise's voice made Chapa wonder.

"There is something, isn't there?"

"No, not really. I don't think so, at least. A few days ago I got a call from the owner of the building where my shop was located. Someone, a man, had stopped by looking for me."

"Did they describe the man?"

"Tall, maybe had a foreign accent. I thought it was one of my old customers."

"This man contact you?"

"No, I don't think it's anything to be concerned about."

Chapa thought she was trying to convince herself of that.

"You need to be careful, and if anyone unusual, or anything out of the ordinary—"

She squeezed his hand.

"I'm no threat to anyone. If someone is out there, you must tell the authorities, for Annie's sake."

"I've already spoken with the FBI."

Louise gently nodded and smiled, the wrinkles in her cheeks carving a wedge through the heavy makeup.

"Do you have a number for Annie or Angela, an address, anything?"

She flipped through the red journal.

"I don't have an address or any sort of contact information, I'm sorry. Angela just shows up at my door every now and then. We talk about all sorts of—wait," Louise was softly tapping a page she had stopped on. "She mentioned a friend, his name is Donnie."

"Last name?"

"I don't have that, but he's an artisan, and he has a store or a studio in the city." She flipped the page. "It's on Southport, just a couple doors down from an old theater."

Now it was Chapa taking notes.

"And before you ask, she never mentioned if it was a romantic relationship, but I don't think it was."

"Why do you say that?"

"Just a sense I got from her."

"What else?"

"She worked at a club on the North Side, but I don't know if she still does."

"No name?"

Louise shook her head without looking up from the page.

"I'll tell you one thing I know about her," she said and closed the journal. "Angela is better adjusted than many folks I've met who've had a much easier time of it."

That brought Chapa a small bit of comfort. He watched intently as she returned the journal to its place, and then adjusted the other books on that shelf until all of the spines were more or less aligned.

She walked back to her chair, and again went through the process of carefully fanning out her dress before sitting down.

"Has any of this helped?"

"Maybe."

"You know, Alex, it's not unusual for my clients to give me a tip, especially after a particularly helpful session."

Chapa pulled out his wallet. He was all out of twenties, so he drew out a ten and wrapped it around his business card. His next expense report was shaping up to be a doozy.

"If you hear from her again, ask Annie to call me, and then you give me a call."

He let himself out, anxious to jump on the expressway into the city and begin searching for Annie and her friend.

"Alex."

He turned back to look at Louise, framed in the door of her house, and for a moment he wondered if she could survive outside of its confines. The wind had picked up and was muscling its way inside, her gown waving like a psychedelic flag.

"I believe the afterlife has reserved an especially dark corner for those who disappoint the ones who depend on them. Don't be that person again." Then she added, "I also believe in redemption."

With that she disappeared into her house and closed the door. For the first time in days, Chapa was feeling that high he always got whenever he caught the scent of a good story. It was the reason he became a journalist. His drug of choice.

The information Louise had given him was full of holes, but at least he had a name, and a starting point. That was reason enough to pop a fresh CD into the player. Chapa dug into his past and pulled out Aerosmith's *Rocks*. He closed his eyes as the intro to "Back in the Saddle" gradually built up to Steven Tyler's throaty eruption, then he cranked the volume up beyond the legal limit, and slowly headed down the circular drive.

Somewhere in the growing distance behind him, Chapa heard a sharp sound that sliced through the audio haze of electric guitars, and it reminded him of the way his first car used to backfire whenever he tried to start it on a cold day. But this sound wasn't quite like that. When he heard it again, Chapa decided that there must have been some construction work going on near Louise's house, though he'd seen no evidence of such, then forgot all about it as he pounded the accelerator and made for the highway.

CHAPTER 15

Ten minutes later, Chapa was still riding the buzz most successful news writers have been fortunate to know. This was the only life he could ever remember wanting, and though it came with a fair share of lows, the highs made everything else worthwhile.

His mother, like a lot of parents, always hoped she was raising a lawyer. Convinced that her son's ability to think on his feet and his knack for talking himself into and out of situations would serve him well in that profession.

Despite her best intentions, however, it was actually Chapa's mother who was responsible for his love of journalism from an early age. Chapa could remember the stories she would tell him about his father as though he had been there, on the scene, just a few days ago. How a young Francisco Chapa had written for a government-approved Havana periodical by day, while organizing and editing an underground anti-Castro paper by night. She taught him the names of dissidents who had been released and allowed to leave the country after his father had exposed their arrests and inhumane treatment by the communist regime. To her, it was proof of the profound good a journalist can do, a philosophy she had passed on to her son.

But his mother had told him the rest of it, too. How his father had been taken away in the middle of the night when Alex was barely a year old. No word for weeks. Then news that Francisco Chapa had been shot while trying to escape. The authorities had shown his mother a picture of her husband, still wearing the same clothes as the day he'd been taken, with a bullet hole in what was left of his forehead. Instead of scaring Alex into a more sensible profession, it was learning of his father's sacrifice that first made him want to be a journalist.

Chapa had never found the sort of story he imagined would have made his father proud. And though he'd come to accept that he might never find it, Chapa also knew he would never stop searching.

Traffic on the Eisenhower was unusually light, and it wasn't long before the Sears Tower appeared in the distance. Chapa left another message for Nikki, then sent her a text that he punched into his phone while driving through expressway traffic.

Hey Nik I miss you and I wish I could just say hi and talk to you for a few minutes. Please let me know you got this and—

Chapa changed his mind and decided to keep the message simple. He erased the last sentence fragment, punched in, *I love you, Dad,* and sent the message. He no longer expected a response.

Though the divorce had been diffficult, Chapa and his ex had managed to work through most of the issues that arose in the months after it became final. That changed after Carla remarried.

A judge had awarded Chapa joint custody, but it hadn't worked out that way. Whatever role Chapa could play in his daughter's life started shrinking in a hurry.

That became even more of an issue after Carla and her new husband, a real estate developer from Boston, relocated to one of that city's more exclusive suburbs, and Nikki moved with them. The man Nikki sometimes called her "New Dad" had inherited his family's success, then gone out and built some of his own.

Chapa had fought Carla in court until his attorney convinced him he was all out of options. Carla had gotten everything she wanted, and probably more than what she had coming. Over time, the distance between Chapa and his daughter had widened, though he'd struggled to keep that from happening. Every once in a while he would go a week or two without having contact with Nikki. But this current stretch was by far the worst, and Chapa sensed that in spite of his efforts, he was slipping out of his daughter's life.

He'd decided long ago to try and ride out the occasional storms, hoping that Nikki would make the right choices once they were hers to make. But things were starting to spiral.

Chapa met Carla while on assignment, researching a story about insurance fraud. She was working as a legal assistant in a large firm in Oakton. The first thing Chapa noticed were her eyes—clear blue and radiant— no hint of the cold glares that would become familiar in the final months of their marriage. She was blond, slender, and tall. Her natural good looks were the product of a Nordic heritage by way of South Dakota. They hit it off right away, though the attraction was mostly physical.

Chapa knew that, but then he had a moment of weakness.

"We should get married," he said as he watched her getting dressed after a midafternoon tussle.

Two weeks later they did exactly that. Nikki was born in the tenth month of their marriage, even though they had originally agreed to wait before having children. Nikki was the result of a compromise.

There had been some good times. Quiet nights together, and family trips. Chapa still had moments when a deceptively gentle memory would sneak up on him. Those were becoming scarce, however, and easy enough to shake off. All it took was remembering how many quiet nights or family times ended in arguments. And how conflict, much of it without purpose or clear origin, always seemed to have filled the ever widening space between them.

Now Chapa just wanted to put as much distance as he could between himself and Carla. The easiest way for him to do that was by focusing on his work. It's what he had always done. A means of escape.

He found a parking space on Southport, on the same block as the theater Louise Jones had mentioned as a landmark. Now he just needed to find the store that Annie's friend owned. After scanning the storefronts along the busy street, Chapa had a pretty good idea which one it might be. He checked his messages one more time, turned off the phone and slipped it inside a pants pocket, then grabbed his tape recorder, a notebook, a couple of pens, and went to work.

CHAPTER 16

The young man who introduced himself as Langdon, the artist and owner of a store called Intertwined, was tall and athletic, his thick blond hair carefully groomed to appear random. Langdon examined Chapa with eyes that were the color of wet concrete, and greeted him with a smile that seemed easy and authentic.

"Is Langdon your first name or last?"

"Both. It started out as my artist name, but now it's what everyone calls me," he said, handing Chapa a cup of coffee.

He explained his real name was Donald Langdon Young, and he gave Chapa a quick tour of his shop, which was neatly stocked with his creations. Chapa noted a certain consistency to the designs on jewelry, purses, and clothing.

"They all look a little like those old English crosses."

"Gaelic crosses, yes, some people see the interlocking lines and maze-like designs and make that connection," Langdon said. "I suppose I probably drew some inspiration from that, but I've been sketching these designs since I was a kid."

Chapa suggested that some of the designs looked like the intertwined branches of a thorn bush.

"Maybe they're supposed to represent the way our lives are intertwined. Who knows? I just draw what comes to me."

Chapa made some notes, though he had little interest in the guy's artistic history.

The boutique was divided into sections, miniature departments, for each group of products. Electronic music, more machine than human, surged from small speakers perched on the wall behind the register. Photos on the other walls showed off Langdon's work by illustrating women wearing the clothing and jewelry, with one of his designer purses draped over a shoulder.

"You've done all of this yourself? Created the art, started the business, everything?"

Chapa was studying several framed newspaper and magazine articles about the store and its owner.

"I own the shop, and I run it by myself, mostly, though I do have a couple of part-timers. As far as the art goes, I lay out the designs, but I have a partner who actually makes the things you see here. I create the art from my imagination and he makes it a reality."

Chapa moved around the store, but stopped when he saw a familiar face wearing one of the necklaces. The only thing that he didn't recognize was her perfectly black hair.

"I have those in several different styles, if you'd like to get one for a lady friend."

"Who is this woman?" Chapa asked, pointing at the photo of Annie Sykes.

Langdon's demeanor shifted away from cooperative.

"You're not really here to do a story on my art, are you," Langdon looked down at the business card he'd been handed, "Mr. Chapa?"

"No, and I've been doing a really poor job of fooling people, then again, I'm not trying all that hard."

Langdon walked over and stood by the door, and Chapa understood that was supposed to be a cue for him to leave.

"I'm looking for your friend, the one in that picture. I know about her background, and quite a bit more. I would like to do a follow-up story on her and how well she's doing now."

"What if she doesn't want to be part of anything like that?"

"If she tells me to get lost, then I get lost."

The young man remained guarded.

"I haven't seen Angie in some time, not since she left the city."

"Where did she go?"

"She started seeing some guy in Joliet, and got a job down there."

"Do you know where?"

"It was a bar of some sort." Langdon thought for a moment. "I think it might've been called Night Owls."

"Were you two ever involved?"

Langdon shook his head, and relaxed enough to sit down.

"No, I was interested in that, but Angela wasn't. That's how it goes, but it didn't hurt our friendship any."

"Do you know where she lives now?"

"No. Angie isn't easy to find unless she wants to be found."

Chapa poured himself another cup of coffee.

"What's her last name now? I know it's not Sykes."

The hard look returned, and it made Chapa wonder if the last couple of minutes had been a put-on. The reporter sensed he was being sized up, on the receiving end of a practice that had long been second nature to him.

"She changed it to Noir, first professionally, then legally, I think."

"Angela Noir, Black Angel, that's some name."

"It was a good move for her when her paintings began to sell and attract attention from Goths and people into dark art. Though I don't think she's ever really bought into all that, or been part of the scene."

"Did the two of you ever collaborate on anything?

Langdon shook his head.

"She's got her muse, I've got mine."

Chapa smirked.

"You're a writer, don't you believe you have a muse?"

"I got a job to do, a deadline to meet, and a commitment to my readers. That's what drives me to write."

Chapa pointed to his business card which Langdon was still holding, and asked him to call the number on it if he heard from Angela, or remembered any other details that might help.

"You sure you're not going to buy something? Maybe a loved one needs a pendant."

Though he sensed Langdon was holding out on him, Chapa decided Erin might like one of the overpriced T-shirts, and picked out a dark blue one with a silver design. A purchase now could lead to some valuable information later.

"One other thing," Langdon said as he slipped the shirt into the bag, "That photo over there, Angie's hair isn't black anymore. She just dyed it like that when she was starting out."

"So it's her natural red again."

Langdon nodded. "At least that should make her easier to find."

And that's not necessarily a good thing, Chapa thought.

CHAPTER 17

Chapa tossed the open map of Chicago's far southwest suburbs on the passenger's seat so he could focus his attention on the mounting traffic, as well the annoyed federal agent on the other end of the phone.

"You are way out of your league, Al."

Chapa attributed his friend's negative attitude to a bad day.

"There's something very real going on here, and you know you're like a brother to me, but this is our territory. This is no business for a reporter."

The feds had managed to connect the dots on a couple more of the names Grubb had given Chapa, but the details weren't fitting together, and that always made Andrews cranky.

"Wasn't that the case with Grubb's victims?" Chapa asked as he turned onto a southbound ramp and passed under the sign that read, JOLIET AHEAD. "He was the only one who saw a pattern, and whatever it was, you won't find it in any profiler's manual. Isn't that what stumped the cops?"

"The lack of a pattern is not itself a pattern," Andrews responded, and seemed to be growing impatient with both the situation and Chapa. "Where are you now?"

Chapa hesitated before deciding to avoid the question.

"Did you write down the name I gave you?"

"Of course I did, Angela Noir is a hell of a long way from Annie Sykes."

"That could be true in a number of ways."

Traffic was getting thicker on I-355, and Chapa jumped off so he could get something to eat before continuing his trip to the bar that Langdon had told him about.

"Look, Al, and I hope you don't take this the wrong way."

"Ah, so you're about to insult me."

"What's going on here is getting heavy, and it's not another one of those situations where you manage to stumble around for a while until it all finally lines up for you. This is real."

Chapa wasn't insulted—this was not a new line of discussion for the two of them.

"I understand what you're saying, but I'm split here. The reporter in me knows that I can get most of the story I need from the comfort and safety of my office." Chapa fiddled for some change to pay the toll, came up short, and faked the empty handed toss into the basket before rolling through. "But the other part of me is looking for a girl who could be in a lot of trouble, and I can't let her down."

Andrews' silence told Chapa that his friend got it.

"Just be careful, asshole."

Chapa then asked, "Did you find out anything about Jack Whitlock?"

"We did. He moved to a small town in Michigan about six years ago, where he and his wife run an online business out of their home. He's probably just a guy who struggled through a very rough stretch, but he appears to be out of the loop."

"That makes sense." Chapa hadn't expected it would lead anywhere, but Whitlock was still worth checking out.

"You on your way to Erin's?"

"Maybe later, not yet."

"You never told me where you are now."

"Didn't I?"

"Nope."

"I'm driving down to Joliet. There's a roughneck bar there that Annie Sykes might be working at."

For all Chapa knew, Night Owls might be no rougher than a pancake house, but he was embellishing purely for dramatic effect. Andrews came back with a garbled bit of R-rated mumbling.

It was exactly the response Chapa was angling for.

CHAPTER 18

Night Owls squatted down by the river. It was in a part of Joliet that had somehow eluded the influx of money from a riverboat casino, and even more cash from a nearby NASCAR race track. The place sat there like an unearthed relic.

A large neon owl was perched on top of the uneven roof. It was holding a martini glass, complete with a green olive. No matter how at home the bird appeared, Chapa had a feeling that Night Owls didn't cater to a mixed drink crowd.

It was no pancake house, either, and the couple by the door looked like they hadn't seen a breakfast menu in their adult lives. The guy turned his stubbled face away from the artificially blond woman he was talking up long enough to give Chapa one of those looks. It was intended to let the recipient know he was being watched. Chapa nodded to the guy without breaking stride and opened the door.

Wearing jeans and a simple green shirt under his brown leather jacket, Chapa fit right in. He figured as long as he kept his notebook and recorder tucked away he'd be okay. But the moment Chapa walked in he was greeted by an aggressive scent. Like someone had pressed his nose into that ever moist area in a homeless drunk's beard where the spillover collects.

The bar was a little darker than Chapa would've liked, but on the whole it was no better or worse than a lot of others. Its burnt wood paneled walls were littered with posters of race car drivers and pro wrestlers. Chapa couldn't have named any of them even if someone put a gun to his head and ordered him to—a possibility he was not ready to dismiss just yet.

He pulled up a stool and kept it simple, ordering a whiskey on the rocks. The bartender responded by tossing him a coaster that had the neon owl logo on it.

This was the sort of bar that usually cranked out liquor-stained country music or hard core white trash blues. Bad to the bone. Instead, the jukebox was alternating sappy love songs and heartbreak tunes, giving the place an even more desperate vibe.

"I'm looking for someone. I was told she worked here."

"In what professional capacity?" the guy sitting next to Chapa asked, forcing each syllable out as though he were giving birth to it. The bartender laughed, Chapa let it go.

"I believe she has worked here as a waitress, her name is Annie, you might know her as Angela."

The bartender sized him up, and for a second Chapa thought he saw a glimpse of something the big guy didn't want seen.

"Buddy, if you're a cop you've shown up at the wrong place, and the force must really be hurtin'."

Chapa handed the bartender his card, it disappeared between thick fingers. Something about the guy's demeanor didn't seem quite right. It was as though he was adopting an attitude just for Chapa's benefit.

"I'm not a cop, I'm a reporter doing a story on this woman who I'm looking for."

"What makes her so special?"

He slid the drink in Chapa's direction, the glass left a slug's wet trail across the counter.

"She's a local artist who's gaining some notoriety, but she can be hard to find."

Faces filled with curiosity and a little too much interest had turned his way, and Chapa figured there had to be a few more he couldn't see in the shadows that poured into every corner. His welcome, such as it was, was wearing out in a hurry.

Chapa wasn't the sort to be fazed by being the round peg in a room filled with square holes. Maybe he never had been. Or maybe he'd grown used to it. When he was in seventh grade a group of boys cornered him on the way home from school. Chapa didn't know them, couldn't understand why they were calling him a *communist*. Apparently their parents had taught them a lot more about bigotry than world politics. He managed to shield himself when one of the kids, an angry piece of work in greasy jeans and a dull white T-shirt, threw the first punch, but couldn't do much to save himself when two more joined in.

He went home bloodied and humiliated, cleaned himself up before his mother saw him, then refused to tell her what had happened. But over the next two weeks Chapa tracked down each of the three kids, got them one-on-one, and squared things. He bloodied one bully's nose, broke another's, and his third fight earned him a suspension.

That was a long time ago, and though he'd never again engaged in an act of cold-blooded violence, Chapa knew he could take care of himself. With any luck he wouldn't have to prove it tonight.

"Buddy, the servers here come and go almost on a weekly basis," the bartender said as he wiped the counter. "The pay is lousy and the tips are a disgrace."

The guy next to Chapa grunted in approval.

"Most of them take the job hoping to meet some guy who will take them away."

"Lots of love in the room, can you feel it?" Chapa's scruffy neighbor said, enunciating every word again, like a college English professor, though he looked more like the school's garbage man.

An avalanche of blond invaded Chapa's space, followed by a wave of dollar store perfume. It was the woman he'd seen on his way in. Her bright, artificially colored hair might have been considered artsy in some parts.

"Buy me a drink," she said and licked her thickly painted lips. "Anything you want."

She was big all over, and Chapa had no interest in figuring out which parts were natural and which were the result of scientific breakthroughs.

"I'm not going to be here long enough to do that," Chapa said, just before someone gripped his shoulder and spun the barstool around.

"You're damn straight about that." It was the surly piece of trash who was hitting on the blonde when Chapa walked in. He cocked a boney fist, then suddenly vanished from Chapa's sightline before he could throw it.

"We've talked about this too many times before, Skyler," the enunciator was telling the guy as he held him down against the creaking floor. "You should know by now that Janet is everybody's baby."

"Hey!" Janet said from somewhere in the shadows. Chapa thought he saw her sitting on some guy's lap.

"And that ain't even it, there's not going to be any

fighting here. Now you go back there and drink your-self blind." With that he tossed Skyler into the darkness at the far end of the bar, and extended his hand.

"I'm Munson, I own this establishment," he said and returned to his stool like nothing had happened. "I apologize for Skyler. He's what you might call a linger-ing concern. Skyler's got a streak of mean in him, but I let him hang around because last year his bar tab paid for my new sundeck. This year, I think he's gonna send the wife and me to Cancun."

Munson and the bartender laughed, a few others joined in.

"But you know how it is," Munson said, lifting his glass. "There but for the grace go any one of us. It's like that, isn't it?"

Chapa watched as Skyler used the beer-soaked edge of a cardboard coaster to pick something out of his teeth.

"Maybe." Chapa pulled out another business card. "Anyway, thanks for the help with Skyler. This woman I'm looking for came to work at your place because she was dating someone here."

"Do you mean Cody?"

"I don't know his name."

"He used to tend bar for me, real son-a-bitch, but he brought the girl on, I remember."

Munson stared at Chapa's business card like it was about to do something interesting.

"Do you know much about her situation?" Munson asked without looking up from the card.

"Some."

Whenever possible, let the subject believe he knows more than you do.

"I looked into it quite a bit when one of my employ-ees"—he tossed a nod at the bartender—"told me about her background. Real sad."

One of the waitresses joined the conversation. She was a little older than the others and looked like most of the romance in her life never made it off a turntable.

"I remember Angela, she was a sweetie."

Munson grunted in agreement.

"She got a job at some club in Chicago after she dumped Cody. Said she missed the city."

"What was the name of that place?" Munson asked no one in particular.

"Was it Panthers?" the waitress responded.

"Let's put on our thinking caps," Munson said, and Chapa became a spectator as the two of them, plus the bartender, silently searched their memories for the answer.

"Prather's," Munson said finally.

"Is it a men's club?" Chapa hated asking the question.

"She didn't seem like the exotic dancer type," the waitress answered without hesitating. "It was somewhere way up north in the city."

Chapa finished his drink and thanked them both for the information, then started to leave, but Munson grabbed his forearm and pulled him close.

"I know a lot of things, I've gotten around," he said. Chapa was surprised that he could smell no liquor on the guy's breath. "Lots of people take my calls. You seem like a right guy, you need some information, I can probably help. Maybe we'll have lunch sometime."

Then Munson looked around the bar. The shadows seemed more active than before.

"But you can just call me here, you don't have to drop in," his words were crisp, like a typewriter key striking cheap paper, and his meaning was clear. "We got some crazy folks here who might want to bring the night down on you. How far away did you park?"

Chapa had been in enough situations to understand

that Munson's powers of persuasion were limited to inside the four crooked and time-beaten walls of Night Owls. As he walked out, Chapa heard the late 70's disco hit "Heaven Must Be Missing an Angel" playing behind him, but he was certain no one remotely matching that description could be found in this place.

CHAPTER 19

Erin had dinner waiting for him. Her chestnut brown hair was pulled back into a ponytail, suggesting that she might have been cooking a full meal. Dinner turned out to be a frozen pizza, but Chapa didn't care. More than anything he wanted to look into her eyes and feel her warm arms around him.

But before he was able to indulge in any of that, he played a game of Chutes and Ladders with Mikey, then they watched a kid's television show together. The five-year-old had taken to him right away, and Chapa knew he was the closest thing the child had to a father figure. Chapa had already been around longer than the boy's natural father.

"I wish you were here more," Mikey said.

"I like being here with you and your mom." That earned Chapa a quick hug.

Mikey was a sweet kid who reminded him of Nikki at the same age. A playful force of nature wrapped up in a small but gangly package. Chapa enjoyed being around the child, but in a way it was bittersweet. Every minute he spent with Mikey was another he didn't spend with his own daughter. That seemed selfish, and he worked to bury those feelings. But Chapa had noticed how much Mikey had changed in just a few months, and wondered how Nikki was changing. Chapa knew he was missing out on so much.

"Mommy is happier when you're here."

The child stopped playing long enough to watch a toy commercial on TV.

"It makes my heart happier too," Mikey said finally, and the game resumed.

Chapa worried sometimes that Mikey was getting too attached too quickly. Maybe it was a natural thing for someone that age. But there were no plans to make any of this permanent, and he wondered how much of a hit the child would take if it eventually came to an end.

From early on in their relationship he had explained to Erin that he wasn't ready to try marriage again. Maybe someday, maybe never. Too much left to figure out about what went wrong the first time. Erin was nothing like Carla. But he worried that he was still the same guy who struck out once, and he wasn't in the habit of repeating his mistakes.

After the show was over and Chapa had read him a book, Erin put her son to bed.

"I'm pretty sure Mikey likes you," she said with a smile.

"I like him too," Chapa said and slumped into the couch.

"Difficult day?"

"Yeah, I met some different sorts of people today. It was a day for guys who go by one name, Langdon, Munson, and I even met a psychic. It's a strange, screwed-up world out there."

He'd decided to leave out the part about the green sedan.

"So let's just stay in here for, oh I don't know, how

'bout a lifetime," Erin said in a way that made the idea seem perfectly reasonable.

That made Chapa feel good. He wasn't necessarily closed to the idea, just not ready to commit to it yet.

"We have this night, we have now, and that's more than nothing," he said, gently touching her warm cheek.

"I know, Alex."

Erin leaned in and kissed him on his left temple, then gradually moved down until their lips met. The sweet taste of her mouth had become something Chapa thought about every day, and its memory sometimes caressed him as he drifted off to sleep. They exchanged delicate kisses until she pulled back, undid several of the buttons on her white blouse, reached in and unsnapped her bra, exposing the tender skin between her breasts.

"Okay Mr. Reporter, is there anything in here that you might want to investigate?" Erin asked as she pulled her blouse open enough to show off her cleavage.

They rushed to her bedroom, and he hastily undressed her, then took her even quicker. It was fast and it was fun, and when it was over they both knew they were not finished yet.

"What are you thinking about us?"

This again, is what Chapa thought.

"You know how I feel about you," he said.

"Do I? Let's double-check. Why don't you tell me."

Chapa kissed her, and though this went on for a while, when it was over he could tell she was still waiting for an answer.

"Should I rent a plane and have something written in the sky for you?" Chapa asked.

"Why would I want you to say something from way up there when I've got you right here in my bed?"

She was waiting, giving him a *ball's in your court* look. He diverted her attention by slowly and gently running his hand down to the base of her right breast, then up and over to the left one.

"I'm not going to forget we were having this conversation," she partially said and mostly moaned.

They made love again, this time more gently and passionately. He took his time and explored every beautiful inch of her, lingering wherever his touch elicited a soft moan. Damn, it turned him on when she responded like that.

A female college professor once told Chapa he had the sort of face that would age well, and that women would appreciate him even more as he got older. The way Erin looked at him, not just when they were making love, but even in the most mundane moments, had Chapa believing that professor had known what she was talking about.

Afterward, they quietly lay on the bed, arms and fingers softly touching warm skin. But it was clear he wouldn't be staying. Chapa had only slept over twice, and on both occasions Mikey had been spending the night at his grandparents' house. He had explained to Erin how he didn't want the child to ever see him walking out of his mother's bedroom in the morning. Chapa was never going to be one of those men in Mikey's life.

Chapa liked how it felt when Erin rested her head on his bare chest, as she was doing now. He let his fingers get lost in her hair.

"You should be more relaxed than you are," Erin said, a day's worth of tired in her voice.

"I'm going to lose my job next week. I'm no longer considered *vital*," Chapa said.

She raised her head to look at him, and he immediately wished he hadn't said anything about it, though being able to see the warmth in her hazel eyes made the trade-off worthwhile.

"You were told that?"

"There are cutbacks coming. A shortage of ad buys, shrinking of home delivery subscriptions, a drop-off in newspaper readership, it's all true. It's a bad time for the newspaper business, and it's not going to get any better."

She caressed his face with her long, narrow fingers, then put her head back down on his chest.

"Don't worry, you're a survivor. You're the kind of guy who can figure it all out."

Her confidence in him never got old.

"All I know is this story may end up being my swan song and calling card all at the same time."

She kissed his chest in a way that under different circumstances might have led to more lovemaking.

"You're Alex Chapa, the Chicago area's best investigative reporter, a heck of a writer, and one of the world's greatest lovers. Two of those qualities will have employers knocking at your door."

"Actually, I'm Alex Freakin' Chapa, but that's another story. Or maybe it isn't. I don't know, I'd be willing to do stud work too. For even less money."

Erin laughed, kissed his chest again, and said nothing more. A few minutes later he felt her breathing grow steady as she fell off to sleep. Chapa was tired but not sleepy, so he decided to stay just a little longer. He lay there and stared off into the darkness, trying to make the mismatched pieces from several different puzzles fit together.

Four Days Before the Execution

CHAPTER 20

Chapa was relieved to not get that *dead man walking* vibe as he made his way through the newsroom to his office. The work had started piling up, which was to be expected, and he had more than a dozen phone messages, which was unusual.

Half of those were from Andrews. The FBI agent had a bad habit of hanging up as soon as he heard the message. Chapa figured his friend wanted to make sure he had survived the trip to Night Owls. Or maybe something was up.

Chapa started dialing Andrews' cell phone number, but stopped when Matt Sullivan appeared in his doorway.

"Hey Alex, how are you doing? I need a minute."

Sullivan had been moved over from sports just a few weeks earlier, and though no one realized it at the time, his transfer signaled the beginning of the paper's internal realignment. His friends and coworkers in the sports department called him "Sully." Chapa didn't know him that well, and now realized he probably never would.

"We haven't seen much of you these past few days."

"I know, Matt, but I did let you know I was going after

this one, and this is how it is when I'm doing one big story."

Sullivan helped himself to a chair, and Chapa put the phone back down in the receiver.

"I want you to understand that I trust your judgment. You've been doing hard news longer than most people in this town. But are you certain this story is big enough to justify the attention you're giving it?"

"It's big enough." Chapa was starting to get pissed off.

"I mean, Alex, I know it's sensationalistic and maybe even a little lurid and that can sell papers, but—"

"There might be more bodies."

Sullivan slowly sank into the chair, like someone who had just received bad news, but Chapa watched as the newsman in him then rose to the surface.

"From before or more recent?"

"New ones, a copycat, but I haven't told you that and you never heard it."

Sullivan got up and paced a little, about as much as he could in the cramped office. The wind from the ceiling fan lifted a few thin strands of his mostly gray hair each time he turned.

"If this story is going to get big and maybe even go national, we should probably assign a team of reporters to it."

"No team. Never needed one, don't need one now."

Chapa knew he had drawn a line. Maybe Sullivan was ballsy enough to cross it—Chapa didn't think so. Maybe the editor would decide to use this moment to put the writer in his place. Chapa was hoping he'd try it.

The two men looked at each other for a short but uncomfortable moment.

"I'm on your side, Alex, and we'll do this your way."

Chapa figured that saying "thanks" could sound

trite, so he didn't say anything. Sullivan gave him a friendly slap on the shoulder and headed out the door.

"You'll make this one count, won't you, Alex, for everyone involved," Sullivan said, then closed the door behind him.

CHAPTER 21

After leaving a message on Andrews' voice mail and another at his office, Chapa decided to take another swipe at online research. There were a few hits for the name Angela Noir, but none of those seemed to have anything to do with Annie.

Through a narrow rectangular window, Chapa watched as Carston Macklin walked past his closed door, not bothering to look in. Maybe he'd grown accustomed to Chapa's office being empty.

His office had served as a safe harbor Chapa would escape to when he wanted to be somewhere other than home. During his married years, Chapa put in as many hours as anyone on staff. He'd slept in his office on more than one occasion, even kept a change of clothes in a drawer for a time, back when things were especially bad between him and Carla. But there was no comfort here for him anymore.

Marching into Macklin's office and having it out was an option, and in many ways an attractive one. But Chapa understood how that would end, and he had to think of the story. Of Annie. He shut down his computer, and gathered some things together. He wouldn't be back until he had a reason to be there.

Opening a large bottom drawer in his desk, Chapa reached in and dug around until he found something that had been buried under files, papers, and notebooks. Right after the divorce he'd bought a blank journal that he planned to write in, then give to Nikki. Chapa figured this was one way his daughter could get to know him.

Chapa had forgotten all about it until his visit with Louise. It seemed like an even better idea now than when he came up with it. He ran a finger along the smooth vinyl cover, wiping some dust away, revealing the bright colors beneath, and remembered taking time to pick out one he thought his daughter would like. But flipping through the small volume, all Chapa found were blank pages. The only notation was on the first page, which he remembered writing the same day he bought the journal.

It read, *Your daddy loves you more than anything in the world. We'll always be together in our hearts.*

Chapa began to put it back in the drawer, then decided to take it along.

CHAPTER 22

"Louise Jones is dead, someone put two bullets in her skull." Joseph Andrews' voice was calm and steady. "A family member stopped by to visit and found her on the floor of the hallway just beyond the front door."

Chapa turned off the car radio and took a moment to process what Andrews had just told him. He imagined what Louise's lifeless body must have looked like sprawled across that same hallway he had walked through only a day before. Now he understood the urgency, and why Andrews had phoned so many times.

"When were you at her house, Al?"

"Yesterday morning. Shit, Joe, the woman was harmless."

"Maybe she gave someone bad advice, or had family problems, you never know about people."

Chapa understood that Andrews' dry detached cop persona was a survival mechanism, one that most law officers develop. But it still annoyed the hell out of him.

"Or it could be that it has something to do with Annie Sykes," Chapa said as he waited for the light to turn and wondered if he should change direction and head to Louise's house.

"Let's not get ahead of ourselves. The locals are already investigating, and I'm on my way to the crime scene now. But if you're right, it supports my opinion that you need to back off."

Back off, my ass, Chapa thought.

"Have you found out anything more about Annie Sykes?" Andrews asked.

"No, nothing new."

Chapa wondered if Andrews was holding something back, and decided he would prefer talking to him in person.

"I'll meet you at Louise's house."

"No, Al, you won't."

That was the answer Chapa expected, but he figured it was worth a try.

"The coroner hasn't set the time of death. Right now his best guess is sometime yesterday, late morning or early afternoon. The locals will be all over you if they know you were there. She probably kept an appointment book."

That triggered Chapa's memory, and he pulled over into a grocery store lot and parked in the first space he came to.

"There's a journal you're going to want to get your hands on. You can't miss it, it's red."

Chapa explained how Louise had pulled it off a shelf, and that it seemed to contain information about Annie Sykes.

"It's in the middle of a bottom shelf along the north wall, I think. You sort of get turned around in there."

Chapa watched a loose shopping cart roll across the parking lot, hunting for a target.

"This will give me an excuse to pick up Grubb's brother for questioning."

"I know you want me to back off, Joe, but I would appreciate it if you let me know what you find in that journal, ASAP."

The rusted cart finally struck hard against a new model SUV, leaving a mark, then caromed off and went in search of another victim.

"There's lots of dangerous shit everywhere, Al. I'm just trying to keep you from falling into something you won't be able to climb out of."

CHAPTER 23

After swinging by his house to drop off a few of the things he'd gathered from his office, Chapa stopped in at the Golden Sea for some fried rice. He was seated by himself in a far corner of the old-style Chinese restaurant, but the weight of his thoughts made him feel like he wasn't alone. He couldn't stop thinking about Louise Jones, and wondering if her killer had been in the house while he was there. Her murder had to be tied to Grubb, and her friendship with Annie. Why else would a federal agent be on his way to investigate?

Chapa was squaring his bill and wondering if the thin, dark-haired guy sitting in the corner booth looked familiar, or could be he was just getting paranoid, when his cell phone starting playing "Guantanamera"—a rare nod to his heritage. He recognized Erin's number, but turned the phone off, deciding to call her back from the car. His phone kicked into a reprise the moment he stepped out of the restaurant. This time he answered it right away. Chapa could tell by her voice that something was very wrong.

"Where are you right now, Alex?"

"Tell me what's going on," Chapa said, rotating through his key chain several times before finally managing to concentrate long enough to isolate the one he wanted.

"I found something taped to the front door of my house when I got home."

Chapa watched a green sedan pull out of the parking lot and thought it looked familiar.

"It's a note with a map, but there's something else, too."

He tried to get a look inside the vehicle as it sped away, then quickly turned a corner, but couldn't see the driver.

"What kind of note?"

"All it says is *Mr. Chapa, The answers you seek.* The piece of map shows some area way past DeKalb, in the middle of farmland out there. They've drawn a red star on a spot between two rural roads."

Chapa looked around like a startled animal, certain he was being watched, though he was alone in the parking lot.

"You and Mikey need to get out of there, get out of town. Pack for a few days and go to a hotel with a swimming pool, or one of those with an indoor water park. Take vacation time, call in sick, whatever you have to do."

"Alex, the other thing that's on here, it's like a lock of hair, several, maybe a dozen, long strands of red hair."

A bead of sweat broke loose and streamed down Chapa's forehead, around his brow, and into his eye. It stung badly, but a moment passed before he thought to wipe away the pain.

"Are you coming over?" Erin asked, more resolute, as though the maternal instincts were overtaking her fear.

"No. I'm going to force whoever did this to make a choice between worrying about me and stalking you."

"Stalking me?" Erin's voice cracked a little. "Why? Why leave this here?"

"Whoever it was wanted me to know that they could get to you and Mikey."

That's how it works. The last time someone delivered this sort of message was a few years back, long before Erin knew who Alex Chapa was or that his problems would someday become hers.

"I'm sorry about all this."

"It's not your fault, Alex. But you've seen something like this happen before, haven't you?"

He had, and the memory was still fresh, though many years and columns had come and gone since then. Nikki was just a baby, and Chapa was still working on figuring out how to balance his new responsibilities with the old ones. He was piecing together a series of stories destined to shine an unflattering light on the dealings of a restaurant mogul in the suburbs. Sure, the guy was organized, but he was also a major advertiser with the *Record*, so whatever heat Chapa brought on him got reflected back.

The man who was the subject of Chapa's story and his associates cranked up the pressure one afternoon, just a few days after Nikki's first birthday. Carla was watching her play in the backyard when the phone rang. Ducking back into the kitchen to answer it, she had a clear view of her daughter the entire time, with only brief interruptions as she took down a message for her husband.

When she hung up, Carla noticed something was hanging from Nikki's neck—a plastic bib from one of the guy's restaurants. Message received. She begged Chapa to drop the story, not understanding that was the way the bad guys operated.

It spurred Chapa to quickly finish the piece, know-

ing what thugs often forget—it's only a stand-off until
the moment their faces color the front page. Then re-
venge takes a backseat to self-preservation, and the
journalist slides to the bottom of their to-do list.

One hour after Carla told him what had happened,
Chapa informed his editor the story would be set to run
later that night. Two days later, the wealthy owner of a
dozen popular Chicagoland eateries was hiding behind
lawyers. A year and a half after that they outfitted him
for an orange jumpsuit.

Chapa got a special kick out of seeing that photo on
the front page, above the fold.

Erin wasn't saying anything, but she didn't have to.
Chapa knew she wanted him to ignore the map, the
threat, and just turn all of it over to the police. He considered doing that, but all the cops would likely do at
this point was file a report. And Chapa had no idea
what sort of a response that might trigger, or how it
could put Erin or maybe even Annie in greater danger.
No, there was no percentage in playing it that way, not
yet, anyway.

He was just ten minutes from Erin's house, and the
urge to rush over and throw his arms around her and
Mikey, then carry them off to a safe place was so
wrenching it hurt. But Chapa understood that whoever
was doing this would now shift their attention to him, at
least for the time being. That would certainly change if
he did not show up wherever the map led him.

"I've gotten their message. Now, Erin, as carefully
and with as much detail as possible, I need you to give
me directions to that spot on the map."

CHAPTER 24

Chapa waited in the parking lot and stayed on the phone with Erin until she was in her car with Mikey tucked safely in his seat. She headed north along a two-lane highway that would give her a fair chance of spotting another car if she was being followed. The plan was for Erin to spend a couple of days at a resort near the Wisconsin Dells, but as Chapa had suggested, she did not phone ahead to make reservations.

"Stay rural for a while, and if you see any cars that draw your attention go ahead and jump on the interstate when you get up by Elgin."

This was yet another reason Chapa had been reluctant to get involved in a more permanent way with Erin, no matter how strong his feelings. Mothers needed stability, children even more so. They needed the sort of man who hopped on a train each morning and rode it to work. The sort of guy who wore a suit, maybe even a tie, and didn't take either off until he returned home at the same time he got home yesterday. That wasn't Chapa. And though a part of him wished he could settle into something that resembled a stable life, Chapa knew he never would. He had tried to explain that to

Erin, and wondered if what was happening now would make it easier for her to understand.

The minutes passed slowly, and he imagined her car steadily moving away from danger. Once he was certain that all was as well as it could be with Erin and Mikey, Chapa called Andrews to let him know the latest, but only got his voice mail.

"Hey Joe, I know you won't take my call when you're on a case, but this is big. Call me."

Erin's directions would take him far from the suburbs, to twenty miles past nowhere. Chapa again considered driving straight to Louise Jones' house and bringing Andrews up to speed in person. He thought about going home or over to Erin's and waiting there for whoever might show up.

But that's not the way he wanted to handle this threat to people he cared about. Chapa looked at his key chain, which had Nikki's photo on it, dangling from the ignition. Rocking gently from side to side almost gave it a three-dimensional quality, and that made him feel a little less alone. He glanced one more time at the directions, clipped them to the inside of his visor, and drove out of the lot.

CHAPTER 25

Chapa spent the first part of the drive talking to Erin, which made the time pass quickly. They lost the connection at one point, and the next time the spirited chorus of "Guantanamera" filled the Corolla, Erin and Mikey were calling from Wisconsin.

That provided Chapa with some much welcomed comfort, and he loosened the death grip he'd had on the wheel. But that slight ease of mind didn't last. When the connection dropped again, Chapa knew he could be out of range for a while, and it gave him the opportunity to think about his own well-being.

Ten miles after he crossed into Ogle County, Chapa turned north on highway 14. Five miles later he passed through the town of Hunters Ridge, which was little more than a feed store surrounded by farms on lots that were so big the houses in the distance looked like Monopoly game pieces.

A brown pickup truck pulled out behind him as he passed a long gravel road. Chapa kept an eye on his rearview mirror, but the truck turned off onto a side road a couple of minutes later.

The directions next called for a turn onto an unnamed road. *Turn left at the dark green house, there's a*

pretty little swing dangling from the tree in the front yard.
Chapa felt the muscles in his stomach tighten when the
house emerged on the horizon. As he slowed down,
looking for the road beyond it, he noticed the swing
was swaying just a little, as though a child had recently
been playing on it, though the yard was now empty.

He turned left and picked up his phone, hoping to
get a call through to Andrews. *No Service.* From there
the landscape opened up so much it made the previous
fifteen miles seem crowded by comparison. Chapa had
never been fond of wide open spaces, and he believed
just as much trouble could find you in the country as in
the city. The only difference was that out here the soil
and wind conspired with an endless sky to do a better
job of hiding it.

"This is where the chainsaw murderers come from,"
he had once informed his wife when they were staying
at a bed and breakfast somewhere in the wilderness of
Minnesota, part of a getaway that was designed to help
their marriage. "You realize if someone breaks into this
place and chops up everybody it could be days before
the bodies are found."

It seemed darkly funny to him then. Not so much
now. Chapa tightened his grip on the wheel again, and
the hard and unforgiving rubber pressed against his already sore hands. He reached his next turn-off four
miles and two farmhouses later.

Turning onto an unnamed road that was designated
by a number, Chapa saw more of the same. A row of
trees in the distance provided the only contrast in this
otherwise featureless place where nature seemed to
have run out of ideas.

Chapa now had a terrifying thought. What if he was
being led out to the middle of nowhere so that someone could get to Erin and Mikey? Deep down he knew it
probably didn't make a lot of sense, but none of this

did. His tires screamed in protest as Chapa abruptly pulled off the road, and stopped the car, kicking up a cloud of dirt and gravel in the process. He tried to call Erin. *No Service.* He rolled down the window and held the phone out, then slowly moved it around hoping it would find a signal that might've wandered far from home. *No Service.*

For a moment, Chapa wanted to turn the car around and head up to Wisconsin to be with them. He was sure he hadn't been followed, and by now Erin and Mikey would be far away from anyone who wanted to hurt them. Then, in the distance, he saw the last landmark in the directions. It was a large red barn with an enormous smiling pumpkin painted on its backside. It was looking right at him from a couple hundred yards away.

Take the first right after the barn with a pumpkin on it. Drive a little more than two miles. The address is 802, it will be painted on a white post.

Chapa kept an eye on the pumpkin as he drove past it. A guy was standing by the barn. Out of place in his business suit, he stared as if Chapa's was the first car he'd seen in some time. He was still staring as the barn faded in the distance behind a sheer of open and barren farmland.

The next chance to turn right came about half a mile later, onto a road that was narrower than the tight one he had just been on. He watched as his odometer clicked past the first mile. Everything that was anything kept its distance from this road.

The second mile came and went and civilization hadn't gotten any chummier. A wild goose chase? Chapa was certain now that this was about getting him away from Erin and Mikey. Again, he thought about whether it was better to turn around and retrace his movements back to the interstate, or forge on until he hit a major road.

Then something unusual rose out of the country-side. From a distance it looked like an enormous shoe-box. It was so out of place, surrounded by acres of flatness, that Chapa knew it must be his destination. As he got closer he saw it was an old trailer home, one that had seen better days, maybe back in the 70's. It sat in the middle of a field, isolated from anything else except the white post by the road. The number 802 had been crudely painted in red.

Chapa brought the car to a stop just beyond the post. Reaching into the glove compartment, he dug out his recorder from under a pile of bills, junk mail, unpaid tickets, and fast food restaurant napkins, and slipped it into his inside coat pocket.

Studying the open landscape, Chapa looked around for any sign of movement before leaving the car, but couldn't see any reason not to step out. He opened the door and got out quickly, fearing someone might sneak up on him if he took his time. Sneak up from where? A crooked old path ran from the road, past the post and in the direction of a farmhouse at least a half a mile away. Thick tire marks had gnawed into the soil near the path, which explained how the sixty-foot mobile home got to where it sat, about fifty yards from the road.

Keeping his distance, Chapa looked for any move-ment around the trailer, but everything was still, just as it was for miles around. That stillness was the only way that the trailer blended into its surroundings. The win-dows were covered by dark curtains, and its beige and chrome exterior was specked with rust that had taken up permanent residency in some of the cracks and ex-tremities. It gave the impression of having been there for some time, though the tire marks that led up to it suggested otherwise.

The after-harvest smell of decay rose from the dormant soil, and it helped Chapa remember more of what he didn't like about the country. He walked to the back of the Corolla, surveying his surroundings with every step, and opened the trunk. Chapa looked around again, and made certain he saw no movement before leaning in and throwing back the thick carpeting that lined the bottom.

Inside the space that held the spare tire he found the only weapon at his disposal, a small crowbar. It was wedged between the tire and the jack, but with a little bit of effort he managed to work it loose. It was cold, but it felt good in his hand.

Chapa was feeling confident that he could protect himself if need be, when the sound of laughter made him jump back away from the car. Crowbar in hand, he was ready to strike, and then saw a black bird sitting atop the white post. It looked at Chapa and called out again, mocking him, warning him, or maybe both.

The bird flew away when Chapa slammed the trunk shut. He imagined that if anyone was watching him they'd be laughing right now. He climbed back in and drove the car off the road and far enough up the ragged path to get it out of the way, then started for the trailer.

The ground was coarse and uneven, and his all-sport shoes were not suited for this terrain. He approached the trailer with caution, pausing a few times to look back at his car, or to make sure there was no movement in the area.

Chapa was no more than twenty feet from the trailer as he watched the black bird fly overhead and return to the post. It called out to him again as he walked up the badly dented metal steps.

Careful not to be too obvious, Chapa tried looking

through the curtain that covered the small, dust-caked window at the top of the door, but all he saw was darkness.

He knocked on the scuffed and dented aluminum frame of the screen door, and was surprised by how the tinny sound echoed around him.

"Hello?"

No answer. He knocked again. A few more seconds slowly passed without a response and Chapa wondered if he was supposed to have gone to the farmhouse. It was so far away it seemed to belong to another part of the state altogether. He decided to walk around the trailer and maybe get a look inside of one of the other windows.

But as he started back down, careful to make sure his now dirty black shoes found what little solid footing the steps offered, Chapa noticed that the interior door was not shut tight. Gripping the crowbar in one hand, he turned the cold and crusty knob of the screen door with the other. It screeched open, and Chapa again tried to look inside without success. Holding the screen door open with his knee, he pressed the fingertips of his right hand against the beige door, and pushed.

The door slowly swung open, as though it were doing so on its own, giving Chapa his first glimpse of what lay beyond.

CHAPTER 26

At first glance, the interior appeared to be as dark as the depths of a cave. But after a few seconds Chapa could see a shred of daylight slipping in though a narrow crack in the curtains from a side window. The sparse light revealed a collection of objects on a small table, and not much more.

Chapa stuck his arm inside the doorway and swung the crowbar back and forth, just in case someone was waiting for him. But it only sliced through the black air, making a dull *swoosh* sound. He gripped the weapon with both hands, and took a tentative step inside. A gust of wind raced up from the field and brushed against the back of Chapa's neck. Startled, he jerked forward and into the trailer.

The screen door slammed loudly behind him, and he heard what sounded like a generator kick on somewhere outside the trailer, then an electric sizzle from above. Yellow and purple fluorescent lights suddenly swept away the darkness, and the trailer was awash with color. Clutching the crowbar as tightly as his adrenaline would allow, Chapa pivoted from side to side, ready for an attack that wasn't coming.

Display cases and framed pictures covered the walls

above several small tables with a variety of items on them. The one Chapa was standing in front of had a sign on it that read WELCOME—PLEASE BEGIN AT THE REAR.

The arrow pointed to Chapa's left. The trailer had been gutted, and was not divided up into rooms the way most mobile homes are. It was basically a large rectangular box. A narrow door at the back probably led to the bathroom. To his right, at the far end, he saw a television set poking out between thick indigo curtains.

Electrical wires along the length of the ceiling led from small boxes to the front of the trailer and behind the curtains. Chapa guessed they were sensors, responsible for starting the generator and turning the lights on. He took a closer look, but couldn't tell if cameras had been tucked into shadowed corners.

The stale smell of damp wood swam in thick air and seemed to cling to every surface. Chapa worried that it might attach itself to him. Someone had been smoking, but with all of the windows closed it could have been last week or last year.

Not wanting to turn away from those curtains, he shuffled toward the back of the trailer, stopping at the first display case. Above it a sign read: THE MYTH OF AGE-PROGRESSION. Chapa recognized the term as referring to the process by which a missing child's photo is aged in order to help in identifying them years after they've vanished. Beneath the sign, the case was filled with computer-altered pictures that had been crudely cut out from the backs of ad fliers, next to what he assumed were actual photos of the same victims. Some were police photos of corpses, a few others had been defaced with the profane addition of satanic horns, or grotesque features.

His instincts were telling him to get the hell out of there. But something on the small table a few feet far-

ther toward the back caught his eye. The collection of
worn leather straps with buckles was laid out like a work
of art, something that could be the subject of a still life.
The sign above it read: THE MASTER'S TOOLS.

Chapa was beginning to understand what this place
was. But why would anyone go to the trouble of creating
a memorial to Grubb? Chapa followed the displays
along that wall to the back of the trailer, scanning the
chronology that began with photos of Grubb as an un-
happy child, sitting by himself on a stoop, staring off
into nothing. He reached the door near the back of the
trailer. Chapa retracted his hand into the sleeve of his
coat and using the cuff to grip the knob, he twisted.
The door was locked.

"Annie, are you in there?" His voice muted but firm.

Silence. Only the call of a bird in the distance, and
the constant hum from whatever was supplying power.

Chapa made certain he didn't touch anything for
fear of disturbing possible evidence and replacing one
set of fingerprints with his own. He did not want to
leave any part of himself in this place.

He was squatting down, more closely examining the
unusually secure lock, when some movement at the far
end of the trailer caught his eye and prodded him into
attack position. Holding the crowbar in front of his
body like a sword, he leaned against what he assumed
was the bathroom door and waited.

Outside, the wind was pushing against the sides of
the old structure. Primed for the fight, he watched as a
breeze slipped in through the screen door and the
curtains swayed in response. Then Chapa saw how one
of the lights flickered spastically, the beginning of its
death dance. Movement—just a trick of light and
wind.

Chapa stepped away from the door and tried the
knob once more without success. He would use the

crowbar to bust it open, but first he needed to see what was hiding behind those curtains at the opposite end of the trailer.

Wanting to somehow document whatever happened to him next, Chapa reached into his coat. Refusing to take his eyes away from the rest of the trailer, he fumbled around for a moment until his fingers located the tape recorder. He wrapped his hand around it and pushed the record button, leaving the device in his pocket so he could keep his hands free.

Chapa continued moving toward the curtains at the front of the trailer, measuring each step, stopping to look through the door and make certain his car was still there. The light outside the trailer had changed somehow, as though daylight decided to give up the fight a little earlier than usual. His Toyota appeared to be part of another reality, like something on the outside of a snow globe.

Or maybe he had it backward. It could be that what most folks think of as normal society is just a ruse encased in a protective but fragile shell. The only thing separating them from a brutal reality. It was hard to believe that only a few minutes had passed since he'd entered this real world house of horrors.

He thought about running to his car and getting away from there. Getting to a landline and calling in the cops. But the thought passed just as quickly as it had arrived. Leaving that temptation behind, he continued to move toward the front of the trailer, splitting his time between the curtains and the displays on the wall.

The Grubb tribute ended with a collage of his victims' photos stemming out from a larger one of Annie Sykes in the middle. Chapa noticed a second photo of Annie had been slipped into the corner. She was an adult in this one, a candid taken at a restaurant. A small sign beneath it read: *A creature so vile even the ground spit her out.*

A series of manifestos followed, with titles like MYTHS ABOUT VICTIMS and LEGAL HYPOCRISY. Photos of other murderers, both as adults and when they were children painted a grotesque mosaic. The whole thing seemed to be an attempt to put Grubb into some murderous historical context.

The wall immediately to Chapa's right was papered with drawings. Some were renderings of clowns, others of distorted faces, and some had no form at all. Poems and long, handwritten pages crowded with very small print had been carefully fitted into the gaps. The ranting of lunatics. Above it all a sign read: MISUNDERSTOOD ARTISTS.

Chapa was trying to read some of the writings when he bumped into a small bookcase full of photo albums. He opened one to a crime scene photo of a shattered young body. He flipped through it and found more of the same. He tossed the gruesome scrapbook on the floor.

Then he noticed a small beige plastic box sitting on the footstool in front of the television. It looked like something that had been rigged from parts purchased at a strip mall electronics store. The quarter-size red buttons on it were labeled *1* and *2*. Probably having something to do with the TV.

As Chapa moved closer to the curtains he decided to attack the one on the left first. He stabbed at it several times with the sharp end of the crowbar, then stepped back. The curtain put up no resistance, waited until he was finished, then eased back into place. He watched for movement behind the other curtain as well, but saw none.

Leaving nothing to chance, Chapa swatted hard at

the other one, ignoring the fact that he was starting to feel a little silly beating the crap out of a cheap pair of drapes. He stopped when he struck something solid on the other side.

Slipping the pointed end through the slit between them, Chapa pulled back the curtain on the right with one swift jerk, revealing a plywood wall that stretched across to the other side. A hole, about two inches in diameter, had been drilled through the wall, about a foot off the floor. Cables ran from the television and disappeared into the hole.

Trying to avoid leaning against it any more than he had to, Chapa pressed his ear to what he guessed was a relatively thin piece of wood. He had no idea what he was expecting or hoping to hear, but it didn't matter, he got nothing for his effort. Squatting down to floor level, he peered through the hole as much as he could, and poked around at the cables to create more space, but still couldn't see anything.

That left the television and the locked room. Maybe one would hold a clue about the other. Chapa again tucked his hand up into the sleeve, then pressed down on the red button labeled *1*. The television switched on with an electronic *pop* and snow filled the screen. The unit was only a couple of feet off the floor, the footrest even lower, and he felt like a child as he sat down on the undersize furniture.

Chapa pressed the second button and the screen went black, though the TV was still turned on. The odd shapes of the tables and displays behind him reflected on the blank screen, creating an oddly artistic pattern. He was thinking about how crowded and cramped it looked when an image replaced the shadows.

A camera tilted down along a whitewashed brick wall

while muffled sounds could be heard beyond it. A moment later it stopped and focused on the man in a jumpsuit, who was sitting in front of the wall. Then Kenny Lee Grubb looked into the camera and released a slow crooked smile.

CHAPTER 27

I am so very proud of you Alex, Grubb began, the smile still pasted across his face. *I'm glad that we have this opportunity to become better acquainted. I hope you did as instructed and carefully studied the information here at this shrine. I know that if you did that, and did so with an open and clear mind*—Grubb poked at the middle of his forehead—*then you have a better picture of my mission, and perhaps you will even allow yourself to become an advocate, a convert. Am I asking too much? I don't think so. If I could make you see things through my eyes, Alex, you would understand everything.*

Grubb appeared as he had just a few days earlier. In fact, the video could have been shot that same day. Chapa knew that prisoners found ways to get their hands on all sorts of things. But smuggling a video camera into a maximum security prison and getting the recording back to one of Grubb's zealots was a bit beyond the pale.

I was portrayed by the folks in the media, like yourself, as someone who chose his targets at random, but that wasn't the case. I did what had to be done to those who needed it done to them.

A noise from somewhere off-screen captured

Grubb's attention, and he turned toward it. A look of concern replaced the smugness, but only for an instant.

I performed a service that would earn me hero status if the simple people understood. I would get a fucking parade down State Street if they understood. I rendered monsters that, though small, would have eventually brought more horror and misery to the world than I ever could. I'm not a murderer. I am a crusader who prevented evil creatures from committing future crimes.

My work was far from done when Red turned on me. I was fooled by her, and tried to make her cleansing as painless as possible. Grubb leaned in toward the camera in a way that distorted his features. *I made a mistake. And you made her into a hero, but that's only because the people don't understand. When that cop shot me I was trying to show them how Red had been bound. No normal child could've escaped. I was disposing of a creature so vile that the dirt itself spit her back out. I know now that was only temporary. My work continues.*

I am like a parent, and a good parent nurtures his offspring because he knows they are the ones who will continue his work. I have always been a good parent. My work continues because of that.

Grubb reached inside the front of his jumpsuit and produced a photo. He looked at it for a moment before turning it so that it faced the camera. It was another candid of Annie Sykes, different than the one on the wall of the trailer, but probably from the same day.

I hope you understand now, and you are ready to take what must seem like a large leap of faith. I don't believe it is. There is such little time left for you to come around. You must tell the truth about Red.

Grubb looked around as though he was making sure no one was nearby or walking in his direction. His eyes locked in on the camera. Then, without as much as the slightest hint of difficulty, the killer pushed himself up and out of the chair until his elbows locked. Grubb's lips parted, creating a jagged chasm that no sane person would've labeled as a smile.

Chapa was mesmerized by the sight of a crippled animal rising from its trap, wondering if he'd just seen the killer's right foot move on its own.

Me and you, we'll talk again, Grubb said, no strain in his voice, then reached up and stopped the recording.

The television switched off, and the uneven shapes returned to the dark screen. It took a moment for Chapa's eyes to adjust back to the muted light of the trailer. Wanting to watch the video again, certain that he had missed something, Chapa pressed the buttons without bothering to cover his fingers this time. Nothing happened. He tried again, holding the buttons down longer. But the television did not respond. Maybe he could pry open the wall behind the curtains and get at it that way. That, however, might take a while. The light outside was in full retreat now, and he had no desire to be anywhere near this place once night came.

Chapa decided he would take some of the displays with him, for fear that they, along with the trailer, might vanish after he left. He didn't like the idea of leaving the video behind, and wondered how long it would take him to tear up the plywood wall and get at it. Chapa considered his limited options as he sat there for a moment, staring at the reflected shapes on the television.

And then one of those shapes moved.

Chapa gripped the crowbar and bolted to his feet. In one desperate motion he brought the weapon up to an attack position and turned to see who was behind him. But before he could do that, a sharp pain stabbed into the soft area between his neck and collarbone. He lost all feeling in that arm and dropped the crowbar without knowing he had released his grip until it clattered against the floor.

Slumping forward, Chapa was certain he was going to fall. But he knew that would be a mistake, so he willed his upper torso to work with his suddenly rubbery legs, and Chapa again began to turn in the direction of his assailant.

But his attacker, more shadow than human in Chapa's hazy view, was moving much faster. Something metallic and heavy slammed into Chapa's forehead, blinding him for a moment as shards of pain ripped through his skull. He was already too far gone to realize he had lost his balance, and was now completely out of options.

As he fell backward, his eyes at half mast, Chapa saw that the bathroom door was now open. His left shoulder hit against something hard and unforgiving. The last thing Chapa heard was the sound of the TV crashing to the floor, but it registered several seconds after it fell, and at that moment the noise sounded like it came from somewhere far away.

CHAPTER 28

The child who would become Kenny Lee Grubb was barely a dozen years old when he committed his first murder. It happened the summer after fifth grade. His family had moved to Illinois from Mississippi the week before, so Kenny knew no one and no one knew of him.

He met Cliff, who was two years younger and liked to smile a lot, while playing behind a nearby junior high school that had been abandoned for the long summer break. Cliff had found a large pile of bricks along the back of the school and was carefully stacking them to build a fort.

"Can I help?"

"Okay, just keep putting them on top of each other the way I started to."

They spent the next half hour building the make-shift and unsteady wall. Kenny had altered the pattern just a bit, and they wound up with one extra brick.

"Here, I'll put it right on top by itself," Cliff said. "That way if any bad people show up, we can use it to scare them off."

Cliff's family lived in Ohio, and he was spending the summer with his grandparents while his folks were going through a divorce. Grubb envied his new friend.

He had often wished that his truck driver father would never return from the road. Maybe then one of his mother's boyfriends would stick around for keeps, or even better, they'd stop coming by altogether.

Sometimes when Kenny's father was around he would try to engage the child in a conversation about sports, or tell him stories from the road. These always started out well enough, with his father calling him over and tossing a beefy arm around the boy's shoulders. But Kenny had been through this process enough to understand that in the same way a smattering of clouds and a gentle breeze out in the Atlantic start out with good intentions before they merge into a raging storm, so it was with his father's occasional interest in him.

Eventually, the man would manufacture a disagreement, or create a reason to complain or pick on Kenny. Things would deteriorate in a hurry after that. Before long the child's pleas were as useless as yelling into a roaring hurricane as it blows the house off its foundation.

The boys avoided trouble, but not mischief, and for the first time in his life Kenny had a sense of how friendship could feel. Though they had very little in common other than their loneliness.

"Have you told your grandparents about me?" Kenny would ask every few days.

"Nope," always Cliff's response.

"Good, don't. Like I've told you, I'm like a ghost."

The deserted school became a favorite hangout, and they would ride their bikes to it several times a week. The three-story brick structure had been built in the 1930s, and originally used as a high school until a more modern version replaced it. Kenny had found a way inside through an old storm shelter, and left a basement window unlocked so they could get back in any time they wanted. The building, full of odd hallways and secret spaces, served as a giant playroom. Cliff was always the first one to run into a strange or dark place, and he came out laughing every time.

Kenny liked climbing up to the old brick building's third floor, its scuffed, uneven boards creaking beneath his feet, and looking down at the world below. Everything he hated seemed so small and far away from up there. He wanted to open one of the large windows and scream out as loud as he could.

They would end each day by going down one of the fire escape chutes on the top floor to the blacktop below. The tubular slide was dark and rough and it scared Kenny just a little each time, but he liked that rush.

They were about to end another day that way when Kenny called Cliff into one of the third floor classrooms.

"You don't have to go yet," Kenny said. "You're just trying to get home to watch some stupid TV show."

Cliff laughed and followed Kenny into a classroom that was full of pictures of animals, molecules, and other illustrations detailing various parts of the human body. An impressive mobile of the solar system sat on a lab table in the middle of the room. Cliff pressed his index finger against one of the planets, gave it a push, and the whole solar system spun.

"I like science," he said.

Kenny had opened a large window, and the breeze that invaded the room blew papers around and threatened to knock the mobile over.

Cliff couldn't imagine how he had not noticed the open window before.

"That wasn't like that, was it?"

"Nope. I like to open it and stick my head out."

"Well, you'd better close it, and let's get going."

"Wait, check this out."

Kenny climbed up on a desk that sat next to the window. Paint chips fell to the pavement below as he carefully placed his feet on the ledge and squatted, folding his knees out toward the opening. He then slapped his hands open palm against the glass above, and eased his head and as much of his upper torso as he could out into the void.

This had to be the bravest thing he had ever done, though Kenny had never been able to coax himself into looking down from this vantage point.

"Careful, somebody might see you," Kenny barely heard Cliff say from inside the room.

After the wind had blown his hair around a bit, Kenny slipped back inside.

"Your turn."

Cliff hesitated for just a moment, then smiled and walked to the window. Kenny was surprised that his friend had hesitated at all, but Cliff made up for it by not being as cautious once he got to the opening.

Kenny came up behind him, figuring that he might have to catch Cliff if he fell off the table, but he saw that his friend was laughing. Of course he was. Cliff got bolder, and began separating his hands from the glass pane above his head, rocking back then allowing himself to fall forward a little before slapping them back into place.

Now it was Kenny who thought it was time to go.

"You stay up there too long and somebody is going to see you."

"Okay, one more time," Cliff said and pushed his body away from the opening until his head was the only part of him that was still outside, before letting himself fall forward.

And then he was gone.

Kenny saw how Cliff's hands reached for the glass but instead landed on the wooden frame, then slid off, but for a moment it didn't seem real. He ran to the window, expecting to see his friend smiling up at him as he dangled from a ledge. But all Kenny saw below was Cliff's small contorted body.

He ran down the stairs, forgetting about the chute which would have been much faster, and bolted through a door he'd never used before. Kenny was disoriented and it took him a moment to figure out where he was in relation to where Cliff had landed.

Kenny heard Cliff before he saw him. It was a labored groan unlike any sound he had ever heard a person make. He came up around the side of the building and found the boy. From several feet away it was not easy to tell where Cliff's body ended and the pavement began.

Hoping this was just another gag, Kenny turned his friend over. Cliff let out a scream from somewhere deep in his throat. Blood was escaping from Cliff's head as well as the rest of his body.

"Help."

"Yes Cliff, what can I do?"

The boy swallowed hard as though he had to get something massive out of his throat before he could speak again.

"Get help."

"Okay, okay, I will."

Kenny touched him on the shoulder and it felt wet and warm. He looked down at his hand as he stood up and saw that it was painted with blood.

"I'll be back."

He hopped on his bike and started for the edge of the playground, hoping that he could get help at one of the houses in the adjacent neighborhood. What would he tell them? He could always say he was playing at the school or maybe riding his bike past it and saw Cliff fall out of a window.

Would they believe that? Adults thought he was lying all the time, sometimes even when he was telling the truth. They might even think that he pushed Cliff out of the window. And what would Cliff say? Would he still keep their secrets?

Kenny brought his bicycle to a stop a few feet shy of the opening that led out from the playground. He turned around and started riding back toward the school. He planned on asking Cliff to go along with his story. Everything would be okay if they agreed on what they would say happened.

Another idea crept in as he passed the fort. Kenny rode over to the uneven structure that was held together by gravity and little else. Then he reached down and picked up the brick that his friend had placed on top of the wall.

The shattered child was trying to say something as Kenny got off his bike and walked toward him. A dreadful look of panic swept across the boy's face when he saw that Kenny had not brought anyone with him.

"Cliff, I need to be sure that you're not going to tell anyone that I was playing here," Kenny said, struggling to make eye contact. "Do you understand?"

Cliff's eyes revealed a mix of confusion and fear. The broken child struggled to respond.

"Help," he finally forced out.

"No, I need *you* to help *me*," Kenny said, once again looking away from Cliff's bloodstained face.

This time the response came quicker and with less effort.

"Get help now, Kenny."

Something about hearing his name spoken through the bloodied gurgling in Cliff's throaty voice made Kenny feel very vulnerable. He hated that feeling, wanted to rip it right out of his body. And then Kenny knew what he had to do next.

Cliff did not react when Grubb raised the brick over his head. The first blow sent blood spraying from the sides of Cliff's head. Grubb did not look away as Cliff spit out more than a mouthful of fluid.

He wasn't moving after Grubb slammed the brick down a second time. The third blow only served to further disfigure the tiny carcass. Beneath the blood and distorted flesh, Grubb could still make out Cliff's thin, discolored lips.

He appeared to be smiling.

Grubb rolled Cliff over before getting back on his bike and riding away, holding the bloody brick like it was of no significance. He took the long way home, through a small but dense patch of trees near his house. It was there that he buried the brick beneath some dead leaves, twigs, and as much of the dry dirt as his small fingers could scrape up.

For the next couple of days he waited for the police to come to his house and take him away. But that did not happen. In fact, he heard nothing about it until his mother told him that a boy had fallen out of a school window, and added that he should never go to that playground alone.

Cliff's grandparents had told the police that he was a troubled child who always got into things, and they were devastated but not too surprised something like this had happened.

When his mother recounted that to him, Grubb wondered why anyone would describe Cliff in that way. Perhaps his grandparents knew him better than anyone. It could be that they were relieved he was gone. Maybe Cliff was evil, in which case it was a good thing he was gone. Grubb concluded that he had done them a favor.

During the two years that he attended Franklin Junior High School, Grubb had just one class in the science room on the third floor. When it got warm, the teacher would open the windows. Every once in a while, Grubb would walk over to the one Cliff had fallen out of and look down on the pavement below. And sometimes he would smile.

Three Days Before the Execution

CHAPTER 29

Ten-year-old Annie Sykes had been buried in the damp October ground for nearly an hour when she awoke from a frightening and confusing dream. Whatever breathable air was left beneath the heavy soil would get used up in a hurry if the child panicked.

She couldn't understand why the darkness wasn't going away, the way it always did when she woke up in her bedroom. Her head hurt so much she thought for a moment about going back to sleep, but somehow knew that would be a very bad idea.

Annie tried several times to turn her head, but she managed to move only slightly. With each abbreviated twist, the coldness pressed harder against her face. Breathing was becoming more difficult. Annie knew that she had to do something—and fast.

Shifting a few inches on knees that ached, and which she imagined were badly scraped, Annie groped around awkwardly with delicate fingers that she could not see. Everything felt hard and cold. Her trembling hands moved slowly in toward her shoulders and upper back, to where her head and neck had been swallowed up by the ground. With a difficult, contorted stretch she touched a mound of soft dirt where the rest of her body should have been.

Now Annie knew what was happening, and fear began to take hold. She had been buried, but not all of her. Wiggling just enough to free her shoulders a bit, she pressed her palms to the ground and pushed. Pain, like that of a thousand jagged razor cuts, tore across her chest, and up through her neck. She tried to scream, but that effort only let a couple more tablespoons of dirt slide into her mouth. Something large and heavy clawed into her chin and behind her ears. Annie started crying, but the tears pooled in her eyes, and made them feel sticky and heavy.

Don't move too much and it won't hurt at all. Sit in one place Annie, motionless, still, like an object. Until someone comes and sets you free.

Where had she learned that? Those words were familiar, and comforting in a way. But now she realized that no one was coming to rescue her.

Annie pushed again, but whatever was digging into her chin slid a little and started choking her. She tried to catch her breath, but there was too little air to be had and the dirt burrowed up, filling her nose until it was gnawing into the tight spaces behind her eyes.

What limited strength Annie might've normally had in her slender arms was just about gone and she started to cry again, thinking of her parents, her brother, and how badly she wanted to be back in her house. Again she brought a hand to where her body ended and the dirt began.

Willing frigid fingers into the ground, Annie started digging. It was easy, at first, as her nails sank into the recently upturned earth. But then she reached the area where the ground had been packed more tightly by the weight of the dirt above it. By that point, however, her hands weren't quite as cold. The feeling was returning to her fingers, and Annie started to believe she was going to be able to free herself.

The child strained to pivot her head from side to side. She dug farther down along her neck until she touched something hard and completely foreign. Moving more of the dirt aside, Annie felt her way around what she at first thought was a belt, then recognized it as a thick dog collar.

Again, Annie tried to pull her head out, desperate to get free, but the collar wouldn't budge. She slipped her fingers between the coarse leather and the smooth skin of her neck, until her hands struck metal objects that were somehow attached. Using her index fingers and thumbs, Annie followed the smooth, curved metal on either side of her neck until it straightened and vanished into the dirt.

She knew what these things were. Just a few months earlier, when the Sykes family went on its annual Memorial Day camping trip, Annie and Tyler had helped their father put up the tent. Now she recalled how Dad had scolded Tyler when he pulled a long spike out of the duffel bag, explaining to the seven-year-old boy how dangerous those things were.

Annie remembered watching her dad pound the spikes deep into the ground, then challenging each of them to try and pull one out. They couldn't, and Annie knew that she wouldn't be able to now.

She felt lightheaded and nauseous. It would be so easy to just let go and slide off to sleep. Her head hurt so much, and the pain seemed less intense whenever she stopped moving, or quit thinking about getting out.

Don't move too much and your head won't hurt. Sit in one place Annie, motionless, still, like an object. Until someone comes and sets you free.

Maybe this is how she would be set free, by letting go. Annie let herself relax and in an instant she began to drift off. She had just about lost consciousness when her knees slipped and she fell to her side. The fall wrenched her neck, jolting Annie back into the moment. More determined than before to get free, she began to feed off the pain, imagining it was a tangible thing that could be directed right into her muscles and bones.

Annie groped around until she found the buckle, just behind her ear. Moisture from the damp ground had caused the leather to swell and tighten its grip on the metal. She ran her fingers along the buckle until she touched its sharp narrow prong, then forced her right thumbnail under it while holding the buckle still with her other hand.

When her thumbnail had gone as far under as it could, she pulled up on the prong and managed to create a slight separation. It was just enough for Annie to be able to grab hold, and maybe pry it open. She pinched the prong between her index finger and thumb, then tried to coax it away from the strap. The slender metal tooth was about halfway there when it slipped from her tender fingers.

Annie managed to jam her index finger under the prong before it fell back into its original place. She pushed up on it—more slowly this time—until it was sticking straight up from the collar. Grabbing the metal sliver with one hand, and the end of the strap with the other, Annie pulled in opposite directions, freeing the prong from the damp leather.

Once she had unfastened the buckle, Annie willed her head out of the collar, and then the hole. But she didn't have full control of her body right away, and fell back hard against the ground. One nightmare had ended, another was beginning.

Alex Chapa stood on the same ground just a few days later and tried to imagine what that image must have looked like. For him, it represented a moment of extra-ordinary courage and strength. He had an instant admiration for the little girl who would not give up when she was supposed to.

The image of Annie Sykes standing alone in that field, cold and wounded, but also defiant and determined, was slipping through his mind now, as were dozens of other seemingly unrelated images. A giant black bird screeched at him before disappearing in the distance. A bleeding heart with a knife through it undulated as it drifted through a dark landscape, only to double back and come around for a second pass. A tangle of thick branches turned into a swatch of red hair that floated across the edges of his mind.

At first the images seemed disconnected and random—Annie's face and the faces of some of the other children whose photos he had seen in the trailer. Chapa thought he was chasing Nikki through dense trees, but couldn't catch her. The parade of disturbing images came then went, only to sweep by again.

A marginally conscious part of him feared he would not be able to escape this nightmare.

But then he opened his eyes.

CHAPTER 30

The first time Chapa heard the voice he wasn't sure if it came from within the room or somewhere out in the dark, cold field that Annie Sykes had managed to escape years ago.

Chapa was certain something heavy had been fastened to his eyelids. Forcing them open even a little made his head scream at him just for trying. After a few painful attempts, he managed to let what sparse light there was in the room slip in through the narrow slits, and that hurt even more.

He brought his hand up to rub his face, but it felt as though the arm belonged to someone else. Digging his thumb and index finger into the corners of his eyes, Chapa managed to work some of the haze out. His forehead felt like it was misshapen somehow, but the last thing he wanted to do right then was look in a mirror, since that would mean having to get up.

Though Chapa's eyes were more or less open, he was far from fully conscious. He focused on a figurine sitting on a shelf just a few feet away. Just enough specks of light from the hallway were creeping into the room and he was able to make it out. A small porcelain girl in a blue checkered dress with a teddy bear tucked under one arm was handing a book to her father.

"Tell me a story, Daddy," Chapa softly said to himself, having read the inscription a thousand times since Nikki had given the fragile gift to him on Father's Day when she was just four. It had sat on the same shelf, within reach of his bed, ever since then. *I could tell you a story, but I don't think you would understand it*, Chapa thought as he began to understand that he was back in his own bedroom.

"From what I've seen, Mr. Chapa, your stories are nothing more than a disappointing collection of lies."

The voice came from Chapa's left, and he gradually willed his head to move in its direction. It was as easy as rolling a large boulder up a steep mountain using nothing but the muscles in his neck.

"How did I get here?"

"I don't know how much longer you will be conscious, so you need to listen."

The voice was coming from a shape in the far corner of the room. Chapa squinted and tried to see beyond the darkness, but it was no use.

"This is where you let go, Alex. You write your story, and this time tell the whole truth about what happens over the next few days, and leave the rest alone."

He had some sort of accent, Eastern European, maybe.

"What did you do to me?"

"Nothing that wasn't done to Red."

Flooded by images of violence, Chapa now realized that the stabbing pain he had felt back at the trailer was caused by a needle being jammed into his neck.

"I can get to you any time I want. I can come into your home. The cops get involved with Red, and you will find me here waiting for you."

The voice was drifting across the room, and the shape was no longer tucked safely into the corner.

"I know where your loved ones live, that woman you screw, her cute little boy, your daughter too. What's her name? Oh yeah, *Nicole*," he said it as though he was ordering his favorite meal. "You call her *Nikki*, with two ks. Cute."

A large hand gripped Chapa by the throat, tightening around his neck like a collar. He couldn't breathe.

"It's only out of the kindness of my heart that I don't drive over to your woman's house and peel the skin off the little boy's tender body while she watches. But my kindness is conditional."

He came in close, and Chapa could smell his stale breath. The shape of his face became visible, but the features remained a blur.

"Maybe I'll just stop by now and hang around to watch her get the boy ready for preschool before she goes off to work."

Then the thick hand released its vise grip. Chapa coughed, and it hurt like hell to do so.

"I like the way your woman moves."

Chapa closed his eyes and drifted back into something less than consciousness. A short while later, or maybe an hour, he lacked the lucidity to be certain, he heard footsteps calmly retreating down the stairs, then the sound of the front door closing.

He needed to get to a telephone and call for help. But that meant figuring out how to make his body do what he wanted it to. His shoulders were numb, but he had some sensation in his legs. Chapa started trying to rock his hips, which proved much harder than he expected, and he was not certain that any part of his body was actually moving.

Suddenly, enough weight shifted and he rolled over. The jerking motion made him feel nauseous. He blacked out, falling into a deep chasm, desperately trying to reach back as his bedroom vanished in the distance.

CHAPTER 31

When he opened his eyes Chapa again only saw whatever was pressing down against his face. Something was putting pressure on the whole front of his body, as though he was lying under a lead-lined comforter.

After a couple of minutes of staring into the beige fabric while trying to get a sense of how much it would hurt to move, Chapa realized that it was he who was lying on top of something. The weight he was feeling was his own.

The ringing in his head was abruptly replaced by a muted series of seemingly random sounds. Then the ringing returned and this time Chapa made out the sound of his answering machine message, followed by Joseph Andrews' voice.

Alex, damn it, where are you? You need to answer a phone and you sure as hell better call me before you set foot outside of whatever rock you're hiding under.

Chapa brought his hands up along the sides of his body, then pushed and separated himself from his bedroom carpet. He sat there by the side of the bed and rubbed the back of his sore neck, wondering what other injuries he would have to deal with.

Tiny but determined demons were kicking at the

skin on his forehead. Chapa slowly reached up, and with an unsteady hand felt a massive welt above his right eye, just below the hairline. Eventually, he walked over to the answering machine on the dresser and pushed the messages button while he took stock of his appearance.

Chapa found six messages on his answering machine and two bruises on his face.

Al, it's Joseph. Hey, give me a call at the office or even better on my cell.

Andrews had called again two hours later, almost to the minute.

Al, it's Joseph again. I checked the blotter so I know you haven't been picked up yet. Call me!

Blotter? Picked up? Chapa now remembered Andrews had warned him about going out in his most recent message.

Um, hi Alex, this is Matt Sullivan. Wow, what a morning, huh? Well, obviously we have a situation here and Mr. Macklin would like to move up his meeting with you. Can you give me a call as soon as you get this so we can schedule that? Thanks.

How long had he been out? Chapa looked at the clock. *11:28.* How much can happen to a guy in roughly eighteen hours?

The next call was from Erin, describing all of the things that she and Mikey were doing at the indoor water park. After what Chapa had been through and the messages from Andrews and the newspaper, hers seemed to come from another dimension.

The one that followed brought Chapa back to his new reality.

Okay, Al, I just now got around to playing back your message from yesterday. You didn't give me much information, just enough to have me worried. The local police have identified you as a person of interest in the death of Louise Jones. I've managed to put them on ice for the time being, but that won't hold. If I haven't heard from you by tonight I'll try to get out there and stop by your house.

Chapa looked outside through the slats of his bedroom blinds. The bright sunlight stung his eyes, but everything below looked as it should. That is, except for the police car doing a slow cruise past his house.

Good thing I didn't leave my car parked out there, he thought, and then, *Where the hell is my car?*

As he walked to the bathroom to throw some water on his battered face, Chapa remembered what the guy had said about going over to Erin's house. That meant he didn't know she and Mikey had gotten out of town. He felt a small bit of relief.

The cold water didn't do him much good, but at least it wasn't painful, either. He returned to his bedroom and dialed Andrews' cell.

"Jesus, Al, where were you? Are you okay?"

"I was asleep on the floor of my bedroom."

Chapa explained as best he could everything that had happened to him since Erin found the note on her door.

"The Traveling Killer Museum? That's an urban myth."

"Really, then that would make the purple ping pong ball on my forehead the stuff that dreams are made of."

"Were you able to gather any evidence?"

"I had planned on it, but that wasn't on the curator's agenda."

Andrews told Chapa quite a bit about the museum, and how there was a running debate within the Bureau as to whether or not it was real. Believers claimed that it popped up in deserted areas. A few months earlier it had been seen at a remote spot in the wilds of Southern California called Slab City, but folks claimed to have seen it in many parts of the country.

"According to the creeps who follow this stuff on the Internet, the process is a lot like what you've described. A person gets an invitation with a map. When they arrive at some remote place they find the trailer unlocked. There's never anyone around, but a few people claim they felt like they were being watched."

Chapa gave him the directions as he remembered them, and Andrews told him he would send a forensics team to check out the area where the trailer had been.

"It won't be there anymore," Andrews said.

"No, but my car should be. Tell your guys to be gentle, it's a family heirloom."

"That trailer is the least of your problems right now."

Chapa watched as another squad car rolled down his street. Two in less than half an hour, that couldn't be a coincidence.

"How the hell am I a person of interest to anyone?"

"Well, let's see, there's your business card which had Louise's blood all over it. Your name is in her appointment book. Also, you left a message on her machine stating that you would be there at a time that closely matches the coroner's preliminary report for the time of death."

"And on the other side of the ledger is my complete lack of motive."

"They're not accusing you of anything. They just have some questions."

"Like what?"

"Did you get any sense that there was someone else in that house?"

Chapa thought for a moment and tried to put himself back there again. Was that really just two days ago?

"No, but I guess there could've been."

"To make matters worse, every paper picked up the story today."

"Every paper?"

"Actually no, your employer chose to ignore it, but two of your competitors ran it on the front page."

Chapa looked at himself in the mirror and wondered what his mug shot might look like.

"You've got about a twenty-four hour window. But I'd like you to come here to the office and I'll take your statement."

They agreed on an 11:00 A.M. meeting the next day. Andrews said that would give him enough time to have Grubb's brother picked up for questioning on the murder and everything else that had gone down in the past few days.

Then Chapa remembered something else.

"Did you find the red journal I told you about at Louise's?"

"It wasn't there. Lots of other journals and notebooks, but no red."

Chapa wasn't surprised.

CHAPTER 32

The warm water cascaded through Chapa's dark brown hair and down his face, revealing more wounds than the mirror could. But he didn't care. It felt good to simply stand still and quiet and clear his mind of everything. Though that was hard to do.

Chapa wondered about the missing journal. Had someone murdered Louise just to get their hands on it? And how did they know about it? Maybe she told her killer about the journal before she was shot to death.

He was allowing himself the luxury of lingering a while longer, letting the water wash away some of the hurt, and trying to decide whether to finish before the hot water ran out. Then he remembered his tape recorder.

Toweling off as quickly as he could, Chapa threw on a robe and stumbled out of the bathroom as his head reminded him about the night before. He gripped the railing tightly and took measured steps down the stairs.

His living room looked exactly as he'd left it, like nothing out of the ordinary had happened. The same was true of the dining room, as well as the kitchen, where he paused long enough to say good morning to Jimmy and refill the bird's water bottle. All the doors

were locked. Everything was in order. But when he
turned toward the front door Chapa saw the black cloth
coat that he'd worn the day before neatly folded and
resting on a small table. His wallet and keys were on top
of it.

As far as he could tell, all of his credit cards and cash
were still there. The only thing missing was a small
photo of Mikey that Erin had given him a few weeks earlier.

"Sick bastard," Chapa said to himself.

All of his keys were there, including the one for his
car. He made a note to have the locks to his house
changed as soon as possible. Erin's too, since her key
was also on his chain.

He patted down his jacket and felt nothing but the
soft worn cloth. Then he reached into a side pocket
and touched the small plastic recorder. Had they
missed it, or intentionally left it there for him?

Chapa pushed the power button, rewound a few
minutes, then pushed Play. Silence. Fast Forward—
Play—more silence. The timer read *94:02*. That meant
he had recorded for more than an hour and a half, but
where was it?

This time he rewound all the way back to the beginning of the recording. Chapa heard muffled sounds,
then the click of the television, followed a minute later
by Grubb's voice, muted but clear. On the one hand,
Chapa wished he had taken it out of his pocket and gotten a better recording of Grubb's diatribe. Then again,
if he had thought to do that, whoever drugged him
would've seen the recorder.

Grubb's voice was gone, and an instant later he
heard a crash, a groan, then silence. Chapa was surprised by how quickly it had all gone down, much faster
than it seemed at the time. After a couple of loud jolts,
like someone had kicked him close to where the

recorder was, he heard another round of muffled shuffling sounds, then other noises a distance away, followed by more silence.

He picked up the recorder and was about to fast forward when he heard something else. Was that a voice? It was faint and distant. Chapa cranked the volume, but that only distorted the sound. Who were they talking to?

The voice, if that's what it was, sporadically faded in and out over the next few minutes. Then he heard what might have been a second voice. At least two people were with him in the trailer.

Chapa grabbed the recorder and his keys, slipped his feet into a pair of dusty tennis shoes, the same ones he was wearing the day before, and headed for the back door. He didn't much care if any of the neighbors saw him in a bathrobe as he walked to his garage.

He pushed a button on his key fob and the garage door opened, revealing his blue Corolla neatly parked inside. Chapa could almost hear Andrews' voice telling him to leave it as is until a forensics team could go through every inch of the vehicle.

After considering that option for a moment, Chapa said, "Screw it," then closed the garage door and hurried back inside to get dressed. He had to get to Pennington Correctional before visiting hours were over.

CHAPTER 33

All it took was a call to the warden, reminding him of how well the *Chicago Record* had treated his facility, and within seconds Chapa was cleared for a visit. He listened to the rest of the tape as he drove the forty miles to the prison. The quality of the recording ranged from very bad to poor, but it did reveal several new details. They had carried Chapa to his car in silence, then deposited him in the rear seat. The recording had cut out before they got to Chapa's house.

He had no reason to expect answers from Grubb. But unanswered questions weren't the only thing driving Chapa. More than anything, he wanted to show Grubb that he had no intention of backing down.

The sun was hiding behind one of the guard towers as Chapa drove onto the prison grounds.

"This is an unscheduled visit," the guard at the gate said.

The old man inside the security booth had a Marine Corps buzz cut, a beer league gut, and an attitude that suggested his workday would soon be over and he saw no reason to make what was left of it memorable. Chapa explained the situation, and a call was placed to the warden's office. The guard was still on the phone when he waved Chapa through.

Harker recognized him from the last time.

"Grubb may not see you. I understand he hasn't been talking much lately, which is unusual."

"Let's find out."

Chapa followed him through a familiar set of doors and back to the antiseptic room where he'd spoken to Grubb four long days earlier. The walls were so white they almost glowed, and the only thing hanging on them was a calendar, which Chapa thought was odd. Maybe it was a cruel joke on the part of the guards.

"You know the drill," Harker said.

Chapa sat in the same chair as before, though it seemed like weeks had passed since he was last here. He took out a notepad that was strictly for show, and a long thin metal pen which immediately rolled to the middle of the uneven table. Then Chapa casually reached into his pocket and felt for his recorder. He wasn't going to push Record this time, but he needed to know exactly where it was.

When Grubb finally arrived he had the energy of a man who was on his way to a business meeting, one that he felt very good about. He rolled his chair over and stopped directly across from Chapa, then tossed his cuffed hands on the table. The chains connecting Grubb's wrists, waist, and ankles rubbed against the wheelchair's metal frame, the sound echoing off the thick walls.

"Are you a bit more enlightened, Alex?" Grubb asked, putting the emphasis on the word *enlightened*.

Chapa thought for a moment. "In a way, I suppose."

Grubb smiled.

"I want to know who the hell is screwing with me and threatening the people I care about."

"Yes, maybe someone got a little overzealous. But I wanted you to understand, Alex."

"Why?"

Grubb leaned back in his narrow chair.

"Because no one in the press has treated me fairly for some time, and you're my last hope. Maybe I'm your last hope too."

"How do you figure that?"

"I have respect for you. That's not something you're accustomed to. Not in your marriage, probably not even at work."

Then Grubb conjured up a look of empathy and concern that would have made any psychiatrist envious. Chapa let it all sink in, knowing his silence would give Grubb the impression that he was getting through. When enough time had passed, Chapa reached into his inside pocket and produced the recorder, then set it down on the table.

Chapa looked over at Harker, who gave him a *what the hell are you thinking* look.

"I promise I'm not going to record anything."

Harker thought about it for a moment, then went back to reading his magazine. Chapa pushed Play. In an instant, the killer's recorded voice filled the cramped room.

"You really ought to tell your cohorts that they should check every pocket after knocking someone out."

"Searching your things wasn't part of their mission," Grubb said with a look of concern. "You were given a great privilege in being allowed to see the shrine."

He was going through some sort of complex transformation, it was unlike anything Chapa had seen before. The cold façade slipped away, revealing what no mask could ever fully conceal.

"Maybe I'll invite you back from beyond the grave,

Alex, and the next time you visit the shrine I'll make sure the exhibit includes some pictures of your daughter."

With the tape still playing, his recorded voice drifting across the table and around the room, it was as though Grubb was doing a bizarre duet with himself each time he spoke.

"Her name is Nikki, isn't it? Tricky Nikki. I'll name her *Tear*, after that tasty little birthmark of hers."

Chapa abruptly stood up, not fully realizing that he was doing so, and the chair tumbled to the floor behind him. Its crash echoed through the sparsely furnished space. Fists clenched, Chapa closed in on Grubb, uncertain about what he would do next.

"Hey! Mr. Chapa!" Harker, already in motion, yelled from the other side of the room.

Grubb was smiling.

"You sick piece of shit, I should push the teeth you have left through the back of your throat," Chapa said with some effort.

Harker's heavy paw landed on Chapa's shoulder, which hurt like hell, but he did not flinch. The guard waited until Chapa finally looked at him.

"Would this be a good time for me to take a coffee break?" Harker suggested as much as asked, then he raised a thick eyebrow.

It took a moment for Grubb to understand the guard's offer.

"That's one definition of justice," Grubb said.

Chapa was aching to take Harker up on it, but worried that he wouldn't be able to stop himself once he started.

"Thanks, but I'll go ahead and let you guys deal with him."

Grubb laughed hard and clapped his hands.

"There you go, Alex, someone else raises your child,

and someone else can slay your dragons. Maybe we're not as alike as I'd hoped."

"Glad you finally figured that out, asshole."

Chapa gathered his recorder and tucked it back into his pocket as Grubb followed its movement like a shark tracking bait.

"How did you manage to make a video inside a prison?"

"When you have friends and admirers, the rest is easy. Besides, I'm resourceful. We have that in common, you and I."

"I'll tell you another thing we have in common," Chapa said. "Just now I made the decision to clear out my calendar, so you and I will both be here on the morning of your execution. Too bad for you that's where the similarities end."

Chapa leaned back, and away from his darkest temptation. Grubb finally tore his eyes off the pocket the recorder had disappeared into and returned Chapa's gaze.

"One more thing before they wheel you back to your death cell. How long have you been able to stand?"

Grubb tilted his head to the side just a bit, like a confused dog, or a wolf sizing up his prey.

"C'mon, Alex, you know I've been trapped in this chair ever since a cop wrongly put me here. It was in all the papers." Grubb moved in as far across the table as his chains would allow. "I heard Officer Rudman retired, how's that working out for him?"

Chapa's fist clenched involuntarily. He took a calculated breath before responding.

"Tell me, how do you think your time here might've been different if they had known what you and I know about your legs?"

Grubb's eyes narrowed to dark slits and nothing more.

Chapa continued, "What sort of fund do you think folks on the outside would've started then? I'm guessing even some of the really sick fucks who've supported you might have thought twice once they realized you'd been playing them. And that you're just a piece of shit, and nothing more."

This was making Chapa feel good, better than he had for some time.

"You know what, Kenny, my deadline is still hours away. Maybe I should do like you said and tell everyone the truth."

What happened next could have been measured in fractions of seconds. But for Chapa, who noted how each of the muscles in Grubb's upper body moved as one, the whole thing played out in slow motion. Like a scene that's happening somewhere else to other people.

In one uninterrupted move Grubb lunged for the pen that still rested where it had stopped rolling near the center of the table. As Harker called out for help and rose from his chair, Grubb clutched the pen like a knife and raised it up over his head in a stabbing position. He strained to get as close to Chapa as he could, but the reporter refused to flinch.

Grubb froze for an instant. His dark eyes vacant. Then he fell back into the chair. As Harker drew closer and another guard raced into the room, all expression abandoned Grubb's face.

Harker was just a few yards away and yelling something when Grubb lifted his arm up over his head, then plunged the pen into his right thigh with a force that made his chains rattle like wind chimes in an angry storm. Harker was almost on him when Grubb yanked the pen out of his leg and tossed it on the table. As it rolled toward Chapa, more than an inch of its tip painted with blood, the pen left a scarlet trail across the white top. Grubb's face revealed nothing.

The guards engulfed and restrained Grubb, who did not put up a fight or take his eyes off Chapa. And then the room erupted into a scramble of activity as more uniformed men hurried in and wheeled Grubb out. Chapa saw the slick dark stain that was spreading across Grubb's leg, discoloring the orange fabric.

Harker, hands on hips, glared at Chapa but didn't say anything. He didn't have to. The reporter gathered his notebook and got up to go. The bloodstained pen was still on the table when Chapa turned and walked out of the room without looking back.

CHAPTER 34

There were certain key pieces of information which Chapa had kept from Andrews. He had not told him what he'd learned about Annie from Munson down at Night Owls. He had not yet told him about the tape recording, or that he'd gone to visit Grubb a second time this week.

Chapa knew it was time to come clean, and he would do so when he met with Andrews the next morning. That meant he still had a lot to get done with what was left of today.

When he walked into the offices of the *Chicago Record* shortly after 5:00, he hoped that the folks from the night crew, most of whom he knew only in passing, had replaced his more familiar coworkers. That turned out to be the case, for the most part.

"Stop the presses, the fugitive has come to turn himself in," Duane Wormley said, looking up from his keyboard with a shit-eating grin on his face.

Chapa started to walk past Wormley's cubicle, then decided he'd rather do something else. He turned and leaned in close, invading Wormley's space.

"I had planned on bringing my killing spree to an

end, but maybe I'll make an exception," Chapa said coldly.

Wormley searched Chapa's eyes for the punch line, but when he found none the lower part of his face started trembling slightly. Chapa noticed the subtle jerking of the man's narrow, neatly shaven chin and started laughing in a way he hadn't for some time.

Zach came out of the copy room. Though he'd missed the joke, he immediately understood that it was on Wormley, and started laughing. The few others who were left all looked over to see what was so funny, and witnessed Wormley's entire upper body trembling with anger.

Matt Sullivan emerged from a corner office, he seemed confused.

"Mr. Macklin is gone."

"For good?" Chapa asked, feigning optimism. "Don't worry, I'm not here for any meeting, I'm here to do my job."

Chapa slapped Wormley on the back, damn near knocking him into his keyboard, and walked to his office with Sullivan following in his wake.

"You've been out of touch, and with that story today, well, there's been some concern."

"I can certainly understand that," Chapa said as he sat down and flipped his computer on. "The story is bogus, it's already been cleared up with the authorities, and I'm going to make sure the papers that ran with it end up eating some serious shit over this."

Sullivan raised his palms in a calming gesture as he sat down across the desk.

"Let's keep our heads, this is not personal."

"The hell it's not."

"The *Record* will, of course, support you, but I think we need to all have an open dialogue about this situation and the story you're working on."

Chapa rocked back in his brown leather chair which squeaked whenever he moved.

"I'll be glad to meet with you and Macklin, but first I have to finish what I'm working on. I have to see this Grubb story to the end."

Sullivan sat with his meaty arms folded, competing for space across his chest.

"A lot of people are worried about you, and what you're up to. That's all."

"Look, we've already had this conversation."

Chapa stood up and walked around to the other side of the desk, then sat on the edge.

"No one else is on this. I haven't sniffed any coverage from the other papers. Sure, they'll all be at the execution, but that's just the most basic part of it. This story is going to be huge, and I'm going to be the only one who gets it."

Sullivan pushed his chubby fingers around his eyes and rubbed hard. When he stopped, his face looked red and tired.

"Off the record, Alex, I would strongly recommend that you not set foot in this building again until you're ready to file the story."

Chapa understood.

"You missed Macklin by no more than fifteen minutes tonight, and Duane will make certain he knows you were here," Sullivan said, then stood up to leave. He was almost all the way out of the office when he leaned back in.

"Alex, he's going to fire you."

Chapa let those words sink in. This was no longer an editor talking to one of his writers. It was just one regular guy warning another, and Chapa appreciated that.

"I know, Sully. Thanks."

"Folks don't want their news this way anymore, doesn't matter how soft we go or what we try."

"I know. We're dinosaurs and the comet's bearing down on our little blue world."

"Do you have a clip file, a portfolio, or a résumé, something that's going to help you land on your feet?"

"No, I've got something better. My reputation for being one hell of a reporter."

Sullivan nodded and walked out.

CHAPTER 35

Chapa was wrestling with the reality that he would soon be unemployed, when things found a way to get worse. He received an email from Carla.

Alex,

Over time you have chosen to become a less and less significant part of Nicole's life, and that's fine.

My husband has agreed to adopt Nicole as his own, and I am grateful for that. If you care about your child's well-being you will see this is what's best. Our attorney is currently preparing the papers, but there's no reason for this to stir things up again between us, and the process should not be too difficult. Hopefully, for once, you will think of someone other than yourself.

In case that's not possible, let me add that after the adoption goes through you will no longer be responsible for paying child support.

Chapa printed the letter and tossed it into a file with all of the others. A major part of him wanted to pick up the phone and have it out with Carla. But he knew that wouldn't do anyone any good, especially Nikki.

They had been mismatched from the start, though Chapa had done what he could to bridge the gap between them. Should he have seen the potential for how it would all turn out back when they were dating? Was there something that he'd missed? A look, an inflection, anything that might've offered a glimpse. Chapa prided himself on his ability to read people—a vital trait for any reporter—but he'd been blind when it came to Carla.

It wasn't easy, but Chapa had admitted to himself some time ago that it was never all that good between him and Carla. It bothered him now that he carried some of that gun-shy fear into his relationship with Erin. It wasn't fair, and he knew it.

Chapa pulled up Carla's cell number on his computer, took the phone out of its cradle, and held it while he rocked back in his chair. He got the squeaks going in a syncopated rhythm with the sound of the ceiling fan, and thought about what to do next. After he finally put the phone down, Chapa turned back to his computer, and looked up the address for Prather's in Chicago.

CHAPTER 36

Finding an address for the club Munson had told him about was easy. Chapa then spent a few more hours researching the trailer, sensing that he'd missed something. He tracked a few threads that led nowhere, before finally discovering a series of sites dedicated to what was commonly referred to as the TKM, short for Traveling Killer Museum.

Numerous reports detailed what others had said about the trailer, while a few accounts purported to be firsthand. Only two seemed remotely credible. Still, Chapa was surprised and more than a little disturbed by how fascinated some folks were about an elusive mobile home that served as a shrine to the murderers of the innocent.

Just reading about it stirred up feelings from the night before that he was working hard to bury. He wondered if those memories would ever scab over, and eventually be replaced by scarred skin.

Wormley and Sullivan were gone by the time Chapa left the building. An hour later he was navigating through lazy traffic on the way to Chicago's far North Side. Prather's was somewhere between the lake and the expressway. There was no guarantee Annie would be working there at all, let alone tonight, but Chapa figured it was worth a shot.

He'd considered calling ahead and asking for her, or rather, for Angela. But anyone who was so determined to make herself difficult to find could get spooked by that sort of phone call. Better to take a chance and drop in.

A green neon sign probably dating back to the early 60's announced Prather's. From the outside, the jazz club looked like it could have been there for a generation or two. But it was not run down, something that the ten dollar valet parking made clear.

Chapa passed on the lot and took his chances with street parking around the corner on Sunnyside Avenue, just a couple of blocks north of Irving Park Road. From there it was a short walk past the nearly full lot that flanked the building, and another thirty feet to the front door.

He was greeted by a bouncer who was big enough to have smaller bouncers orbiting around him.

"Gimme six bucks."

He didn't make it clear whether that was the cover charge or if he was just collecting lunch money. From the looks of him, it was a safe bet the man needed a lot of lunch money. He wore a black T-shirt that might've been spray painted on. It was so tight that the large cursive P in the middle was stretched to the point of distortion. Chapa ignored the heavy temptation to crack wise and just gave him the cash.

Prather's looked like one of those places where you didn't let your guard down, but not for the same reasons some watering holes have a way of bringing one's survival instincts to the surface. While Night Owls had projected the threat of physical violence, Prather's suggested intrigue and the kind of private negotiations that could change lives, or destroy them.

There was money at Prather's. It walked around and had enough of a physical presence that at any moment it might pull up a chair and join you for a drink. Night Owls had waitresses, Prather's had servers who brought drinks with exotic names and foreign objects in them like plastic birds or umbrellas.

The room was bathed in subdued swipes of amber, green, and violet, and every color in between. Prather's served food, liquor, and jazz, though not in equal measure.

Round tables crowded in near the cramped stage, while curved and heavily padded booths ringed the perimeter. No stains on the walls or cracks in the upholstery. A long bar filled one end of the room, behind it a tall heap of muscle with rock star hair was serving drinks. Chapa was seated at a booth in a far corner that offered a decent view of the rest of the room. He was underdressed and out of place and he didn't much care. The discreet lighting was intended to hide a variety of sins.

"Are you waiting for someone?"

She was tall, thin, and very blond, all of which appeared to come naturally. Her neatly manicured nails curved around the edge of the tray she was holding.

"Aren't we all waiting for someone?" Chapa responded.

"So true."

He ordered rum on the rocks and asked what her name was. She told him it was "Denise" and slipped away into the discreet darkness. A four-piece band was cruising through a no-nonsense rendition of "Harlem Nocturne." While it served as background music for most of the booth dwellers, the folks sitting at the tables treated the performance as though it was religion.

Chapa watched a server cross the floor, navigating around the tables and chairs. She was medium height with a pleasant figure and dark hair. He stared at her, hoping she would turn his way.

"Would you like me to start a tab?" Denise said as she placed his drink on the table.

"Sure."

She seemed pleased with that answer, rewarding him with a smile, and letting her eyes get in on the action. The other server was gone from view by the time Denise left Chapa's table, and he began surveying the rest of the room. He counted a total of seven employees, including four servers, all of whom were women.

Chapa scanned the area from one side of the floor to the bar, then the other side, and the entryway. When he'd done this for several minutes and was satisfied that Annie Sykes was not out there, he decided to ask Denise about her.

Before Chapa could do that, he noticed a woman who had joined the tall brawny guy behind the bar. Her hair was neither black nor red, but something in between. It was the color of a rich merlot. When she turned, the light from above the bar slipped down to touch the woman's face. It was Annie.

He dropped a ten on the table, figuring that should cover his drink and the tip, then picked up his glass and headed for the bar, Denise caught his eye on the way and he shrugged and mouthed, "Sorry."

Chapa sat near the end of the bar, a few stools away from where the woman stood by the register. She was counting money and writing figures down on a sheet of paper. Any kind of work at this place was a major improvement over whatever she'd been doing at Night Owls, Chapa figured.

But the more he saw of her, mostly profile, the less certain Chapa was that he had found Annie/Angela Sykes. He tried not to stare or be too obvious. Chapa had been in enough saloons of various stripes to understand that you never know who's watching you. A quiet stranger paying too much attention to one of the servers can be suspicious. That same stranger staring at a woman handling money can eliminate all doubt.

She finished whatever accounting she'd been doing and turned in Chapa's direction. He raised his head and smiled as she passed, hoping to get her attention, wanting to get a better look at her face. Her eyes were fixed straight ahead, as though the rest of the room wasn't there, as she walked toward the end of the bar.

She was almost to the service doors when Chapa said, "Annie."

He said the name just loud enough for her to hear it above the music and chatter. She stopped. Chapa slid off his stool and walked over closer to her, expecting the woman to turn around. But she stood motionless, her back turned to him.

She stayed there for a few seconds, anchored in place, and didn't respond in any way. Then she disappeared through a set of black swinging doors.

CHAPTER 37

Chapa sensed that no one else at the bar had heard him when he called out to Annie Sykes, or at least the four other drinkers had chosen ignore it. He eased back onto the stool and motioned for the bartender to come over.

"That server, will she be coming back?"

The bartender's features had been chiseled by an uncertain hand, giving him something of a 40's tough guy look beneath his shoulder-length hair. He shook his head without making eye contact and continued wiping the bar.

"Nope. She just closed her money out," he said in a barrel-deep voice.

"Let me pay for my drink."

The guy looked up from what he was doing. He probably knew Chapa had already paid, but said nothing about that when a twenty dollar bill appeared on the counter.

"Could you ask her to come back out for a minute."

He studied Chapa for a moment.

"Sure, unless you're her father, or a cop, or something."

"No, I just know her from way back."

The twenty disappeared from the top of the bar, then the guy vanished through the same doors that had swallowed up the woman a couple of minutes earlier. Chapa could hear voices coming from the other side, not yelling, but loud enough to suggest an intense discussion.

When the bartender returned he had a much less accommodating expression on his face.

"She's left already."

Chapa looked over at the doors and wondered if Annie was standing on the other side, listening.

"Will she be working tomorrow?"

"No idea, sport, why don't you stop by and find out."

Chapa thought about asking for his twenty back, but knew there was no point in it.

"Can you tell me her first name?"

The bartender looked around like he was worried someone was watching him.

"C'mon buddy, it wasn't that great of a drink," Chapa said.

The guy checked out his immediate area a few more times then leaned across the counter and wiped its front edge.

"Angie."

Chapa finished his drink in one quick tilt, thanked the bartender with a silent nod, and made for the door. He noticed how the bouncer's gaze followed him. When Chapa stepped outside, the thick steroids case in the undersized black muscle-T was just a few casual but calculated steps behind.

The sun had ducked beneath the buildings, and dusk would soon give way to night. Chapa walked around the side of the building in the general direction of his car, but also toward a door he had seen on his way in that was labeled SERVICE ENTRY. As Chapa casually glanced back to check if the bouncer was still hanging around, he heard the door squeal open.

By the time he saw her, the woman was already headed in the opposite direction at a steady clip. She was wearing the same navy blue outfit that all the female servers had on. A large purse dangled from one shoulder. Though she walked like there was somewhere she needed to be, Chapa sensed that the woman hadn't seen him standing there.

"Angela."

The woman paused without turning, just as she had back inside. Chapa watched as she slipped her hand inside the baggy denim purse. Then she turned, but continued digging around in the bag.

"What do you want?"

Chapa assumed that she was trying to get her hand on some mace or pepper spray. He kept his distance.

"I'm Alex Chapa, I did a story about you a long time ago, back when you went by the name Annie."

She had stopped searching, but her hand was still inside the purse.

"That's ancient history. Why are you here now, and how did you find me?"

Her makeup brought out the most dramatic aspects of her face. Though only in her midtwenties, Annie's eyes, green and framed by full lashes, were those of a person who knew more than most.

"I need to talk to you." Chapa didn't have to turn around to know the bouncer was moving in their direction. "One of your friends, Langdon, helped me find you."

"You need any help, Angie?" Now that he had expanded his vocabulary, the bouncer spoke with a Caribbean accent that did not fit his light features.

"Not yet," she answered without taking her eyes off Chapa.

"I'll stick around just in case you change your mind." The glow from a nearby lamppost was reflecting on the guy's shaved head, giving him the appearance of a bloated flashlight.

"Look, Angela, or Annie, what would you like me to call you?"

She didn't respond.

"Have you noticed anyone hanging around, here, or near where you live, anyone?"

"You mean, besides you?" She smiled a little which took several difficult years off her face. "Not that I've noticed. Why?"

This was not going as Chapa had imagined it would. He handed her his card, and was pleased when she took it and slipped it into a front pants pocket, even though she hadn't bothered to look at it.

"I have a very good reason to believe that with Grubb's execution—"

"Oh no, this is about some story you're doing."

"No, that's not it."

"You've come a long way for a whole lot of nothing."

Chapa again tried to explain himself, but she had checked out on him.

"Hey Chico," she said, raising her voice, the bouncer already on the move. "This gentleman might need some help finding his car."

With that, she withdrew an empty hand from her purse, turned and walked off into the rest of the city.

CHAPTER 38

On his way out of town Chapa replayed his en-
counter with Annie Sykes. He couldn't believe how
poorly it had gone down. What had he expected? The
woman had survived the kind of experience that keeps
parents awake deep into the night, and makes thera-
pists wealthy.

The first time Chapa had seen her was the night of
Grubb's capture when he managed three vital minutes
with Annie and her parents. A few days later, he
stopped by the family's house to interview the parents
for a follow-up story. Chapa had not spoken to her
then, he did not want to. Though he had not quoted
her directly in his original story, or at any other time,
his brief conversation with Annie had blown his comfort zone of detachment.

He remembered everything about that visit to the
Sykes. Annie stood in the doorway of the kitchen as
Chapa interviewed her parents. She never spoke a
word, never appeared tempted to join in the conversation. But Annie didn't look away, either. She stared at
him in a way that was intense, but gentle somehow, without a hint of anger, hostility, or fear.

There was something different about Annie Sykes,

even then. She seemed stronger than most. Not just tougher and more resilient than any other child Chapa had ever met, but emotionally stronger than most adults as well. But now that strength and the independence it produced might get her killed. Chapa was not about to let this go. He would approach her again, but next time he'd have to be much better prepared.

He gave himself twenty-four hours to get Annie's confidence and figure out what sort of trouble she was in. After that, he'd make a phone call to Andrews and let the feds take it from there.

Chapa lowered his window and let in a slap of crisp autumn wind. Old brick buildings and city traffic had started giving way to strip malls and the open road when Chapa's cell phone started serenading him. He picked it up out of the cup holder he'd dropped it in and checked to see who was calling.

Unknown

He closed his window and flipped the phone open.

"This is Chapa."

"Mr. Chapa?"

The voice was small but steady.

"This is Angela, you know, Annie Sykes. I expected to get an answering machine."

Chapa took the next exit, wanting to give himself the opportunity to pull over quickly if he needed to write something down.

"I'm never home, and my cell is always with me even when I'm at the office, so it's the number I had put on my card."

"I need to apologize to you, I'm not usually like that, but you caught me off guard."

"You don't need to apologize," he said, pulling into the parking lot of an old movie theater that had closed down a few years earlier. "But you need to listen to me, there could be some trouble for you."

She sighed, like it was all old news.

"I know there are a lot of creeps out there, Mr. Chapa, but I live a very private life."

"I found you."

Silence.

"Maybe we shouldn't be having this conversation on cell phones," she said, and Chapa sensed he'd gotten through to her. "Do you have time tomorrow to have lunch with me here in Chicago?"

They agreed to meet at a restaurant on Clark, around 12:30. That would still give Chapa time to sit down with Andrews in the morning.

"Miss Sykes, I need you to understand that you must take some precautions. I will explain more of it to you tomorrow, but please believe me, my concerns are well founded. Don't hesitate to call the police if you see anything or anyone unusual."

"I live in Chicago, sometimes it's not easy to figure out what *unusual* means," she said. "I understand, but I ask that you let me be the one who makes that decision for myself."

"Okay, Miss Sykes, tomorrow then."

"Call me Angela."

He signed off, then spent the rest of the drive home trying to determine how much information to hold back from the feds.

CHAPTER 39

Chapa's house was as dark and still as the rest of the neighborhood. He turned off the car radio in the middle of Billy Joel's claim that only the good die young, and tried to recall whether he'd left any lights on. It had been such a long day that he could not remember either way.

He made a habit of leaving a lamp lit in the living room, and sometimes wouldn't bother to turn off the kitchen light for several days. Chapa didn't like walking into dark empty houses. They always felt lifeless and cold.

The newspaper was resting in the middle of the yard. He picked it up, knowing that he should have done so earlier in the day, then retrieved a handful of letters from the mailbox. Usually when he got home, Jimmy would greet him with a song, but with the house being dark the parakeet had probably fallen asleep.

Chapa flipped the three switches that were by the door, and light filled the living room, entryway, as well as the landing at the top of the stairs. He dropped his keys on a small table by the door and flipped through the letters, stopping when he got to an envelope with a

Boston postmark. It had been addressed by a very young hand.

He tossed the rest of the mail on the table, and carefully opened the letter from Nikki. The lined pink paper had been folded, not too carefully, into thirds. As Chapa opened the letter, a small photo slipped out. It was a school picture that he had not seen before. It had been cut in such a way that he knew his daughter had been the one holding the scissors.

She was smiling, which always brought her cheeks out. But the child's eyes told him something else, and at that moment Chapa missed Nikki so badly that he had to lean against the front door to keep from crumbling to the floor.

He opened the letter and immediately recognized Nikki's handwriting from the all too few other times he had seen it.

> *Daddy,*
> *Why won't you ever come to see me?*
> *I miss you sometimes.*
> *Love Nikki*

Only fifteen words in length, Chapa had the letter memorized after he'd read it a second time through. But he read it again anyhow. Part of him wanted to respond, *Ask your mother*, but he knew he too had failed Nikki, and he saw no point in passing off his share of the blame.

He decided right then that getting so caught up in Annie Sykes' problems had been a mistake, considering how many of his own issues remained unresolved. The best solution at this point was to turn everything over to Andrews and let the feds do their work. Maybe he could still salvage his job. Chapa had a feeling that Macklin was the sort of guy who would get a kick out of seeing one of his highest paid writers begging on bended knee.

Chapa was creating a mental to-do list as he walked toward the kitchen. Jimmy didn't like dark rooms any more than he did, and the poor parakeet had been alone in that kitchen for much of the past three days. As he approached the door, Chapa heard a rustling sound. Jimmy was awake. But when he turned on the lights Chapa noticed that the curtains from a large window against the back wall were flapping in the wind. The countertop below it was littered with broken glass. When he shut the window Chapa saw that someone had broken the glass above it so they could flip the lock open.

His senses on overdrive, Chapa knew this wasn't a random break-in. He needed to call Andrews first, then maybe the local police, though he feared they might bring him in for questioning. The phone was on the wall near Jimmy's cage, but Chapa never reached it.

At first he thought the bird had gotten himself tangled up in the string from a toy, but that was not the case. Jimmy was hanging in the middle of the cage, strands of bright red hair had been twisted together and tied around his neck like a noose.

His feathers were badly tangled, as though the bird had been abused before it was killed. Maybe Jimmy had fought back, that's what Chapa hoped. A small spot of something on Jimmy's beak might have been dried blood, and Chapa imagined the parakeet taking a piece out of the bastard's hand.

The cage door was open, and as Chapa reached in and cupped his hand around Jimmy he could see that the hairs had been tied so tightly they had cut into the bird below the feathers. Whoever had done this probably tied the hairs around Jimmy's neck, then watched as the bird strangled itself trying to get free.

The parakeet felt rigid and cool, his feathers stiff and brittle. Chapa realized he'd have to cut him down, there was no way to untie the knot. He was fighting to not think too much about that, when he heard what sounded like someone walking around upstairs.

Chapa was not alone in the house.

He hesitated for a moment, and listened. But the noise was gone. How many sets of footsteps had he heard? Chapa tuned out the ambient sounds of a typical house, and waited.

Nothing.

As he took a cautious step out of the kitchen he heard another sound, then several more. He concluded there were probably two or more people moving around upstairs, or a single large one. A showdown had some appeal for Chapa. He was in the mood to kick the shit out of someone, and whoever had broken into his home and killed his pet seemed like a perfect candidate.

But Chapa remembered the heavy hand pressing against his neck. The terrible feeling of helplessness. After his confrontation with Grubb earlier that day, it was a safe bet that whoever was up there didn't stop by to negotiate. They were here to inflict some pain.

His house was starting to feel like a trap. They had heard him come in, and seen the landing lights turn on, but did not rush downstairs because Chapa was exactly where they wanted him. He didn't own a gun, and there were too many ways to trump a kitchen knife—the best weapon available at the moment. As hard as it was for him to accept, Chapa understood that his house offered him no tactical advantage.

He heard the footsteps moving across his bedroom and into the hall. They were heading for the stairway.

Chapa raced through the dining room and into the foyer, then heard another noise from above, this one much closer to the stairs. He grabbed his keys off the table, spilling the bills and junk mail on the floor. Still clutching the letter from Nikki, he opened the front door as a shadow appeared in the landing at the top of the stairs.

CHAPTER 40

The three-mile drive to Erin's house took much longer than usual. Chapa avoided a direct route in favor of the side streets and wide open avenues that offered a long look in the rearview mirror.

A couple of times along the way, a set of headlights a few blocks back seemed to mimic his turns. But they eventually went their own way, and Chapa would then continue to narrow the distance to his destination. Chapa had a feeling the person in his house was probably the same one who left the note on Erin's door. In which case, all of his deceptive moves would only serve to give them an advantage if they got there first.

When he was certain no one was following him, at least as certain as he could be, Chapa slowed down to just a mile or two above the limit and headed toward Erin's. Her house was dark, and there were a couple of newspapers resting near the front steps. It almost seemed like a repeat of Chapa's arrival at his own house. He hoped the similarities ended there.

Erin's house had a simple but effective alarm system she'd had installed a few years earlier after her ex capped a night of drinking by showing up at her door. Chapa figured that the broken window in his kitchen

meant that whoever was doing this had not made copies
of his keys or hers during the hours he had been unconscious.

He would know for sure soon enough.

The simple ranch had very little landscaping, for
which Chapa was grateful at that moment. He kept his
distance from the house as he walked across the front
yard, trying to get a look behind the smattering of
shrubs that decorated the left corner. The streetlight directly across from Erin's house projected his elongated
shadow against the beige aluminum siding.

A car was parked on the street three houses down,
but Chapa hadn't seen anyone inside when he had
driven past the vehicle. Otherwise, the neighborhood
looked deserted. When he was satisfied that no one was
hiding anywhere near the front door, Chapa picked up
the newspapers and quickly slipped the key in the lock,
then stepped inside without looking back. He locked
the door behind him and reset the alarm.

Another dark house. He took stock of his surroundings, even though he'd been there many times, then
turned on the lights. Mikey's green aluminum Little
League baseball bat was sitting in an umbrella rack by
the door. Chapa pulled it out and started searching
each room and closet in the house.

Erin's tastes were simple, but not crass. With the exception of Mikey's room, the place had a definite feminine feel to it. She kept it cleaner than most stay-at-
home moms could ever dream of, and there wasn't
much clutter. That would make Chapa's task easier.

After checking the back door and searching each
room, Chapa decided he was alone. He made sure that
no windows were broken, and that the house was secure, then returned the bat to where he'd found it.

Chapa took off his coat and pulled his cell phone out
so he could call Erin. But first he had to lock his car

door, something he'd intentionally avoided doing when he got there just in case a quick getaway was needed. He searched his coat for the keys, then looked on the living room coffee table and various places in the dining room, but came up empty.

Now Chapa realized that in his haste to get inside he could've left his keys in the lock. He gave the door a nudge with his shoulder, which brought a jolt of pain to the back of his neck, but it also told him what he wanted to know when he heard the jingle on the other side.

He turned off the alarm, unlocked the door, and opened it. Retrieving his keys, Chapa opened the screen door and took two steps in the direction of his car before he saw the man standing in the yard.

Chapa froze, then asked, "Can I help you?"

No answer.

"Who the hell are you?"

Chapa waited for a response, but none came. The guy was tall with wide shoulders framing an imposing torso that rested on thick legs, neither of which was moving.

This was not a friendly neighbor coming over to make sure everything was okay. Maybe he was a distraction, there to give someone else the opportunity to creep up along the side of the house, or break in around the rear.

A chill moved in on Chapa and vise-clamped on the muscles in his back. He ducked inside, closed the door behind him and locked it before turning the alarm on. If Chapa's heart had been equipped with teeth it would have chewed its way out of his chest. He was so tense his ribs ached, and the back of his neck felt as though someone had lit a series of small fires just below the skin.

If another door was open or a window had been broken the alarm would have been screaming right then, but it wasn't. He thought about turning the lights off, figuring that he knew the house well enough to navigate it in the dark, and that could give him an advantage over someone who'd never been there. But Chapa was starting to sense that whoever was outside was acting alone. Maybe it had been just one creep all along.

Coaxing a front curtain open just enough, he got a look at the area where the figure had been standing. No one there. Chapa moved to the other side of the window and scoped the rest of the yard. It was empty.

From that vantage point Chapa's visibility was limited and he could not see the corners of the house. He moved into the dining room and looked out through a side window. Except for his car, the driveway was empty and quiet. What the hell?

Chapa wasn't going to just let this ride, he wasn't the sort to cower behind locked doors and windows. He remembered Mikey's bat. It was small, just a little more than a couple of feet in length, and Chapa would have gladly traded it in for a full-size Aramis Ramirez model, but it would have to do. The other guy had a size advantage, but Chapa knew that would change if he could connect just once.

Up until now, guns had not been part of the equation, and Chapa believed there was a reason for that. Like Grubb, his followers preferred the intimacy that more up close and personal forms of violence offered. He was counting on that particularly twisted preference when he bolted through the front door and raced for the middle of the yard, the bat cocked and ready for a swing.

He appeared to be alone. Still, Chapa kept looking back toward the front door in case someone emerged from the shadows and made a dash for it. He moved slowly from side to side, as he had done when he first got there, but saw no movement that wasn't caused by the wind.

The street remained quiet, apparently none of the neighbors had noticed the strange goings on in Erin's front yard. One thing was different. The car that had been parked a few houses away was gone.

CHAPTER 41

Chapa had not told Erin about the night before, or this night, or what someone had done to Jimmy. Even without that information, it was a struggle to convince Erin that it was best for her and Mikey to stay away for just a few more days.

"I feel like I belong next to you during all of this."

Those words lingered long after the conversation had ended. Chapa felt guilty that he had not told her the truth about everything. Not only was he deceiving her, but he also felt a need to share it with her, the way partners are supposed to do. But more than anything, Chapa knew his life and the sort of people who populated the professional end of it, had now invaded hers. He had to find a way to keep that from ever happening again. Chapa already knew how to best deal with the problem, but he didn't like the solution.

She had offered to take Mikey to her mother's house in Rockford, then drive back to be with him. Chapa knew if he told Erin much more about what was happening there would be no stopping her.

As they said their goodbyes he surprised himself by adding, "I miss you." Then he realized the connection was gone. Had she heard it? When she did not call back he assumed she hadn't.

Two more unread copies of the *Chicago Record* had been discarded near the umbrella rack by the door. Chapa added those to the ones from outside. Erin had confessed that she was never into newspapers before they met. She now subscribed to the *Record* because she liked reading his column and seeing his picture above it.

Chapa took a four-day-old newspaper off the small stack. He opened to page two of the first section, where his column had been located for the past seven years. After all that had gone down he could barely remember the story about a local landmark that was scheduled to be bulldozed in the name of progress, even though it had only been a week since he'd written it.

The next day's paper carried a reprinted story he had written several months earlier, preceded by: *While Alex Chapa is on assignment, we invite you to enjoy this story he wrote earlier in the year.* This was standard procedure when a columnist was working on a longer piece, or off on vacation. Chapa wasn't sure why they picked this particular column over others, and wished someone had asked for his input.

He opened a two-day-old paper. No column this time, just his standard photo above the words: *Alex Chapa is on assignment.* They must have sold more ad space than usual and did not need to use one of his columns. But when Chapa flipped to his usual page in yesterday's edition he did not see his name or photo. He rifled through the rest of the paper. Nothing. For the first time since he started working there, more than a decade ago, Alex Chapa's name did not appear anywhere in a weekday edition of the *Chicago Record*.

The same was true for that day's paper, and Chapa knew then that it was over. He was like a stiff no one had yet bothered to bury. He wondered how Erin would react once his firing became official, then felt like a heel for thinking it might make a difference in the way she felt about him.

Rather than wasting any time worrying about whether anyone would ever run the story he was working on now, Chapa's thoughts returned to his to-do list for the meeting with Andrews. But instead of accumulating information to pass on to the feds, Chapa was editing, trying to determine what he would and would not tell Andrews.

The process had the same effect on him that counting sheep has on others. It wasn't long before Chapa was asleep in his dress clothes, with all of the lights on, and Nikki's letter pressed against his chest.

Two Days Before the Execution

CHAPTER 42

Chapa's underwear had wedged itself into places where it didn't belong. It took him a few partially conscious minutes to remember where he was. Erin's house, hopefully alone. He looked at the clock on the mantle, it read 6:55. Chapa was fairly certain it was A.M.

When he sat up, the muscles in his lower back let him know he was past the age where crashing anywhere other than a bed would be easily forgiven. Chapa showered, though not as quickly as he knew he should, and that meant he would be fighting traffic all the way into the city.

At that moment, he didn't care. As his thoughts drifted away from the events of the past several days, Chapa remembered the note from Nikki, and that spurred him into moving on to the rest of his day.

A couple of Chapa's shirts were hanging in a hall closet, right next to a pair of pants. They had been there since August, when the three of them had gone camping. Leaving extra clothes at her house had been Erin's suggestion.

"You never know what can happen."

She had no idea.

He passed on a Big Dog T-shirt, and settled for a simple dark gray polo. Chapa wasn't quite dressed for success, but good enough, he figured. After he'd read Nikki's letter again, Chapa folded the note and tucked it into his wallet. Then he flipped past his credit cards and press credentials to where he kept her photos so he could add the one Nikki had cut out for him.

It had been more than a year since he'd received a new photo, and in that time he had memorized everything about the last one. The sweater Nikki was wearing—purple with small red apples—and that tiny little gap between her two front teeth, as well as the way her long hair was down, covering one shoulder but not the other.

That photo had become extremely important to him, a direct link to his daughter. He flipped past the cards and credentials a second time. The photo was gone.

Fist clenched, Chapa fought to harness his anger, sensing that if he lost control, it could be a while before he got it back. They must have taken it while he was unconscious. Chapa could only imagine why, and knew it was best not to.

It was one of those October days that remind Illinoisans of why they love living in the Midwest. Dead leaves crunched under Chapa's feet as he walked to his car. The neighborhood was quiet except for a couple of people at either end of the street who were getting in their cars.

Chapa checked to make sure the Corolla was still locked, then used the automatic key. He was about to turn the ignition when he noticed something taped to the middle of the steering wheel. It was the old photo of Nikki.

He quickly stepped out of the car and surveyed the

area for anything out of the ordinary. Chapa was getting better at this than he ever wanted to be.

Even standing outside, in the brightest of autumn mornings and just a few dozen yards from the kind of neighbors who would respond to a call for help, Chapa felt no sense of comfort or safety.

CHAPTER 43

"It's too bad about your bird, Al."

Andrews was wearing the standard navy blue suit and red tie outfit, though in what Chapa assumed was a moment of unbridled wackiness, the agent had gone with a tan shirt instead of the usual white.

"I know how we can all get attached to our pets, no matter how small."

"It was an act of pure cruelty, Joe. We're not talking about someone killing a guard dog."

"It wasn't just cruel," Andrews was shaking his head. "I know it seems that way, but they were trying to let you know they will hurt those you care about. They can't get to Erin or Mikey or Nikki right now, so—"

A much younger agent handed Chapa a cup of coffee, then started walking back to his desk.

"Hey, Brandon," Andrews said, "Is that the good stuff?"

The young agent shook his head. His brown hair cropped close, Brandon reminded Chapa of a GI Joe action figure.

"What are you thinking, kid?" Andrews took the cup out of Chapa's hand and gave it back to Brandon who at that moment looked like a scolded puppy.

"Just like a rookie to give you perp coffee."

Chapa had recounted in detail what happened at the trailer, as well as his visitor the following morning. He left nothing out about those experiences, and made Andrews' day when he played the recording for him.

"Our lab will pick this thing apart."

"Is there any way you can make a copy of the recording and give me back my recorder?"

"That will take a few days."

Under normal circumstances, Chapa would have anticipated this, but nothing about the past week had been normal.

"Then you need to let me transcribe my notes first," Chapa said and put his hand on top of the recorder, but waited for Andrews to respond before removing the device from the meticulously organized desk.

Andrews thought for a moment, then agreed.

"I'll do that today and then your guys can have at it," Chapa said as Andrews sifted through a small pile of files before sliding one out.

"We found the field where the trailer had been, but all that was still there were several sets of tire marks, and the indentations from where the trailer sat."

The agent turned the file so Chapa could see it, and flipped to a photo of the empty field.

"Was this the place?"

There weren't many landmarks for Chapa to identify, but he recognized the white post with the address painted on it. He also remembered the farmhouse in the distance.

"Did you find out who lives here?" Chapa asked, pointing to the two-story structure fading into the background.

"A retired farming couple who fly off to their winter home in Phoenix each year right after Labor Day."

"So whoever parked the trailer there had to know

that. They must've been familiar with the area," Chapa said as Brandon handed him a fresh cup of the good coffee.

"If the newspaper thing does go belly up, you might have a career in law enforcement."

Chapa passed on the opportunity to share his work troubles with his friend. This was not the time or place.

"We still haven't had any luck tracking down Annie Sykes, or Angela, or whatever the heck she wants to call herself these days. How about you?"

"A couple of leads here and there, but I'm still waiting for it all to come together."

Chapa knew that down the line he would have to deal with the way he'd held back information, and Andrews would not be happy with him. But he was concerned that Annie might go even deeper into hiding if the feds started hanging around. Then she'd be beyond anyone's protection. He had to gather some more details first, and figured that would happen in the next few hours.

Andrews was staring at him, waiting for more. When none came he said, "You do realize that you're in over your head?"

"Maybe."

"Al, you were drugged, and they could have killed you. They killed your pet, and threatened your girlfriend right out of town. This is not all in a week's work for any journalist."

The constant shifting of papers, murmur of conversation, and clacking of keyboards quieted for a moment.

"I expect to know more after today."

"Why? What's today?"

"You've got to trust me here, Joe. I will check in with you as soon as I know anything. Hell, I'll call you tomorrow either way."

"In the morning."

"Yes, first thing." The coffee burned a little on the way down, but that pain offset all the other ones Chapa was dealing with. "I'm just trying to get this one thing right, Joe."

Andrews put the files back together in a perfectly rectangular pile. Then opened a drawer and carefully slid them inside.

"That is the quietest file cabinet drawer in history," Chapa said, then reached over and opened and closed it several times. Not a sound. "Remarkable."

"You have to grease the hardware in your drawers from time to time if you want it to work right," Andrews said with his usual lack of irony or humor.

"Isn't that sort of thing illegal in a couple of southern states?"

Andrews ignored that crack, as he had ignored thousands of others through the years.

"How long are Erin and her son going to stay away?"

"Until this is over. They're having a blast."

Andrews nodded his approval, then produced a small photo and slid it toward Chapa.

"Here's something that will make you feel better. We picked him up early this morning."

It had been a while since Chapa had seen Lance Grubb. He remembered him from the trial. The killer's brother was there every day, but never reacted to the testimony or spoke with the media.

Chapa stared at the new photo, looking for something, anything in the man's eyes that might give him a sense of the person. He failed, just as he had years earlier. The man's artificially dark hairline had receded, exposing parallel rows of deep grooves in his forehead. His eyes were heavy, as though they had to be hand-cranked into place every morning.

"What did you get him for?"

"We've started with questioning. He hasn't lawyered up yet, so that will continue for a while. We're also looking into his movements over the past few days."

"How long can you hold him?"

"We can find all sorts of reasons to hang on to him until after his brother is executed. Let's just say that the rules have been softened since 9-11."

Chapa tried to remember back to the trailer, his bedroom, and Erin's front yard just the night before. But he had never managed to see a face.

"He's not going to miss work. The guy lives off some bullshit disability for psychological problems," Andrews said. "No job, no family. Sounds like the sort of person who might end up doing some very bad things."

Another victim of Kenny Lee Grubb's crimes, Chapa thought.

"We have him in an interrogation room," Andrews said as he stood. "Let's go find out if he looks familiar."

CHAPTER 44

The man on the other side of the one-way glass was sitting with his hands clasped together on the long table in front of him. Lance Grubb wore workman's clothing, a blue denim shirt and dark baggy pants. Surrounded by concrete walls, he looked straight ahead, focused on something only he could see.

"Have you seen him lately?" Andrews asked.

Though Chapa felt much better knowing that this man was in custody, he could not make the connection. He looked at Andrews and shook his head.

"I can't say."

"Try again, Al. We're going to keep him here anyway, but you could give us a stone cold reason to."

Chapa wondered what could be going through Lance Grubb's mind as he just sat there, doing nothing but staring off into nowhere.

"Any idea how his brother managed to shoot a video while inside a maximum security prison, then somehow get it out to one of his followers?"

"Not yet, but officials at Pennington are carrying out a discreet internal investigation. A couple of my guys stopped in to talk to Grubb. They were there for a couple of hours, but got nothing useful out of him."

"This guy acts like a drone, just waiting to be told what to do," Chapa said, pointing to the glass.

But before Andrews could respond, Lance stood up, as if on cue, and walked to a far corner of the cramped room. He was much more solid, not as wiry as his brother. His upper body tilted forward just a bit as though the bulk of his shoulders was losing the battle against gravity.

"Hey Sandro," Andrews barked at one of the two agents who were standing a few yards down the hall.

Sandro's dark gray tailored suit may have been the most expensive piece of equipment in the building. His shoes, which no doubt had come individually protected in velvet bags, had been polished to a black chrome finish. He reminded Chapa of a younger, Mediterranean version of Andrews. The agent walked over without hesitation, but sauntered a bit, as though someone was judging his level of cool.

"I want you to go over by the door to the room, something might be happening and I need you to be ready if we have to make a move."

Sandro took a position, and waited for a signal. Lance Grubb was facing the corner, his back turned to the window.

"What the hell is he doing?" Chapa asked.

Andrews just shook his head.

"Some guys take a few minutes to crack, some take hours, some never do. When the moment comes, it's rarely the same for any two people."

Andrews was about to continue his discourse on criminal behavior when Lance suddenly turned and faced the mirror. He looked right at it, and Chapa sensed the man could see through it.

"Get ready, Sandro."

The agent nodded in response. But the subject of all this attention did not charge the window or snap in any way. Instead he just stood in that spot, unnaturally still. And something about that was clawing its way inside of Chapa.

"It's him." Chapa spoke abruptly, before he realized that he was going to say something. "He's the man I saw last night."

CHAPTER 45

"How did you find me?" she demanded, even before the waitress had come around to get their drink orders.

Annie Sykes was wearing a loose-fitting, sky blue hoodie and had just enough makeup on to suggest that she cared about her appearance. It was a far cry from the night before, and made-up in this way she looked much younger. Chapa had no trouble seeing the small child he had met years before.

"Your friend Langdon."

"Donnie? Yeah, I think you told me that last night. But I haven't seen him in months."

"Well, not him, exactly. He sent me to Night Owls, and from there I was able to get to Prather's."

She was nodding, and seemed a bit more at ease now knowing which tracks she had not yet covered. The waitress was wearing a name tag shaped like a human skull, in keeping with the name of the restaurant.

"Welcome to Boneheads, you two out for lunch today?"

Her name was Alesia, and Chapa judged she was trying to gauge whether this was a father-daughter situation or maybe something a bit more interesting, as she set glasses of water in front of them. Boneheads was one of those family-oriented theme restaurants where all of the employees are forced to sing some sort of annoyingly upbeat song at the slightest hint of a birthday.

"So I understand you were led down to Night Owls by a boyfriend?"

"Cody? Wow, *down* is right. I wasn't there for long before I ditched him and got out."

As they placed their orders, Chapa could see that Annie was processing something.

"But how did you find Donnie Langdon?"

Chapa took a long sip of water before answering.

"I interviewed Louise Jones about the visions, or whatever they're called, that she had around the time of your kidnapping. She told me you two were friends."

Annie was smiling.

"Louise is a sweetheart. I remembered my parents telling me about her. I looked her up a few years back and we've been friends ever since. Haven't talked to Louise in a while, either. I'll have to give her a call."

Chapa held off on telling her the rest about Louise.

"You said I might be in danger?"

"I'm afraid that's true. Have there been any changes in your life? Has anything out of the ordinary happened in the past few days or even weeks?"

She thought for a moment.

"My life is a bit unusual, but pretty consistent. I live simply and quietly. How about you?"

"What about me?"

"What in your life brought you to this point?"

Chapa wasn't used to being the subject of discussion, and his instincts were telling him to keep the conversation on Annie.

"It's been a strange week for me. I've spent time with a wide variety of people, but that's the job."

Their drinks arrived.

"Do you have any children?"

The question came out of nowhere, but out of habit Chapa reached for his wallet anyhow. Flipping to his most recent photo of Nikki, the one he'd just gotten in her letter, he handed Annie the wallet.

"Cute girl."

She studied the picture like a student prepping for a test. Something about the way she stared at it made Chapa a little uncomfortable. Maybe she was trying to get a better fix on him.

"How's your brother doing?"

"Tyler is a bit of a wandering soul. I think he's a craftsman of some sort or a handyman, something that doesn't pay too well. He tracked me down a couple of months ago to ask me for money, and then he took off. That's just Tyler, he comes and goes."

She finally gave Chapa back his wallet.

"Has anyone unfamiliar come around lately?"

"No, no, no," she said wagging an index finger back and forth, which she then tilted forward and pointed at him. "What sort of *variety* of people have you spoken to? Louise, Donnie, and who else?"

"I've spoken with Grubb twice in the past week. He's told me some things that make me think you might be in trouble."

She looked out the window, and he followed her gaze. Clark Avenue was filled with lunchtime drivers fighting to get back to work.

"He's insane," Annie said.

"And extremely dangerous."

Alesia returned with their food, setting a sandwich down in front of Annie that was big enough to feed half the people in the crowded restaurant. Chapa wondered how often Annie ordered off a menu without worrying about the cost.

"Have you talked to the cops about what Grubb told you?"

"Not yet, they would probably tell me to quit listening to an insane man on death row."

Chapa saw no need to tell her about Andrews, and he didn't want to get into the other reason he couldn't go to the local police.

"My job is to observe, record, analyze, and report. I make a point of keeping a safe distance between myself and the subject of the story I'm working on. That approach has served me well over the years."

"Like the defense mechanism a psychiatrist uses to keep from going nuts."

"In a way, yes. But over time it's become somewhat of a burden for me. With this story, I've had to get my hands dirty and then some."

"What happened, did you and Grubb go at it?"

"Just about."

Chapa could sense that possibility intrigued her, and he followed up with an edited account of what had transpired at the prison.

"I've got flesh and blood in the game this time, Annie. So do you."

She had already finished half of her sandwich and Chapa was just getting started with his.

"Why did you go into hiding?"

Annie responded as though she had been expecting that question.

"At first, it wasn't a conscious decision. I knew there were people I should be afraid of. Your story all those years ago made me something of an underground cult figure."

Her attention returned to the window, but Chapa knew she was looking far beyond the street outside.

"First, I changed my name and that felt good. I read how the members of some Native American tribes adopt new names for each stage of their lives, and that made sense to me. So I buried Annie Sykes."

Chapa wondered if the unfortunate choice of words had been intentional.

"I moved around a lot over the course of two or three years and just stopped forwarding my mail. An old boyfriend left his cell phone behind, so I use it as my own and pay the bill every month."

None of this explained why she cut her family off. It was a subject Chapa wanted to get into, but wasn't sure how to do it.

"I spend a lot of time online. I'm an illustrator, and I sell my art that way."

"Did you ever hear from Jack Whitlock, that father of one of Grubb's other victims, again?"

"You don't have to remind me, I remember him." She sipped the last of her water, then crunched down on a piece of ice. "I thought I saw him once near my high school, but it probably wasn't him. He was just another person in pain."

Chapa was committing as much of this conversation to memory as he could in case he decided to use any of it in a story. He knew Annie would not agree to be recorded.

"So you talked to Grubb, Louise, and Donnie."

"And Munson at Night Owls."

Annie laughed. "That guy."

"Also Dominic Delacruz, the convenience store owner."

"I remember him. He was a nice man."

That meant that she must still remember a great deal of what happened the night she escaped.

"Anyone else?"

Chapa had a good idea of what she was hunting for. He took a bite of his Reuben, trying his best to not make it look like a stall.

"I spoke with your mother."

Her demeanor underwent a sudden change, and the

person who had wanted nothing to do with Chapa was back.

"Why did you do that?"

Alesia returned. She started to say something upbeat about their dessert options, but read the mood at the table and told them their check would be on the way.

"Because when I started out my focus was entirely on doing a story."

"And what's changed since then?"

"I've been threatened, so have people I care about. I've learned that you're in danger, and I've seen the look of loss in your mother's eyes."

No emotion registered on Annie's face, though he was certain that the anger was building.

"You should think about getting in touch with her."

"Says the man who took my father from me."

"What?"

"Haven't you figured it out?"

She was waiting for a response, but Chapa did not have one ready.

"He didn't withdraw when I was taken, and certainly not after I got away. It happened slowly, over time, and it started when you wrote that story about us."

"I should've written that story differently, and I've beaten myself up over it for years, but I can't believe that's the reason—"

Annie got up and grabbed her purse. It jingled as she tossed the strap over her shoulder.

"You sacrificed me and my family for your work then, and you're doing it again now."

She dug into the faded blue denim purse and pulled out a couple of bills. Chapa shook his head. She hesitated for a moment, then pushed the money back inside.

"Thanks for buying lunch," she said, and turned for the exit.

Chapa threw some money on the table, enough to cover the check, and headed after her.

Annie was out the door in a hurry.

"Where are you going?"

"Home, to kick back for a few hours before I go to work."

A Chicago city bus rumbled past him as Chapa picked up his stride. Its loud roar drowned out everything else he said. It came to a stop ahead of him and she hopped on. Chapa reached the bus before it took off and saw Annie sit down by a window that was halfway open.

"Annie." She turned and looked at him. Chapa hesitated for a moment, then continued, "Louise is dead. She was murdered a few days ago."

Chapa stood on a broken piece of sidewalk, and watched the bus roar away until it turned out of view a few blocks later. He couldn't stop thinking about how pale Annie had looked when his words sank in.

CHAPTER 46

Compartmentalizing was something Chapa had become good at when he was younger. It was a skill that came in handy any time the problems in his personal life threatened to spill over into his work. It was not quite as useful when he was trying to save his marriage.

He was thinking about that as he read a text message he'd received while his phone was turned off at the restaurant.

Dad, I know Mom is going to talk to you some more about letting Stephen adopt me, and I think it's a good idea. Stephen has been more of a father to me than anyone, and if you love me you won't turn this into a long drawn-out process. Nicole

What ten-year-old would use a phrase like, *long drawn-out process?* If Carla had sent the text from Nikki's phone, that was bad. If she had put her daughter up to it, that was much worse. Not knowing was the hardest part. What was his daughter thinking? What was she feeling? Those questions could rip him apart.

Chapa wasn't going to let that happen. He decided it was best to table this problem for the time being. Like tossing an unpaid bill into a junk drawer, then forgetting about it. He closed his phone without responding to the message and tossed it on the passenger seat.

Elvis Costello's *My Aim Is True* CD ripped through his car's speakers as Chapa drove to a familiar coffee shop. He was determined to put everything else out of his mind for the next few hours and just worry about being a reporter. It's what he got paid to do, and the one thing he knew he was good at. Even during his hardest times, Chapa had always managed to keep everything else from getting in the way it was time to write.

As he pulled into a parking space a few doors down from Beans to You, Chapa checked his watch. It was just after 2:00 on the East Coast, and that meant Nikki wasn't home from school yet, did not have access to her cell phone, and could not be sending text messages.

CHAPTER 47

Chapa took a slow sip of hot black coffee and adjusted his earpiece as he looked at the first notes he'd transcribed on a half-used legal pad. They came from a recording he had made for himself earlier that week as he drove to his first meeting with Grubb. The notes no longer made much sense. Questions about how the killer was facing his own death, remorse, and his experiences in prison now seemed to belong to an entirely different story.

But he jotted them down anyway, and then moved on to the recording of his interview. Listening to it now, Chapa got the sense that Grubb knew he was recording it, even though the guard had told him not to. The killer would draw in closer during key points in the conversation, his voice clear and steady. Chapa listened as Grubb told him to go ahead and pick up the pen that had fallen to the floor, as if he was saying, *We both know you don't need it.*

Next, he examined his notes from conversations with Dominic Delacruz, Michelle Sykes, and Louise Jones whose voice Chapa had difficulty listening to now that he knew what had happened to her a short while later. He continued the process of transcribing the few recordings he'd made, along with the notes from his meeting with Langdon, and the visit to Night Owls, but stopped when he reached his trip to the trailer.

This would require a fresh cup of coffee. He returned to the counter, where a young, shaggy-haired male barista offered to refill his cup. While he waited, Chapa looked around at some of the faces in the half empty shop—none were familiar—then he returned to his table and got back to work.

Chapa turned up the volume on the recorder, pressed an index finger to his earpiece, and shoved a thumb into his other ear, then pushed Play. A few seconds later he was listening to the muffled rustling of the recorder shifting around inside his pocket. Hearing his movements took Chapa back to that place. He remembered pressing against the locked door, wondering if Annie was trapped behind it, and calling out her name.

Then he heard the *click* of the television being turned on, followed by Grubb's voice. The recording made from inside a jacket pocket wouldn't please an audiophile, but Chapa was able to make out most of it. Grubb spoke deliberately, and Chapa got the sense that he was somewhat rehearsed. He'd missed that the first time.

Chapa could feel the muscles in his chest contract as Grubb's recording came to an end, and he decided it might be a good idea to stop drinking coffee. While he was being assaulted, the recorder banged against something but did not shut off.

He cranked the volume up as high as it would go and forced a thumb into his naked ear until the pressure became uncomfortable. After more than a minute of silence, Chapa heard what might have been a voice. Then he heard it again, though it wasn't at all clear.

This was the same portion of the recording he had

listened to the morning after. He'd hoped that using the earbud might make a difference. It didn't. Still, he wanted to be sure he hadn't missed anything before turning the recorder over to Andrews.

Chapa fast-forwarded thirty seconds in the recording. Nothing. Then thirty seconds more, and the rustling was back. But now there was something else in the background. Laughter.

A few seconds later he heard a word. At first it sounded like "old" or "mold." But when he played it again Chapa realized it was "told," and it came in the middle of a sentence. He rewound back ten seconds and played it again. He closed his eyes and tried to shut out everything else. This time Chapa heard the words *I* and *he* sandwiched around the other word. He slowed the playback just a little and tried again.

I told he could.

He slowed it down a little more and locked in on the voice.

Just like I told you he would.

Chapa turned the recorder off and stared into his half empty cup of coffee until all of the remaining steam had burned away. What the hell was going on? Before Chapa could answer that question his cell phone started vibrating.

"It's Chapa."

"Is this Alex Chapa, the newspaper reporter?" The labored voice, though young, was tinged with exhaustion.

"That's right."

"Why was my father murdered last night?"

CHAPTER 48

Eddie Delacruz's voice was trembling as he recounted how someone had held up his father's convenience store, then shot Dominic Delacruz.

"I'm so sorry to hear about this, Eddie. Your father was a good man."

"He cooperated with the robber, and got shot anyway."

"Was he alone?"

"Yes, so was the gunman."

The journalist's instincts were kicking in. Though he'd told himself he wouldn't pursue another story until after Grubb's execution, Chapa sensed an opportunity to get deeper into this story than any other writer in the area would be able to.

"How do you know your father cooperated?"

"You can see it on the security tape. The cops are treating it like just another holdup."

"What, exactly, can you see on the security tape?"

"Not the holdup guy, not much at least. His face is covered. But my dad gives him the money straight away. The cops are tracking down the usual assortment of junkies and bangers."

"But Eddie, you do understand those are the people who commit a lot of these crimes."

Chapa realized the words came out hard and cold, and wondered if he would be approaching this differently if he wasn't in the middle of a bigger story.

"My father didn't like you personally, Mr. Chapa. But he thought you were a great newspaper writer."

Chapa slumped down into his chair, rubbed his tired eyes, and flipped his notepad open to a fresh page.

"What do you want me to do?"

"Look into it. Write one of your investigative stories. Don't let them bury it."

"I'll probably end up exactly where the police are. You understand that, don't you?"

"Maybe, but you should get a look at that security tape. There's something strange about it."

"Strange how?"

Chapa could hear the young man take a deep breath and gather himself, like he was trying to tap into a dwindling reserve of strength.

"There's a hesitation after my dad gives him the money. The two of them are standing there like they're talking, just before the gunman pulls the trigger."

Several seconds of silence.

"That's unusual, isn't it?" Eddie asked, finally.

Another silence.

"Yes, it is."

In large letters Chapa wrote the word *pause* on his notepad, followed by an even bigger question mark.

"Which police department has the tape now, Eddie?"

CHAPTER 49

Shana Reynolds answered her cell phone on the first ring.

"Hey newshound," her usual greeting for Chapa.

The two had been friends for more than a decade, and Shana was one of the few contacts Chapa had inside the Oakton Police Department.

"I'm guessing you've got a security video from a holdup that went down last night."

It wasn't a guess. Shana was a one woman hub for all of the electronic information that flowed through the department.

"It wasn't ours to begin with, but yeah, it came across the server a couple of hours ago."

"I need to see it."

"I can burn a copy and give it to you when you buy me a really nice dinner tonight."

"Sorry, Shana, that's not going to work."

"Which part?"

"Both. I'm in Chicago and I've got to get a look at that video right away."

Shana thought for a moment.

"I can put it up on the *Record*'s server and you should be able to access it from there."

Chapa heard Shana clicking away on a keyboard as they caught up on what was happening in their lives. Both agreed that Chapa's was far more interesting at the moment, and for that Shana expressed her sympathy.

"You know the ancient Chinese curse?" she asked.

Chapa did.

"May you live in interesting times."

"That's the one," she said. "Okay, the video is on its way. It'll take a few minutes, but you should be able to access it."

"You're the best. Tell you what, I'll talk to Jerry Rossiter over in sports about wrangling a couple of Bulls tickets."

"Are you trying to bribe an officer of the law?"

"Yes."

Shana laughed.

"How are the various departments treating this shooting?" Chapa asked as he logged on to the *Chicago Record*'s site.

"Just like any other typical late night hit." There was a pause, and Chapa could almost hear the wheels turning in Shana's head. "Wait, there's more to it, isn't there? Otherwise, you wouldn't give a damn about some holdup, would you? Damn it, Alex. I take back everything I said about feeling bad for you."

The image was loading on Chapa's computer.

"Why?"

"Because it's your own damn fault."

CHAPTER 50

The black and white image was grainy and a bit blurred. A typical low-resolution video shot with an old camera. Shana had explained that a better version would've taken much longer to send, and Chapa sensed time was more vital than picture quality in this case.

Everything he would need to see was there, anyhow. The camera was suspended above the counter, with Dominic Delacruz on the left side, the gunman on the other, and the cash register in the upper right corner. All of it documented and measured by a time log across the bottom.

The silent film began with Dominic organizing the area under the counter. He stood, probably alerted by the sound of the door opening, then froze. The other man, already wearing a ski mask, made it to the counter in just over two seconds.

The gunman appeared to be about the same height and build as Dominic, which meant average across the board. He wore a dark coat, gloves, and mask to match. It was a typical, almost clichéd outfit for a common street thug holding up a store, but there was nothing ordinary about what was happening.

Inching toward the screen, Chapa wanted to make

certain he didn't miss whatever Eddie Delacruz thought he'd seen. The image became distorted the closer Chapa got to it, and he didn't mind that. Knowing what was coming wasn't going to make watching it any easier. He was hoping the more distorted the picture, the less real it would all seem.

Dominic Delacruz emptied the drawer, making as little eye-contact as possible. He put the money on the counter and stepped away. The gunman shoved the bills into his left coat pocket, never taking his eyes off the frightened store owner.

This was the point where most other armed robbers would make a dash for door. But that's not what happened. What Chapa saw matched Eddie's description in a way he had not expected.

Instead of taking off, the man in the mask seemed to be talking. Slowly, Dominic Delacruz raised his eyes and looked at his killer. The expression on his face changed. It shifted from the passive blank gaze of a frightened man who simply wants a bad situation to end, to something altogether different.

It could've been misinterpreted as a smile, but that was just a cruel trick played by a slightly garbled image. What Chapa saw was a look of sheer terror. And something else. A sense of what was about to happen to him, and maybe even why.

And then it happened. Though there was no sound, Chapa still recoiled in his chair, as though the gunshot had gone off inside his head. In an instant, Dominic Delacruz lay dying on the floor behind the same counter he'd used to shield Annie Sykes sixteen years before.

Chapa closed the laptop and buried his face in his hands. For several minutes he fought to erase what he'd just seen, knowing that would not happen for a long time. Not until that day when it would mercifully blend into the mosaic of pain-filled images that many veteran newsmen carry around like tattoos only they can see.

A waitress wandered over, probably to see if everything was okay. Chapa sensed her being there and waved the well-meaning young woman away. When the sharp edges of shock had dulled enough for him to return to the moment, Chapa picked up his cell phone and called Joseph Andrews.

CHAPTER 51

It took some coaxing by Chapa before the office assistant at the other end agreed to pull Andrews out of a meeting. Getting the agent interested in the video was much easier.

"I'm a little surprised the locals are treating it like just another holdup since there isn't a lot of crime in that area," Andrews said. "Then again, every department seems to be running a little thin on manpower these days."

"I can understand why they think it's just another random crime, but take a closer look. There's something else there. The thug says something to Dominic Delacruz after he has the money."

"That doesn't happen in a run of the mill grab and go. But it still doesn't mean that any of this is connected to Kenny Lee Grubb."

"Uh huh," Chapa said, knowing Andrews didn't believe in coincidence.

Andrews told Chapa he would call the local police later that afternoon and have them forward a copy of the tape. An agent would be sent to the crime scene the next day.

"Why wait until tomorrow?"

"Can't do it today. We've got too much going on right here in town. A lot of agents are in the field at the moment."

"One more thing, Joe, when did you say Lance Grubb was picked up?"

"Yesterday morning."

"So that's at least twelve hours before the shooting."

Chapa sat back and let Andrews process that information.

"I know what you're thinking, Al. You just do your job, and let me do mine."

CHAPTER 52

"Refill?"

The server was back. She had probably seen Chapa looking off into nothing and wanted to make sure he hadn't passed away mid-thought. The twenty-something was lean, brunette, and pretty, and Chapa might have gone for her in a simpler time.

"No thanks, can I just get some water?"

Chapa had agreed to call Eddie Delacruz the next day. He wouldn't have anything new until then, anyhow. Andrews had told him to get back to doing his job, and that seemed like an excellent idea right about now.

He quickly finished transcribing his notes and recordings, then wrote down the title for his series— *The Death of a Killer*. When the glass of water arrived, Chapa downed it all in one extended effort. He thought about splashing some of it on his face in hope that it might snap him back to sanity and reason, but resisted that temptation only because he knew it wouldn't work.

In a little more than an hour, he had banged out the first installment, as well as the leads for the next three. The final two parts had yet to be determined. Chapa re-read his story, did a quick rewrite, and emailed it directly to Sullivan. He would check in later and play it cool, as though it was just another day in the newspaper business.

He shut down his laptop, then tore out each sheet of notes and laid them across the table in chronological order. They looked like pieces of a puzzle and as he studied one, then the next, some connections began to emerge. Much of what he had encountered over the past several days were not random acts of madness.

Chapa now understood he had been manipulated, a process that started when he interviewed Grubb four days ago. He had been followed more than once. At other times he'd been nudged in one direction or another by whoever was orchestrating this, in the same way an experienced pinball player muscles the machine just enough to get the ball to go where he wants it to.

The server returned. Chapa asked for another glass of water and squared up the check. But he didn't leave for a while, not until he knew what his next move would be. Chapa had decided it was time to tilt the works.

CHAPTER 53

Paul LaRang was never in whenever Chapa called his office. The attorney had represented him since the initial divorce procedure, and through the series of still unresolved custody issues. As far as Chapa could tell, he had not managed to win anything that Carla wasn't willing to concede.

"I see, well I'm sure he's busy, but this is important."

"Um hmm."

Chapa could tell the woman with the nasal voice at the other end was doing something else while pretending to care about his phone call.

"Just let him know I called."

"Um hmm, Mr. Chapa."

"And that he's fired."

"What? Excuse me, what?"

"I will no longer be needing Mr. LaRang's representation."

"You know what, you should tell him that yourself. I think he's just out in the hall."

Chapa had been to LaRang's office at least a dozen times, there was no hall.

"Let me try and chase him down."

He was put on hold and subjected to a rendition of

"Every Breath You Take" played on native South American instruments. Having grown tired of this treatment, and fearing that a didgeridoo-driven version of "Roxanne" would follow, Chapa was about to hang up when LaRang picked up on the other end.

"Is there a problem, Alex?"

"You mean other than the fact that I don't get to see my daughter even though the court says I'm supposed to."

"I understand that you're angry, and I'm angry for you. But as I've explained to you in the past, our justice system favors the mother and for us to be able to—"

"We're finished, I'm getting a new lawyer."

"That is, of course, your right, but I must advise you that—"

"I've had enough of your advice, I think you're full of shit."

"I would like to know what occurred that has set you off like this, or perhaps a cooling off period might be—"

"The next sound you hear will be you losing a client."

It felt good to cut him off like that. Chapa wondered if the attorney, who was never at a loss for words, would call back. Part of him hoped LaRang would, just so he could hang up on him again.

As soon as the Grubb saga was behind him, Chapa would find himself a new attorney. This time he wouldn't settle for anything less than a heartless, badass son-of-a-bitch, a real street fighter.

Everybody bad-mouths lawyers, until the day they need one. Then, you might as well go get the meanest asshole on the block. If you need to hire a gunslinger, you don't go looking for one with a knack for diplomacy. Chapa had paid a stiff price for that hard-earned knowledge.

He wasn't sure where the money would come from

to pay for a more aggressive lawyer. How big would his unemployment check be? That concern could be set aside for a couple of days. Right now Chapa needed to focus on his immediate future.

Every reporter encounters obstacles from time to time. Most wrap up their stories with as little drama as possible or walk away altogether. Chapa always played through, and over the years he'd discovered that the best way to wrestle back control of a situation was to do something that no one expected.

The most unlikely thing he could think of doing was going back to Prather's, so he turned onto Clark from Belmont and headed north, in the direction of the club. He had no way of knowing if Annie Sykes would give him one last chance, but figured it was worth a shot. Chapa sensed he was running out of options, and knew he was running out of time.

CHAPTER 54

The bouncer recognized him, and not in a good way. The guy's shaved head accentuated the thick rolls in his neck that were neatly stacked like barbell discs all the way up from his shoulders. He raised one of his bloated paws, but Chapa stopped before it made contact with his chest.

"You were here last night."

"Yes, I'm becoming a regular."

"I didn't like you the first time I saw you."

"I grow on people."

"I doubt that."

"It's Chico, right?"

He glared at Chapa, then pulled out a walkie-talkie from a small holster.

"You stay there, I gotta check on you."

But before the bouncer could do that a voice from inside the doorway captured his attention. Though Chapa strained to listen, he couldn't hear what was being said.

"You sure?" Chico the bouncer asked, continuing his conversation as he reemerged. He then stepped aside and pointed to the doorway with a jab of his thumb.

"It's your lucky day, pal."

"Maybe I should go buy a lottery ticket."

"Gimme six bucks."

Chapa slipped him the money and walked inside. Annie Sykes was waiting for him.

"You're not exactly someone I expected to see here tonight."

"What can I tell you? I just can't live without live jazz."

She smiled and that went a long way toward easing the tension.

"Seriously though, Annie," Chapa started, then moved in closer so no one else could hear. "I need to talk about what's going on and how to keep you safe."

"I went online and read about Louise."

"I didn't want to have to tell you that way."

Her look hardened, and she folded her arms and shifted her weight to one hip. The toughness was back.

"I also read that you're a suspect."

Annie said it just loudly enough that the bouncer heard it and took one sizeable step in Chapa's direction.

She shook him off. "It's nothing, Chico."

And the guy obediently retreated to his post.

"I know you didn't have anything to do with that," she said as her demeanor seemed to shift again. "I'll seat you in my section. I'm not sure how much we'll be able to talk before I get my break."

"How long will that be?"

"Little over an hour."

"Lead me to a table."

There weren't as many people sitting near the stage as the night before, but more of the booths were filled, and as far as Chapa could tell, fewer employees were moving around the place.

"My boss calls this a slow night. And I guess it is, once the dinner crowd moves on."

Annie guided him through the maze of tables, at one

point waving to another server who apparently had expected to get the next customer.

"What are you going to have?"

"Get me something with rum in it, the best you've got."

Chapa turned his attention to the crooner who was mumbling his way through "A Man Alone." He was wearing a tie that he'd already undone and was spending more time looking at his shoes than his audience. Too cool by half, Chapa thought.

Annie brought him a rich brown drink on the rocks, and told him she would return as soon as she got the chance, then went back to making the rounds. Except for the other two or three men who appeared to be flying solo, the booths and tables were populated by couples engaged in romantic conversations, and groups carrying on lively debates.

The place had a good vibe, even if the evening's entertainment was cheesier than a small town fair in Wisconsin. Chapa was tapping his fingers to a less than enchanting rendition of "That Old Black Magic" when Annie slipped into the other half of the narrow booth and slid another drink in front of him.

"That one's on me."

Chapa smiled and knocked down what was left of the first drink.

"What is this, turn back the clock night?" he asked, pointing to the stage.

"That's just Billy, he's a friend of the owner who lets him perform here once a month. His stage name is Buddy Chuck, and he's convinced he's going to Vegas."

"He'd better buy a plane ticket," Chapa said.

"Like I said, it's a slow night."

"Do you have a few minutes?"

"Just a few."

Chapa took a slow sip of his new drink. It tasted sweet and smooth. She'd made a good call.

He locked in on her eyes and said, "Dominic Delacruz was shot last night while he was working alone at his store."

Chapa had determined that there would be no easy way to break the news. Now he watched as fear and understanding swept across Annie's face.

"You think it's all connected?"

"Yes, Annie, I do."

She slumped back into her side of the booth.

"The police, what do they believe?"

"They think it was just another robbery, but I've seen the security tape."

"And you don't believe that it was?"

He shook his head.

"First Louise, now Dominic Delacruz . . ." Annie's voiced trailed off and Chapa imagined her completing the rest of that sequence in her mind.

"I saw Louise the day she died, and we talked about you."

"She helped me through some things. Louise was a good friend and I miss her already."

"Any thoughts on who might want to kill her?"

Annie shook her head. "She was a kind and truly unique person who never hurt anyone."

"Someone didn't think so. Did you know she kept a journal of your conversations?"

"Yeah, Louise did that with everyone she knew. She thought it helped her understand her visions."

Chapa described his exchanges with Grubb and the threats that were made, filling in the blanks that were left after their earlier conversation. He looked for any changes in Annie's demeanor that might suggest fear. But her face was a wall of neutrality, and he wondered what might be hiding behind it.

"Could someone have gotten their hands on a few strands of your hair?"

"I don't know how. I cut it myself, have for two or three years now. Why do you ask?"

He explained about the message on Erin's door that led him to the trailer, and also how Jimmy had met his death.

"That's so sick."

"It's odd, isn't it, how violence to animals hits us at a deep level."

"It's not odd at all. It's because they're defenseless and trusting. The way children are."

The squat candle flickering in the middle of the table was drawing attention to the lines on her young face.

"There was a locked door inside the trailer, and I was worried that someone had drugged or hurt you in some way, then put you there."

"Why would anyone have done that?"

"Maybe to get me out there, I'm not sure. I wasn't exactly thinking straight."

Chapa polished off his second drink and realized that he'd have to pace himself if he had any hope of seeing the evening through to the end.

"From what you've said, if someone comes after me it will be as a sacrifice, not a hostage."

He was struck by the matter-of-fact way that she was approaching all of this.

"Where is your lady friend now?" she asked.

"I sent her away for her own protection."

"Your child is with her?"

"No, *her* child is, mine lives out east."

She seemed confused, but Chapa did not want to get into the details.

"Annie, you act almost as though you expected something like this."

"I'll confess that these past few years I've spent much too much time online looking up websites, news, and discussions about Grubb and other monsters like him."

"A lot of sick people out there."

"Can't deny that. I always sensed someone else was there with Grubb, hiding in the shadows, watching the things he did to me. But now they hide behind their screen names."

Buddy Chuck kicked it up a notch for his rendition of "Spanish Eyes," a favorite of Chapa's right up until that moment.

"You told the authorities about that second person being there with him, didn't you?"

"I'm pretty sure I did. But they didn't find any evidence and blamed it on the drugs Grubb had given me. My folks didn't pursue it. They were much more interested in getting back to being a normal family."

Chapa had hoped he would get a chance to talk about her family, but now that they were into it he wasn't sure if he wanted the conversation to head in that direction.

"Families are complicated, and sometimes fragile," he said, finally. "It's a lot easier to break one than it is to put it back together."

He was about to apologize, but she reached across the table and pressed her fingers to his lips.

"You didn't destroy my family," she said, looking so deeply into his eyes that Chapa worried she might see everything. "An insane murderer did that."

"Still—"

"No, there's nothing else. We're all alone, every one of us. We lie to ourselves about it because it's comforting to do so, but no one is coming to save any of us. No one is looking out for anyone but themselves."

He wanted to argue that point with her, but knew it

wouldn't do any good. A couple of tables away, a man and woman were looking around for their server.

"I think you're wanted," Chapa said.

"I'll see you during my break," she said, snapping right back into character.

CHAPTER 55

Chapa considered switching to rum and Coke, but thought better of it and settled for the nonalcoholic half of that combination. Annie would pass by every few minutes and send a look in his direction. He figured that her break couldn't be more than fifteen or twenty minutes away.

The crowd thinned out some, and only a few new faces had wandered in since Chapa got there. Maybe a late night rush would follow, but he doubted it. The folks who were there alone now outnumbered the groups.

Annie passed by again and mouthed the words, *ten minutes*. He was anxious to ask her a few more questions about the mysterious other person at Grubb's house. Chapa watched as she swept across the floor, past the stage and the bathrooms, on her way to the bar.

Someone else was watching her too. Chapa had first noticed the man twenty minutes ago, when he sat down at the other end of the room. He was big, but not over-weight. Still, when he leaned forward and pressed his heavy forearms against the tabletop, the floor below must've felt it. He was wearing a wool coat that hid everything except what appeared to be extremely hairy hands. He didn't seem to be interested in the other patrons or the music. Just Annie.

Chapa was trying not to stare, but couldn't help it. Something wasn't right. The guy's drink was tall and dark. He lifted the glass to his mouth, then it followed the movement of his head as the guy slowly pivoted when Annie walked past.

She seemed unaware of the set of heavy eyes trailing her from one end of the room to the other, and maybe it was no big deal. The servers probably dealt with creeps on a nightly basis. Could be this one was a regular. Chapa planned to ask her about him the next time she walked by, then he saw that the guy was staring straight at him.

Chapa wanted to play it safe and look away, but a growing part of him was feeling confrontational. He studied the guy's face for anything that might be familiar, but came up empty when the stranger looked away.

A minute later, his large frame emerged from behind the table as he got up and walked to the men's room. Chapa decided it was time for him to take a bathroom break as well. He would give Andrews a call after he got a better look at the guy.

As he made his way toward the restroom door in a back corner of the club, Chapa looked for Annie, hoping to give her a heads up, but she wasn't around. He considered walking over to where the bouncer was shaking someone down for another six bucks, but knew he had nothing of any real significance to tell him. Maybe that would soon change.

Chapa hoped there would be other guys in the men's room besides himself and Annie's biggest fan. Safety in numbers. On any other night he might have gotten his wish.

That hope vanished as he pushed the door open and walked into the cramped, well-lit room, consisting of one stall, two urinals, and two sinks that shared a double mirror. He didn't see the man right away, but as the bathroom door creaked to a close behind him the guy in the wool coat emerged from the stall.

Chapa tried to not act startled, but knew he probably looked every bit as surprised as he felt. They did not make eye contact as the man walked over to the sink, pushed his sleeves up as far as the heavy fabric would allow, then washed his hands. Chapa squared up at a urinal and pretended to take care of some business of his own. He realized that by now the guy might be thinking his interest in him was of a somewhat more personal nature. So Chapa pulled down the plunger and headed over to the sink.

He was about to turn the water on when the man abruptly reached into his coat. Without thinking, Chapa took an uncertain step back, then felt like a fool when a comb appeared in the man's right hand.

Both men looked into the mirror, but not at each other. Chapa was starting to feel he had made a mistake when the man slipped the comb, which looked like a toy cradled in his enormous hand, back into his coat pocket. The guy took a step toward the door, then seemed to notice a few strands of hair that were still badly out of place, and raked his left hand across his forehead.

This was the hand that Chapa had earlier thought was covered with hair, but in the mirror he saw that was not the case. A tattoo that Chapa found as startling as it was familiar spread across the back of the stranger's hand. Though he only caught a glimpse of it, Chapa instantly recognized the image of a bleeding heart with three knives through it as the same one that had haunted his drug-induced dream two nights before. He remembered how it had wandered across the murky landscape of his subconscious.

Then Chapa looked directly at the reflection of the man standing next to him. Their eyes met for a split second before the guy left the bathroom like he was late for an appointment. Chapa's anger and determination began to take hold.

A call to Andrews from inside the bathroom led to the usual conversation with his voice mail. He left a detailed message including the location of the club and a description of the guy. Then Chapa slipped the phone back into his pocket and headed straight for the man's table.

CHAPTER 56

Chapa was aching for a confrontation, but one was not immediately available. The guy was gone. He had left a couple of bills on the table. Some folks had decided that Buddy Chuck's second set was worth dancing to, and their movement obscured Chapa's view of the bar.

He headed in that direction, figuring it was the only other place in the club where the guy could be. But when he got there all Chapa found was a couple of businessmen talking to some women who were hoping they might improve their odds of a happy retirement.

This vantage point gave Chapa the opportunity to carefully scan the room from one side to the other, while ignoring the bartender's offer to get him a drink. There was no sign of the guy, and Chapa didn't see Annie either, so he dropped a twenty dollar bill on the table as he passed his booth, and headed for the door.

"Did you see a big guy walk out a minute ago?"

"I'm a big guy, and I stepped outside a minute ago," Chico the bouncer responded with a forced smile.

Was he trying to be friendly or just a smartass?

"He was wearing a thick wool coat, and might have been in a hurry."

"Lots of people coming and going, many of them have coats on." He left both hands open, palms up like some religious statue of a steroid-addicted saint.

Chapa got it. He was being a smartass, but one who wanted to get paid. Chapa's last twenty fit nicely into the bouncer's hand, like parking a Matchbox car into a two-and-a-half-car garage. He slipped the bill into a back pocket and pointed down a side street just beyond the left end of the two-thirds empty parking lot.

"He might've gone down that street."

Chapa almost thanked him, but decided the over-tip was thanks enough.

CHAPTER 57

Argyle Street was darker than the rest of the night. It was barely wide enough for one large car, and crowded with trees that reached higher than the houses they fronted. Parked vehicles crept in on both sides, but there was no traffic, and none of the usual city chatter of casual conversation.

Several blocks in the distance, Chapa saw cars moving down busy Lawrence Avenue. But shadows, thick like old curtains, were wedged into the obscure spaces between here and there. A man might easily be hiding in one of them, and that could lead to a bad result.

Chapa walked in the direction the doorman at Prather's had pointed. He looked from side to side with each step, knowing that at any moment the man he was chasing could emerge from the darkness and come after him. As big as the guy was, there were still enough gaps between the brownstones to hide a dozen like him.

After he had walked a little more than half a block, Chapa started wondering if the bouncer had been on the level. Maybe the guy with the tattoo bearing an image from Chapa's worst nightmare never left the

club in the first place. Or could be he was in the parking lot when Chapa came out and was tracking him
right now.

Chapa picked up his pace until he was half-jogging,
but stopped when he reached the corner. As he scanned in every direction, searching for any sign of movement, Chapa considered what he would do if he found
the guy. Like the dog that finally catches the car.

Except for the movement of a few defiant leaves still
clinging to otherwise barren trees, the street was still.
One intersection over on Chapa's right, a car paused
briefly at the corner before turning in his direction. As
it did so, the headlights swept across a large figure who,
though not running, was definitely moving away from
Chapa at a no-nonsense clip.

Chapa kept his eyes on the guy as he crossed the
street to the other sidewalk. The car passed slowly and
parked at the end of the block. Chapa heard a door
open and close behind him. He couldn't decide
whether to call out to the guy and maybe force a showdown, or continue to give chase and hope this led to a
more public place.

The large figure maintained a steady pace, moving
into and out of the shadows. Chapa was still gaining
ground, no longer caring how much noise the soles of
his shoes made as they scraped the pebble-ridden sidewalk. He closed the gap between them to half a block, a
manageable distance. But a moment later, the guy was
gone.

The next corner was at least four houses away, so
Chapa figured that he had taken cover somewhere.
Chapa walked out into the street, fanning away from the
shadows, hoping that would give him a little more time
if someone came at him from behind some bushes. But

the street did not feel any safer than the sidewalk, and the parked cars blocked much of his view.

Slowing down a little as he got closer to where he'd last seen the man, Chapa was starting to wonder if he lived in one of these houses. Just beyond another dark two-story, Chapa found a long alley that led all the way to the next street over.

The light from a lamppost at the other end of the narrow passageway was doing a fair job of illuminating the far half. But it had no effect on the sixty feet of alley that lay before Chapa. Shadows sketched that portion in varying shades of night, making it difficult to detect any movement.

Chapa strained to see beyond its mouth, and deep into the brick and concrete corridor. He wondered if the guy could have already sprinted the length of it. Maybe. But then Chapa should have heard footsteps beating on the broken pavement, and he hadn't.

Having gone this far, Chapa found no reason to wait another second. He could feel his pulse climbing as he walked into the alley. In all likelihood the guy had come out the other side and could already be in a cab, cruising down Lake Shore Drive.

Chapa was being a bit more cautious now, but no matter how carefully he stepped, the sound of his footsteps echoed off the walls, eliminating the element of surprise, if he ever had it to begin with. Though it had not rained in days, there was a dampness there that probably never completely went away, and a smell of filth Chapa would not soon forget.

He stopped when he thought he heard a noise, like something scraping against the pavement, coming from somewhere not too far away. The light from beyond the other end of the alley cut a diagonal line across its base and up the side of the left wall, about forty feet from the opening. It also cast several crooked shadows that Chapa kept an eye on as he got closer to the better lit end of the corridor.

Ahead on his left he saw a large Dumpster, easily big enough for anyone to use as cover. A few feet beyond that, a steady stream of smoke rose from behind a tall stack of wooden crates. If the man he was tracking was tucked behind either of those, things could get ugly.

Again Chapa heard a sound that might have been footsteps, but could not tell which direction it came from. He rushed to one side, and pressing his back against a grime-caked wall, Chapa made himself as hard to see as possible. His left heel slid across some muck in the elbow between brick and pavement, and Chapa almost fell, managing to balance himself in a squatting position.

From that vantage point he was able to get a better look back toward the dark end of the alley, where he had started. Was someone there? *It had to be him.* How easily he could've hidden in the dark bushes or behind a porch near the entrance of the alley and waited for Chapa to wander in.

Chapa stood and started moving fast toward the light at the far end, looking back every few steps, until he finally saw someone moving in the dark, coming faster, matching him step for step. As he passed the Dumpster, Chapa stumbled over one of the crates, but managed to stay on his feet, though he scraped his hand on the rough pavement as he fought to keep his balance.

A wave of hot smoke caught Chapa flush in the face, blinding him for a split second. He wiped the burn from his eyes and was only thirty feet or so from getting out of the alley when the light from beyond silhouetted a large figure.

Chapa came to a dead stop. Though he could not see the man's face, he knew it was the guy from the restaurant. He was also a carbon copy of the figure Chapa had seen the night before in Erin's front yard. Chapa had made a mistake earlier when he identified Lance Grubb, and now it was going to cost him.

The stranger slowly lifted his left arm until it was perpendicular to the rest of his body, and pointing at Chapa.

"You are a slow study," he said in a thick voice that was laced with an accent.

The man was digging in his coat pocket with his right hand.

"You're so fascinated with Red, I'll show you what she will experience. I'm going to hurt you, drug you a little, then hurt you some more."

With his right hand still buried in his pocket, the man took a measured step forward, and the light from the street flashed for just an instant across an object in his extended hand. Chapa wondered if the gun this guy was holding was the same one used to kill Dominic Delacruz.

Knowing there would be no room for negotiation at this point, Chapa started backpedaling, hoping to slip into the shadows before the first shot. The guy was closing the gap in a hurry, chewing up yards, not feet, with each heavy stride.

Chapa slammed into the Dumpster and felt a jagged edge tear through his coat and into the soft skin of his back. No time to worry about small wounds. He spun off from the blow and continued to back away from the man with the gun.

As soon as he was out of the light he would turn and run zigzag. He was about to do that, when a shot ripped through the alley and Chapa fell backward, his head slammed into the dirty pavement. He lay there, groggy, unable to move, and wondering what a bullet wound was supposed to feel like.

CHAPTER 58

A second shot followed, this time from the other end of the corridor, the one Chapa had walked through back when he still thought following dangerous men into dark alleys was a good idea. Then another, and the large man's forehead exploded into blood-slicked shards of torn flesh an instant before he crumbled into a mass of muscle beside the Dumpster.

"Were you hit?"

The voice seemed to be coming from another area code.

"Can you hear me, Mr. Chapa?"

Closer now, but still not in the same neighborhood where Chapa lay, sprawled across a dank bed of filth.

"We're going to need an ambulance and the coroner."

Chapa wondered which one was coming for him.

"Is he shot?"

This voice was different.

"I don't think so, I'm pretty sure I saw the bullet bite off a piece of brick along that wall."

Chapa opened his eyes and took a moment to process the face that was looking down at him with a moderate degree of concern.

"Brandon."

"Yes sir."

"You brought me the shitty coffee this morning."

The agent smiled and turned to his partner.

"He's okay, Eisenhuth. Looks like he just scrambled his brains a bit when he went down."

They told him not to move until the paramedics got there, but Chapa did not listen. Willing himself to stand, he stumbled over to the body. He had to get a closer look at the face of the man who had tried to kill him.

"Actually, I'm not sure he was shooting at you," Brandon said.

"I think he was aiming at us," his partner, Eisenhuth, a well-worn man in his fifties, added.

The body seemed smaller now that it was folded up and resting there, like just another piece of refuse. An undersized yet dedicated drum and bugle corps started playing in Chapa's head when he bent down to get a better look. Eisenhuth quickly stepped in and slipped a gloved hand beneath the dead man's chin.

"Let me help you here, Mr. Chapa."

He tilted the head up, and Chapa studied what was left of the guy's face. He had seen what a bullet could do to a body a few times over the years, but it wasn't the sort of thing you ever got used to. The shot had removed the upper half of the man's forehead and several inches from the front of his scalp.

"I just don't know. Maybe I never saw his face," Chapa said, then fell back into a sitting position, and Brandon knelt behind to keep him from going all the way down.

"But I remember that," Chapa said, pointing to the distinctive tattoo.

Eisenhuth picked up the dead man's flaccid hand and examined it.

"It's a tarot symbol."

Brandon leaned in, across Chapa's shoulder.

"What does it mean?"

"Damned if I know, but a crazy in-law of mine was into this shit."

"They're not into it anymore?" Chapa joined the conversation.

"They're no longer my in-laws. Divorced."

"Been there, still there," Chapa said and forced himself to stand as he heard the sound of sirens rushing down a nearby street.

"The ambulance should be here any second now, we'll get you down to the hospital," Brandon said, cradling Chapa's elbow for support.

"The hell you will," he responded and shook his arm free. "You need to get a statement from me, down at your office. Just get a doctor there to look at my head, and maybe my back."

"Andrews warned me you'd be—his words, not mine—a stubborn pain in the ass."

Chapa nodded as he tried in vain to wipe off some of the grime.

"Get him down there too. Tell him his old pal will buy him a drink if he drags his sorry carcass out of bed."

"He's already on his way to the office."

Chapa closed his eyes and tried to get his mixed up thoughts to quit doing cartwheels.

"Check his other pocket, he was reaching in it for something," Chapa remembered. "But be careful."

Using a thin pair of silver tongs, Eisenhuth removed a syringe that was half full, and also what appeared to be a ceremonial dagger.

"I wonder if that knife is a match for the ones in the tattoo," Brandon said.

"Doesn't look like it," Eisenhuth responded as he slipped the items into clear plastic evidence bags.

Paramedics were making their way into the alley, but Chapa's thoughts were finally starting to come together. He turned to Brandon, who was busy directing all of the people who were suddenly flooding into the area.

"So Andrews got the call and sent you down here?"

"What call?"

"I left him a message a short while ago."

"He didn't say anything about that."

Some pieces were still missing, and Chapa gently ran his hand along the back of his head to see if maybe a few of them had tumbled out.

"I don't get it, then how did you find me?"

With a sternness and sense of authority that belied his age, Brandon ordered the growing crowd of onlookers to step back and clear both ends of the alley, before giving Chapa his full attention.

"I'm sorry to break this to you, Mr. Chapa, but we've been on your tail since you left the office this morning. Boss' orders."

With that, Brandon returned to his duties, leaving Chapa to face a trio of paramedics who were anxious to get him on a stretcher.

"Not a chance," he said, and walked off in search of Eisenhuth and a ride back to his car.

CHAPTER 59

"What, exactly, in our long and sordid history would lead you to believe I would listen when you tell me to trust you with something like this?"

Chapa was already feeling like an idiot, sitting there with his shirt off, fourteen fresh stitches where the edge of the Dumpster had sliced off a small piece of his back. Now he was getting lectured. He deserved it all right, but that didn't make it any more pleasant.

"Look, Joe, can this scolding wait until the next time my head feels like it has something, anything, in common with the rest of my body, other than hurting like hell, that is?"

"You have a minor concussion. Maybe it will do you some good."

"Like I told you this morning, I had it all under control."

Brandon walked up behind Andrews who was lining up the half dozen or so perfectly sharpened pencils on his desk. The young agent was all business, and he carried himself in a way that suggested a veteran who had seen a few things during his years with the Bureau.

"You got lucky, Mr. Chapa. My partner was in Prather's, I was in the car and everything was cool.

Then all of a sudden you came tearing out of there and vanished down a side street."

"The doorman told us where you'd gone and that you were chasing some guy," Eisenhuth said as he walked past.

"Did you have to pay him for that info?" Chapa asked.

Brandon reached inside his suit pocket, "No, I just showed him my credit card," he said, flashing his badge.

Though it was already pushing midnight, the office was buzzing with more than a dozen agents and other employees all moving around like bees in a hive. Chapa looked down at his bare chest and stomach. Was he starting to get a little flabby? Must be the lighting.

"Why did you go after him?" Andrews asked, taking one of his pencils out of formation.

"Instincts, maybe. I had to know who he was, and what he was doing. Don't you ever act on instinct?"

"No."

There was a reason why Chapa trusted his instincts. Andrews thought it was because his friend was impulsive and unfocused. But that wasn't it. Chapa's instincts were good, damn good. When he was on a story Chapa was in his element, moving through a maze he already had the key to.

"What about Dominic Delacruz, anything new?"

"Yeah, quite a bit, Al. He either died in a botched robbery or his killer's cold body is lying on a slab."

"So you think it could've been the same guy?"

"When we get the ballistics we'll know for sure. Now it's my turn to ask the questions."

Over the course of nearly two hours Chapa gave them a full report, holding nothing back this time.

Andrews slid a copy of the dead man's ID in front of

Chapa. At first glance it looked like a driver's license, but it wasn't.

"Lorn Strasser, ever hear the name before?"

Chapa shook his head, and immediately regretted it.

"I think I know what kind of car he drives," Chapa said, then did his best to describe the green Dodge sedan he'd seen a few days earlier, leaving out the part about the chase through suburban neighborhoods.

"This ID is probably a fake. A couple of our guys are headed over to the address on the card."

Chapa took one of Andrews' pencils and a square off a notepad, and wrote down the guy's name, and other vitals.

"So why not kill you? He certainly had enough chances."

"I think he wanted to make sure I gave Grubb the sort of press he's looking for. Apparently they see me as their ad hoc PR guy. For someone who murdered children, Grubb is really image conscious."

"And apparently you're going to do that, you're going to give them the coverage they want," Andrews said, pointing to the slip of paper that Chapa had filled with notes.

"Not a chance. Don't forget, Joe, we're both pretty damn good at our jobs."

Chapa felt his cell phone vibrate in his left pants pocket, then "Guantanamera" started playing. He checked to see who was calling.

"I've got to take this," he said to Andrews who responded by rolling his eyes and organizing the items on his desk again.

"Hey, Matt. Sure, read it back to me."

Matt Sullivan had been on his way out of the *Chicago Record* office, heading home to watch a Jim Carrey movie his wife had rented earlier in the day, when he got a phone call from the back of an FBI car. It had been some time since Chapa had last called a story in from the field, and the reporter got an unexpected rush out of it.

"No, wait, we have the assailant's name now," Chapa said, ignoring his own scribbling and reaching across Andrews' desk for a legal pad that was full of neatly written notes. "It's Lorn, no *e* at the end. No, not *Greene*, though that too would be a hell of a story. The last name is Strasser, double *s* in the middle."

Andrews figured out what was going on. "You called in a story?"

Chapa nodded, and signaled for Andrews to be quiet.

"We've held back every other paper, even the Chicago PD isn't entirely in the loop yet."

Chapa pressed his hand over the mouthpiece. "I know, and I so appreciate that," he said, then turned his attention back to Sullivan. "Yep, that's the name of the agent who gave me a quote."

"Who the hell gave you a quote?" Andrews was half out of his chair.

Chapa mouthed the name *Eisenhuth*, then whispered, "He did an excellent job, he was really good, you'll be proud of him."

After he'd signed off and slipped the phone back into his pocket, Chapa took another square from the paper cube and wrote down a couple more notes. When he glanced up at Andrews, his friend was staring back at him with a look that could melt steel.

"Joe, did I ever tell you that I write for a newspaper? At least today I do, I think. And my responsibility is not to protect the law or help anyone do their job. It's up to me to tell people what's going on outside their front door."

"Just you? You're the only one out there doing that?"

"That's the way you have to approach it, the only way.

Otherwise you start negotiating with yourself and pretty soon you've become something else, just an air-taker with a byline."

"Are you done preaching?"

"It's the same with you, Joe. You put a tail on me because you were doing your job."

Andrews sprung forward, leaving his cool against the backrest of his leather chair.

"I put a tail on you because I was worried about a friend."

The two men nursed a precarious silence until an assistant brought them fresh cups of coffee.

"Did you get anything else from Annie Sykes?" Andrews asked after swallowing a mouthful of steam and a sip of black heat.

"No, just what I told you."

"We didn't get much from her either."

"You talked to her?"

"We brought her down here," Andrews said, opening a folder and pulling out a formal looking sheet of paper. "She gave us a statement, but she didn't recognize your assailant, or Lance Grubb."

Chapa got up and swung around to look at the official FBI form Andrews was holding.

"May I?" Chapa asked as he slipped it out of the agent's hand.

Andrews hesitated for a moment, then shrugged, "Help yourself, there's not much there."

There wasn't, but Chapa did find Annie's contact information near the top of the sheet.

"Why are you writing that down?" Andrews asked as he tried to casually retrieve the document.

"You never know."

"Just wait a damn second, Al."

"Joe, her family has been trying to find her. Maybe they deserve the opportunity to do that."

"Maybe you should mind your own damned business."

"What are you going to do about Lance Grubb?"

"We'll hold on to him for a couple of days, probably until after the execution."

Eisenhuth walked up with two photos in his hand—a close-up of Strasser's tattoo, and one of the knife. Chapa looked at the weapon's ornate handle.

"I think he was going to threaten me with this, but not use it. His plan was to drug me, not kill me with some fancy show knife. At least not right away."

"I got some info on the tattoo from the Internet." Eisenhuth seemed a bit confused and a little taken aback by the way Andrews was glaring at him. "Like many occult symbols it can mean several things, in this case a dark female spirit, or a broken heart."

"Or it could be that the crazy bastard liked the design," Andrews said, taking the photo from Eisenhuth, then sending him off with a dismissive nod.

Chapa added that information to one of the already crowded pieces of paper he'd been using for notes. He then folded the squares, as if he were preparing to slip them into a pocket, and remembered he was missing something.

"I need my shirt."

A young woman dressed in a gray skirt and black blouse brought it to him. Chapa surveyed the four inch hole in the back, surrounded by a bloodstain the size of a salad plate.

"You can't drive home," Andrews said as he watched Chapa cautiously slip the shirt on.

"I'm not staying here," Chapa said, hoping he could stand long enough to tuck the shirt in, but doubting it was worth the effort.

"You know you're welcome at our place. We always keep the guest room in ready condition."

Chapa dropped back into his chair. "Thanks."

"I'll call Jenny and let her know you're on your way. One of the guys will drive you."

"Eisenhuth?"

"No. Decidedly not Eisenhuth."

CHAPTER 60

It was just past two in the morning when Chapa got dropped off in front of the Andrews' two-story home in Wrigleyville. Jenny was waiting for him at the door. She looked tired, but welcoming. Jenny had always been more cute than beautiful, and she hadn't lost much of that to age.

"You didn't have to stay up, Jen," Chapa said, dragging himself up the steps. "Joe gave me a spare key."

"From what I understand, you could probably use a small welcoming committee."

Chapa politely turned down her offers of food and beverage.

"I just need to lie down. A couch, the floor, your front step, I don't care."

Then she noticed the blood on the back of his shirt, so Chapa had to go over some of the highlights of his day.

"Joe told me things got rough. But of course, he couldn't go into detail. Let me get you one of his shirts." She was on the move before he could tell her not to bother. "You know where the guest room is. It's ready for you."

Chapa had stayed in the Andrews' guest room before

when a party or an outing had run long. It was nicer than a suite at the Ritz, complete with fresh linens, a TV, and a private bathroom. All Chapa wanted to do was ruin the neatly made bed.

Jenny knocked before entering, but Chapa had not yet harnessed the energy to draw up a plan for undressing.

"Here's a comfortable shirt to sleep in, and a pair of sweats I don't think Joe has ever worn."

The navy blue T-shirt had one of those motivational slogans on it.

Each of our days is a self-portrait of who we are.

"I've seen this kind of—" he started to say *crap,* but caught himself, "stuff on posters before, but not on clothing. How innovative."

"It's just one of Joe's comfy shirts, he doesn't wear it very often."

Chapa made a mental note to give Andrews shit about having "comfy shirts." She showed him the clean towels in the bathroom, and the ironing board in the closet.

"Really, Jen, my clothing would probably burst into flames if a hot iron came within six inches of it."

She smiled politely.

"If there's anything else you need—"

"Just go back to bed. I really didn't want to be a bother."

"You're a friend and a guest, not a bother." She smiled again and closed the door behind her as she left.

CHAPTER 61

Chapa was still lying awake when Joseph Andrews got home a little more than an hour later. He waited to hear if Jenny would wake up to greet him. When that didn't happen, Chapa willed himself out of bed and wandered to the kitchen.

"Strasser was taller," Chapa said as he walked into the room where his friend was digging around for a snack.

"Taller than?"

"The guy in the video."

"C'mon, Al, are you telling me that you can discern a man's height from a grainy security video?"

"Delacruz was about the same height as me, and not much shorter than the holdup man. But Strasser was taller."

Andrews said nothing, and just stared at Chapa, then shook his head and said, "You look even worse than you did at the office. Have you slept?"

The kitchen was done up in a 1950's theme complete with vintage napkin dispensers like the ones in a diner, and old signs and magazine ads on the walls. The subtle smell of fresh apples gave it a homey feel, and though the only light at the moment came from a fixture above the sink, Chapa could see that this room was as colorful and warmly decorated as any in the house.

"No, I've been lying in the dark for more than an hour trying to figure out what the hell this is supposed to mean," Chapa said, pointing to the slogan on the front of the T-shirt.

Andrews laughed.

"That shirt does look kind of ridiculous on you."

"I'll take that as a compliment. What did you find out about Lorn Strasser?"

Andrews shook his head, "Still looking. He either left no tracks, anywhere, or did an expert job of covering them. We'll know more in the morning."

Chapa watched as Andrews carefully constructed a sandwich, allowing none of the purple jelly to escape its white bread boundary.

"You hungry? Should I make you one?"

"Thanks, but I'm too damn tired to be hungry. Did Jenny decorate the kitchen?"

Andrews nodded and mumbled something unintelligible through a mouthful of sandwich, then swallowed.

"She's into all this vintage antique stuff. I don't care for it, but you work things out. You know?"

Chapa stared at a wall that was half covered with photos of the Andrews family taken during various trips and special occasions. An old sign above the collection of thoughtfully framed pictures read, TODAY'S SPECIALS.

"No, actually, based on my own experiences, I don't know," Chapa said as he dumped his tired ass into a vintage metal and vinyl chair. "I fired my lawyer today."

"I know a good one, a winner. I'll leave his card by the door."

"Is he expensive?"

Andrews shrugged.

"Because you're looking at a soon to be unemployed writer."

That spurred Andrews to finish his sandwich in one large bite, and pull up a chair as Chapa brought him up to speed on what was happening at the *Chicago Record*.

"The thing about tonight was that I needed to get my name at the end of a byline again. Besides, after being in an alley shootout and winding up with a concussion for my troubles, the least I could hope for was to get a story out of it."

"Everybody has a job to do, Al, I'm good with that. But you're too damn fine a reporter to be on the street for long. Have you already started sending out feelers?"

Chapa shook his head.

"First I've got to see this thing with Annie and Grubb through to the execution. Right now it's the only assignment I have."

"As far as that goes, the hard part is over. In less than thirty-six hours Kenny Lee Grubb will be a corpse."

"There's still a story to write, and it has to be a great one."

Chapa got up to help himself to a glass of water, but immediately regretted his decision to move. Andrews motioned for him to sit back down and got his friend a drink.

"Once that's all in the rearview, I'll turn my attention to Nikki and dealing with her mother. After that, there's the work thing."

"Ever heard of multitasking?"

"I do it all the time, but the stakes are higher now. I need to stay focused."

Chapa took a long drink of ice water and let the coldness bring a dull ache from deep inside his throat to the surface.

"Joe, do you ever struggle to figure out what you're supposed to do next?"

The old metal frame creaked a little as Andrews leaned back in his chair.

"No, not really."

Chapa nodded knowingly, picked up his glass of water and raised it, like a toast, in the direction of the wall of photos.

"Then count your blessings, my friend."

Andrews copied the gesture.

"Believe me, Al, I do."

The Day Before the Execution

CHAPTER 62

Chapa's memories of his few early years in Cuba were not so much a series of events that told the story of his childhood as they were individual highlights, like the clips in a movie trailer designed to show you just enough to whet your appetite for more.

In this case, however, there was no more. And over time the pictures in his head had become one with the photos in old albums and the handful of stories his mother had passed on to him. As a result, he wasn't always certain where one memory ended and a collection of blended images began.

He was a solitary child playing on a long, hot beach, his parents watching from a safe distance. Another day, walking with his father along the edge of Morro Castle, the centuries old structure built to guard the entrance of Havana Bay. There he was, standing next to his mother at the corner market, staring at the empty shelves.

Or maybe those were just fragments of someone else's recollections. Faded pictures in black and white, like a scratchy old silent film, or newsprint on torn bits of brittle paper.

Some moments were, however, more complete than

others. He was lost in one of those now, remembering sitting on a sun-drenched granite step that was hot to the touch but not uncomfortably so. In front of him, a street lined with perfectly maintained nineteenth-century homes. Women in colorful dresses and men sporting the sort of hat you don't see anymore except in retirement homes, on golf courses, and throughout the tropics, strolled by as though going for a walk was the only thing on their minds.

A Cuban song that he'd learned as a child was play-ing in the distance, and the smell of croquetas and pastelitos from a street vendor's cart was tempting him to run home and ask his parents for money. But the peaceful street scene was disrupted when two men in dark suits walked up to a woman who was minding her own business and began to drag her away.

Something inside of Chapa was telling him to go help the woman, and he couldn't understand why everyone else was ignoring her cries. He yelled out for the men to stop, but he couldn't hear his own voice. He tried again, this time straining his throat, but the effort was rewarded with silence.

Young Alex wiped the hot sweat from his face as he stood and started toward the street. The music grew louder, and kept increasing in volume until he opened his eyes and realized that the ring tone on his cell phone was playing.

He had only recently switched it to "Guantanamera," and the change was more out of a sense of irony than national pride. The ring stopped mid-note, and Chapa noticed the clock on the dresser read *10:04*. When he flipped the phone open he saw that he'd slept more soundly than he had in days.

Three phone messages were waiting for him. The first was from Erin to let him know she and Mikey were planning to be home that night, and they would be expecting him for dinner. She added that she was wearing the new T-shirt he'd bought for her, and it took Chapa a moment to remember having done that.

The next two messages were from Andrews. A standard wake-up call at exactly 8:30 had missed its mark, and Chapa couldn't remember asking him to do that. The other one logged in just after nine and consisted of, "Just call me ASAP."

Andrews had also sent him a text which read simply, *Call me ASAP*. After he had checked out the clothes that were left for him, Chapa followed orders, and Andrews answered on the first ring.

"I probably made a bigger deal out of this than it really is," Andrews said calmly. "But I also wanted to make sure you didn't sleep later than you planned to."

"I appreciate that, but what's up?" Chapa asked as he worked the remaining drowse from his eyes and started getting himself together.

"Lorn Strasser might not be that guy's name."

"Then what might his name be?"

"No idea, nothing's checked out. The address on his identification card was for a city owned parking garage."

"It's a sure bet he didn't randomly pick that location," Chapa said as he unwrapped the brand new toothbrush that Jenny had left in the guest bathroom.

"Right, and we're going through the employee lists as well as those who regularly rented a space there. But so far this bastard is just a ghost, and I wanted to make sure you knew in case you're writing another story."

"That's a good thought, thanks. Fingerprints?"

"Turned up nothing. We'll figure it out. What are you eating?"

"Nothing. I'm brushing. Thanks for the clothes."

"You're welcome, and there is one more thing. Lance Grubb's lawyer got him out this morning."

Chapa stopped brushing and processed that bit of information.

"Al, you there?"

"Are you shitting me?"

"Nope. Judge said we had to let him go, but it's going to be okay."

"How do you figure that?"

"I got two top guys tailing him and they're not being subtle about it. If he so much as tries to fart in church they'll be on him before he leaves the pew."

Chapa laughed.

"What's funny?"

"Don't worry about it, Joe, you wouldn't get it."

CHAPTER 63

By 11:00 Chapa was showered, wearing one of Andrews' crisp white shirts as well as a pair of expensive blue slacks, and an older sports coat. After tossing yesterday's clothes into a bag, he was ready to get back to the suburbs and have that meeting with Macklin.

Chapa checked in with Matt Sullivan as he walked down the street, searching for his car.

"This would probably be a good day for you to come in. The boss really liked your story."

Sullivan confirmed that Macklin would be around all afternoon, at least until 4:00, most likely as late as 5:00.

"Should I tell him you'll be in?"

Chapa hesitated.

"Sure, but let him know I won't be there until after four."

There was a pause, Sullivan was writing it down.

"You were left a message by a Mr. Munson."

Chapa closed his eyes trying to place the name, waited for an image to appear in his mind, and then it did.

"Oh no, Night Owls. What's it say?"

"'*Let me know if I can do anything to help. Hope to see you soon.*' He left a callback number, you want it?"

"No. Really, no. Just leave it on my desk." *Assuming I still have one.*

The Andrews lived in a neighborhood that included some newer homes with small but well-kept front lawns. Most of the SUVs and foreign cars that were parked on the street the night before were now gone. Parking there, like a lot of residential areas in Chicago, was by permit only, and Chapa hoped he hadn't gotten enough tickets to earn a tow.

As he passed a Neighborhood Watch sign Chapa noticed a middle-aged man whose graying hair had grown long. The man was standing by a silver Chrysler across the street, and wasn't being at all coy about staring at him. Chapa greeted the curious onlooker with an exaggerated wave, but the guy did not respond.

The Corolla was parked near the end of the next block, and just as he had feared, Chapa saw something in the windshield. At least the car was still there. But what he initially assumed was a ticket turned out to be an official federal vehicle parking sign that had been left inside the car, on the top of his dash. This could come in handy, he thought, hoping Andrews did not expect to get it back.

Chapa unfolded one of the small pieces of paper that he had filled with notes the night before and found Annie Sykes' phone number and address. He decided to give her a call just to see how she was doing. He started punching in the number, but was startled by an abrupt knocking on his window.

It was the guy he'd seen across the street, and he was signaling for Chapa to lower the window. He brought it down about halfway.

"You don't look like a federal agent."

"Why not?"

"The way you walk, this car, the clothes are right, but the pieces just don't fit."

"I'll have to work on that," Chapa said and began to raise the window.

"Wearing the clothes and having that sign in your car don't change anything if the rest of the pieces don't fit."

Chapa smiled as agreeably as he could manage, waited for the man to step away from his car, then drove off. He immediately remembered how much more comfortable it felt to be on the move. While he searched for a place to grab a sandwich, Chapa called what he assumed to be Annie's cell phone. After four rings he was greeted by a computer generated voice.

He'd planned on hanging up if she didn't answer, then thought better of it and left a simple message. There was still enough time before his meeting with Macklin that he didn't need to rush out of the city. So Chapa decided to find Annie's place and leave a note for her. That would also give him the opportunity to get a better sense of what her home life was like. It wasn't the sort of thing that he would ever use in a story, but a little more background couldn't hurt.

She lived just off Lincoln Avenue, not too far from Prather's. It was about a fifteen-minute drive and Chapa would be able to hop on the Kennedy Expressway from there. That gave him enough time to get some lunch, stop by Annie's, then still knock out tomorrow's story.

He turned north on Halsted, then jogged over to Clark and stopped at Johnny's Real Italian for a beef sandwich. He was wiping an errant bit of juice from the left side of Andrews' shirt when his phone went off.

"What's up, Joe?"

"No biggie, Al. Just so you know, in case you see anything out of the ordinary, Lance Grubb slipped our guys a little."

"How does someone get away from a tail *a little?*"

"Don't get cute, they know where they lost him and they think—"

"Where did they lose him?"

"Up near Evanston."

"That's only a few miles from where Annie Sykes lives."

"Yeah, and there's a lot of city between her and there."

Chapa still had some sandwich left, but he'd lost the appetite to do anything about it.

"Here's the thing, Al, Lance Grubb has a lady friend in Niles, that's where we think he was headed. Our guys and the locals are moving in that direction now." Andrews hesitated. "Even through the phone I can feel you worrying."

Chapa cleaned up his mess and headed out to his car, which he had confidently parked in a conveniently located tow zone, thanks to the permit Andrews had left for him.

"I'll give you something to worry about, a real odd character hanging around your neighborhood."

"Kinda scraggly, long hair?"

"You know him, really curious about the comings and goings?"

"That's just George Initch. We call him 'Crazy George,' but not to his face, he wouldn't like that. George claims to be psychic, talks in code a lot, but he's harmless."

Some idiot in a Lexus was waiting for the illegal parking space, but drove off in a huff when he saw the tow zone sign, flashing Chapa a look as though he were somehow responsible for it being there.

"I'll let you know when we've reestablished contact with Lance. Are you out of town already?"

"Oh yeah, I'm on the Eisenhower, just a few minutes from my exit."

"Good. You go deal with your work issues, and just write another kick ass column. We've got this down tight."

Chapa signed off and pulled out into midday traffic, some forty miles from where he had told Andrews he was. He then drove up Clark as fast as the traffic would allow, changing lanes whenever it bought him a second or two. His chest tightened and the stitched-up tear in his back burned a little more every time he hit a red light.

CHAPTER 64

He found Haas Street on the first try, though that was just the result of a lucky turn. It was located in a part of the far north side that developers and young professionals had not yet taken over. It still belonged to the artists and new couples who moved in after their first taste of success, and the elderly who could never afford to leave.

The area wasn't unusual or particularly unique, just a lot of quiet. As he drove past, Chapa checked out the parked cars for anyone who might be watching the street, but it looked like just any other day.

Annie Sykes' address was in the middle of the block. The tan, eight-story apartment building needed a paint job, and a few of the rusty air conditioners had barely enough metal left to keep them in the window.

Chapa took the first space that he found, and slipped the parking permit back under the windshield just in case.

In the distance he heard the sound of traffic, and children playing at a nearby schoolyard. But walking down the sidewalk, the loudest sound was the one made by Chapa's labored steps. He tried to envision this place through the eyes of someone who was stalking Annie.

A mailman emerged from Annie's building and walked past Chapa as though he wasn't there. As he did, Chapa looked down at his bag, which was filled beyond capacity, and noticed the label on an oversized envelope that was sticking out.

"Excuse me," he said, and the mailman stopped but continued sorting the envelopes in his hand. "That envelope, are you delivering it somewhere around here?"

Finally looking up at Chapa, the mailman searched his face but found nothing familiar.

"Just picked it up. You know these people?"

The mailman pulled the envelope out of the bag and Chapa got a better look at the symbol on the mailing label. Chapa had seen it before, recently. The apartment number was 7G, two floors above Annie's. He withdrew a small notepad from the inside pocket of the sports coat and wrote down the number.

"Do you pick up mail like that from 7G often?"

"Sometimes, I guess. What are you, some detective?"

Chapa coolly turned and pointed to the sign under his windshield. The mailman looked over at it, then sized up Chapa, and determined he was the genuine article.

"Well, sir, yes, this is your standard yellow business envelope, a little larger than a regular envelope."

He gave the envelope to Chapa, who studied it more closely. It was all he could do to not open it.

"We at the USPS handle these as we would any other."

Chapa almost told the guy he was confiscating the envelope, which might've worked. But he drew a line, albeit a thin and sometimes barely visible one, at committing a federal crime.

"Thank you."

Chapa started to walk away.

"Hey, sir, is there something in here I should be worried about?"

"Nothing at all."

"I'm always happy to help out our government."

He was still talking when Chapa walked into the building and started scanning the directory.

CHAPTER 65

The label for box 5C read ANGELA NOIR, but no name was listed for 7G. The building had a door with an old, but durable security lock, so Chapa pressed the button for Annie's apartment and waited, then pressed it again. Beyond the thick decorative glass door he saw a woman getting out of the elevator with a large dog in tow.

She wasn't Annie, but she would do. Chapa pretended to be finishing a conversation with the dinged-up metal speaker as the door opened and a German shepherd walked through it, followed by the woman. Chapa offered a friendly nod, held the door for her, then slipped inside.

There was no security guard. Chapa hadn't expected there to be one, but it was still a relief. The lobby would never be featured in any fine living magazines, but there were signs that suggested it once looked a lot better than it did now. The fixtures and some of the tiles dated back to the forties.

He passed on the elevator in favor of the stairs. The marble steps had been so worn down that they were concave in the middle. By the third floor he was thinking that maybe he should get his old treadmill out of the garage. Something else for the bottom of his expanding to-do list.

The building was quiet, and his heavy breathing filled the stairwell. He paused for a moment when he got to the fifth floor, wanting to make sure he walked down the hall in the right direction the first time. Like he knew what he was doing. Like he belonged there.

Annie's apartment was two doors down from the stairs. Nothing about its dark brown wood door set it off from any number of other apartments in aging buildings throughout the city. But at that moment Chapa knew that the events of the past week had led him to this place, as though he were being directed by an unsteady but determined hand.

He was alone in the fifth floor hallway, and had not seen anyone on his way up the stairs. The muffled sounds of children playing in one of the other apartments filtered up from a couple of floors below. There was no sound coming from behind Annie's door.

Wrapping his knuckles against the solid oak door did not produce an echo, and that surprised Chapa. But something else surprised him even more. The door had moved, just a little.

"Annie? It's Alex Chapa. You home?"

Chapa waited for a response, but when none came he pressed against the door with the tips of his fingers. It gave a fraction of an inch. He pressed again, applying just a bit more force this time. The door slowly opened, and gradually came to a stop at a forty-five degree angle.

That was enough of a gap for him to get a decent look inside. From where he was standing outside the door, Chapa could see a hallway that led off into darkness, and a small portion of what was probably the living room.

He wanted to call for her again, but worried that a

neighbor might start getting concerned. So he stepped inside just enough to close the door behind him without shutting it.

"Annie."

No longer expecting a response, Chapa started looking around, even though he was now way beyond his comfort zone. What he had assumed was a living room turned out to be more of an artist's studio. A large drawing table at one end of the room was surrounded by supplies. Over on the other side sat a couch with uneven cushions that had been re-covered with a flowered cloth.

The light from a large window at the far end spilled into the room and onto drawings on the walls. Several of them were of solitary people doing nothing of particular interest besides being lonely. A dark stillness haunted the images, and Chapa found them quite unnerving. The drawings were being treated with little reverence. No frames, just tape and tacks to hold them up.

The kitchen was to the right, and Chapa allowed himself enough steps in that direction to confirm there was nothing out of the ordinary. He could almost hear Andrews yelling at him to get out of there. *What the hell was he doing?*

But Chapa couldn't leave until he'd made sure that nothing had happened to Annie, that she wasn't lying somewhere, wounded, or worse. He started down the hall, toward the bedroom.

Before he got there, Chapa passed a large room along the right side. He stuck his head in and flipped the light on. The bare dim bulb still had enough juice to reveal a room that was being used primarily for storage. Boxes were stacked against the walls, and the only thing in the middle was a futon.

The wood floor creaked beneath Chapa's feet as he walked across the room to a closet in the far corner. He turned the knob slowly until it clicked, then opened the door without hesitation, retreating a step as he did so. Empty. Looking inside, he was surprised by how large the closet was, and figured that most of the boxes crowding the room could easily fit in there.

Chapa was shutting the door when he noticed a small rectangular box sitting alone on the top shelf. It was white, about the size of a pad of paper, and just a few inches tall. Chapa carefully retrieved it.

The box was old, and all four of the lid's corners were torn. But the photos he found inside were even older. The first one he saw was faded toward the yellow and red end of the spectrum. Chapa guessed Annie was probably in second or third grade when the picture was taken. Beneath it, he found a couple dozen others, a few of which were from roughly the same time as the ones he'd seen in her parents' house.

Unlike those, however, none of these photos showed Annie as a teenager. Every one of these images exuded happiness and wonder. It was as though time had stopped for Annie at a very young age.

He put the pictures back in the box as he had found them, then returned it to the shelf. Chapa was becoming more uncomfortable with each passing minute. Voyeurism was never his thing.

Chapa shut the closet door and retraced his steps, turning the light off as he left the room. The bedroom was just a few feet away. The door was open.

"Annie?"

Again he waited for a response that was not coming, then stepped into her bedroom. The bed was unmade, and clothes were stacked in neat piles on the floor. Nothing seemed out of the ordinary. Just a messy bedroom, left that way by someone who wasn't expecting a relative stranger to be walking through it.

The closet had one of those sliding doors with the

full-size mirrors. Chapa opened it, and found that this closet was every bit as cluttered as the one in the other room was empty. Shoeboxes, a few hats, and several purses lined the floor and crowded the one shelf. Her clothes were hung on the rod in no particular order, except that they became gradually more Goth on the right side. Apparently, that half of the closet belonged to Angela Noir.

As he shut the door, Chapa noticed something in the mirror's reflection. A notepad on the nightstand. He walked over and picked it up. It looked as though she had started to draw a figure in black pencil, then scratched it out with a series of thick, dark, angry strokes.

He had to get out of there, but first he stepped across the hall, and looked into the bathroom. When he saw that the shower curtain was closed, Chapa called out to her again and got the same result as before. He drew the curtain back just enough to poke his head through. It needed a good cleaning, but besides that there was nothing noteworthy going on. In some ways the place reminded him of something he might've seen while visiting a friend at college.

She had left her medicine cabinet open, and when Chapa noticed the feminine products inside, he walked out of the bathroom and straight toward the front door. Annie wasn't there, and this was feeling like a very unsettling waste of time. He had to get back to the office and ready for his meeting. If he was going to get fired, he might as well take the initiative.

Chapa decided to leave a note for her on the door, and stepped into the kitchen to use the counter top as a writing surface. He pulled out his notebook and a pen, and began to write.

But he stopped before he'd finished his first sentence.

Sitting on the counter, next to an open newspaper and a half-eaten Pop Tart, were Annie's cell phone and keys. *Who would leave without those?* He closed the notebook and put his pen away. Then Chapa returned to the living room and scanned the area slowly, until he spotted what he was looking for.

Annie's purse. It was the same one she had been carrying the day before.

Chapa flipped the notepad open to the other apartment address he had written down, *7G.* He thought about what that nutjob from Andrews' neighborhood had said.

The pieces didn't fit.

CHAPTER 66

Apartment 7G was the last one at the end of the hall, toward what Chapa at first assumed was the back of the building, but then realized he had gotten turned around. When he looked out through a large window, a few feet beyond the apartment door, he saw a shorter building's rooftop across the way, and an alley below.

That window and another at the opposite end of the hallway were responsible for what little light there was. It was just as well, the faded blue walls and chipped tile floor looked bad enough in the limited visibility.

Chapa leaned against the door, then pressed an ear to it. He heard nothing. Retreating a couple of quiet steps, he looked for any signs of light escaping through the bottom of the door, but couldn't see anything.

He took a deep breath, and knocked. Nothing. Another knock, same results.

Then again, harder this time, followed by, "Annie?"

After several seconds had passed, he heard a sharp noise from deep inside the apartment. It sounded like a door slamming or something heavy falling to the floor. Maybe he had frightened the tenant's pet.

Chapa twisted the doorknob, which did not budge, so he knocked again, but the silence had returned. He dialed Annie's cell number, figuring that if she had simply gone over to a neighbor's apartment she might have returned to her own by now. He knew that was unlikely, but still worth a try. His call went straight to voice mail. Chapa thought of Annie's phone still sitting there on the kitchen countertop, and remembered the layout of her apartment.

He walked over to the large hall window, and noticed that it was not sealed shut. Still, it refused to open without a fight. Jagged paint chips dug into Chapa's palms as he gripped the bottom and lifted with all the force his wounded shoulder would allow. He'd coaxed it up about two feet when he heard a noise coming from the other end of the hall.

"Hello, is someone there?" Chapa asked.

There was no answer, or any movement as far as he could tell. He waited another minute before going back to work on the window. When he did, Chapa found that it gave in to his efforts much more so than before. Maybe the short break had given him an energy boost, or more likely, it was a jolt of adrenaline delivered by the sensation that someone might've been hiding in the shadows.

The alley below was larger than he had expected. A cement ledge, a foot and a half wide, maybe less, jutted out from the building a couple of feet beneath him. To his right, Chapa could see what he guessed was the living room window for apartment 7G, suggesting that it was probably set up just like Annie's.

He had to get a look inside that window. Then he could call Andrews and give him some idea of the situation.

Most people know whether or not they have a fear of heights, but Chapa had never given it much thought. He had never done any crazy daredevil crap like jump out of airplanes or off bridges. But it was more something he simply hadn't gotten around to, rather than avoided.

At this moment, he wished he'd tried a few of those stunts. Not that leaping from a bridge with a safety cord tied around your torso would prepare anyone for standing on a narrow ledge, seven stories up.

Chapa swung his left leg through the opening, then carefully found the ledge with his foot. He sat on the windowsill, half in half out, and pressed against the concrete to make sure it was solid. A small part of him wished the whole thing had crumbled to the ground below, but the strength of the ledge would not be a concern.

If he could shimmy the thirty feet or so, Chapa might be able to get a peek inside the apartment. He saw no obstructions between the two windows, and no errant bricks that could trip him up or nudge him off.

Chapa swung his other leg through the opening, then ducked under and out. A moment later he was standing outside the building, and leaning forward against it without a harness or a chute to provide him any sense of comfort or security.

He found it easier to take short steps, left, right, chest and cheek pressed against the brick building. Focusing on the narrowing distance between his suddenly heavy feet and the target ahead, Chapa struggled to keep his mind off the long drop that was one miscalculated step or shift in balance away. But he ran into a problem ten feet into his trek. That's where he discovered an area of the ledge where time and water decay from a spout directly above had taken a triangular bite out of the concrete. The gap was roughly twice as wide as his carefully measured steps.

Turning back was an inviting option. But the more Chapa looked at the gap, the more certain he became that he could get across. Inching as close as he could, Chapa stopped when a handful of small pieces of concrete chipped away and tumbled out of sight.

Chapa knew that if he stood there any longer the section under his feet might give. In one calculated, continuous motion he extended his left leg as far as it would go and reached footing on the other side of the gash. But just as he did that, another portion of the ledge gave way and he was now straddling the gap, each foot just inches from the void.

There was no room for his right foot next to his left, just air where concrete had been a moment earlier, and the prospect of hopping a few desperate inches on one foot held no appeal for him. So without giving it any more thought, Chapa shifted all of his weight to his left foot and pirouetted on it, swinging his right foot across in an arc as it dangled above the precipice until it slammed into the brick wall.

In that instant, as Chapa turned his body to face away from the building, he half expected to see his life flash before his eyes, but instead he had to settle for the rooftop across the way and the sudden flash of muted sunlight.

His back slammed into the brick, and Chapa had to react quickly to balance himself. A few stones slipped free, then an inch or two of concrete fell from sight. The gap was widening. No time to worry about balance and footing, Chapa quickly shuffled away from the unstable edge of the opening, and kept going until bits of the ledge finally stopped getting swallowed up by gravity. He got his new bearings, and realized after one glance that looking down beyond his black shoes was not a good idea. Moving across the ledge with his back to the wall was more difficult, slower, and far more dangerous.

Chapa was a little beyond the midway mark when he heard a sound coming from the direction where he had started. It was the hall window. Chapa watched as it slowly slid closed.

Leaning forward as much as he could without tipping, Chapa tried to look into the window, searching for a face. Maybe it was the person he thought he'd heard in the hallway shadows, or someone who just happened by and saw it had been left open. More likely, it had returned to its natural position on its own.

"Hey! I'm out here!"

He was also completely alone.

Chapa thought about retreating, but that would mean crossing the gap a second time, and even then he wasn't sure he'd be able to get the window open again. For the first time since he'd climbed out, Chapa felt a rush of panic. If it overtook him, he would be in desperate trouble.

As Chapa fought to get his breathing under control, life went on beyond the end of the alley that led to the street where his car was parked. A pair of commuters on their way home from work walked past, too locked into their conversation to hear Chapa's call. He closed his eyes, and waited for a comforting image, then thought of Nikki, and wondered if all of this was for her. Nothing else meant as much.

His right hand found a space between two bricks. Chapa grabbed hold, steadied himself, and started moving again. The window was no more than five feet away when Chapa saw the dark blue curtains. They looked heavy, and were drawn tight. Once the window frame was within reach, he slipped his fingers around it and inched closer.

Standing next to the window, Chapa looked for an opening in the curtains. He found it, but not where he was hoping it would be. The window was closed shut, but just a few inches from the bottom, and no more than a foot above the ledge, a small potted plant had forced the curtains apart enough to allow him a look. But first he would have to get down there.

As he slid into a squatting position, each movement carefully measured, Chapa could feel the bricks scraping against the back of the suit, and across his wound. Getting his folded legs out from under him was more difficult than Chapa had expected. His shoes didn't budge without an effort, and he had to tilt to each side, fighting to keep his balance as he rested on one elbow, then the other.

Once Chapa's legs were dangling from the knees down above the alley, he leaned back against the window and tried to get a look inside. The glass was in need of a good cleaning, inside and out, and there was just enough sunlight to create a glare. He leaned in, but all he saw was darkness. There was not enough light coming through to reveal anything else.

He tried it again, this time cupping his hands by his eyes in order to block out as much of the glare as possible. It took a few seconds for his vision to adjust, but it worked. Scanning as much of the room as he could see, Chapa paused on a couple items of interest. He was squinting, trying to get a better look, when he felt a tingling in his right pants pocket.

Digging his phone out proved to be relatively easy. He flipped it open to find that Andrews had left a text message.

Lance Grubb located in Evanston. We're on him right now, but nothing out of the ordinary going on. Also,

ballistics tests show Delacruz was not shot with
Strasser's gun, it was just a holdup. I told you there was
nothing to worry about.

That brought Chapa no comfort. What little he had
been able to see through the window was enough for
him to suspect that the greater threat was still loose.

CHAPTER 67

This window, like the one Chapa had climbed out of, appeared to be original, meaning that it was more than half a century old and built to last. He wondered how much force it would take to break the double-thick glass, and how much of a racket it could make.

No doubt he had already broken a law or two by climbing out there and peeking in through a window. But it couldn't be anything too bad, not yet at least. Calling Andrews back and carefully and calmly explaining his actions, then asking his friend for help was an option.

It was not too late to do that, but he worried it might be too late for Annie. Explaining his situation in a way that would make sense to a federal agent would not be easy, and by the time Andrews got people together and up to the North Side, twenty, thirty, maybe more precious minutes could be lost.

He lifted himself back into a squat. Then Chapa coaxed his left arm out of its sleeve and slipped his shoulder free, then bunched the sports coat around his right elbow. Remembering what Mr. Swinn had taught him in his high school physics class, Chapa aimed for as close to the middle as he could reach, and drove his elbow into the glass with one sharp strike.

The window shook just a little, but the impact did more damage to Chapa's arm and shoulder than to the glass. He struck it again, then again, six times in succession, until he heard a faint cracking sound.

He ran his hand along the pane but could not locate the weak spot. Tapping on it, Chapa realized the glass was even thicker than he had anticipated. Greater force was needed.

With each blow he had risked losing his balance, and then everything else. Besides, his elbow was throbbing, and the cut in his back was barking at him in a big way.

He rolled his upper body inward, turned his head away, and drove his right shoulder and elbow into the glass. Once again, he heard an encouraging though faint sound, but there was no give. Chapa looked closely at the window to see if there was some way to pry it open. It was sealed tight. Deciding that he had not given it his all the last time, and knowing that his options were less than limited, he leaned forward until he could see the alley below, then threw as much force as he could generate into the stubborn glass.

For a moment, the entire window seemed to bow, allowing Chapa a split second to consider what might happen if the whole thing gave. Then the glass shattered and he tumbled into the darkness beyond.

He fell to the floor, taking with him the small table and the plants on it. His shoulder struck hard against the wooden slats, and was immediately sandwiched by the full weight of his body. Chapa lay there for a moment, and wondered how the stitches in his back were holding up.

The window remained in place, and Chapa knew he was lucky to have avoided the jagged pieces of glass that were still clinging to the top and bottom of the frame like teeth to badly damaged gums. There was more light in the room now, but it was all coming from outside the broken window. Chapa looked back in its direction and wondered if this is what live prey sees just before the predator closes its mouth.

CHAPTER 68

Knowing he was in a vulnerable position, Chapa quickly rolled to his knees, then stood and looked around before brushing off bits of glass and surveying for blood. He waited for the sting to set in, knowing that razor cuts can take a few seconds to show. But the only fresh wound was the one he'd earned by landing on his shoulder, and there would be time to worry about that later.

His heart was sprinting, and that was comforting in a way, as though his body and mind were in perfect sync. At that moment, Chapa's awareness of everything around him was electric. He was in the zone.

The apartment was set up a lot like Annie's, but with much less stuff in it. Chapa did not bother calling out to anyone, figuring that half of Chicago had probably heard him crash through the window, and anyone in the apartment already knew he was there.

He took a moment to look around as much as he could. Across the way, Chapa saw the opening to what he assumed was the kitchen, but it was too dark to see anything else.

In the limited light, he saw a mattress pressed against one wall of the living room. It had no box springs or

frame, but looked well-slept in. Across from the makeshift bedding stood a neatly organized work center that
included a large, cheap wood desk.

An envelope Chapa had seen through the window
was sitting on top of the desk. He picked it up and studied the label. It was just like the one the postman was
carrying. Next to the envelope was a magazine that
Chapa had noticed from outside as well. He flipped
through it and confirmed his suspicions.

In one of the drawers he found packing supplies, in
another a ledger and a smattering of files. The largest
drawer was heavier than the others, and filled with
video and audio tapes. Most were unmarked, a few had
dates scribbled on neatly applied labels.

An old trunk sat on the floor. It had been painted
green at some point, but that was probably not its original color. Chapa tried to bend down and examine it,
but that hurt like hell, so he compromised and settled
for a full squat.

The wooden trunk was unlocked, but the lid was
heavy and it opened unevenly. He tried to look inside,
but none of the light from the window could reach it.
He switched on a small lamp that was at the far side of
the desk, and was able to see more of the room, though
there wasn't much there. The lamp's cord extended
just enough that Chapa was able to hold it over the
trunk.

Inside he found a series of ropes and bindings, as
well as a pair of pliers, some cutting tools, and a gray
metal tackle box, which he carefully removed and set
on the floor. It was old and heavy, and reminded him of
one that he'd had as a kid.

This one, however, was not packed with lures. Chapa
flipped the lid open and found syringes, including one
filled to capacity. He rubbed the back of his neck and
wondered if that needle had been used on him. Three

of the small bottles, the kind a doctor plunges a needle into, were labeled, *Perc, SP,* and *Rohy.* Under a half-full bottle, Chapa found a list of drugs with various amounts assigned to each. A medicinal cocktail recipe—a pinch of this, two drops of that, mix well, inject into victim.

He also found some gauze and suture tucked along-side a pair of surgical scissors. At the bottom, he discovered some medical clamps and a larger, unlabeled bottle that was half filled with a clear liquid.

Chapa was reaching inside the trunk for the bottle when a noise stopped him. It was not like the one he'd heard when he was listening through the door. This was more of a shuffling sound that came from back in the far darkness, not too close, but definitely somewhere in the apartment. Maybe a pet moving around, or a breeze sneaking through an open window. Maybe something else.

He took the shade off the lamp and used it like a low grade flashlight to scan the room until he found what he was looking for. There was a light switch on the dividing wall between the kitchen and a hallway that led to the rooms.

After putting the lamp back on the desk, Chapa returned the tackle box to the trunk, then quickly moved across the room and flipped the switch on. A single bulb that should have been replaced long ago illuminated much of the walls and most of the floor, but left the corners and far end of the hall to the imagination.

He looked back toward the front door and confirmed that it was locked, though the deadbolt had not been turned and the chain lock dangled freely. The floor creaking beneath his feet, Chapa started down the hall.

The first door on his right opened to a small bathroom. A single beige towel hung over the shower curtain. Chapa pressed his hand to it and found it was damp. He pulled the curtain back, revealing an empty tub, but the scattered drops of water clinging to the porcelain suggested it had been used earlier that same day.

Chapa left the bathroom light on as he continued down the hall. He stopped about halfway down, at a narrow closet door on his left. Inside he found a single empty hanger.

The bedrooms would be at the far end of the hall, one on each side, just like they had been down in Annie's place. A pungent smell was coming from that end of the apartment.

Standing between the two closed doors for a moment, Chapa tried to quiet his thoughts and listen for any sound. He heard nothing. Remembering the layout of the other apartment, Chapa decided to check out the room on his left, the one that corresponded with Annie's bedroom, first. The smell hit him full on as soon as he opened the door. Not being able to see anything inside increased the putrid odor's impact.

It was a combination of sulfur and rotting food, blended with a bleachy medicinal tinge. The windows were covered with thick dark curtains, and the only light he could find had to fight its way through a filthy ceiling fixture that was caked with dead insects. Several black garbage bags, some filled to the breaking point, others no more than halfway, were strewn around the room in no particular fashion.

Chapa assumed they were the source of the smell, but decided to leave that for the cops to confirm. A large slab of wood, longer than a door and just as wide, rested on a pair of sawhorses. The makeshift table was stained various shades of brown and red with a few white splotches mixed in.

More pieces of hardware, including a couple of saws, a set of screwdrivers, and a length of chain were scat-

tered across the table. A navy blue ski mask that
could've been the one Chapa had seen the gunman
wearing in the holdup video had been casually tossed
beside the tools, but there was no gun on the table.

At the end closest to him, several unmarked gallon
bottles were lined up behind a series of paint trays.
Chapa picked up one of the bottles, unscrewed the cap,
and took a whiff. Rubbing alcohol.

He noticed one item that was out of place with everything else on the table. It was the photo of Mikey that
had disappeared from his wallet while he'd been unconscious. Chapa picked up the child's picture and
slipped it into his shirt pocket without giving a damn
about fingerprints or any other possible evidence.

The wall above the work area was covered with newspaper and magazine stories. Time had yellowed many
of them, others appeared to have been photocopied.
The oldest and most brittle was Chapa's original piece
that ran the morning after Grubb's capture. Annie's
name had been circled in black pencil, and the newspaper story was neatly taped in place, next to a page out
of a *TV Guide* from the late-nineties that listed a cable
documentary on Kenny Lee Grubb.

There were several other photos on the wall, including one of a man Chapa recognized as Officer Pete
Rudman. In the picture Rudman was mowing the front
lawn of a simple ranch home, apparently unaware that
someone was watching. Two additional photos of an unsuspecting Rudman showed him coming out of a grocery store with his wife, and casually getting in a few
holes of golf.

Chapa now realized, maybe for the first time, that
staying with the Kenny Lee Grubb story all of those
years had probably saved his life. Dominic Delacruz had
been murdered, and Pete Rudman's death certainly deserved another look. He didn't want to think about

Annie already being dead, but knew it was more than a possibility. So there it was, like a circle formed by connecting the dots. The girl, the store owner, the cop, and he had to place himself in that group, the reporter. Chapa was still alive only because Grubb wanted him to finish telling the story. What had Grubb said to him a few days ago? *The circle will be complete.*

He spotted four more of his stories taped to the wall. After a couple of minutes of searching for his byline, and trying to make some sense out of something only a lunatic could understand, Chapa realized he was making a mistake by getting drawn into the grizzly display. He forced himself to turn away and examine the rest of the room.

The wall-length closet at the other end was closed, and Chapa decided to leave it that way. Getting to it would mean stepping around one of the garbage bags, and over another, and the foul combination of odors was starting to get to him. His senses were still torqued from the buzz of navigating that ledge. Everything was keen and right on the surface.

Chapa left the room and shut the door tightly behind him. The smell had clawed up into his nose and seemed to be following him closer than his own shadow. He walked over to the other door and turned the knob without hesitation.

Locked.

He tried it again to make sure it wasn't just jammed, but it would not budge. He jiggled it up and down. The lock felt new, but had some give to it. A few years earlier Chapa had written a series on the various techniques that criminals regularly used. It earned him an award, but the recognition did not land him the raise he'd expected. The trophy itself, a gold hand clutching a quill, served as a paperweight for several months until he finally tossed it in a box with the others. But now he would finally get something of value from that experience.

He tapped on the door and determined it had a hollow core. This would not take long. Chapa stepped back, then slammed his foot into the thin wood, just a few inches from the knob. He didn't worry about the mess or noise. What's a flimsy door after you've already scattered the living room window all over the floorboards?

The second time, he heard the wood around the lock begin to crack. His third kick sent the door swinging open. As the light from the hall made its way inside, Chapa could see that this room was different from any he had ever been in. The high voltage sensation was still jetting through his system, but now there was something else happening too.

Instincts or intuition, whatever its name, was telling him that things here were even more twisted than he could imagine.

He reached through the splintered door frame and groped around for the switch, determined to get a better look before going any farther. When he found it, Chapa hesitated for a moment, then flipped the switch, and light filled the room.

Chapa stood fixed in the doorway, trying to decide whether to step into the room or get out of that apartment as fast as his bruised and adrenaline fueled body would allow him to.

CHAPTER 69

All four of the walls had been painted a deep shade of red. It was a thick glossy coat that reflected the overhead light and gave the impression of a fresh bleed. Chapa looked inside before entering.

The center of the room was completely empty, as though it had been hollowed out. But that was not the case with the walls. This place lacked the other room's rancid smell, but it was replaced by a heavy stillness that was every bit as uncomfortable. The stale air embraced Chapa the moment he stepped through the doorway.

He studied the carefully spaced rectangles that lined the walls. There were nine of them in all—three along the wall that led from where he was standing to a closet door, three more across the room, two on the wall directly to his right. There was just one, perfectly centered, on the back wall.

As he walked toward the nearest one on his left, Chapa saw these were not merely flat collages inside rectangular frames. Each of the nine wall hangings was a small medicine cabinet. The mirrors had been covered with photos and drawings of children.

A yellow-haired boy, about the age of nine, looked

out at him from a photo on the first cabinet. His blue eyes perched above cheeks full of freckles. He was standing in front of a playground and seemed confused that someone was taking his picture. The child appeared more at ease in the other two. He had a kind, winsome smile as he stood there in the clothes his mother had picked out for him that morning.

Chapa did not have to wonder if the boy would ever get the chance to grow up, and he began thinking of this room as a streamlined version of the trailer tour. When he opened the cabinet he knew it was something far worse.

The latch was tight and Chapa had to give it a firm pull before the mirrored door swung open. Inside, on the second of three narrow shelves, he found two shirt buttons matching ones in the photos. A small toy truck that the boy had been holding in the pictures sat on the bottom shelf.

Chapa gently placed a finger on top of the toy and pushed it the length of the shelf. It clickety-clacked all the way across and he imagined how much the child must have loved that sound.

Extending just beyond the edge of the top shelf was a newspaper clipping. It detailed the search for James Allen, age eight, who had been missing for two days. This had to be one of the children Grubb told him about.

As he closed the cabinet door, Chapa saw a face reflected in the mirror. He quickly turned around, but found no one there. His imagination had conspired with the images on the other walls to send a rock-hard bolt through his system.

This was not a place for browsing. He needed to get moving. The next cabinet had pictures of a solemn-faced little girl whose dark frizzy hair had gotten the better of her brush that morning.

A drawing of a child who bore a passing resemblance to the girl was included among the snapshots. Waiting for him inside was a sock and a bracelet. Chapa didn't bother with her newspaper clipping. He already knew what it was from the first one he'd read. Those stories were always the same. At first hopeful and desperate, but ultimately tragic and devastating.

The boy in the next series of photos had nothing in common with the little girl. He was smiling and playful, sticking his tongue out at the camera in one of the shots. Unruly strands of light brown hair poked out from underneath his baseball cap. Two rocks rested on the bottom shelf of his collection. A piece of paper, wrinkled and curling up at the edges, had been placed on the middle shelf. It was a drawing, a self-portrait of the little boy. Chapa could feel his heart breaking, then noticed the red crayon inscription in the bottom right corner. *For my new friend Mr. Grubb.*

Chapa slammed the door shut with so much force the whole thing shook against the wall. At that moment he wanted to punish someone, to avenge the world of hurt that Kenny Lee Grubb and his gruesome followers had inflicted on so many innocents and the adults who loved them more than life itself.

He was certain now that Annie was gone. Her cruel life reduced to butchered remains and trinkets in a madman's trophy collection. But Chapa also knew that if he was right about Annie, his hunt would not end until every one of the monsters responsible was found, tried, and executed.

His stomach was churning even worse than before. Turning in the direction of the remaining units, Chapa decided it was best to not imagine what they might be hiding, let alone continue his search. The closet door was less than ten feet away, but first Chapa wanted to check out the one cabinet that had been given a special place on its own wall.

Chapa had a pretty good idea whose pictures would be on it.

CHAPTER 70

There were four photos of Annie, and it was clear she had no idea someone was watching her when they were taken. Two seemed recent, while the others were a couple of years older.

He hesitated before forcing the cabinet door open. Annie would be the prize of this collection—the room had been painted in her honor—and that meant the souvenirs of her death would likely be the most personal.

What he found inside surprised him, not because of how horrible it was, but rather, how ordinary. Bright orange hair lined the bottom shelf, reminding him of the way Jimmy had died.

A red journal, the same one that Louise Jones dedicated to Annie, sat on the middle shelf. Chapa wanted to flip through it, but that would have to wait. That shelf also contained a black drawing pencil, and a small piece of soft pink cloth. It had been cut or torn away from a larger section without much care, and bits of thread dangled from uneven edges.

There wasn't a newspaper cutout anywhere in the cabinet, so he ran his fingers along the top shelf until they found something cold and sharp. He closed his hand around the small object and brought it closer. It was an apartment key, most likely Annie's.

Chapa slipped it into the pocket of his sports coat and reached for his phone as he walked across the room toward the closet. Explaining the reasons for his being here to Andrews was no longer on his list of top ten concerns.

With the phone in his right hand, he reached for the knob with his left, but stopped when he noticed the closet door was not shut evenly. The lower third was bowing out, as though something was putting a great deal of pressure against it.

Chapa took a step back and gripped the knob. It did not turn easily, whatever was pressing against the inside of the closet door had jammed the latch. After a quarter turn, he heard the thick snap of a bolt pulling free, and the door swung open on its own.

The first thing he saw was the well-worn bottom of a woman's tennis shoe, and an ankle that had been bound to the wooden leg of a chair. Both belonged to Annie Sykes, and she was not moving.

CHAPTER 71

The chair lay tipped on its side, which explained the pressure against the door, as well as that loud noise Chapa had heard when he was outside the apartment.

"Annie, it's Alex Chapa. You're going to be okay."

She did not respond.

Chapa slipped his phone back into his pants pocket, then reached around the backrest with one arm while wrapping the other across the front of her shoulders. She was heavier than he expected, and as he pulled the chair to a sitting position it became clear why.

Annie's ankles were fixed to the legs of the simple chair with what appeared to be a small belt, and her hands were bound behind her back in the same way. Her mouth had been duct taped shut. But that's not what captured Chapa's attention.

Two thick chains led down from both sides of a dog collar that had been tightly fitted around her neck. Chapa followed the chains to where they disappeared under the chair. Squatting to get a look at the setup, he saw that a padlock was holding it all together beneath the seat.

He checked to make sure it was locked, which it was. The collar resembled the one Chapa had seen the DA introduce as evidence at Grubb's trial, except this one was wider and thicker.

"Annie, can you hear me?"

He touched the side of her neck, just below the jaw line and above the collar. A pulse rose to meet his fingers.

"Come on, Annie, I'm going to get you out of this chair."

Peeling the tape from her mouth was difficult, and Chapa stopped when tears began tracking down Annie's cheeks and onto his fingers. Since it didn't seem to be affecting her breathing, Chapa decided to leave the tape for her to remove.

"Annie, I'm going to unbuckle the collar, and it might get just a little bit tighter at first, but I'll do this as quickly and gently as I can, and then you and I will get the hell out of here. Okay?"

He waited for any sort of reaction, but none came. Annie's eyes were half-open, and she appeared to be conscious. Chapa softly pressed his hand to her face. She was warm, almost feverish.

"Can you hear me? Were you drugged?"

Nothing.

He went to work on the collar, careful to not let the chain links that were wrapped around its side dig any deeper into Annie's neck. The buckle grabbed a pinch of skin as Chapa turned it just enough to loosen the leather tongue and slip it through, but Annie did not react.

The process was slow and entirely out of sync with Chapa's sense of urgency. The prong proved even more stubborn, but he steadily worked it free, then wasted no time opening the collar and peeling it away from Annie's skin.

Her neck was lined with ugly and uneven indentations where the collar or chains had tried to gnaw into

Annie's flesh. He carefully ran a finger along one of the marks. The bruising had already begun.

Chapa thought about all of the work and time he had spent trying to find Annie to warn her, and everything he had gone through. And still, here she was, on the eve of Grubb's execution, drugged up and either near death or at least scheduled for it. Just as Grubb and his minions had planned all along. Chapa had failed.

"I'm sorry this happened to you, Annie."

He slid the chair out of the closet a few feet so he could get to her wrists. Those were fastened in place with a smaller collar. Chapa shifted her hands just a bit, and unbuckled it. But even after they were free, Annie's hands remained in place.

Clutching her elbows, Chapa gradually brought Annie's arms around and folded them across her lap, like a father with a sleeping child who had half fallen out of bed. Her right arm was red, probably from landing on it when the chair tipped over.

Chapa was calculating how he could carry her out of the apartment. Annie was fairly slight, and should not be too heavy. Once free, he planned to take her straight to the elevator, then out the door and into his car. He would then create as much distance from this place as possible, and put a call in to Andrews.

But first he had to release her from the chair. The belt around her left ankle had been pulled at least one notch too tight, and its buckle turned toward the back of the chair, making it harder to reach. Chapa blindly picked at it until he finally determined there was no gentle way of doing this. He yanked the tongue back hard, and freed the prong.

Annie hadn't made a sound.

"After I undo the buckle around your right ankle, I'm going to help you up. You'll need to stand," Chapa said, looking up at her as he shifted to the other side. "I'm hoping you'll be able to—"

Something was different.

He sat up and looked into her eyes, searching for some sort of recognition, but saw something else. Annie's eyes grew wide, wider than he would have imagined they could. She didn't say anything. She didn't have to.

They were not alone.

From somewhere behind him Chapa heard the floor creak like a thin off-key note played on a busted instrument. Annie continued to gaze into some great beyond as Chapa slowly stood.

Even before he began his deliberate turn in the direction of the door, Chapa already knew who would be standing there.

CHAPTER 72

Two hours earlier

Annie tore herself away from the newspaper she was reading to retrieve the Pop Tart that her toaster had just spit out. It was far from an ideal breakfast, but she planned to give them up soon and start that exercise routine she read about last year.

She'd slept well, no dreams to remember. A good thing. A blessing, after everything that had gone down the night before. Three hours of questioning by the FBI and the possibility of a threat on her life had earned Annie a small rectangle of comfort food.

Only two bites were missing from the pastry when someone knocked on her door. That didn't happen very often, few people knew where she lived. The cops?

Looking through the peephole, it took Annie a few seconds to recognize the smiling face on the other side.

"Langdon?"

She unfastened the various locks without hesitation, then opened the door.

"What are you doing here? Did you read in the paper about what happened last night?"

"No, but it's great to see you, Angie."

She gave him a firm, friendly hug. That's all it was, nothing more, never had been.

"C'mon in, I was just hanging out. What time does your store open?"

Annie stepped away from the door, but Langdon did not budge.

"Thanks, but I've got something really exciting to show you upstairs."

"What's upstairs?"

"A surprise. I've gotten my own place here in your building."

Langdon was always upbeat, but Annie thought he seemed a bit more so today. Could be business was going well. The last time she'd seen him his store was becoming quite popular, and Internet and mail order sales of clothing and accessories were growing. Or maybe he was just one of those annoying morning people.

"I'm using the apartment for work, mostly. C'mon, I'll show you."

Annie tugged at her oversize sweatshirt.

"I'm not exactly dressed to go out."

"We're just going upstairs."

She threw on a pair of slippers. Her keys were somewhere in the kitchen.

"You won't need them Angie, we'll just run up there for a minute," Langdon said then reached across and flipped the lock so it wouldn't bolt. "There, now you don't have to go scrounging around for your keys. C'mon, I want you to see what I'm working on."

"A new design?"

"You'll see."

She nodded, and closed the door behind her. There was something odd about the way Langdon was acting. They were never truly close, but she did consider him a friend, though they had not seen each other in some time. Still, leaving her door unlocked would give Annie an excuse for cutting the visit short if she wanted to.

Annie was never a big fan of Langdon's designs, though she had bought a few of his things, mostly to be supportive, and agreed to pose for a series of ad photos. She had always been a little self-conscious about the framed picture of her displayed in Langdon's store, but he had explained that it could have the added benefit of helping generate some business for her artwork. That hadn't happened so far. In fact, as far as Annie could tell, the only person Langdon had ever sent her way was Alex Chapa.

She meant to ask Langdon about that, but he did all the talking on the way up to the seventh floor and down the hall to 7G. Annie thought it odd that the only thing Langdon wanted to talk about was his business.

"I'm planning on achieving a long term goal very soon."

"I'm thrilled for you, Donnie. I know how hard you've worked at your art."

Langdon smiled a bit too broadly and keyed the lock.

The apartment was dark. The only light came from one of the bedrooms, except for a shred of sunlight forcing its way in through a narrow slit in the living room curtains. But she recognized the layout as being not too different from her own.

Annie noticed the work table and mattress.

"Have you been here a while?"

"Not too long."

He was digging around a large old trunk that sat on the floor.

"Go ahead and check out what I've done with the room at the end of the hall, the one on the right. I think you'll be impressed."

Annie started down the hall, but something wasn't

right. She looked back at the front door. Langdon wasn't by the trunk anymore.

"Donnie?"

"Go ahead, I'll be there in just a moment."

That sense that something is wrong, a child's sense of danger, the same one that told Annie to run to safety on a cold black night so many years before, was beginning to take hold of her now. *Make an excuse to leave, Annie.*

Each step down that hall was taking her farther away from where she wanted to go—out the door, down the steps, and back to the comfort of her own apartment. Why was she reacting this way? She'd never felt threatened around Donnie before, but there was something strange about the way he was acting today. Something wasn't right.

The smell hit her in nauseating waves when she was just a few feet from the end of the hall. It seemed to be coming from behind the closed door on the left. She turned to go back, but Langdon was right behind her.

"Sorry about the odor. The previous tenants weren't the best housekeepers."

Still smiling, he put a hand on Annie's back and nudged her toward the room where the light was coming from. She had spent all of her teen years and adult life waging war on the marrow-deep fear that Kenny Lee Grubb had injected into her.

Annie told herself, *There is nothing here to be afraid of, Donnie is a friend.* But why would he need a workshop when he had plenty of space in the backroom of his store? And why would a *friend* wait so long to let her know they shared a building? It was clear that he'd been here for some time.

Who was Donnie Langdon, anyhow? How much did she really know about this man who had darted around the edges of her life since she moved away from home?

How had she met him? That's right, they seemed to always be at the same places and events. He introduced himself to her as a fellow artist, and took a great interest in Annie's work. She found that flattering, but he also asked a lot of questions about her personal life and background. Annie had never been bothered by that. Langdon had a way of easing into and through difficult subjects. Annie had never given that much thought, really. Until now.

Who was Donnie Langdon?

Adrenaline was punching its way through Annie. But she couldn't let it take hold, she couldn't let it show. She refused to surrender to an undefined fear.

Then she stepped inside the room. Annie felt the red walls rush in on her, and saw the pictures on the cabinets.

"What are these, Donnie? What have you done?"

As she turned to face him Langdon wrapped his arm around her shoulders. In a flash of brown cloth, movement, and force, he covered her nose and mouth with a moist hand towel. The more Annie struggled, the harder Langdon pressed the wet cloth against her face. She tried to bite his hand, but got a mouthful of drug-soaked towel for her troubles. Its medicinal smell washed over Annie until she couldn't fight anymore.

Langdon was standing over her when she awoke, bound to a chair in the middle of the room. He was looking at Annie like a lover who had awakened a few minutes earlier than his partner following a night of passion, as he wadded up a small, greasy old rag, shoved it deep into her mouth, and sealed it with several long strips of duct tape.

"Look at this."

He had a drawing in his hands of a small boy with a troubled look on his face and a slump in his shoulders.

"He has been rendered. They all have."

Annie recognized the drawing, the others too, they were all hers. Pictures of the sad children from her dreams.

"Little demons, who won't get the chance to grow up and become killers. Preventive law enforcement, that's what Mr. Grubb called it."

No, not killers, Donnie. Victims. They haunt my sleep. Ever since that night—

"Just like you. Mr. Grubb knew you would grow up to become a killer, just like all those other little monsters whose families he spared the horror of seeing what they had created."

Victims.

Tears slid down Annie's cheeks.

"C'mon now. You fulfilled your destiny. By drawing them you helped destroy these little demons."

She tried to scream through the filthy rag in her mouth, but it came out as a low-pitched grunt.

"At first, I didn't know how to find the right children," Langdon said, then leaned in close. "I don't have Mr. Grubb's gift. But then I saw your drawings, and I understood everything."

Annie tried to scream again, but Langdon poured a clear liquid on the brown towel and once again pressed it to her face. When she regained consciousness, Langdon was dragging the chair and her with it across the floor.

"Okay, here's the problem, Lorn was supposed to pick up some tarps and garbage bags, but you went and got him shot. So I have to run out for a short while."

Something was gripping her neck, and she heard a clanging sound competing with the noise of the chair scrapping across the wood floor.

"Don't worry, Red. I'll be back before you know it."

He steadied the chair, then pushed it the rest of the way into the closet. When she tried to move her head,

Annie knew right then what was around her neck. Then she looked down and saw the chains.

Just before the door blocked out the light from beyond, Langdon leaned in so close that Annie could feel his breath on her face. Still smiling, he slid along the side of her cheek until his lips brushed against her ear.

And then he whispered, "Sit in one place Annie, motionless, still, like an object. Until someone comes and sets you free."

In an instant, she felt all of the hope, and confidence, and courage, as well as everything good that had blossomed from those strengths she had worked so hard to cultivate, drain right out of her. It all cascaded down the chains and seeped through the floorboards below.

Sit in one place Annie, motionless, still, like an object. Until someone comes and sets you free.

Eyes closed, she began a slow drift down into an endless cavern, until a knock on a faraway door pulled her back like rescuer's grip. Was it Langdon? Then a voice, muffled by walls and distance. Then nothing.

Annie was fading away again when the voice returned. This time she recognized it. How had Alex Chapa found her? She tried to call out, but couldn't. Then she had another idea. Maybe Langdon hadn't shut the closet door all the way.

She started rocking from side to side, hoping to tip toward the door and use her weight to force it open. But Annie miscalculated the third time she swayed to the right, away from the door. The weight of her body combined with the chains pulled her down, and the chair slammed to the floor.

Much of the weight had landed on Annie's right arm, and pain rifled through her shoulder and down her back. The fall had made her even more light-headed than before. Clouds began to gather.

Annie lay motionless, refusing to close her eyes, but still allowing herself to go for a long stroll deep into that endless cave.

CHAPTER 73

He crowded the doorway, the embodiment of confidence, as though he owned not only the room itself, but even the lifeless air inside it.

"You picked a very good day to stop by, Alex."

Donald Langdon seemed to have filled out a bit, and had much more presence than when Chapa had met him back at his store. The fact that he was clutching an eight-inch knife added to the overall effect.

Chapa pointed at the weapon.

"Let me guess, it's got one of your fucked-up designs on the handle."

Langdon grinned.

"Just like the one they pried out of Lorn Strasser's hand last night, right?"

The grin vanished in an instant.

"I feel like an idiot for not having recognized it then," Chapa added, then looked back at Annie who did not return the glance.

"Lorn was a valuable partner. Pure id."

Langdon was wearing a simple blue shirt, slacks, and a pair of latex gloves.

"Was that his real name?"

"I don't know, that never mattered to me. I met him online two years ago, we were both chatting about Mr. Grubb. We soon realized we had . . . *mutual interests,*" Langdon said with a smile that seemed as natural as taking a breath. "After a few months of emails and messaging the two of us finally got together at a truck stop along I-80. Once he knew who I was we began talking about how we could make the world a better place."

Chapa wished he had taken some sort of weapon from the tool box in the living room, or the work table in the room next door.

"You didn't seem surprised to see me there in the doorway."

"I wasn't."

Chapa weighed his few legitimate options.

"How did you know?"

If Langdon made the first move, Chapa would see this through until one of them was no longer breathing.

"I walked past the mailman on the way in. Saw one of your tangled designs on an envelope. Then another one out there in the living room, along with that magazine you cut an article out of. I saw the missing story, along with Annie's photo framed on a wall in your store."

Langdon looked down and nodded.

"I've been spending more time here lately, doing more work out of this place so I can keep an eye on Red as the time neared." As he spoke, Langdon slowly drifted away from the doorway, either daring Chapa to make a move for it, or hoping he would. Or perhaps both. "You made quite a mess of my living room."

"So what happens now? You try to carve me up and then perform a ritual sacrifice on Annie?"

Langdon seemed surprised.

"You're not supposed to be here, but you did see the archives. Didn't you understand?"

He waited for Chapa to respond, but the reporter switched to interview mode. In this case, that didn't mean hitting Langdon with a barrage of questions that might put him even more on the defensive, or hasten an attack. The key was letting him talk his way into something of a comfort zone while Chapa figured out what to do next.

"Mr. Grubb hoped you would write about all of this in a truthful way. But maybe this is even better. You're going to be able to give your readers a firsthand account."

"So you're not planning on getting away with it."

"Of course I am. See, I'm your source, and you'll protect me."

Apparently Langdon had confused client-attorney privileges with something having to do with reporters.

"That's not how it works. Besides, the cops will be all over this place."

"Why, did you call them?"

If Chapa thought Langdon might run, he would've lied and said "yes." But he knew Langdon wasn't going anywhere.

"No, I didn't," Chapa said and noticed how Annie responded to his words with a narrow shudder. "But the broken window, the smell in the other room. They'll be here, they'll find you."

"The place is rented in Strasser's name, and it won't take me more than an hour to remove everything that could be traced back to me."

So far Chapa had not taken the bait, and he'd resisted making any sort of move for the door, but this would not last much longer. If one of Annie's ankles wasn't still fastened to the chair, he could grab the piece of thrift store furniture and use it the way a lion tamer would against a rabid animal.

"And what about all this?" Chapa extended his arms like a realtor trying to sell an upscale house.

"I come in here, to this room, for inspiration."

Langdon's tone had shifted, and he spoke like a celebrity who was the subject of a magazine profile. "I probably wouldn't have taken some of the artifacts that Lorn did, but everybody has their kink."

"Where are the bodies?"

"I suppose they're buried all over the Midwest." Langdon smirked and shrugged. "But that's Strasser's department. You'll have to ask him yourself sometime."

"So you were more or less the brains behind all this."

Langdon offered a long silent stare, and Chapa knew he was being sized up.

"I suppose you could put it that way, though Lorn could be hard to manage sometimes. Like I said, not a lot of self-control there."

"Is that what explains his killing my bird?"

"What can I tell ya, Lorn didn't much care for small animals."

Chapa leaned against the wall by one of the medicine cabinets and casually looked to see how it had been hung in place.

"How long ago did you find Annie?"

"I began tracking her when she still lived at home," Langdon said through a small, tortured laugh. "Getting close to her was easier once she moved to the city. I even became her friend."

Langdon took a long stride in Annie's direction, extending the knife toward her pale face.

"Isn't that right, Red?"

Chapa struggled against the urge to rush him.

"Donnie," Chapa said is a crisp staccato voice meant

to draw Langdon away from Annie. It worked, at least for the moment. "Why these children? How did Lorn choose them?"

Langdon—calm, confident—narrowed the distance between himself and Chapa by a couple of steps.

"That was Red's doing, she chose them."

Chapa didn't let his confusion show, and instead nodded as though all of this madness somehow made sense to him.

"What do you mean, *she* chose the victims?"

"It was her drawings of children. She once told me how she had seen them in dreams. I knew right away that it was a message, so I began searching for someone else who understood. Someone who could find the children in those drawings. Shouldn't you be writing this down or recording it?"

"Don't worry, I won't forget any of this." Chapa, stone-faced, cold.

"I made copies of her drawings and sent them to Lorn. He tracked down the creatures."

"Did he kill Dominic Delacruz?"

The question seemed to nudge Langdon out of the moment and a new expression was cast on the man's face. *Not self-confidence*, Chapa thought, *something worse—pride*.

"Would you believe I actually doubted that I would be able to do it? I've wanted that man dead for a long time."

Chapa was looking for an opening, an edge, even the slimmest chance to make his move.

"For weeks Strasser and I took turns driving all the way out there until we'd nailed down his routine. I could've killed him a dozen times at his house. But it needed to be done at the store."

"Why? Dominic Delacruz was a good man."

"He gave shelter to the beast," Langdon said and

looked over at Annie. "He should've seen Red for what she was, what she still is, and thrown her back into the night."

"And Louise?"

It took Langdon a moment to recognize the name.

"Oh, yeah, that was Red's fault. She told me about that crazy old woman once, how she had confided in her, talked to her about me. When Lorn followed you to her house we realized she had become a problem."

"I see, Louise was crazy, but not you," Chapa said, gradually raising his voice with each syllable, hoping the neighbors were home and that the walls were not too thick. "No, not the fucking psycho bastard responsible for the deaths of all these children."

Langdon tried to get a word in, but Chapa was not about to slow down.

"Not you, not the goddamned freak who has an innocent woman chained up to a chair as a way of honoring a condemned serial killer."

Chapa stopped, but not because he had no more to say. It was the way Langdon was laughing, as though he was the only one who was in on a big joke.

"Alex, man, you've got to get a whole lot smarter."

"Listen to me, Annie, I need you to reach down and undo the buckle and free your right ankle."

Chapa knew he was taking a chance, but sensed it might be the last time he could make that choice.

"I was about to give you the option of leaving until all this is over, but not now."

"C'mon Annie, you can do this. It's just like when you were a child and—"

Langdon laughed harder, loud enough for anyone next door to hear.

"Weren't you listening before? I told you to write this down. Look, Lorn rendered the little creatures like I told him to, but who do you think told me which ones needed killing?" Langdon stopped laughing and pointed at Annie with the knife. "I'm starting to think Mr. Grubb might've given you way too much credit, Alex."

Chapa coaxed his eyes off Langdon and over to Annie. The expression on her face had changed. It was not the blank stare from before, nor the mask of terror Langdon's entrance had triggered, and it wasn't anything in between.

What Chapa saw in Annie's eyes shook him to the deepest reaches of his soul.

CHAPTER 74

As Chapa thought about how he could disarm the single-minded man with the long knife, he wished he hadn't given up wrestling midway through his sophomore year in order to become the youngest editor in the history of his high school's newspaper.

Chapa had quickly built a small cove in a distant reach of his mind, and there he stored away whatever doubts Langdon had created about Annie. At least for the time being.

"So with Lorn on ice, you had to step in and go after Annie yourself, is that it?"

Langdon tilted his head to one side and looked at Chapa as though he'd never seen him before.

"No. Red was always going to be the exception. The last tribute. My own little demon."

"Annie, I need you to focus right now."

Langdon's face became a tint of raw hostility, his grip on the knife's handle so tight Chapa thought it might snap in his hand.

"Stop it!" Langdon said, taking a decisive step toward Chapa and shaking the weapon at him.

Chapa backed off just enough to get a look behind

the next cabinet. Langdon hadn't bothered to carve out a hole in the plaster to embed the units. They were each held in place by two screws. The first one he'd looked at had been bolted tight against the wall. But this time Chapa saw a small gap.

"This isn't a new thing between Red and me. If you had been a better reporter all those years ago you'd already know that."

Annie started rocking rhythmically—forward and back, forward and back.

"I see I've got your attention now." Langdon moved closer to Annie. "As a child I stood right in front of you, Alex, trying to get you to notice me, but you didn't care."

"I have no memory of that."

"Of course not. You were more interested in talking to my parents, and all of Mr. Grubb's other neighbors. My folks didn't know much about anything, but they knew enough to avoid mentioning that their son delivered the newspaper to Mr. Grubb's house."

Chapa searched his memory and Langdon's face, but came up empty. There had been so many interviews and stories since then.

"Yeah, I probably should've asked you a couple of questions."

"I'm glad you didn't. I might've told you everything and that would have been a mistake. I would've told you all about how Mr. Grubb took me in, and made me feel important. He taught me that some children are evil little demons whose families spend their nights praying for someone to come along and put them in the ground."

Chapa now understood that Langdon and Annie were both Grubb's victims. One got away, the other didn't. He recalled how the police had found comic books and a Game Boy in the basement and assumed those things belonged to a child that Grubb had murdered. But the police had made a mistake.

"Watching her whimper in the dark whenever Mr. Grubb wasn't around, I learned her weaknesses, Red's soft spots, and that made it so easy to work my way into her life," Langdon said. "I remember more about what happened to Red in that basement than she does."

His eyes trained on Annie, Langdon then began speaking with a child's voice.

"*Don't move too much and it won't hurt. Sit in one place Annie, motionless, still, like an object. Until someone comes and sets you free.* I used to whisper that to her from a dark corner of the basement whenever Mr. Grubb left the room. Red was so drugged up most of the time she probably thought the voice was in her head."

"Why would you do that?"

"Because I liked watching her struggle to hold on to a little bit of hope that someone was coming to save her."

Langdon smiled and leaned in toward Chapa like a bar buddy with a secret.

"Did you buy that stuff about Mr. Grubb making me feel important, like he was some father figure?"

Chapa didn't feel a need to respond.

"That's all bullshit. I just enjoyed seeing the terror in those other kids' eyes." Langdon's smile vanished like ice on hot pavement. "But the part about them being demons, that was true. Especially this little monster."

Annie was rocking faster now—forward and back, forward and back.

"I owe this to Mr. Grubb. See, I'm responsible for her being alive."

"Why is that?"

Most of Langdon's attention was now on Annie, and Chapa knew his chance, the only one he would have, was coming very soon.

"I got off on Red's fear because she tried so hard not to show it. That scared Mr. Grubb, and I enjoyed that too. But that afternoon, when he told me he was going to render her and showed me the bottle of fluid, I knew that I didn't want her to stop hurting just yet. So I poured some of it out and replaced it with saline solution."

Langdon shifted the knife in his hand from a stabbing position to one better suited for cutting.

Then he looked at Chapa with eyes that were void of any humanity.

"Watch—"

The fragile distance between Annie and her executioner was thinning with each of Langdon's forceful steps.

In one continuous motion, Chapa reached for the medicine cabinet that he'd been eyeing, and tore it off the wall, taking a slab of plaster with it. Though ripping it free had proven easier than he expected, Chapa had not accounted for the sudden shift in the weight balance. He barely managed to hold on as the cabinet nearly hit the floor and threatened to take him with it. Bent over in a near squat, Chapa looked up at Langdon who was now standing no more than ten feet away and creeping toward him.

"Think long and hard about your next move, Alex."

He didn't have to.

"If you can hear me, Annie, cover your face."

Chapa swung the cabinet up as though it were a golf club, and in an instant the look of confusion on Langdon's face vanished in a shower of broken glass and splintered wood.

The cabinet fell out of Chapa's hands and Langdon tumbled to the floor, but managed to keep his grip on the knife. Chapa lunged for him, but Langdon waved the knife back and forth in front of him, his other hand covering some of the blood that colored his face.

Chapa spun away as the blade sliced through the thick air, no more than an inch from his ribs. Before Chapa could find another weapon, Langdon scrambled to his feet and bore down on him.

Leaving Annie behind was not a choice Chapa wanted to make, but they would both be dead in a hurry if he didn't find a way to defend himself. He backpedaled through the doorway, and Langdon kept coming.

When he reached the bathroom door, Chapa realized he was alone in the hallway. He stopped, imagining the horrible things Langdon could be doing to Annie. But those thoughts were shoved aside when the killer blew through the doorway and closed in on Chapa.

Langdon's face was painted in shades of pale flesh and fresh red like some malevolent clown. His voice was throaty.

"You are going to bleed, Alex. A lot."

CHAPTER 75

The nearest weapon of any kind was thirty feet away, somewhere in that trunk in the living room. Langdon was much closer. Realizing he would never make it, Chapa turned and faced the bloodied madman who was charging down the hall.

Langdon was a frenzied bundle of rage and pain. His neat appearance had vanished, the dark blue shirt matted with even darker bloodstains. But Chapa's focus was on the knife that extended from Langdon's right hand.

The blade was sleek and clean, and if Chapa was going to keep his own blood from getting on it he would have to anticipate the first stab, then make certain there wasn't a second. He stood in the middle of the tight hallway and readied himself.

Chapa made a grab at Langdon's wrist, but missed. He sidestepped as much as the space would allow, but felt the blade bite into his left arm, just above the elbow.

Langdon tumbled forward and to the floor, the knife still in his hand. As Chapa made a move to pin him, Langdon flipped around and tossed him off.

The living room was within reach now, and Chapa scrambled to get to the toolbox. Out of the corner of his eye, he saw the small red dots of blood that were marking the floor with his every move.

He reached the trunk an instant before Langdon's shadow eclipsed the light from the hall. Just as Chapa had feared, the lid was closed. At least it wasn't locked. He threw the lid open as Langdon's grunts filled the room, and grabbed the first thing his hands could grip.

The tackle box was heavier than Chapa remembered, or maybe it just felt that way because the strength was steadily flowing out of his arm. He ignored the howls of pain from the fresh wound as well as the sting from the slightly older one on his back and lifted the heavy tackle box.

There was no time to search for something more conventional, so he swung around with as much force as he could and threw the metal box into Langdon's chest. It struck him just slightly off-center, then crashed to the floor, its contents spilling across the hardwood.

Langdon fell back against a wall, nearly tripping over the mattress, and gasped for air. Chapa made a move for the knife, but Langdon withdrew it a second before he got there and blindsided him, driving a heavy fist into the back of his head.

By the time Chapa managed to scramble into a half-squat, Langdon was rushing toward him again. His only chance was to go for Langdon's knees, and tackle him. The killer would still get a stab in, but with any luck it would only slice flesh and muscle.

He waited for Langdon to be right on him, so he could see where the knife was going. Chapa's body was spring-loaded, ready to absorb the pain and take control of the situation. Once the blade was in his hands, he would kill Langdon. No second thoughts.

Then everything stopped.

Langdon's head jerked back and his neck stiffened

like someone had just shoved an iron rod up his ass and kept pushing till it reached the base of his brain. He stood there frozen in place, a wax figure in a house of horrors, so lifelike, yet not entirely convincing. Chapa held his position, crouched in full-on attack mode as Langdon took a couple of involuntary steps to the side, in the direction of nowhere.

Annie was standing behind him, still holding the hypodermic which was now empty except for the single drop that clung to the tip of the needle. The duct tape dangled from her right cheek, her left cheek raw and red. She was breathing heavily through her mouth.

In an instant, Langdon got his bearings back and threw himself at Chapa, who was ready for him. Chapa took a snap step to his right, then drove his shoulder into unprotected ribs as Langdon passed, sending him spinning and falling out of control in the direction of the window.

Unable to slow his movement, Langdon slammed into the window frame and the momentum sent his upper body through the shattered opening.

As Langdon lay there across the sill, his head outside the window, his feet planted to the floor, Chapa scrambled to find something in the scatter from the tackle box that he could use as a weapon. He settled on a length of chain and waited for Langdon to rise up and make his move.

And waited.

"Is he dead?" Annie's voice, an uneven mix of hope and fear.

Chapa was just glad to hear the sound of it again.

"I don't think so."

Slowly, Chapa moved in on the wounded animal. The links were coiled tight against his knuckles, leaving a two-foot pendulum of steel swinging from side to side with each cautious step.

He was no more than four feet from the window when he saw why Langdon was not moving. A triangular shard of glass had pierced his back and gone all the way through. Three blood-soaked inches were sticking out just under his left shoulder. He was pinned in place.

Chapa remembered how that ledge was lined with jagged glass stilettos after he had fallen through it, and wondered how many of those had sliced their way into Langdon.

"We can't leave him like that," Annie said and meant it.

Langdon was making a desperate gurgling sound and it wasn't clear whether he was trying to speak, or even if he was still conscious.

"Drop the knife and I'll help you," Chapa said as he got closer than good sense told him he should. "You're going to die, otherwise."

Langdon instead raised the knife and waved it at him. A dying animal whose only remaining instinct was to kill. His head jerked unevenly, as though his neck was hardening concrete.

"This is over, just give up the knife, Langdon."

Chapa extended his free hand until his fingertips rubbed up against the side of Langdon's knuckles. His hold on the knife remained firm, but that couldn't last. Chapa had just about wrapped his fingers around the handle when Langdon jerked it free and started flailing at him.

The tip of the blade clipped Chapa's palm, but as he stepped away he realized Langdon wasn't looking at him. Langdon's eyes, like his hatred, were fixed on Annie. He was still glaring at her even after all of the fight was gone from his body.

CHAPTER 76

Annie cupped her hand over the phone before Chapa could finish punching in Andrews' number.

"We've got to talk first."

"It can probably wait."

"No, it can't," she said and pointed at Langdon's motionless body, "but he can."

"Annie, trust me, I have to do this."

She nodded and stepped away. As Chapa made the call, he noticed Annie looking around the room like she was seeing it for the first time.

"Don't touch anything." Andrews was more shaken than angry, but Chapa knew that would change by the time he got there. "I'm already on the move and I'm bringing my team with me, so don't call anyone else. And for goodness sake, don't do anything crazy."

Too late, Chapa thought, looking down at the knife he'd pried out of Langdon's still warm hand. Chapa had been anxious to let go of the weapon the moment he touched it. It was the first time he had ever seen a blade with his blood on it.

"I assume you're going to need medical help up there."

"Yes," Chapa said, thinking about Annie, then himself, but not Langdon.

Annie was standing by him again when he finished
his brief conversation with Andrews. He put the knife in
the tackle box and took it along as she led him back to
her apartment. Easing down the steps, Chapa surveyed
his wounds, trying to not be too obvious about it. With
Langdon incapacitated, Chapa's thoughts returned to
what he'd said about Annie being a part of it. Chapa
didn't believe Langdon, he knew better.

Annie stopped at her door for a moment before she
remembered it was unlocked.

"Seems like a long time since I was last here."

Chapa was thinking the same thing, but opted not to
tell Annie yet that he'd been in her apartment.

"We probably should've stayed upstairs, Annie."

She turned and faced him full on.

"There's something you have to know."

The look on her face was equal parts compassion
and concern. He followed her in and she closed the
door behind him, then locked it.

"Those things Langdon said about my being involved in all of this."

"C'mon Annie, he's insane, I know that."

"It's true."

Those two words had a three-dimensional quality, a
presence that filled the space between them. Chapa
waited for more, there had to be more.

Annie walked over to a file cabinet and pulled out a
thin black portfolio.

"Those were my drawings that he used to find those
kids."

She laid out a series of them on a table, Chapa recognized a couple of the faces from the medicine cabinets.

"But I had no idea he was doing that. I hope you can believe me." Tears began to cloud the softness of her eyes. "I didn't know."

"Of course I believe you, but how?"

"I don't how he got them, maybe he broke in."

"I know how he got in, that's not what I meant," Chapa said, reaching in his pocket to retrieve her key. "I found this in the cabinet that had your pictures on it."

She took the key from him.

"I meant, how did you choose to draw these children in particular?"

"You're going to think I'm crazy, and you'd probably be right."

"Doubt it. After the past few days, I've got a pretty good idea of what crazy looks like, and you're not it."

Annie sank into the couch and buried her face in her hands.

"I see them when I'm asleep."

"In your dreams?"

"Not quite. You know that snapshot of time, just before you wake up, when you sometimes have absolute clarity, and you can see all the truths you've been avoiding?"

Chapa knew.

"They come to me then, their faces. I never told my parents the reason I started taking drawing classes in college was so I could make a record of what they looked like. It felt like I owed it to them."

"How long have you been having these dreams?"

"It started sometime after that night I got away, and I always believed horrible things were going to happen to those children, all of them."

"Is it the same kids over and over again?"

"Sometimes. That's why I started going to see Louise."

"What did she have to say about it?"

"She thought part of me had crossed over that night."

Chapa suppressed a smirk.

"You don't believe that?" Annie asked as though she wasn't ready to except that explanation either, and was hoping Chapa could provide an alternative.

"Nope."

"Any of it?"

Chapa didn't answer. He was locked in on one of the drawings. There was something familiar about the small boy with the ratty hair.

"I know who this is."

"What?" Annie was off the couch in an instant. She came around the table and stood next to him.

"This is Ryan Miller, he was one of Grubb's—"

"Victims," she finished his sentence, staring at her drawing as though she was seeing it for the first time. "I remember their names. My parents tried to hide your stories from me, but I found them. I knew the names after reading them just once. But I never understood why mine was in there with theirs."

Chapa found another familiar face, then another.

"You must have seen the pictures of children that we ran with the story, because you've copied them."

"I don't remember seeing those photos."

"You didn't really forget, either."

She started tipping back, and Chapa put his hands firmly on her shoulders, sensing that if he did not hold on she would crumble, bit by bit.

"You'll be all right now, Annie."

Tears streamed from her eyes as she turned and hugged him in a way that no one had in some time, the way only a child can.

"When Grubb had me, all I ever thought about was my father showing up to rescue me. I couldn't understand what was taking him so long. As far as I was concerned, he was my dad, and he could do anything. But he never came, and I was too young to really understand why."

She looked up at him with a smile which, though genuine, was still laced with pain. "You came for me today."

They hugged again until Chapa could hear the sirens in the distance.

"They're going to ask us a lot questions. They're going to want to know about your drawings. I'll talk to Joseph Andrews about that, he'll be the lead agent."

"I feel like I'm partly responsible for—"

"Nothing, Annie. Not any of it. That's exactly how these monsters malfunction. They're like time bombs walking around just looking for a reason to go off. The Beatles make a record and Charles Manson uses it as an excuse to murder people. The Son of Sam claimed he was taking orders from his neighbor's dog. Donnie Langdon sees some drawings that have nothing to do with him and believes he's receiving a message."

Annie wiped the tears from her face as Chapa turned his attention to another drawing. There was something about this one, a girl about eleven years old, that captured his attention.

Whatever resemblance there might've been to Nikki was mostly in the eyes, though the girl in the drawing had her chin, too. Chapa knew it well—he saw it in the mirror every day.

"When did you draw this?"

"About two weeks ago."

Chapa was focusing on an area in the drawing, just below the child's left ear.

"Is this some sort of a mark, or just shadowing?"

Annie leaned in and studied the girl's face.

"I don't know, I can't tell. I just draw what I remember."

It wasn't Nikki, Chapa knew that. Maybe it was someone Annie had walked past, or seen on that playground down the street. Could be that over time her memories of those original photos of Grubb's victims had faded. Some of the faces captured in uneven shades of black and white had morphed into someone different, unfamiliar.

But seeing this drawing sent a pitch-black wave of fear through him. It's that fear every father knows too well. The one that keeps a father's eyes pinned on a van as it cruises by a front yard where children, his children, are playing. The same fear that prods him out of bed to look in on his kids, double-check the smoke detectors, make sure the doors are locked. And also the one that reminds him from time to time that even if he does everything he can to keep his children safe, it still may not be enough.

In the time since Nikki moved away, those concerns had become more diffused, but no less powerful for Chapa. Now a rough drawing of an unidentified girl had brought those sharp feelings, and the insecurity they carried like a virus, back to the surface. And Chapa knew that fear would always be there. No matter how far away his daughter lived, no matter how old she was.

Five floors down, a team of federal agents was making its way into the building and not being coy about it. Chapa didn't hear them, and it was left to Annie to open the door. He was still lost in the drawing when Andrews walked in.

CHAPTER 77

Outside of Annie's apartment, Andrews was fighting a verbal turf war with a Chicago cop. He had already won the debate, the feds almost always do, but he was letting the captain get his two cents in. It was his way of giving a fellow officer an opportunity to save face.

"He's pissed at you," Chapa said once Andrews had sent the guy to the sidelines.

"Baum's a good man, he'll get over it. Quite a mess up there."

"Have you found out what's causing that smell?"

"We're still working on that, but I have a feeling some animals in this neighborhood have gone missing lately."

Chapa sighed. "Strasser," he said under his breath.

"Let's just say that apartment won't be going back on the market anytime soon."

"I think while you're up there you might find a reason to revisit the Rudman murder." Chapa was feeling lightheaded as he slumped against a wall.

"The EMTs have patched you up as best as they can for now," Andrews said. "But this time you are going to the hospital."

"Not before Annie."

She looked over at Chapa from the other side of the room where she was sitting, still answering Sandro's questions, and gave him a tight smile. A minute later the young agent was helping Annie to her feet.

"I'm going to ride with her in the ambulance, Chief," Sandro said.

Chapa wondered if the agent was putting the moves on Annie, and felt oddly protective of her. But after noticing how the guy swaggered for no one in particular, Chapa decided it was just a case of Sandro being Sandro.

Annie walked over to Chapa and gave him another hug, not quite as all-encompassing as the first, but still substantial.

"Take good care your little girl. Be there when she needs you."

Chapa watched her walk away as Sandro hurried to keep pace.

"Tough kid," Andrews said.

"Yeah, she is. But she's fighting a mountain of survivor guilt."

"I can't say I'm surprised."

Chapa was staring at the bloodstains on the shirt he was wearing.

"About these clothes you loaned me."

Andrews reacted as though he had forgotten all about them, then stepped back and surveyed the wreckage. The sports coat was so soiled and torn that he was probably unable to recognize it as anything that could have ever hung in his closet. The shirt, one sleeve having been cut away by EMTs anxious to treat Chapa's wounded arm, resembled the beginnings of a Jackson Pollack painting. The impeccably dressed agent grimaced as he forced himself to look at the slacks, but only got as far as the blood smears across the right front pocket.

"Tell you what, consider this my donation to the Alex Chapa museum. I have no doubt there will be one someday."

"I can have it all dry cleaned."

"No need."

"What about the shirt? A needle and thread and—"

"It's yours."

Chapa could tell Andrews had something else on his mind.

"I am going to need that parking permit back."

"Oh, Joe, I tossed it, you know, back somewhere."

"Funny, I could've sworn I just saw it on the dash of your illegally parked car."

Chapa rubbed his chin as though he was searching for some wisdom, or maybe a way out.

"Hmm. Yeah, how 'bout that."

"You know, Al, with everything that's happened, I could put you away for the rest of your natural life."

"Probably, but then you'd spend the rest of yours searching for a new role model."

Andrews smiled and nodded, then struck his best David Caruso pose. If he'd had a pair of sunglasses with him, he would have put them on for Chapa's benefit.

"You did good, Al." He started to pat Chapa on the shoulder, but thought better of it when his friend flinched. "It was messy, but you got this one right."

Execution Day

CHAPTER 78

Thick, green-gray tubes pushed out through a wall of whitewashed concrete bricks. They led to the gurney, which lay empty and ready in the middle of the execution room.

A large rectangular window separated the witnesses from the instruments that would soon render the condemned. If he stretched forward from where he was sitting on the far left side of the front row of the gallery, Chapa could see the small black video camera directly above the gurney.

Beyond the two-foot square window in the back of the chamber, just above the tubes, sat the technician who would push a series of buttons and end Kenny Lee Grubb's life. The control booth was a hive of activity, and it reminded Chapa of a television studio.

He made a note of that. The only other time Chapa had covered an execution he'd been a last minute replacement, and given very little prep info. As a result, he never managed to get his head around that story, especially when it all turned out to be so anticlimactic. That prisoner was brought in, he said something about speaking to God the night before, and five minutes later society had one less threat to worry about.

This time, however, Chapa was locked in. Annie seemed much less curious about the process. She was silently taking inventory of the whole scene, like a quality control expert who wanted to make certain nothing could go wrong.

The two had not spoken to each other since they were ushered into the witness observation room. The seating area consisted of five rows in all, each a bit more elevated than the one before. Chapa would have preferred to sit farther back, instead of in the front row. But that's where Annie wanted to be, and he had promised to stay right next to her.

Andrews was standing in back, at the opposite end of the room, next to reporters from two other papers, as well as a network TV guy. They all turned and looked when Lance Grubb was shown to his seat in the middle of the first row.

He had a look of absolute resignation on his face, as though he'd known this day would come but had not gotten around to preparing for it. Still, Chapa wondered, there had to be a certain amount of relief now that it was almost over, something that could be a very hard thing for anyone to admit.

Chapa watched as Lance dusted some lint off the dark brown sleeve of his dated sports coat, the one he probably dug out for the occasional wedding or funeral. The condemned's only living sibling then folded his hands on his lap, eyes straightforward. It was as if he was getting ready for church to begin.

Fifteen silent minutes passed before Kenny Lee Grubb was brought in. A last minute attempt at getting a judge to grant a stay based on the self-inflicted wound in Grubb's leg had failed. Though courts had delayed executions in the past based on a prisoner's health issues, the judge in this case determined that since Grubb had no feeling in his injured leg, and therefore no discomfort, there was no justification for putting it off any longer.

From the confines of his wheelchair Grubb looked at the setup and nodded. A trio of muscular guards with dour expressions surrounded him. Then two of them lifted Grubb onto the gurney and strapped him down, as the third one wheeled the chair out of the room. After that, a team of much less physically imposing technicians went to work.

A sheet was pulled over Grubb's body, covering him all the way up to his neck. One of the tubes protruding from the wall was hooked up to his left arm. A tech took the other tube and slid it under the bed sheet, connecting it to a catheter.

The expression on Grubb's face was vacant as an empty grave. He occasionally looked over at the gallery without focusing on anyone in particular. Chapa wondered whether the light from inside the execution room kept Grubb from being able to see beyond the glass.

After they attached a heart monitor, it was places everyone, then the warden stepped forward.

"Kenneth Lee Grubb, you have been condemned to die by the people of the State of Illinois by means of lethal injection. Do you have any final words?"

Grubb slowly surveyed the witnesses again, this time he studied every face on the other side of the glass, and stopped when he saw his brother.

"Is it done?" Grubb asked as though Lance was the only other person in the room.

Lance trembled just a little, and Chapa wondered if Kenny Lee Grubb could see that.

"Bro, did it get done? Is it over?"

A moment later, the levers and pulleys in Lance's face began to coax a nod. A final twisted gift to a brother on his deathbed.

Kenny Lee Grubb was smiling when the warden gave the signal to begin. His gaze continued to drift until it reached Chapa. His smile grew broader, and it might have stayed that way had he not seen who was sitting next to him.

As the sodium pentothal began its journey from the control room to Grubb's vein, the expression on the killer's face turned from satisfaction to fear, then to terror as he looked into Annie's eyes. The first drug would ease Grubb into unconsciousness. The next would paralyze him and stop his breathing before the third delivered a knockout to his heart.

In his life as a journalist, Chapa had absorbed dozens of images he'd trade a year's pay to erase from his memory. But in that moment he understood that nothing would ever haunt him as much as Kenny Lee Grubb's last facial expression. The look of all-consuming horror and desperation was so complete that it seemed unnatural. It came from somewhere beyond anyone's reach and would travel with the killer to his next stop.

CHAPTER 79

There is something sad yet comforting about October rain in the Midwest. It's cold, but not threatening, and usually not accompanied by thunder and lightning. It's just nature crying for another lost summer.

Chapa listened to the tiny drops clamoring for attention as they slapped Erin's bedroom window, only to blend into one shapeless sheet of water. His week of full moons was finally drawing to a close, and he wondered whether he would ever get around to telling anyone half of all that had happened.

"I saw a man die today."

Erin stopped massaging the few areas of Chapa's upper body that weren't bruised, or stitched, or bandaged.

"You don't seem too bothered by it."

"Wasn't much of a man."

It was hard to believe Grubb's execution had also been part of this day. The past twelve hours had forged a chasm between those events and the warmth of Erin's touch.

On their way out of the prison Chapa and Annie had agreed to stay in touch. She seemed to mean it, but he knew it wouldn't happen. Their connection to one another had been left back in that room when the heavy doors of the prison closed behind them. They had nothing in common that either of them wanted to spend too much time thinking about.

Erin leaned down and pressed her lips to his wounded back. Kisses that burned. As soon as she stopped, he rolled over and wrapped his arms around her. Chapa meant for it to be a quick, forceful, and seductive move. But in his present physical condition he was forced to settle for gradual, tentative, and amusing, though in a way that engendered a sexy sort of sympathy.

Chapa slipped his hand beneath Erin's lush, shoulder-length hair, gently massaging the back of her neck, and met her mouth with his. He kissed her like he might never get the chance to again, because that's the way he'd felt, just like that, twenty-four hours earlier.

"I think you missed me," Erin said, her lips full and wet.

"Yeah, sure looks that way."

"I missed you too."

He did his best to hide the intensity of his need to be with her. As much as he wanted her at that moment, Chapa also felt a need to protect Erin and her son from ever brushing up against the sort of trouble he'd brought them over the past few days.

"There's something we should talk about." His words didn't sound the way they had all those times he'd played this conversation out in his head.

Erin nodded, and asked, "Are you going to spend the night?"

He gave her a look that gently suggested, *you know better.*

"I'd love to, but I can't," Chapa said and tipped his head in the direction of Mikey's room. "Besides, tomorrow is going be here in a hurry."

The soft look in her eyes told him that she understood.

Then she said, "We could talk about that something and still make the most of what's left of the evening," and kissed his chest. Her kisses held the promise of a great deal more to come, until Mikey called for her from his bed.

Chapa sat up faster than he should have, and managed to get his shirt on before the door opened. The child's well-rubbed eyes were nearly as red as his Transformers pajamas.

"I can't get to sleep, Mom."

"Honey, you have to be wiped out. Go back to bed."

In the background they could hear chirping coming from Mikey's room. Hobbs was still awake.

"And you need to say good night to your new friend."

The bird actually belonged to Chapa, a replacement gift to ease the loss of Jimmy. He'd named it Hobbs after the main character in *The Natural*. Chapa had decided to leave the bird with Erin for a few days, but was already starting to think that maybe it belonged here.

"I was hoping Alex could tell me a story."

"Alex is exhausted too."

Chapa forced himself to his feet, successfully masking his discomfort.

"I'm not that tired."

He put his arm around Mikey's shoulders.

"Let's see if we can conjure up a tale or two."

His mind was a barren wasteland and coming up with a decent story would be a challenge. But Chapa got over all that as soon as he looked back at Erin and winked as they headed out the door and into the hallway. The look on her face made him feel like he was the most amazing man who ever lived.

Three Days Later

CHAPTER 80

Nikki's letter was tucked into its own pocket inside Chapa's wallet. He had thrown out one of his old press credentials to make room for it. He unfolded the delicate piece of paper and read it again.

Daddy,
Why won't you ever come to see me?
I miss you sometimes.
Love Nikki

Some questions are best answered in person.

Parked halfway down a block where the homes were fronted with Greek columns, and the yards stretched big enough to host a music festival, Chapa's Corolla stood out like a pair of cut-offs at a black tie affair.

He didn't give a damn. Chapa had felt out of place his whole life. Over the past three days, as he made the drive from the Heartland to the coast, Chapa had decided that in spite of everything that had happened, he'd done all right for himself.

Job security was temporary, but at least he knew where the sucker punch would be coming from. Macklin was keeping him on to write a series of pieces about his experiences with Grubb, Langdon, and Annie. Once those were finished he would be helping out with local election coverage. Beyond that lay the great unknown, a place Chapa was actually looking forward to visiting.

Dominic Delacruz's obituary, personally written by Chapa, had filled more than a half page, the sort of space usually reserved for celebrities. The next day he received an email from Eddie Delacruz which simply read, *Thank you.*

Langdon would not be reading any of Chapa's stories, or feasting on all the Internet traffic surrounding his capture, or Grubb's execution. He was still in intensive care, unconscious and being kept alive by a network of tubes. Chapa wondered how they compared with the tubes that had channeled streams of death into Grubb's veins.

The injuries, in particular those caused by the drugs Annie had injected into his body, had left Langdon with no measurable brain activity, and were determined to have been the result of defensive actions. The feds could find no connection between Langdon and Strasser, and the trailer, which had vanished as though it never existed.

Likewise, no trail had been drawn between Lance Grubb and any of it. Still, Andrews remained certain Lance had served, at the very least, as a link between his brother and the outside world. When he moved out of the state two days after the execution, it created even more concern among authorities, but there wasn't much they could do.

The investigation into Pete Rudman's death had been reopened. The feds were in the process of tracking Strasser's movements in the days leading up to the retired officer's death. It wasn't easy. Even in life, Strasser had been like a ghost.

Chapa's new attorney, the one Andrews had put him in touch with, went to work before his retainer check had been cashed. A day later, Chapa received an email from his ex filled with words like *cooperation, misunderstandings,* and *communication.* It ended with a plea to work together like adults with a common interest.

There's no reason for us to ever be in court again. We should begin the healing process. We should talk.

Carla had no idea just how soon that process would begin.

Her new approach made it a good time for his first visit to Boston. But that's not what had triggered Chapa's decision to take a trip. Those wheels were in motion even before he had written the lead to his story the day of Grubb's execution.

Chapa checked his look in the rearview, like he had done five minutes earlier, and ten minutes before that. Then again in the driver's side mirror which worked like it was showroom new now that he'd had it fixed. Was this what a dad was supposed to look like? Why not.

The sleek green shirt he'd bought for this moment gave him a sense of distinction without overwhelming the casual vibe he was going for. Drawing the collar out a bit from inside his black leather jacket, he made sure both sides were even. Chapa wondered how much he still looked like the man Nikki once saw on a daily basis.

He reached over to the passenger's seat and shoved aside the maps that had cluttered there. From inside a gray satchel that he used to carry important papers any time he traveled, Chapa pulled out a small, neatly wrapped package.

It had taken Chapa three stops and several hours back in Cleveland before he finally settled on the perfect journal for Nikki. Its cover was decorated with smiley faces, hearts, and flowers, and for a moment he feared she might have outgrown those things. His hope

was that she would fill it up with her day-to-day doings
and thoughts. He had already done that with the one
he'd picked out for himself years before. Chapa had
stopped a number of times along the road, and stayed
up late in hotel rooms trying to write down those things
that would best tell his ten-year-old who her father was.
Maybe, over time, this could become a long distance
way to get to know each other again.

Families are complicated and fragile, but some can
be fixed, or at least jerry-rigged to function in a way.
Chapa had received a note from Michelle Sykes the
morning before he left. While Michelle failed to specify
whether Annie had reached out to them, the tone and
sincerity of her gratitude suggested she had.

He'd sat there long enough, but still gave the house
one more long look. The three-story colonial wasn't the
neighborhood's most impressive, but it certainly wasn't
doing anything to lower the seven-digit average for
homes in this secluded part of town.

Everything about the place, from the wrought iron
fence that ran the length of the property, to the front
door that was taller than some houses, didn't just suggest wealth, it hollered it from the top of a recently
painted gable.

After casually tossing the federal parking permit on
the dash just to be on the safe side, Chapa emerged
from the car and locked it, more out of habit than ne-
cessity, then started up the driveway which led to a cob-
blestone walk. With each step, Chapa's determination
fought to silence his anxiety.

Strategically placed Halloween decorations marked
the coming holiday with precision and not the unbridled enthusiasm that was celebrated in most American
neighborhoods. A designer witch and her matching fe-
line fashionably haunted the spaces on either side of
the front door.

The margin between everything in Chapa's past and that imposing door had narrowed to just a few feet, and he thought back to his first conversation with Annie, and how badly it had gone. He would approach this situation differently, more directly. Though Chapa knew he would make some new mistakes, he was determined to not repeat his old ones.

ACKNOWLEDGMENTS

Many people provided valuable advice and vital encouragement. Their contributions are woven into the pages of this book.

My agent Scott Miller immediately saw what could be, and then worked to make it a reality. A huge thank you goes out to him and the staff at Trident Media.

John Scognamiglio, my editor, saw beyond what was on the page and helped me find the story within. The talented folks at Kensington took it from there and did first class work at every step.

I am fortunate to have received generous advice from a number of veteran writers. Much gratitude to all of the fine and giving authors who make up Chicago's mystery writing community. A loud shout out to Marcus Sakey, Anne Perry, James Rollins, and David Morrell, my old college professor, who two decades later helped me make my first book better.

A special thank you goes to Joe Konrath, whose wisdom and insight are matched only by his generosity.

Before any of the pros got a look at the manuscript it was well vetted by my first readers. Leslie Rocha can spot a missing word or misplaced comma like the best of them. Valuable feedback from Greg Varney, Maria Konrath, J. D. Smith, Tina Varney, Joe Rocha, and Alesia Hacker influenced subsequent drafts of this book. I am indebted to each of them for caring enough to tell me when I still had work to do.

Sometimes you have to change your surroundings in order to get back on track. John Sandrolini, a great friend for more than thirty years, handed over the keys and generously allowed me to turn his wonderful Southern California home into a writer's retreat for the better part of two weeks.

Some of my biggest supporters can be found in my family. Tops among them are my mother, Magaly, and my brother, Ed.

Of course the warmest thank you goes to my wife Cheri, and my daughters Maggie and Kate. They are the ones who give meaning to it all.

ABOUT THE AUTHOR

Henry Perez has worked as a newspaper reporter for more than a decade. Born in Cuba, he immigrated to the U.S. at a young age, and lives in the Chicago area with his wife and children. *Killing Red* is his first novel.

Readers can visit him at www.henryperezbooks.com.

More Nail-Biting Suspense From Your Favorite Thriller Authors